"Chris Cander's debut novel is a multigenerational epic about religion and obsession in a West Virginia coal-mining town. A terrible moment in 1916 echoes across decades, shaping the way an entire community understands good and evil. Beautiful prose and unique, well drawn characters make *Whisper Hollow* one of the most auspicious debuts of the season."

—JEREMY ELLIS,
BRAZOS BOOKSTORE
(HOUSTON, TX)

"*Whisper Hollow* explores the complex lives of three very different women: Myrthen harbors a cold heart behind a face of piety, Alta is torn between duty to her family and the man she truly loves, and Lidia is a loving young mother who harbors a dark secret. When town scandals that are buried as deep as the mines threaten to come to light, each woman must test her courage. This riveting story with an explosive ending makes for an 'unputdownable' read, and a great novel for book clubs to discuss."

—PAMELA KLINGER-HORN,
MAGERS & QUINN
(MINNEAPOLIS, MN)

"Oh, the secrets in Verra, West Virginia, run deep and deadly. This multigenerational saga of families holds love, sorrow, and religion up to a mirror and then turns on itself. Myrthen loses her twin sister at a very early age and spends the rest of her life trying to atone for the accident. Alta loves and loses. Lidia has a secret that is causing her nightmares. Set in treacherous coal-mining country, this novel will be perfect for book clubs."

— VALERIE KOEHLER,
BLUE WILLOW BOOKSHOP
(HOUSTON, TX)

ALSO BY CHRIS CANDER

11 Stories

Whisper Hollow

by Chris Cander

Other Press
New York

Production Editor: Yvonne E. Cárdenas
Text Designer: Julie Fry
This book was set in Van Dijck by Alpha Design & Composition
of Pittsfield, NH

10 9 8 7 6 5 4 3 2

Library of Congress Cataloging-in-Publication Data

Cander, Chris.
   Whisper hollow / by Chris Cander.
      pages cm
     ISBN 978-1-59051-711-6 (paperback) — ISBN 978-1-59051-712-3 (ebook)
1. Female friendship—Fiction.   2. Religiousness—Fiction.
3. Ambition—Fiction.   4. West Virginia—Fiction.   5. Psychological
fiction.   6. Domestic fiction.   I. Title.
   PS3603.A53585W48 2015
   813'.6—dc23

                        2014010051

For Dorothy Welshonce, in memoriam

And for Joshua, who told me his ghost stories
while he still remembered them

Nothing is covered up that will not be revealed,
or hidden that will not be known.

—Luke 12:2

~ PART ONE ~

October 17, 1916

Myrthen's mother and father had carried more hopes than means with them when they crossed the Atlantic Ocean in the middle of January 1910. Rachel Engel was just sixteen when she left her home and family in Saxony, Germany, brave and willing and fiercely in love with Otto Bergmann, but nonetheless glancing over her shoulder all the way to the southern shore of the river Elbe, the gateway to the world.

Myrthen's grandparents disapproved of Rachel's choice for a mate, and so she and Otto, a twenty-nine-year-old miner with black cuticles and an uneasy cough, stole away in the middle of a star-filled night. She wore all the clothing she owned and packed everything else in her mother's upholstery bag: a photograph of herself with her parents and younger sister, a silver creamer that her mother loved, a hairbrush, her Bible. In her arms she carried an unlikely treasure: a divided cutting of the myrtle tree she had been tending since she was a little girl, dampened and wrapped in muslin for protection from the cold. They traveled north to the Port of Hamburg and boarded the steamer *Scandia* with 804 other passengers. "We Germans are like this tree," Otto said to Rachel three nights into the hard, dirty twenty-four-day journey to New York. "No matter where we go, we will take root again."

They were married on the ship by a Prussian Catholic priest, a Bavarian wheelwright and his wife as witnesses. The only bridal accoutrement Rachel wore was a simple wreath across her brow, woven from the thinnest myrtle branches off the cutting she'd brought. Their honeymoon was taken in the bowels of the ship, during a brief interlude of privacy in a cabin that rarely offered it. That night, as the hulking ship moved quickly over the ocean's unknowable depths, Myrthen and her twin were conceived.

"*Was bedeutet das?*" Rachel peered out into the window-framed dawn and wiped her hands on her apron. " 'Red sky in the morning, shepherds take warning'? Is that how it goes?" Otto coughed as he sat down to his breakfast of oatmeal and black coffee. "*Das ist richtig,*" he said. Then, a moment later, after wiping his long, prematurely gray mustache and beard with a threadbare but pressed cloth napkin: "That is correct. Your English is becoming so good, Rachel. I'm proud for you."

"Thank you," she said. It was nearly six years ago that they'd arrived in West Virginia, young Rachel still thinking the morning nausea was leftover seasickness from the journey across the Atlantic. Fueled by their unlikely passion, they'd hastily exchanged the Erzgebirge mountain range for the Appalachian; uranium mining for coal; the town of Niederschlema for the town of Verra. There were many similarities — the metallic cold of winter, the lush patina of foliage in the spring, the graduating blue of the eastward-looking slopes, the toil and promise that awaited underground. But once they slowed down long enough for their breathing to steady and their heat to subside, the differences were too numerous to count.

The local speech that sounded nothing like the English she'd studied at school in Germany was just one of them. She didn't understand when a neighbor said she could hang up a line for her "warsh" or that the likelihood for rain was "chancy." The idea that a man "hain't good for nothing" was not quite as difficult to comprehend—though she didn't believe it in her own case—as the idea that "he don't know no better." Even Whisper Hollow, the small valley across the creek from Verra where the Catholic church was situated, was pronounced in a way that suggested something irreconcilable; they called it "Whisper Holler." She didn't know if it was the lax and tense vowels and the strange conjugations that made her queasy, or the undeniable undercurrent and swell beneath her apron.

It took her longer than she would have liked to adjust to being in another country among so many other foreigners, being married, being pregnant, then becoming a mother. Her husband went to work for the Blackstone Coal Company, and they rented one of the small camp houses. On a rainy night that same year, Rachel gave birth to identical twin girls, Myrthen and Ruth.

Rachel had decided upon these two names early on, liking them equally well. "Ruth" was the name of Otto's mother, the only person in either of their families who supported their marriage and emigration. "Myrthen" came from the title of a work by Rachel's fellow Saxonian the composer Robert Schumann. She liked the story about his opus 25, *Myrthen*—he'd dedicated it to his wife on the occasion of their wedding. The name came from that, and from the myrtle branch she'd stolen from her mother's garden and carried across the sea.

She purchased an English dictionary from the company store with one of Otto's first meager paychecks, and looked up the definitions of the words she learned. Out of curiosity, she decided to look up the names she was considering for her child. There was no entry for Myrthen. But for Ruth:

ruth \\'rüth\ *n. Compassion for the misery of another.*

This made it easy for Rachel to choose her favorite. Ruth it would be. She patted her voluminous teenage belly, full of compassion, imagining the plaits she would braid into her daughter's hair, the piano lessons she would give, the German poetry and history she would recite. Already she knew she would need nothing more: a tiny family comprised of herself and Otto and baby Ruth. It would be perfect.

But after a bloody, waist-down battle on October 20, 1910, two little girls emerged instead of one, identical in every way but their temperaments.

"Come, *Mädchen*," she said to them. "Come look out the window at how red this sky is." Ruth sat with her legs splayed on the floor, sorting buttons from her mother's collection by size. She dropped them in an instant, scattering them like buckshot, and ran to where her mother stood. Dragging one of the wicker-seat chairs over, she climbed on it to have a better view. "Pretty," she said in a reverent voice.

"Myrthen, come look. Stand here and let me braid your hair." Rachel patted the high back of the chair upon which Ruth stood and then turned to follow Ruth's polite gaze out the window. Myrthen cached her own stack of buttons in her pinafore pocket, then walked over to the handful that Ruth had dropped on the other side of the braided rag rug and, glancing to make sure nobody was looking, pocketed them as well. Then she went and stood obediently in front of her mother and allowed her to part and pull her thick, dark hair so tightly off her face it made her eyes water.

"Sit still, Myrthen. Be like your sister. See? She's had her hair done for a half hour already."

"Red sky in the morning," said Otto, thumbing up his suspenders and glancing again out the window. "It will be foul weather today. I can smell something is coming."

"It's fine, it's fine. We have plenty to do inside today, don't we, girls? Plenty canning to do. Squash and zucchini and beans."

"You're a good wife, Rachel." Otto smiled at her, cracking his gaunt, ashen face in two. His white teeth and sparkling demeanor were the only two things about him that didn't seem somber and gray.

"*Danke*," she said, putting her palm against his cheek. "Come home safely."

"I always do." He kissed her first, then Myrthen, who was still standing on the chair. Then he went over to Ruth—who was looking, uncomplaining, under the rug for her missing buttons—and tapped her on the shoulder. She stood up and he bent to kiss her on the nose. Then he pretended to pinch it and sleighted his thumb between his fingers and showed it to her. "I got your nose," he said, and put his hand into his dungaree pocket. "I'll keep it with me for good luck." He winked at her, picked up his brimming dinner bucket and pickax, and was gone.

The day collapsed into darkness as strong winds from the west blew the clouds into huddled masses, thick and cumulonimbus. Throughout the gloomy morning, Rachel worked as she typically did, domestic needs dictating the course of the day while her husband labored in a two-foot-high tunnel underneath the rain-soaked mountain. There was always so very much to do: tending the children, laundry and gardening, mending and sewing, prepping and kneading and cooking and baking. She was forever beginning the next meal just as she finished the last one. And her efficiency was only ever stalled by the twins' nearly constant, one-sided feuding.

"Girls, go outside and play," Rachel finally said. Beads of sweat mustached her lip as she stirred the contents of the pot. A dozen jars lined the narrow countertop. Already she'd put up forty-eight cans of vegetables, taking them down to the cellar four at a time. It was nearly two o'clock; Otto would be home by 3:30 p.m. She hadn't, on this rare day, begun a soup or a meal of any kind to feed him when he came home. "I'll be finished soon, go play. Go down and get your cousin Liam. He's probably awake from his nap by now."

"We can't go outside, Mama," Myrthen said in her flat and factual tone. "It's raining too hard."

Rachel sighed and wiped her face with her tea towel. They heard a rifle report of thunder. "So it is," she said. She tapped the wooden spoon against the pot and set it down, wiped her hands on her splattered apron. "Come along then. Let us see what I have for you in my sewing basket."

A stuffed doll, dressed in a pinafore matching the girls', with blue button eyes and raven hair the same as theirs, but made out of yarn. There was another one, identical, but the hair and eyes had not yet been sewn on, the outfit was not quite ready. Rachel handed the finished one to Ruth. "This is for your birthday, only a little bit early. Almost six years old!" she said, cupping Ruth's face with her hand. "What big girls you are!" Then she turned to Myrthen and cupped her face the same way. "Myrthen, I'll finish yours tonight. I was going to give them to you both on Friday, but perhaps now is a good time to have it, yes?"

Ruth flung her arms around Rachel's waist. "Thank you, Mama!" she said. Myrthen hung her head in a pout.

"Ruth, you share yours with your sister today, yes?"

"Yes, Mama."

"Myrthen, don't be sad. I'll have yours finished tonight after I do this canning." She lifted Myrthen's chin off her chest. "You be a good girl.

"Now go play," she said, and picked up her spoon. She wanted to finish the canning and have something ready for Otto to eat.

Myrthen and Ruth went back to the sitting area and began to play with Ruth's doll. Myrthen sulked on the rug, fingering the buttons in her pocket while Ruth made the doll walk and sit and dance and lie down in a make-believe cradle, all the while delivering her own version of a lullaby their mother sang at bedtimes: *Hush, my baby, do not cry, in your cradle now you sing, then you weep, I softly swing, lullaby, lullaby.*

"You don't know how to play baby," Myrthen said. She snatched the doll by the hair from its imaginary bed.

"No!"

Myrthen turned away and held the baby close to her chest, pinching its neck as she ran.

"Gimme! Gimme her back! Gimmeherback!" Ruth caught up with Myrthen after a few rounds about the kitchen, where Rachel continued spooning stewed beans into glass jars, doing her best to ignore the bickering. Otto could be home any time.

Ruth grabbed the doll's legs and Myrthen hung on to her neck, and the two of them tugged and yanked, back and forth, silent but for the swish of cloth and pant of breath. The pair moved the entire process forward a few inches at a time until they were standing in front of the open cellar door, at the top of six downward steps.

Back and forth they grunted, until the doll's neatly sewn hair was torn askew, its pinafore ripped, its seam allowances exposed at the most private areas. Myrthen stared, unblinking, at her twin, who would normally have allowed her sister anything she wanted—but this doll was somehow different. Mama had given it to her first. Ruth flinched, but this time she would not let go. She gripped the doll's legs as though clinging to life itself.

"She's *mine*. Mama gave her to *me*."

Ruth yanked the doll forward with all her strength, pulling Myrthen off balance and swinging them both around until Ruth was the one with her back to the cellar.

Seesawing, they glared at each other, tethered only by the doll, and Ruth said with all the force she could, "You *meanie*!"

Myrthen's cheeks flushed. "I'm not a meanie! You are!"

Rachel appeared behind them, carrying more jars to add to the four dozen she had already left at the base of the stairs to be stacked later. "Girls, please," she said in a tired voice. "Stop arguing."

"But she won't give me back my birthday doll," Ruth said, holding fast.

"Myrthen!" Rachel said. "Enough! Give the doll to your sister."

Myrthen looked down at the bare, flat legs of Ruth's doll, and felt something she couldn't have described: a mix of shame and self-pity and anger. She narrowed her eyes at her twin and said, "I don't want it anyway. It's ugly." When Ruth gave the doll a final yank, Myrthen opened her hands in defiant acquiescence and let go.

In a slow-motion tumbling backward—doll over ankles, pinafore flying—Ruth's eyes flew open and the doll rammed against her tiny chest from the sudden tug-of-war victory, and then they were both bump bump bump bump bump bump crash splat gone.

Myrthen stopped. Her movement, her breath. She stood at the top of the steps and stared, wild-eyed and speechless. A flash of lightning from the cellar window lit the floor: Ruth, splayed at the bottom of the stairs, one leg bent at a sickening angle; blood pooling beneath one ear; her eyes and her mouth with its perfect baby teeth, open; shattered glass and beans spilled across the dirt floor; the birthday doll lying a few feet away, likewise limp and torn.

"*No!*" Rachel shoved Myrthen aside with one arm and took the stairs in two lurching steps. "*No!*" She fell to her knees next to Ruth, and lifted her limp torso up against her own. The jar glass cut into Rachel's knees like shrapnel, adding her blood to her daughter's as she rocked back and forth, back and forth, begging and pleading with God.

Myrthen looked down, seeing only what the lightning allowed — her mother, rocking her limp twin, like she did when Ruth couldn't easily fall asleep. Outside, the thunder gnashed and roared. Ruth was scared of thunder. Yes, she didn't like the thunder or the rain or the dark. Mama was comforting her because she was scared, and she should go down and get her doll and give it to Ruth because it would make her feel better, wouldn't it, Ruth? It was so dark outside, shepherds take warning, it was probably almost bedtime and she wasn't hungry so she must have eaten and it was probably time to go to sleep.

"Mama, I'll get our bed ready," Myrthen called quietly down to her mother, who was still rocking, rocking with knees bleeding into the spill of blood where Ruth had fallen. Ruth looked so tired; they were both so very very tired, and Myrthen thought she should go and get their bed ready before it was past their bedtime and she heard the door begin to open — Papa's home — and she didn't want to be caught up late; it was so dark and Ruth was already fast asleep, so she ran, quickly, quietly to their room and pulled back the covers and climbed inside, and moved all the way to the wall so that Ruth would have enough room when her mother brought her sleeping body in.

She closed her eyes and promised God that when her mother finished her doll that night after the canning was done, she would give it and all the buttons to Ruthie.

Three days later, it was her birthday — their birthday — but there was no wreath on the table, no burning life candles, no colorful flowers. Instead, six-year-old Myrthen was eye-level with shades of gray. Her mother's flannel dress. Her father's threadbare suit, the one he had worn when they left Saxony for a better life. Father Timothy's cassock. The clothes of mourners, the coal-dusted handkerchiefs that the adults pressed to their eyes.

Beyond them, the morning sky was complementary, with thick, dark clouds. Even the sounds were gray: the low drone of prayer, the sniffles, the throat-clearings, and the belching of the trains, heaving their heaping loads of slick coal down the mountain. But the darkest gray of all — the one from which Myrthen couldn't tear her eyes — was the black casket that hovered over a fresh hole in the cemetery behind St. Michael's.

"We therefore commit Ruth's body to the ground; earth to earth, ashes to ashes, dust to dust; in the sure and certain hope of the Resurrection to eternal life," Father Timothy said. Myrthen heard a steep pitch in her mother's sobs, which sounded both raw and scabbed after three endless days. Myrthen had hardly seen her, but her crying had filled every crack in their small house. It was the sound to which she fell asleep, when she finally did in her suddenly wide bed; the sound to which she woke, always with a few groggy minutes before she remembered why.

Then Myrthen's father and the other men stooped through her line of gray sight, and lowered her twin's body into the ground. Poor Ruthie. Ruth didn't like the dark. Maybe her eyes were closed; maybe she was playing hide-and-seek. Then she wouldn't be scared. She always hid in the same place when they played that game, always under her parents' bed. Myrthen always counted to ten before she went looking, and she had to act like she didn't know where Ruth was. She looked in different places to keep the game fun, and Ruth always acted surprised when she finally found her.

Myrthen tugged on her aunt's dark sleeve. "How many do I need to count?"

"*Was ist das?*" her aunt whispered down at her. Her mother's sister, Agnes, and family—her husband, Ian, and their son, Liam—had joined them in Verra when the twins were two, but Agnes's English still lagged behind.

"Until I can go get her?" Myrthen said, pointing to the hole.

"Shhh," someone said, a man or a woman, Myrthen didn't know. She hung her head, aching. The only sound besides Father Timothy's dulled voice was the grasshoppers clacking, searching for their mates. The sound of loneliness. She didn't know it then, but she would suffer that sound for the rest of her life.

May 21, 1925

"Alta! Stop that daydreaming," Alta Krol's mother called from the kitchen window into the late-May morning air. "Those weeds won't pull themselves."

"Yes, Mama," she called back. Her mother set a *piernik* spice cake on the sill to cool, then waved the towel she was holding at her and turned away.

Alta stood up from her crouched position in between rows of lettuce and spinach, rhubarb and peas, and stretched to her new full height. The ground looked farther away again. Most mornings these days, her legs and back ached. She thought of her grandmother, the tiny, stooped figure with fingers like old tree roots and a pinched expression on her hard, lined face. She wondered if the old woman had ached like that all her life; wondered if she, Alta, now thirteen, would ache all her life, too.

Alta sighed, squatted back down, and forced her hands to perform this small duty. She moved aside the fragile, desirable leaves and, from underneath, pulled out the murderous weeds that threatened to deprive her family at the dinner table. A cool breeze cut through the sun's warmth and raised bumps on her arms, making the short blonde hairs quiver. She stopped to watch her skin settle back down. With her eyes still on her own arm, she reached forward to lift the next tuft of green with one hand and stretched the other out in anticipation of a dandelion shoot. But it was no dandelion that met her fingertips. She yanked back her hand and fell onto the ground with a thump when she grabbed, instead, something with fur.

She blinked hard a few times and then, when nothing else moved, slowly pushed herself back onto her heels, her long legs bent like a grasshopper and her sharp knees pointing at the blue sky. Again she lifted the lettuce leaves, and she found splayed out the fresh-dead body of a small brown mouse.

No insect morticians had yet arrived to claim the body. There was no blood, no apparent cause of death. She rocked forward onto the balls of her feet and craned her head to see if there was anything on the other side of the mouse. She found no stick nearby with which to lift it, so she reached forward and touched it carefully with the end of her index finger. Nothing. Just a warm pelt, softer than she would have imagined. She reached out again and stroked it — first with just the one finger, then with two, then three, and finally, the whole flat of her open palm.

The mouse looked so peaceful lying there, curved in the lettuce shade as though taking a late-morning nap, its tail tucked around its long feet. She pulled up a tiny flower from within the rhubarbs and laid it across the mouse's forepaws. If it wouldn't cause her mother grief, Alta would have gone inside for her sketch paper and pencils to memorialize the dead mouse that looked so serene in his weed blossom funeral arrangement.

Alta looked up, thinking instead she should offer a prayer to send his poor, lonely soul up to Heaven. She wasn't sure it would be considered appropriate, but it was the only ritual she knew for a moment such as this. That's when she saw the scuds of steam rising into the sky above the valley, a chain of train-made clouds signaling that the passenger engine was coming. Was it already almost noon?

She abandoned the mouse as quickly as she'd found it, and took off barefoot down the garden and up the slant of yard and past her own house and past the row of twenty-six company houses that made up her street.

The hard rains had stopped a few days before, but the dirt road was still muddy, especially along the sides. Even though she held it aloft, the hem of her dress would be filthy by the time she reached the station. Still, she wouldn't slow down. She ran hard on her spindly legs, her feet flaring unskillfully out to the sides, keeping her pace by the trail of steam puffs, which she watched over her shoulder to make sure she was ahead of them. There were two reasons she wanted to meet the passenger engine at the yard: the Verra Bears were coming back from their away game after a two-month winning streak, and her uncle Punk and his new bride were arriving for a home visit from New York.

She beat the train to the small station house with just enough time to climb the few steps to the platform and lean forward to catch her heaving breath, her hands clutching the heavy fabric at her knees. The tracks, running parallel to New Creek, lay between Whisper Hollow — which was bursting into bloom with monkey flowers and pigeonwing vines, ginseng and buffalo clover — and the town of Verra, which was comprised of the coal tipple, the coal camps, the company store and a few other shops, the barber's, the post office, and two schools. When she could breathe normally again, Alta stood under the noon-struck clock with her back to the town and waited for the passengers to spill off the train.

The station manager tucked his watch into his trouser pocket, adjusted his hat, and walked through a belch of steam to open the door. A few men stepped onto the platform first, stiff in their wool and blinking into the bright sunlight. Then an elderly woman clutching her daughter's hand, who was in turn helped down the metal steps by a young man in steel-toed boots. Then the baseball players, smiling and proud, their uniforms packed into the cardboard suitcases they carried, descended into the small crowd waiting for them. Their mothers and a few fathers whose shifts in the mines had ended or else not yet begun, sweethearts, and classmates welcomed them home with claps on the back and demure smiles. When shortstop Giovanni Esposito stepped into the light and waved at Alta, she lost her breath again.

Giovanni, or John, as he was called, was fifteen, with dark, curly hair and a smile that turned his eyes into crescents. She'd never been close enough to know what color his eyes were and had never cared to find out until that moment, when they looked right at her. Unlike the other boys, whose faces were slick and spotty or darkened by coal dust, John's complexion was clear and smooth, except for a small mole under his left eye near his nose and the shadowy beginning of facial hair. He was tall for his age, taller than the high school coach who was traveling with them, and his shoulders looked as strong as a grown man's. Under the midday light, he resembled her image of Homer's Odysseus, the king of Ithaca, about whom she'd read nightly for three weeks by candlelight the previous winter. That is, after her chores were done.

He waved again and shouted, "Hello there!" and Alta, suddenly smitten, tentatively raised her own hand to return the greeting. Why was he waving to her? Then, from behind her, another shout: "Hey, Johnny!" She felt the brush of a boy's shoulder against hers as he moved toward John to pump his hand and offer congratulations on a game well played.

Embarrassed, she turned her face as though she hadn't been staring, entranced, at the boy who in that moment became the most beautiful thing she'd seen in all her twelve years. When she moved her gaze beyond him, she found herself staring again, this time at the second-most-beautiful thing: the woman she assumed was her new aunt, Maggie.

Maggie stood so still amid the excited, doting movements of her uncle Punk that she seemed to be floating in the stir of air he whipped up around her. Alta watched as she reached inside her drawstring purse and pulled out a silver case. Maggie took out a cigarette and put it into the end of a long plastic holder. Punk quickly dug inside his pocket for a lighter, then made a cup against the wind to light it. She hardly moved, except to bring the cigarette slowly toward and away from her mouth, but Alta had the impression that all her movements would be as languid and graceful as a cat's. Maggie waited as Punk collected their many suitcases from the baggage car, struggling under their weight and piling them next to her one by one. Each time he appeared, she beamed at him, but made no offer to help.

Alta had never seen a woman with such poise. Had never watched someone stand so elegantly and confidently still. Had never, ever seen a woman smoking a cigarette, nor wearing high-heeled shoes, flesh-colored stockings, a dress with a hem that barely covered her knees, dangling earrings, rouge. In the vague periphery of her vision, Alta realized that other people were staring at Maggie as well. She even heard an audible gasp from somewhere nearby. Nothing like this woman had ever happened to Verra, West Virginia, much less to Alta herself.

Finally, when Punk had gathered all their belongings, he looked around for his brother or nephews, but all he saw was Alta.

"Is that you, Alta?" he called across the platform. Alta came out of her reverie enough to nod. "Well, come on up here and meet your aunt Maggie!"

Alta walked the thirty or so feet without taking her eyes off her new aunt, then stopped in front of Maggie without saying a word.

"I swear you're gonna be taller than any of us, you keep growin' like you do," Punk said; then he turned to Maggie. "This here's Alta. My sister's girl." Then he slipped his arm around Maggie's waist and looked into his wife's sparkling eyes and said, "And this is the lovely Mrs. Maggie Borski."

Maggie smiled at him and leaned away so she could transfer her cigarette from her right hand to her left, then she turned to Alta and extended her hand. Alta blinked in surprise; she'd never before shaken hands with a woman—or anyone, for that matter.

"How do you do?" Maggie said in a tone that was bouncier than Alta would have expected, given her molasses-coated gestures.

Alta slowly reached out and slipped her hand against Maggie's. "Good," she said.

Maggie laughed, still holding Alta's hand, and looked her up and down. "You're a dear!"

Alta smiled but became suddenly aware of herself under Maggie's gaze. She looked down again and, with chagrin, observed the contrast between her aunt's shiny leather Mary Janes that lifted her two inches off the ground and her own flat, bare, dirty feet. The mud had begun to dry and crack along the tops into brownish-gray contours like states on a map. She curled her toes, as though to help at least some of them secede from that unsightly union.

"Listen, do you like motion pictures?" Maggie asked.

Alta looked up. "I don't know."

"You don't know? Haven't you ever seen one?"

Alta shook her head.

"Oh, you'll love the pictures. We go all the time, don't we, Punk?" From within her poised exterior, a girlish enthusiasm erupted. Maggie closed her eyes for a moment and smiled. "The Silver Palace. It's simply divine," she said, drawing out the last word. She looked back at Alta and continued. "You can see the picture screen from any of the seats, but I prefer the balcony. We just saw *The Gold Rush* and oh, that Charlie Chaplin! Isn't he fantastic? The way he pretends to eat the shoe!" She looked at Punk and smiled with her mouth open, showing her small white teeth. He smiled encouragingly back at her. Then she took a draw on her cigarette, and leaned in toward Alta. "Listen, I'll take you to one sometime, you and me, okay?"

Alta nodded, still bewildered by this elegant and unexpectedly friendly creature.

"You don't talk much, do you?" Maggie asked, still smiling. She turned to Punk and said, "Baby, get me my train case, would you?" Punk held it out for her so she could unzip it without having to bend over. She took out a magazine with a picture of a dark-haired woman with fair skin and a rosebud smile that matched the background. She handed it to Alta.

"That's Colleen Moore. She's a screen star. Maybe I'll take you to see her in one of her pictures sometime."

Alta looked at the magazine, its title *Motion Picture*, written in bubble letters above the date and price: *May, 25¢* "Thank you," she said.

"Oh," Maggie said, reaching into her bag. "Here." She took out another cigarette and handed it to Alta. "Don't smoke it yet. I'll teach you how sometime."

"Maggie!" Punk said. "She's too young for all that. My sister'll have my head you start her smokin' cigarettes!"

"Oh, baby, it's fine." She put her hand on his coat sleeve, then turned to Alta and winked. "It'll just be our secret, then, okay?"

Alta smiled, broadly now, and nodded again. "Our secret." She slipped the cigarette into the pages of the magazine, which she hugged against her chest just in time to keep it out of her three brothers' and other uncle's view. They'd come to the station to help Punk and Maggie with their bags.

"Mama needs you home to help with dinner," Alta's eldest brother, Kasper, said to her as he passed, but he didn't take his eyes off Maggie as he spoke. "Better get going."

As they gathered around to shake Punk's hand and meet Maggie, Alta stepped backward out of the throng, clutching the magazine, the smile beginning to slide back down into a neutral expression as she slipped out of Maggie's glow. Between the dark-colored shirts of the men in her family, as if looking through fence posts, she could see Maggie lapse back into languor as she met each of them in turn.

Just before Alta reached the edge of the platform, Maggie, who was shaking the hand of one of her new relatives, dipped her head and winked at her. Alta winked back, then turned and ran barefoot through the mud again, all the way home.

May 10, 1927

The scent of tomato sauce clung to everything: the wallpaper, the crocheted doilies on the arms of the couch, their clothes in the narrow closets, even the weekly that his mother kept on the coffee table in spite of the fact she couldn't read a word of it. To John, tomato sauce was equally the smell of comfort and the smell of conflict.

"What are you thinking, I want to know?" said Ciro Esposito, shaking the opened envelope and its contents with his one hand. His chest barreled beneath his thin undershirt, the tempest-tossed gray hairs poking out. "What's this 'Carnegie Mellon'?" He said the name as if it was something not only foreign but felonious, or, at the very least, not to be trusted. Squinting at the header address on the letter, he held it out at arm's length so he could read it. "Carnegie. Institute. Of. Technology." His English halted along with his aging eyesight. "Pittsburgh!" he bellowed, and shook the handful of paperwork at his son John as if he were strangling a chicken.

John stared at the old rug on the living room floor, heard his father's voice boom with disappointment, smelled the sauce coming from the kitchen, the clothes, the wallpaper. "So?" he said, slumping his two strong shoulders, which diminished him by two or three inches and about ten years.

"What are you meaning, 'So'?" His father took a step closer. Even though he was fully half a head shorter, with only a stump dangling from his left shoulder socket, in his mind—in his house—Ciro was Hercules.

John turned his face slightly away, as though from a slap. "I wanted to see if they would take me," he almost whispered.

"Take you? Take you! For what? What you going to do at this Carnegie Mellon, huh?"

"Structural engineering," John said. "Or architecture. I'm not sure yet."

"*Che l'inferno?* Engineering? What, you want to drive the coal train?"

"No. Of course not." John chuffed once through his nose, that unmistakable measure of contempt he'd learned from his father. "I want to design buildings. Tall buildings." Then his enthusiasm strained against the tension and he couldn't help but lift his eyes to meet his father's. "Skyscrapers," he said, and smiled.

He hadn't even seen one. Until three months ago, when the Verra Bears were on their way home from a town close to the border of Pennsylvania, he hadn't even known they existed. Some passenger on the train had left behind a copy of *American Living* magazine, and John was struck by the cover drawing of the Fuller Building in New York City stretching in triangular majesty toward the heavens. It was a giant among its neighbors, and John wondered who could even think up such a thing. Then he read the title—*America's Greatest Contribution to World Architecture, the SKYSCRAPER!*—and spent the rest of the train ride reading about these magnificent structures and the men who designed and erected them. Architects and technical specialists and structural engineers. He imagined himself as one of them, weaving foundations and frames with threads of steel, bearing the burden of responsibility for stability and permanence and human safety. The article said that with no reasonable limit to the height of the steel frame building, skyscrapers a mile high were within the realm of possibility. A mile high! He leaned his head against the window and considered it. His very own Trist Mountain wasn't a mile high, even if one counted from the peak down into the black depths from which his father mined a modest living. Oh, how much nicer it would be to work above ground, building structures that scraped the sky, than to toil underground like an ant, like a mole, only to come back up one-armed and mean.

"*Di che lei parla*, eh?" his father said. His face grew red, from anger or embarrassment John couldn't tell. But he knew his father didn't know what a skyscraper was. Ciro set his mouth and shook his head, darting his eyes across the far wall as though searching for words. Finally, Ciro walked over to his chair and dropped into it, the Carnegie Mellon paperwork crushed in his hand. "Giovanni, you wanted to go have big dreams, you should've stayed pitching baseball."

"I got hurt, Papa." It was a fact, but he couldn't help but plead.

"You seem good to me."

"I can't throw anymore. Not without hurting."

"Life is hurting, Giovanni. You think I don't know about hurting?" Ciro raised his voice and lifted what was left of his arm, and John looked down. "I want *I* could throw a baseball," his father said. "Just one more time."

John had pitched a no-hitter right after he'd read the article on the train, throwing slider after slider that hooked sharp outside the strike zone and confused the batters every time. But in the bottom of the eighth, he felt something snap. He dropped his glove and grabbed his pitching shoulder. Even as the pain shot through like lightning he thought, *Maybe I won't have to do this anymore.*

"I want to go to college," John said to the floor.

"How you going to pay for some fancy college, I want to know? You think your papa going to pay? I can't pay."

John couldn't look at his father, so he looked at the couch. At the doilies his mother had crocheted to cover the threadbare armrests, the uneven wear on the cushions. The couch had belonged to the family who lived in the company house before them; they'd never had the money to replace it with something nicer.

"That University of Kentucky offered to pay if you came to play baseball. But not this Carnegie Mellon. If you not gonna swing a bat, then you swing an ax like your papa."

"It's too late. My arm is bad now. They wouldn't give a scholarship to someone with a bad arm."

"When you finish with high school in a couple weeks, then you come down with me." Ciro slapped down the letter and the envelope with its fine, embossed Pittsburgh address. "Your arm gonna be fine by then."

Later that day John's mother, Lia, knocked softly on his bedroom door. It was their private signal: two knocks followed by three followed by two. John jumped off his small bed, still made, to answer. There she stood, holding a plate of biscotti and a cup of tea, a tender half smile on her face. Under her arm was tucked the Carnegie Mellon catalog. John took the offering and stepped aside to allow her passage. She closed the door behind her and sat down on his bed.

"Giovanni."

John shrugged. He set down the plate and cup and dropped onto his brother's bed, empty because he was out on a date.

"*Amore*, I sorry your father so hard like this on you. He loves you. You know it?"

John nodded.

"I love you. You know it?"

He nodded again.

"I save your drawings, you know it? All of them." Her eyes lit, as though from a memory or a dream. "You always such good painter, since you were little boy. Always making pictures of something! Your buildings drawings, oh I love them. How you think of such things, Giovanni?" She clasped her hands together and sighed. "Some kind of artist."

"That's what I want to do, Mama," he said. "I want to design buildings."

"But what about a family, eh? You don't want to go so far away now, you thinking about a family soon."

"No, Mama, I'm not. Not yet."

"But what about that nice girl you seeing now? Beatrice? No, no. Lucinda, yes?" She tapped her forehead with two fingers. "I keep them...*come lei dice*...confused."

John raised an eyebrow. "So do I."

Lia turned her head and smiled. John knew she didn't understand, and so he explained it: "All the girls are alike, Mama. They don't *do* anything. They don't yearn for anything. Beatrice and Lucinda and Dot and Patricia—they all want the same thing: marriage and babies."

"So what's a matter with babies?"

"*Niente*, Mama. I want a family, too. But not yet. Not yet," he said. He reached out for a biscotti and took a bite. "When I'm ready," he said between bites, "I can find a girl. An interesting girl. A smart girl." He shrugged. "Then I'll have a baby."

"Long as she good Catholic girl. Italian girl." Lia thought for a moment, then smiled. "So maybe not Italian girl. It no matter to me. Long as she good Catholic girl, like your mama." She let her gaze drift past him to the window and—by the look on her soft, round face—through it, beyond the other houses and over Trist Mountain and across the Atlantic, and backward through the years to a country that had once been her home.

After a few quiet moments, she sailed back and landed again in the only other home she'd ever had, and smiled at him. "Giovanni, do you really want to study this...structure... engineer..."

"Structural engineering."

"Even the name is hard!" She laughed quietly. "Maybe it would be better to stay home, eh? Why go so far away where you don't know anybody? And for what, eh? Structure engineer seem like very hard job. Very complicated. Must be, studying for such hard job be very hard, too."

John hadn't thought much about whether it would be difficult or not. It didn't matter; he'd always done well in school. Maybe he wasn't the smartest student in his class, but he never struggled. Anything artistic came naturally.

When he was very young, he wanted to be a painter, but his father said that only girls wasted time on art. He'd hoped his father would think structural engineering a masculine compromise.

His mother raised her eyebrows. "It would be too hard for me for sure. I'm good for cooking, but not so good for school. When I was girl, I wanted to be teacher so much! I used to make my brothers and sisters sit down in the ground like it was school and I was teacher, told them so many things!" She glanced out the window again. "But I couldn't learn to read. All the letters, so complicated. So I stay home and help my mama with cooking and then I meet your papa and we come here." She smiled and shrugged. "I never could be teacher, but still my life is good. I have your papa, and my children."

Soon she was gone, and John sat back down on his narrow bed. He picked up the Carnegie Mellon catalog. There were dark gray smudges on the cover, prints from his father's coal-stained fingers. Everything his father touched turned dark; he never could get all the coal off his hand without the other one to scrub it. And there in the corner was a red splotch of tomato sauce. There were tiny blots of red all over their house. His mother often carried a spoonful of it out into the living room for his father to taste—*more basil, not so much sugar*—or else it dripped off the splatters that covered her aprons. It was as if she was always bleeding, one tomato-red drop at a time.

He flipped open the catalog and looked at the pictures of the buildings, so sturdy and proud. It brought his mind back to the Fuller and the Woolworth, those woven pillars of steel that looked as if they could punch holes in the heavens. He'd read about plans for two more skyscrapers in New York City that would become the tallest in the entire world, possibly even taller than Trist Mountain. John closed the catalog with a sigh, lay back, and closed his eyes. He could hear the low voices of his parents speaking in their mother tongue: his mother, who was not a teacher because she couldn't read, and his father, who would never play baseball because he was missing an arm. They lacked abilities, both of them, but they were brave. He felt as if it was the opposite for him.

He slowly sat up. Looked at the cover of the catalog once more. Then he rolled it up like a set of blueprints and dropped it in the trash.

April 17, 1928

By the time she got home from school, all three of Alta's brothers and her father were at work. She finished cleaning up the breakfast dishes that had been left undone so she wouldn't be late, harvested some vegetables from their garden, and chopped up some meat for their dinner stew. She read a chapter from her tenth-grade history book on how cotton influenced the slave trade, economic policies, the Civil War, and the Industrial Revolution. Then she took off her shoes, lay down on her narrow bed, and closed her eyes against the slaving, both historical and present-day, and began to drift off into a rare and brief and blissful respite — until she remembered that it was Tuesday. Mail day.

She was already three houses down her street, which had been screed with machine-laid asphalt just the previous year, before she realized that not only was she running, she was also still barefoot. She stopped and straightened her long back, and glanced sideways from underneath her lashes to see if anyone had been watching. It wasn't in her nature to take such objective notice of herself, but she'd overheard a comment made several months ago, just before her sixteenth birthday, by a friend of her younger brother: "Your sister gallops like a horse. Kind of looks like one, too. Maybe you could enter her in the Kentucky Derby next spring." Marek had boxed him flat, and the boy stopped coming around, but in that moment she'd painted an unsightly image of herself as a galloping quadruped, fifteen hands high at the withers, and it hung thereafter in her mind no matter how hard she tried to take it down.

She walked casually home, trying to ignore the road emulsion tacking her feet—*hooves*, she thought, and closed her eyes against the image of herself as a Centaur—then went inside and buttoned up her worn, low-heeled leather boots. She would have liked to wear something nicer, perhaps with an elegant Boulevard heel, but her feet were too long to find anything that fashionable, and besides, her father said tight shoes destroy character.

She walked slowly, then, past the row of houses and up to Main Street, where the company store, the barbershop, the jewelry store, and other fronts lined up facing the arterial tracks that chugged coal from the Blackstone tipple out of town and all the basic, daily-life goods in, including the mail. Just past the hardware store, where a few older men were swapping gossip, was the brick-front post office. She pulled open the door and stepped inside the tiny lobby.

Facing the street was the newly installed Formica counter, which, according to the papers, signified economic progress. There were green metal combination-lock boxes on either side of a barred window behind which the postmaster, Mr. Kiser, sold stamps and sorted deliveries and hand-canceled the outgoing mail. At that moment, his place was empty. She walked up to the small ledge and peered in between the green bars, but he must have been at the rear, receiving or disbursing the mail for the trains and rural routes. *Ah well*, she thought, and turned around on her boot heel, propping her sharp elbows atop the

smooth plastic counter to wait. And there, against the east wall
of the shallow room, bent over a tall worktable, his back to her,
was John Esposito.

That broad back was unmistakable. She'd watched it from
afar for the past three years, since he was a high school fresh-
man playing baseball with the Bears. His back was still young
and rectangular then, bony shoulder blades poking out of his
uniform. But as he grew, his shoulders had broadened while his
waist stayed slim, and new brawn concealed his blades and the
archipelagic knots of spine that showed when he bent over to
pick up a foul ball or a girl's dropped schoolbook. And now, as
he leaned over with an expression she couldn't see but imagined as one of thick concentration, she saw that his back had
filled out yet again, muscles straining against his work shirt
as he wrote. After a moment he stood back up and folded his
letter. She wondered to whom he was writing, and why here,
at the post office instead of home, and what his handwriting
looked like—was it deliberate and masculine, like his voice,
based on the few times she'd overheard it? Then she allowed
the thought, the feeling—but only fleetingly—that whatever
he'd written was meant for her: a love letter, a plea, an apology,
a proposal.

She forced herself to stop and looked down at her too-long,
boot-clad feet. The floor that was so far down. She felt the stab
of her elbow joints jammed against the Formica. And in her
mind, she heard the rude, unchanged voice of a thirteen-year-
old boy, suggesting she run in the Derby. Someone like John
Esposito would never bet on a horse like her. He wouldn't even
see her at the gate.

"Miss Alta!" Mr. Kiser said. She spun around and faced the
window. "Today's a good day, ain't it? Beautiful spring weather
we got! And..." He winked at her. "And I got a special package
for you. Just came in today, got it right here waiting. I know

you been expecting something awhile now." He stepped away and she followed him with her eyes, standing on her toes to see the size and shape of the long-belated birthday parcel from New York City that would, in some way, make up for the privation of her aunt Maggie's glamour from her own unimportant life.

Mr. Kiser's high-pitched and cheerful voice pulled John's attention out of his thoughts and to the counter. He still held his half-licked envelope to his tongue. And there, with her back toward him, was Alta Krol.

She was stretched up on her toes, leaning forward on the counter. The hem of her skirt came just above the backs of her knees, which lengthened even further her long, slender legs. Her uncovered calf muscles were flexed and lithe. He quickened at the little swell of flesh inside the delicate curve there. More leg, hidden beneath pleated cotton, a narrow but sturdy waist, a graceful back, an appealing curve of neck, plain but not unattractive hair. She settled, flat-footed again, and the knees were hidden. But the skin between hem and boot was not.

He'd seen her around town, of course. It wasn't a metropolis, after all. She had three brothers; two of them played baseball for the Bears, and he would graduate with one next month. When had she become so...graceful? He tried to think whether he'd ever had a conversation with her in all the years they'd lived in the same small town, gone to the same school, passed each other on the street or in a store.

"Oh, thank you, Mr. Kiser," she said. John listened for the qualities of her voice, surprised by his own interest.

"You're mighty welcome, Miss Alta. Mind if I ask — can't blame me for my curiosity, now, can you — what's got you so excited you been coming down here every week, anticipating?"

Alta smiled and held the package, touching it along the sides as if weighing and measuring the contents or volume or value within. "It's from my aunt in New York City," she said. "She's a society lady. A 'patron of the arts.' " Her eyes grew wide as she said it, as though it were something really important. "She made acquaintances with an artist, someone named Leighton Macrae. She said she was going to send me some new paints and one of his original watercolors for inspiration."

"You paint, Miss Alta?"

She ducked her head and shrugged. "I try."

"Now that's just fine. You keep on doing that, hear? World needs some fine things like paintings and such."

"Thank you, Mr. Kiser," she said, and pulled the package into her arms as though it were a baby. "Oh, I meant to ask—how's Mrs. Kiser doing? Is her leg better?"

"She's doing fine, Miss Alta. Nice of you to ask."

"I'd be happy to come around, see if I can help out in some way."

"You got plenty to do yourself, I know, what with your daddy and brothers needing your attention all the time. But thank you all the same."

"I'll check on you, anyway," she said, smiling, "even though I've already got my package." She hugged it to her aspiring chest.

John watched her, the way she bounced just slightly onto her toes as she spoke, her happiness invading every part of her lissome body. She sounded kind and seemed interesting, and she was beautiful.

She reached through the bars and touched the postmaster on his forearm and smiled and said, "Thank you." Then she turned, jubilant, clutching her package as she strode past John in only three long steps, and lifted it slightly toward him as their eyes met. She said, without stopping, "New paints!" With one final footfall, she shoved open the door with her elbow and stepped into the slant of afternoon sun.

John stood expressionless with his half-licked envelope held in midair, and blinked into the glint of light caused by the closing door.

" 'New paints'?" Alta said aloud to the asphalt. " 'New paints'?" Three years of silence and yearning, and that had been all she could think of to say.

August 11, 1929

It was hotter than usual, even for August, but it was a Sunday afternoon, and they had the day off from the mines, dinner to look forward to, cold Coca-Colas, and the Yankees playing the Indians. The men and boys, about twelve of them, leaned against the counter and sat on wooden crates inside the Welcome Store, straining their ears to hear the play-by-play through the static. Pepper Pollock had offered to set up his kit-built radio set, but everyone knew he hadn't done a very good job on the tuning circuit, and besides, his mother was expecting her in-laws and didn't want a bunch of louts hanging around her tidied living room. So his uncle Lenny, who owned the store and loved Pepper almost as much as he loved the Yanks, agreed to let everyone come down and listen to the game with him there.

Lenny was just certain Babe Ruth was going to hit his five-hundredth homer against the Indians that day, and since there was no way he could get to Cleveland, he wanted to witness it as close to live as he could. He tuned in to Charleston's WCHS on the new RCA Radiola 60 Super-Heterodyne that he'd had in stock since March. It was something he made sure to mention to his customers, even if they were just stopping in for flour or razor blades or Drano or a box of shotgun shells. "It's just like one a them de-luxe cabinet models, except it's small enough you can set it right there on a shelf or a side table. Can even set up the speaker in a different room if you want to." Lenny knew most of his customers couldn't afford a luxury like that radio, even if it did have tone fidelity that was ideal for the kind of altitude interference they had in Verra. Today he was glad nobody had forked over the $147 asking price. As he passed around cold bottles from the icebox like a host, marking them down on people's tabs, he even considered keeping it as part of the store's ambiance.

A few girls drifted in; some were sweethearts and some just friends who aspired to be more. They joined the young men and twittered enthusiastically about the game, although the only thing they knew about batting involved their eyelashes. An older woman hobbled up to the counter with a dozen eggs, shaking her head at the sight of so many idle men.

John Esposito dropped his eyes under her glare. He'd been sitting on his parents' front steps in his undershirt less than an hour ago, bits of shorn grass stuck to his arms and face, trying to cool off after trimming the lawn. Without even going inside for a glass of water, he'd pulled his copy of *A Farewell to Arms* off the rocking chair where he'd left it and opened it to chapter eleven: the priest is taking a glass of vermouth with Fred, who admits that he fears God but does not love him.

> *"You understand but you do not love God."*
> *"No."*
> *"You do not love Him at all?" he asked.*
> *"I am afraid of Him in the night sometimes."*
> *"You should love Him."*
> *"I don't love much."*

Just then, a voice had shouted at him from the street. "Johnny! We're going down to the Welcome to listen to the Yanks clop the Indians. Come on!"

John shaded his eyes and blinked into the bright sunlight. Behind him, his father pushed open the screen door with a long, slow squeak. Ciro stood, barrel-chested in his overalls, a pipe dangling from the corner of his downturned mouth. "Go on, Giovanni. You just waste your afternoon with your nose in that book." The stump waved at him.

"All right," John said. He dog-eared the page and stood up. "Lemme get a shirt," he called toward the street.

The score after the first inning was one to zero, Yankees. The announcer's voice crackled over the Radiola: "Second inning and the bases are empty. Willis Hudlin checking his sign with Luke Sewell. The tall southpaw Babe Ruth ready to go to work again. Look at that! Ruth points his bat at right fielder Morgan. And the windup, and the pitch...He swings, a line shot, right field...The ball is going, going, going, right to the foul line of Cleveland's League Park right-field wall...and it is a home run!"

Three hundred miles south of the field, as Babe Ruth took all four bases with superstitious care, the crowd in the Welcome Store released their collective breath into a roar. The girls cheered, and even John, who secretly preferred Hemingway to home runs, found himself swept up in the whirl of euphoria. Jars shook on the shelves as the men jumped up and down and yelled and slapped. The entire store and everything in it quivered. Everything, that is, but the quiet girl who had entered the store just as the Babe's five-hundredth homer sailed over the right fielder's extended glove and hit a fence in Ohio.

Myrthen Bergmann walked as if she were a ghost, nearly float-ing, silent. She inclined her delicate, brunette eighteen-year-old head, mostly covered by a crocheted lace chapel veil, and paid no attention to the men or the excitement. Her only interest was in heeding the call of the Holy Spirit. In the darkness following her sister's death, Myrthen had found the light of truth from up above, yet kept her face bent mostly toward the ground.

Nonetheless, John, from his reluctant place on an upturned crate of Scott's Emulsion vitamin-enriched cod liver oil, felt an immediate hush within the uproar. The sight of the translu-cent skin of her hands, the cant of her neck against the black lace. An immediate connection to something else, something other than the inconsequence of baseball and Coca-Colas, something reverent and observant and still. This was not a girl who would feign interest in baseball, nor bat her lashes. Here—he could tell just by the unambiguous and taciturn way she approached the counter and asked for "a pound of ground round, please"—was not someone shopping for a husband or even, most likely, a passing compliment.

And yet she clearly deserved one. Her head turned as she reached into her bag for the forty-three cents she owed, and he saw the blue eyes, the full lips, the slap-red of her high cheeks. The straight line of her nose that ended in a tiny, upturned bulb. He had never seen such modest, exquisite beauty, and without meaning to, he rose slightly from his crate to get a closer look. But she bent her head again, saying thank you to Lenny, who handed over the paper-wrapped meat. Then she started for the door.

As the announcer called the next play, "And Gehrig adds a circuit blow...," John stood up abruptly and said, "Thanks, boys. Lenny." He handed over his empty soda bottle. "I'll be seeing you."

"Where you off to, Johnny?" Pepper asked.

"Goin' on home now. Dinnertime." But there was no mistaking the way he hurried toward the door. Pepper saw Myrthen stepping out into the afternoon and he laughed.

"Don't bother with her," Pepper said. "She won't have anything to do with anybody — even you. Besides, there's talk about her. Something funny, about what happened to her sister."

John just shrugged and then nodded to Lenny, who tipped an invisible hat. "Thanks," he said, and pulled open the door. He looked one way, then the other, and found her walking up the street. Picking up his pace after her, he tucked in his shirttails and combed his hair with his fingers. John jogged a few steps, then slowed, thinking, wondering, practicing. He wasn't a cad, but it wasn't his nature to be so uncertain in the approach of a girl. But she wasn't the usual type of girl.

"Excuse me," he said when he was a step behind her.

She didn't pause or falter.

"Excuse me?" he tried again.

She either didn't hear him or pretended not to. Her black mantilla fluttered against her shoulders in the summer breeze.

"Hey you!" he said, catching up. "I said, 'Excuse me.'"

She looked at him from behind the slip of lace, her piercing eyes meeting his and making his heart leap. But there was no smile when she spoke, nor did she slow her step. "I'm in a hurry."

"I can see that," he said. "Let me walk you."

"No, thank you."

He glanced at her ring finger and saw that it was bare. "Where do you live?"

"Why does that matter?"

"I'll see you home."

"I can see myself."

"I have no doubt about that," he said. "Let me see you anyway."

"There's no need."

"My name's John. Giovanni Esposito. What's yours?"

She looked at him again, narrowing her eyes and appraising him from his blue collared shirt down to the scuff of his short boots. Then she fixed her gaze onto the road ahead. "Myrthen Bergmann."

"Myrthen," he said slowly, as though he could taste the sounds. "You sure we haven't met before?"

"I didn't go to your school."

The road inclined a few degrees, and both of them, intent on their pace, began to breathe heavier into the thick air. "You working?"

"I'm a secretary at St. Michael's."

"I do the first shift at Blackstone's. Been down two years now."

She looked at his hands, pumping by his sides. "I could have guessed it."

He held them out in front of himself and looked at his fingers, coal-black at the cuticles. Embarrassed, he shoved them into the pockets of his dungarees. "It's not all I do."

"I can only imagine."

They ascended the hill in silence, then, until they reached a small row of peeling clapboard company houses set off from the road. He stopped at the scrap edge of lawn, and she continued up the steps to hers without so much as a pause.

"Can I call on you?" he asked, loud enough for her parents, if they were inside, to hear.

She swung open the screen door, walked in, and let it slam behind her.

John stood with his hands lax at his sides and stared at the empty doorway. He thought of a shred of dialogue:

"You should love Him."

"I don't love much."

Then, a minute later, the door creaked open again. Once again, his heart leapt. But it wasn't Myrthen who stepped out onto the porch.

A dry sliver of a man, eighty years old or fifty. Hollow-cheeked and gray all over: eyes, skin, hair, clothes. But his beard was neat and his shoes, polished. The man came to the edge of the top step and clasped his hands together at his belt and squinted down at John. In a drowned voice, he said:

"Yes." His German accent was thick. "You may call on her."

Then Myrthen's father smiled, all the way up to his temples, revealing a surprisingly straight and white set of teeth, and stepped back quietly into the tight gray shadows of his falling-down house.

September *14*, *1929*

"Come on, Alta. Listen to me. I been working with him now for three months, he's a decent fellow, really," her brother Marek said.

"He sounds dull."

"He's not dull, he's...he takes his work seriously is all. The other guys respect him a whole lot."

Alta sighed and plunged her hands into the sourdough. She pushed it forward with the heel of her hand, then folded the flattened edges toward the middle and pressed them down. Push, fold, press. Push, fold, press.

Marek sighed back at her. "He's not bad-looking. He works hard. He's quiet, like you. I know he ain't seeing anybody else because he's been taking some ribbing about being twenty and not having a steady girl."

She stopped and looked at her sixteen-year-old brother, younger than she by only a year and two days, and far more adventurous. He'd started underground after school to save money to go to college. "Why are you working so hard to set me up with Walter Pulaski? You've only mentioned him about a hundred times in the past two weeks. I don't need you playing Cupid for me."

Marek reached over to pinch the dough. Then he grabbed a bit of flour and tossed it on the counter between her hands. He dusted his hands together and shoved them back into his trouser pockets. Alta absorbed this addition of flour into the dough without comment. They understood each other well.

"If I don't, who will?" he asked. "Listen, you know Cyryl and Kasper are close to leaving home—I heard Kas say the other night he was thinking about asking for Juliet's hand, and you know it's only time before Cyryl asks for Margaret's. Then it's only gonna be Daddy and me until I get out of here, and I know how to cook as well as you. So what I'm sayin' is, you've been taking care of us since Mama died, and if you don't pick your head up out of the washbasin pretty soon, you're gonna miss your chance to make a family of your own."

"I have a family."

"Alta, cut it out. You know what I mean. I'm not saying do something wild like run off to New York, which I know you wouldn't do even if that old hag Maggie ever did invite you, I'm just saying find someone who'll take care of you for a change," he said. "You're not getting any younger."

Alta narrowed her eyes at him even while a smile played at her lips, and she grabbed a fistful of sourdough and threw it at him. It hit him square in the chest, and he caught it and staggered back, feigning the force of it. "Ah, you got me!" he said.

"Hardly," she said. She opened her hand and waited for him to return the weapon, then she worked it back into the thickening mass. Push, fold, press. "Oh fine," she said. "I'll go to the stupid bazaar and meet Walter."

"Atta girl."

"But then you have to promise to leave me alone. If I don't like him, then just leave me be about it, hear?

"Yessum." Then he dipped his finger into the canister of flour and drew a white line underneath one of her eyes. "Go get your war paint on, we gotta leave in an hour."

That afternoon was the eighteenth annual St. Michael's bazaar, which was always held on the second Saturday in September. Women brought their canned and baked goods to sell at the Country Kitchen; crocheted afghans, baby blankets, handmade furniture, and rosaries went on sale at the Craft Booth. All the proceeds went to pay for repairs to the church and, this year, a new ambry, the case that contains and displays the holy oils.

When Alta and Marek crossed the bridge over New Creek and walked up the turning-leaf path into Whisper Hollow, they found a crowd gathered in the level clearing that separated St. Michael's from the cemetery. Children played carnival games, and parents and older adults visited over plates of kielbasa and sauerkraut and rolls as dense as baseballs. A few parishioners walked around selling twenty-five-cent raffle tickets to win the "Mystery Nine Patch" quilt sewn by quilting bee volunteers.

With one hand in his pocket, Marek shielded his eyes with the other and scanned the crowd. "I don't see him."

Alta stood next to him, a small basket of baked goods looped over one arm. "What's he look like, exactly?"

"You ever heard Daddy describe a pillar of coal in a cut-out room?"

Alta shook her head.

"Big, strong, squared-off. Mostly quiet."

"Sounds dashing."

"He's better-looking than coal, for sure. But maybe not exactly dashing."

Alta shot him a look.

"Listen, a pillar's what's left after we mine out a room full of coal. It's what holds up the mountain after it's been hollowed out. Same could be said about old Walter." Then he tipped his head toward the arc of afternoon sun. "What do you know," he said, raising his hand. "There he is now. Hey, Walter!"

Alta sighed, but at the same time felt a kaleidoscope of butterflies take flight inside her belly. She'd never had a steady beau. She'd never even been kissed. The closest she'd come was when the pimple-faced cousin of their next-door neighbor, who was a year younger and a foot shorter, had walked her home every day after school. That was two springs ago. She didn't feel a thing toward him but pity, yet she'd still allowed him the pleasure of her company for those fifteen minutes each day, since he enjoyed it so much. Thankfully, his family moved to Kentucky as soon as school was out for the summer.

Walter made his way toward them, leaning his bulk forward and moving steadily through the crowd as though hauling his own body, like a train of coal-filled cars. His arms and legs were long; his torso, stout. He was exactly as Marek had described, big and strong and square. And even from a distance, with his chin out and his eyes down, he looked quiet.

When he stood before them, Walter nodded and extended his hand toward Marek. "Good to see you," he said in a voice that didn't match his bulk. Alta shifted very slightly forward to hear.

"Walter, I'd like to introduce my sister, Alta."

Walter nodded at her and started to extend his hand, and then, hesitating, pulled it back entirely. "How d'you do," he said.

"Nice to meet you," Alta said, and looked into her basket as the butterflies settled back down.

Marek laughed out loud. "Now that's done with." He reached out for the basket. "Alta, I'll take that basket over to the ladies at the Country Kitchen and give them your regards. Why don't the two of you go for a walk, get to know each other a little bit?"

Walter smiled and Alta met his gaze. He had a nice smile, she thought. His eyes were a very nice brown. She smiled back and then turned to Marek to hand off the basket. Marek winked at her and she rolled her eyes at him. "I'll see you later," he said.

Alta and Walter stood still, watching Marek walk away, swinging the basket in a manner that suggested he knew they were watching. They waited for him to turn around and wave or shoo them onto their walk, but he didn't. Finally, Walter turned to Alta and said, "Well?"

"Shall we?"

"Yes."

And they set off together down a path. Walter asked her polite questions about herself, the answers to which he no doubt already knew: how old she was, how many siblings, how she enjoyed passing her spare time. He said kind things about Marek, her elder brothers, and her father, whom he'd met underground. He didn't mention her mother. In turn, she asked about him.

He'd turned twenty that June, an only child and half-orphaned at age three after his mother died giving birth to still-born twin boys. He worked as an electrician for Blackstone, and he liked to spend quiet mornings hunting or building furniture with felled wood that he found in the Hollow. He liked to read but wasn't very fast at it, so he favored the *Charleston Sentinel* over books. He spoke clearly but softly, and much of what she gleaned came not from what he said, but from what he didn't.

They meandered around the church grounds and circled the happenings of the bazaar while they talked, until they finally ended up by the edge of the cemetery that had been set up for games.

"Win your gal a grab bag!" called Mr. Adler, the parishioner volunteer. "Twenty-five cents buys you three tries to win her something special! There's some with chewing gum, or soaps, or trout flies, and a few got some fancy items you'd sure be lucky to win!"

Walter looked at Alta and she shrugged, smiling and embarrassed at — but also intrigued by — the idea of her being his "gal." Walter seemed shy about it, too, but ready for the challenge. He dug into his trouser pockets for a quarter.

Six rows of six brown paper sacks had been arranged, each sack tied with twine. The idea was to take a fishing pole and try to catch one of the sacks by one of the tiny bow loops. It was harder than it looked. The loops were pulled small, and the hook was so light that it would take aim and patience and a lull in the autumn breeze to catch one. Walter took the wooden stick and surveyed the thirty-six identical bags. Alta wondered what he was thinking when he chose the one that was in the fourth column, third row from the right. He suspended the hook above the bag, eyebrows knitted in concentration, and lowered it. He missed.

"That's one!" Mr. Adler teased. "You got two more."

Walter lifted the hook and took a breath. He dipped it down, faster this time, and then pulled up, thinking he'd hooked it.

"That's two!"

Walter glanced at Alta. She nodded with what she hoped looked like encouragement. He tried again.

As though it were a canary down a shaft, Walter lowered the hook, steady, watchful. He was just about to connect when a sudden breeze blew the hook away. There was a collective groan among the three of them. Mr. Adler glanced around, checking to see if anyone else was watching, then winked. "That there was an act of God; you'da got it that time. Go on, take one last turn. No charge."

Walter shook his head. "Thank you but no." His shoulders reminded her of some sort of large animal, a gorilla maybe. Or an ox. Alta gave a polite thanks-anyway smile to both of the men and shifted her weight as if leaving, assuming Walter would do the same. Instead, he reached into his pocket and withdrew another quarter. "I'll try again, but I want to pay for it," he said.

Mr. Adler took it and held it aloft like the Host and nodded, pumping it as he did so. "A good man," he said. Then he turned to her and nodded again, one eye narrowed. "That's a good man you got there. You hang on to that one, hear?"

Alta blushed and looked down. She glanced at Walter across her shoulder, and saw that he, too, was blushing, and fighting a tiny smile. Once again, he poised the hook above the chosen bag and waited until the breeze had passed and the line had stilled. All of them watched, wanting him to catch it, wanting to escape the disappointment and embarrassment of another failed attempt, even though the prize was no more than a simple paper bag filled with next to nothing. But it was more than that, too, and all of them knew it.

He lowered the hook to the loop and waited—he seemed to Alta a patient sort of man—and, in that stillness, he outlasted the lusty wind that blew in and threatened to steal his prize. He angled his wrist, and the point slipped into the loop of twine, and he pulled it up carefully, testing the heft of the reward. When the loop held and the bag began to rise, they all sighed through broad smiles, as though the miners had all made it safely upground after a shift or the baby had started breathing again or they had enough money at the end of the month for something special. Walter unhooked the bag and held it out to Alta, who accepted it demurely. "Thank you," she said, and held it to her chest. It weighed very little.

"Well, ain't you gonna open it up? See what your fella got for you? It could be a soap, but it might be one of those fancy ones the ladies packed up." Mr. Adler leaned in and winked. "I heard tell one of them's even got a diamond ring! Now, it's not a real one, o' course. But even still, could be something to get you started in that direction." He winked again. "Go on, open it up."

Alta held the bag close. She wouldn't mind at all if it were nothing more than a chunk of good-smelling soap, but she knew better. It felt like a feather in her hand. A diamond ring, on the other hand, even a plastic one, might give Walter an idea she wasn't sure she was prepared to entertain. But what kind of beggar was she to be so choosy? She wasn't anything like her beautiful and worldly aunt Maggie. She should be grateful that anyone would show an interest in her. And Walter seemed nice enough. She looked at him before she untied the twine, and was surprised to see eagerness in his expression. His eyes were bright and held hers, direct and unflinching, for the first time since Marek had introduced them. She hadn't stopped to wonder until that moment what he might have been thinking about her all this time. If he liked her or if he didn't. By the look in his eyes, she thought there was a strong chance he did.

She smiled at the thought, but the butterflies remained peacefully at rest inside her belly. Untying the bag, she peered in.

Her eyes grew wide, but she immediately forced them back to neutral. At the bottom of the brown sack was nothing less than a plastic diamond in a plastic gold setting. It was oversized, likely from the gumball machine at the Company Store, nothing she would ever actually wear, even if it had been real. She swallowed and smiled and rolled the bag down, making out as if it were heavier than it really was.

"Soap," she said, her voice bright.

"Aw, now that's a darn shame," Mr. Adler said.

"No, no. Soap is great. Soap is perfect," she said, and turned to Walter. "Thank you. For winning it for me."

Walter's smile faded. "You're welcome," he said, and handed Mr. Adler back the fishing pole.

"Want to give it another go?" Mr. Adler's eyebrows lifted like a salesman's. "Try for that diamond ring to give your gal?"

"No, thank you," he said. "She seems happy with the soap for now."

"Next time then," he said.

"Next time." Walter nodded and then turned toward Alta. "Want to go see what's for sale in the Country Kitchen?"

"Yes, that's a good idea," she said, holding the bag in the hand farther away from Walter.

Walter nodded and they began walking, he matching his ambling pace to her long, sturdy one and trying to add more weight to the memory of that fragile sack when he'd hooked it off the ground.

October 20, 1929

Today was Myrthen Bergmann's nineteenth birthday. A day that other girls her age would celebrate with a cake, perhaps a new dress, or a special meal with her family or her husband, if she were already married, as many nineteen-year-olds in Verra were. But Myrthen no longer celebrated her birthdays. She no longer considered such blithe happiness an appropriate indulgence. Instead, she mourned.

St. Michael's Catholic Church was to the left off the path that led from town across New Creek and up into Whisper Hollow. To the right was the cemetery, which was bordered by an iron fence to keep out deer and wolves. And people, too, it seemed, since it was usually empty. On this day, like most, it was just she and all the souls that had been laid to rest there. The earliest dead were men, their stones dating back to 1867, the year the first settlers came to work for Blackstone Coal. Twelve out of a little more than a hundred had died in Verra within the first three months of their arrival from neighboring states: Pennsylvania, Ohio, Kentucky. As the company grew, so did the town. And the death tolls. Within another decade, Polish and Irish and Italian surnames were chiseled by hand into the small grave markers, men who'd crossed the Atlantic to do the hard, dangerous work in the mines. Verra was one of the first places an ex-slave could earn an equal wage, working ton for ton alongside a white man, so they came, too. But when they died, they were buried with their own. All of them—the Negroes, the Catholics and the Jews, the Baptists and the Lutherans—lived their segregated lives, then filled up their segregated cemeteries as they succumbed to illness and accidents. Perhaps some even died of homesickness, because the rough, untamed West Virginia wild was nothing like the countries they'd left behind. Back home, even the poorest had familiarity. The comfort of their own landscape, customs, languages. Their mothers.

Myrthen knew these graves. She'd imagined the entire history of Verra, all the lives interred there, just by walking through the town's cemeteries over the years. The one behind St. Michael's was special, though. Sometimes it seemed as though it might get absorbed back into the lush, savage mountainside it had once been part of. Ashes to ashes, dust to dust. If, during her year-round walks, Myrthen noticed weeds beginning to overtake someone's stone, she would stop and yank them out. She'd stuff them into her pockets and throw them alongside the road later, when she left. It offended her when life threatened to choke off the dead.

She could barely remember her sister's burial, or even much from the days before it. Ruth's actual death, if she allowed herself to think of it, existed as a composite of fractured images in her mind: poor, sweet Ruthie, so fragile, so weak, always, even in that watery world they shared before birth. Myrthen remembered Ruth as having a limp, but couldn't remember why she always listed to one side. Maybe the weight of that rag doll their mother made had altered her gait somehow. Their mother had made that doll as Myrthen's birthday gift, and Ruth wanted it so badly that Myrthen felt she had no choice but to give it to her—wasn't that right? Ruth was her twin, her other half; she would do anything for her. But then Ruthie dropped it down the cellar steps one summer night—she was always so clumsy—and Myrthen heard her cry out, "My doll, my doll!" But she wasn't able to get to Ruth fast enough to save her from trying to go down those steep cellar steps on her own. She got there just after Ruth had tumbled down the stairs. There'd been silence, then Mama crying. Always, Mama crying.

Ten, nine, eight, seven, six, five, four, three, two, one. Ready or not, here I come.

She always thought of Ruth with a desperate mixture of guilt and longing, even though her death hadn't been her fault. It wasn't her fault, was it? No matter what her mother said—or didn't say?

So why did it feel like it was?

Now, thirteen years to the day since Ruth had been buried, Myrthen knelt down at her grave. She kissed the tips of her fingers and ran them across the face of the cold stone as though it were the foot of St. Peter. Immediately, she sank into a depth of calm. The only other time she knew such peace was during prayer. The conjured presence of her dead sister brought her as close to Heaven as she'd yet been able to come. And Ruth's imagined voice was the nearest she'd come to God's.

"Happy birthday, Ruthie," she said.

Myrthen stayed a while in the quiet. When she finally spoke again, louder this time, her voice was filled with contempt. "He's come to call three times. That ruffian, John Esposito, I mean. Papa invites him to sit with us on Friday nights."

She flicked away a leaf.

"I can't imagine why he keeps coming back. I've barely spoken to him. I only sit with him because Mama and Papa have told me I must." She sighed, and shifted her position. "I know they want me to marry, even though they know I don't want to. Papa told me he wants me to be happy, but he doesn't understand." She closed her eyes and shook her head. "I won't do it. I want to be a nun and I want to be with you."

Myrthen had decided the winter she was nine years old that she would never marry. She had been loitering, as she liked to do, in the modest wings of St. Michael's after Mass. While her parents were speaking to acquaintances in the narthex, Myrthen had slipped quietly away.

Father Timothy kept literature on the side table outside his office. He wanted to give parishioners something to distract themselves with so as not to overhear the confessions of the penitents. She'd picked up the book on top of the shallow pile: *Mother Isabel of the Sacred Heart Carmelite Nun of Lisieux. 1882– 1914.* On the back cover was a picture of Mother Isabel wearing a habit and holding a prayer book and rosary, eyes full of benevolent fervor.

Father Timothy tapped her on the shoulder and she jumped. "Have you found something interesting, Myrthen?"

She shrugged. He sat down in one of the rickety chairs and extended a hand toward another one. As he rhapsodized about the order of the Carmelite nuns in France, who prayed together six or seven hours every day for the salvation of the world, she took a seat and listened. "They prayed especially hard for the souls of the priests," he said, and sighed. "Thank heaven for Sisters."

"Sisters?"

"Nuns," he said.

"Nuns are sisters?" She knew nuns existed, but had never seen any.

"Well, if I'm technically correct, all nuns are Sisters but not all Sisters are nuns." In response to her blank expression, he continued. "It depends on the types of vows they take. We can talk more about it later if you'd like, but I expect your parents will be looking for you soon. Nuns consider themselves part of a sisterhood. They live and work and pray together. They choose to serve God above everything else, and so they don't marry, don't have children. But it's a rewarding life for the ones who are called to it."

"How do they get called to it?" She moved toward the edge of the chair.

Father Timothy folded his hands in his lap and closed his eyes. "God speaks to them."

That night, she prayed until her knees ached, and then she lay in bed to wait for Him to speak. She heard the slow ticking of the hall clock, her father's occasional wheezing, and the groan of her parents' bedsprings whenever he sat up to cough. The wind against the screen door, another cough, tick-tock, tick-tock. She'd thought that His voice would be loud, like Father Timothy's, but maybe it would be quiet, like a whisper, so she strained to hear it over the noises in the house. What was that? Was that it? But no, it was only the sound of her own eager heart beating.

During the ten years since Father Timothy had first told her about the Carmelites she listened, but God still hadn't spoken to her. She passed much of that time kneeling at her sister's grave, thinking her proximity to death might better attune her ears to any whisper from Heaven. She learned, too, to quiet the sounds around her: the laughter of classmates, the teasing calls of prepubescent and, later, adolescent boys to girls, the girls' flirtatious answers. So intent was her listening, so ready was she to heed, that she even silenced the pleas of her father, who wished she had a more social life, one that would bring normalcy and color into their dreary home and might someday procure them a son-in-law, grandchildren. It was, for him, as though they'd lost not one but both daughters. Her mother, who always seemed angry at her for something or other, expressed no opinion on the matter.

The letters Myrthen had sent to the convents when she was sixteen had all been politely answered: *Thank you for your interest...I am afraid you are not yet old enough to be eligible for candidacy...If by the time you reach twenty years of age you still feel called to Carmel, then we could begin the process of discernment...*But now she had only one year left to live among the laity, and then she would find her rightful place, even if she had to do it Sadie Hawkins style, if God hadn't yet invited her. There, in the company of Sisters, she could finally reconcile her longing. She would be closer to God and, therefore, closer to Ruth. It seemed Heaven was the only place she might find love; none of her relationships with the living had turned out particularly well.

Myrthen bent her head and deepened her focus. She tried to make herself modest by hiding her appearance behind the chapel veils and dark, heavy clothing she sewed herself. But this only made her seem even more regal, more fine.

This, in fact, was precisely what had captivated John Esposito the day she walked into the Welcome Store, and what compelled him to accept Otto's invitation to sit with them over tepid cups of tea for two months of Friday nights. In Verra, girls learned early, either by some predatory instinct or by direct instruction, to make themselves beautiful and desirable to potential husbands. Girls were to become wives, mothers. The men, miners most of them, needed women to give them a reason to make the daily descent into the bowels of the earth. So they would have something to look forward to, something to come back up for, coughing black lungsful of coal dust on the way. That dirty, dangerous life was worth it when there was a good wife waiting, hearth tended, table full, bed warm. Myrthen, of course, wanted no part of it.

John didn't know whether it was her mysterious beauty or her apparent disregard for domestic captivity that urged him on. But, at her father's surprising encouragement, John returned to Myrthen's house the day after he'd met her and followed her home.

Clutching a fistful of wildflowers, he stood at her decaying doorstep as though at an altar, and waited in the late-summer heat for someone to answer his call.

February 3, 1930

Alta had known what was coming. Her brother Marek had been buzzing around her for a week, hinting at how things were about to change for the better. Cyryl and Kasper had been kinder than usual, saying thank you for their meals and clean work clothes, taking care to remove their soot- and snow-covered boots before coming into the house. Even her father seemed different, quieter and even more distant, as though he was mourning some unspoken sadness. Yet when he spoke to her, it was with new respect. So she almost expected it when Walter showed up for dinner on Friday and — as had become custom in recent months — the other men cleared out with vague excuses, leaving them entirely alone in the sitting room.

Walter balanced his weight on the outermost edge of the couch, his mass crushing the floral cushion. He wiped his square brow with the back of his hand and when he swallowed, she could see the lump in his throat rise up and down. "Alta," he began.

Sitting in the chair across from him, she crossed her ankles and pressed her interlaced fingers so deeply into her thighs her wrists hurt. Outwardly, she held a polite smile. Inwardly, she winced at his obvious discomfort with this rite of passage he attempted to cross with solemnity and meaning. She wished he had just written her a note. *Marry me?* was all it needed to say. *Yes*, she would write back. Of course it would be yes. Theirs was a good match between decent people in indecent times. Nobody could afford to be alone. Nobody wanted to be. It was the natural course to find someone kind and honorable with whom to go forth and procreate. It was expected. It was correct. *Yes* was the only reasonable answer to such a question.

"I've been thinking..."

She took a deep breath and held it.

"You and me."

The clock above his head ticked the seconds. Had his mother ever imagined her infant son's head would someday be so large, so angular? He looked down at his hands.

"Yes?" she asked.

He looked up at her again, held his eyes level with hers, which he didn't often do. What he said next came out fast, his words colliding into one another like train cars in a wreck. "I've been thinking—and your daddy is in accord—that you and I ought to get married, and I was wondering if you thought so, too."

Say yes. She looked back at him, his brown eyes nearly pleading, his mouth wrenched into a forced smile. It had been only four months and twenty days since they first met. She felt for him, this large man sitting so awkwardly on her mother's couch, reduced to such vulnerability. *Say yes.* He swallowed again, his gullet confessing his nerves. What would it be like to kiss those wide, narrow lips? What would it be like to serve him his dinner? Would their children all be as large and straight as he? What would she feel, fifty years hence, on the verge of their golden anniversary? *Say yes.*

"Yes."

"Yes?"

"Yes."

February 19, 1930

From within her life of daily and incessant service to the men around her, Alta lived for the promise of Wednesday afternoons. She spent Saturdays, the days her father and brothers weren't working underground, washing their combustible, bituminous clothes. Sundays were for rest, in theory, but that didn't take into account the next meal to be cooked and the next household chore to be done, mending or darning or cleaning out the water tray in the icebox. Mondays, she did enough shopping and baking to carry them through midweek. She spent colorless Friday evenings in the quiet company of her fiancé of almost three weeks. But Wednesdays, once she'd filled the men's dinner buckets and sent them off into the bowels of the earth to earn their living, then made their beds and put a big stew together to slow-cook until dinner, she would take whatever book she was reading by candlelight late each night after everyone else was asleep, and go down to the library.

The Schulenburg House Library was located in a paid-for company house just up New Creek, and had an impressive number of books on its shelves. The community facility was so named in honor of the widowed Schulenburg sisters, Sonja and Anita, who'd willed their home to Verra in 1924. Their husbands had been, respectively, an aspiring but not promising opera singer and an unaccomplished painter before they emigrated from Arnsberg, Germany, to West Virginia to become coal miners. What they may have lacked in talent, they made up for in passion — and a vast collection of books on the subjects that interested them most.

Over the years, other people had donated books to the library. At first it was mainly the surviving families of immigrants who gave away the few books their parents had brought from their homelands. Even if they could speak their parents' mother tongues, they often couldn't read them. As readership grew — whether because Prohibition forced people into other forms of entertainment or because of a collective yearning for something beyond poverty and coal — so did the number of books, and finally a subsidy from Blackstone allowed the little library to buy magazines and newspapers. To Alta, who tangled with an unrequited lust for life beyond her bounds, it felt like the whole world was contained in those three rooms.

She returned the book she'd been reading — or rather looking at, because she didn't understand French — on Paul Cézanne. By candlelight, she had stared at the reproduction of his watercolor *Still Life with Watermelon and Pomegranates*, searching for the pencil lines upon which he created, trying to understand the overlapping washes of different hues. These days, there was no money for something as frivolous as paints, and certainly none for lessons. Someday, she told herself. Someday. In the meantime, she could read.

The librarian, Renata, was the patronizing wife of a check weighman named Grease, who weighed the coal brought out by the miners and made sure they were credited for the work they'd done. Renata felt equally important in her position, noting in her ledger each weekday who borrowed which book and when, correctly shelving returned items, politely demanding payment of late charges when a reader had been remiss. Long ago, after she had discovered literature, she decided that she was living among mostly simpletons who couldn't appreciate the finer things. Renata showed her contempt by pressing her lips together, severely enough that the flesh around them pinched into dry accordion folds and the cords of her plump neck stood out like ropes. But she could never resist the flush of pride that came from a successful matchmaking between book and borrower, and the sense that she had singlehandedly elevated the reader to new intellectual heights.

"Hello, Mrs. Mansfield," Alta said, handing over the Cézanne book. "This was wonderful, thank you for recommending it."

Renata ran her tongue over her crooked teeth and made a moue of distaste so as to hide her delight in her accomplishment. She made an extravagance of accepting the book and crossing Alta's name off the ledger. "I have something else you might enjoy," she said. "Something fairly new."

"Oh, thank you," Alta said. Renata left to find it, allowing herself a tiny smile once her back was turned.

She handed Alta a magazine featuring a story on the artist Georgia O'Keeffe. "Have you heard of her?" Alta shook her head. "She paints flowers. Big ones, big petals and such."

Alta took the magazine from her and flipped it open to the article. A small reproduction of one of O'Keeffe's paintings was embedded in the text, art so exquisite it made her gasp. She didn't take her eyes off it as she walked backward to the couch beneath the windows. Sitting down, inelegantly, she stared at *Black Iris III.* Even though it wasn't in color, she saw in her mind the black-purple and deep maroon that graded into soft pinks and grays and whites. Something else about it lured her gaze, a fascination of unknown origin, which confused and excited her at the same time. She blinked her eyes and forced herself to read part of the text, learning about the artist's early life in a farmhouse in Wisconsin, her years at different art schools, the watercolors she painted while living in Texas. Skipping down, she read a line at random: "O'Keeffe is America's own. It is refreshing to know that she has never been to Europe, and more refreshing still to know that she has no ambition whatsoever to go there." Alta swooned at that, nestled as she was — trapped — in Verra. Perhaps someday she might visit another place, Wisconsin or Texas, but she couldn't begin to imagine how she'd ever get to go anywhere farther away than that. She didn't have Aunt Maggie's charm or pluck, and Walter wasn't the type to indulge such whimsy, even if he could afford it.

Her eyes drifted back to the iris on the page as a child drifts toward a kitchen filled with sweets, and she tried to understand what it was that pulled her. The petals were oversized, contoured and lush. Had she ever seen an iris before? She was certain that if she had, the flower never confronted her as this one did. It bloomed toward her like an open mouth, like a—

"Hello there," came a voice. She glanced up — *oh!* — and slammed the magazine closed as if she were ashamed of it. She hadn't heard his approach. But there he was, with his weight shifted onto one leg, the other at a jaunty angle. He wore a striped shirt, open at the collar, a swath of skin showing through, tan as though it were summer. Under one arm he held a book, and with the other, he raked his fingers through his dark hair. Then he smiled at her, looking directly, impossibly, into her eyes.

"Hello," she said in a voice that sounded as though it had been stuck too long in her throat.

"You reading about Georgia O'Keeffe?" He tipped his chin, which showed the vaguest stubble, toward the magazine on her lap.

She looked down, as if she were surprised to see it lying there. "Oh," she said, and cleared her throat. "Yes."

"She's one of my favorites, too," he said. Then he stuck out his hand. "I'm John, by the way. John Esposito." His smile turned his eyes into crescents.

She nodded, swallowed away the sentence *I know who you are*, and instead reached out to meet his hand and said, "I'm Alta. Alta Krol."

"Yes," he said, smiling. He gestured to the couch next to her. "You mind?"

Her heart took off when he sat down. Alta glanced up and caught the librarian's eye. Renata pushed her glasses up higher on her nose, then went back to her ledger of accounts.

"This isn't as interesting as that," he said, indicating the book in his hand, *The Style of Wright*. She looked at it, but then noticed the high-pitched angle of his bent legs, the way his knees loomed so far off the floor. Hers were like that, but while she felt gangly and too long, he seemed comfortable in the length of space his body claimed. "Frank Lloyd Wright," he said, tapping the cover. "Architecture."

Alta nodded as though it meant something to her, and they sat there, side by side for a long moment. For want of something to do, she flipped open her magazine, but when the black iris appeared again she felt a new heat rush her face as though she'd just lifted her own skirt and shown John what was hidden beneath it. If he felt provoked, however, he didn't show it. Instead he angled his neck so that he could better see the story in her lap. "Do you know the most interesting part about her, aside from her painting?" he said.

She scanned the article for some clue. "What's that?" she finally said.

"She fell in love with the photographer who discovered her."

Alta looked over at him, and waited for more, but John only smiled. She wrinkled her nose and said with equal measures of sincerity and trepidation, in case she was missing something a sophisticate might know, "Why is that the most interesting thing about her?"

John laughed out loud, and Renata looked up from her busy-work, arched one eyebrow, and realigned her lips into their firm pleats. "You're right. Maybe it's not the most interesting thing." Then he shrugged. "But I heard that story and I liked it, two artists…he even left his wife for her, he loved her so much. Not exactly noble I suppose, that part anyway, but somehow it sounded…nice." He looked over her shoulder through the window, as though whatever he was thinking about was somewhere out there, just beyond his reach.

She could see, finally, that his eyes were every color at once: dark blue and moss green and flecked with something lighter, brown or maybe gold. She looked at the small mole under his left eye near his nose and noticed that it was very slightly raised. She pressed her hand against her thigh to keep herself from reaching out and touching it. Oh, how she wanted to hold his face in both her hands and kiss him on the mouth. It was a desire she'd never experienced in all her eighteen years. The image was so clear, as though it was a memory and not a longing. And right then, she decided something.

"Someday, I'm going to be a painter," she said in a soft voice.

He slid his gaze back to hers until she felt herself trembling. He nodded almost imperceptibly. "I used to draw buildings. I was going to go to college, learn how to make skyscrapers." He shrugged again. "But it didn't work out. I still like to draw and paint sometimes." A slow, easy smile spread across his face. "Maybe we'll both be painters."

A moment passed, and the light outside the window dimmed. John looked up and saw the clouds that had gathered.

"Look," he said. "Snow's coming again." Then he turned to her and said, "I have an idea."

"What is it?"

"Would you go ice skating with me? On Miller's Pond?"

Her head went light and her forehead tingled. Another image formed in her mind, so instantly detailed it seemed to have already happened: the two of them, tall and bundled, skates tied together and slung over their shoulders, walking hand-in-hand down the lane past Old Man Miller's barn to the frozen pond behind it. She could already feel the way his fingers folded around hers, the way their bodies flowed into each other's through the palms of their hands. She looked into his extraordinary eyes and felt the word "yes" forming in her smile, but then it snagged on a sharp hook of memory and yanked her back. She'd been wandering, someplace far beyond her borders, and her mouth and her heart collapsed when she remembered: Walter.

"I...I can't," she whispered. "I'm sorry. I...I'm engaged to be married."

"Oh." John's face fell, too, but then he forced another smile, a different one, that didn't quite reach his eyes. "Well, congratulations. That's wonderful. Who's the lucky fellow?"

"Walter Pulaski," she said, and felt inexplicably embarrassed by saying his name out loud. She remembered him sitting on her family's couch not even three weeks before, looking distressed and awkward, sweat beading on his broad forehead. She'd never even kissed him.

John nodded in a way that made her ache. "Well, he sure is one lucky fellow. You can tell him I said so." Then he pushed himself off the couch and once again stood before her with his hand extended. "It was nice to meet you, Alta Krol. Maybe someday I'll see your paintings in a magazine like that." Then he turned, slowly, and before she could overcome the lump in her throat, he was already out the door.

She turned quickly toward the window, fighting the urge to run after him. The sky had darkened; the sun hid behind a thick embolus of clouds. There he was, walking with his head down against the dusk, his hands shoved into his trouser pockets. *Come back*, she willed him. *Please come back*, even though she could offer him no good reason for doing so. It was too late. Three weeks too late.

She watched as John's figure grew smaller and smaller with each step, headed somewhere without her. And just when he was too far away to recognize, just another point on the landscape, it began to snow.

April 25, 1930

Two months later, on a cool April evening, Rachel Bergmann finished packing a basket of canned fruit, dried rabbit meat, and some fresh-baked *Bauernbrot*, then wrapped her head with a shawl. "I am going to sit with Ava for the night, give her mama some rest," she said to Myrthen, who was sitting on the couch reading Scripture.

Myrthen closed her Bible. "I'll go with you," she said.

"No, you stay. Ava is sick, she needs comforting. I don't think you can help."

Myrthen looked down, picked at the corner of the Bible. "I can sit quietly. I can keep you company."

Rachel shook her head. "You stay. When your father comes home from working, tell him where I am." She opened the door and a bitter wind rushed in and claimed a place in the drab, spare living room, and it stayed, even after Rachel closed the door behind her.

Ava was the fourteen-year-old daughter of one of Rachel's good friends, and Myrthen could tell by the way Rachel fussed over her that she cared for Ava very much. But since she wasn't usually invited when Rachel went calling, she couldn't say exactly why. She wished that she knew, wished that whatever it was, she might emulate it in some way. Ava was sick with a high fever and aches that had gone on for two days. It sounded terrible, and yet Myrthen envied her.

Myrthen lit a lamp, and settled back down onto the couch with the quiet, the chill. But she wasn't totally alone; once in prayer, she felt her merciful God bending over her. *Even if my father and my mother forsake me, the Lord will take me in.* And of course, there was always Ruth.

She had finished Jesus's Last Supper and was well into the Agony in the Garden when there was an unexpected knock at the door.

John Esposito was standing, not perfectly upright, on her porch. "Evening, Myrthen." He thrust a handful of flowers at her. She hadn't seen him at all since sometime after the stock market crashed and before Thanksgiving, after her relentless unwillingness to flirt or even converse became obviously uncomfortable for them all. He'd stopped coming, finally. "It's dark," he said, pointing at the flowers. "Might be a few weeds mixed in by accident."

"What are you doing here?"

"I came to see you."

"Why?"

He cleared his throat. "I've been thinking about you is all." He cleared his throat again. "Do you think I could have a glass of water?"

"My parents aren't home."

"No offense, but we're adults." He cleared his throat a third time. "And I could really use a glass of water."

She sighed, and pulled the door open to allow him in. "Wait here," she said, and went into the kitchen. That's when she caught her reflection in the window above the sink, and realized she wasn't wearing her veil. It had become her habit, covering her head—hiding herself from other people—and now she felt exposed without it. Still, something made her smooth down her hair, tuck in a piece that had gone astray. Was it that mole on his cheek? The way his eyes crinkled when he smiled? She shook her head against such silly thoughts, and the stray lock of hair came loose again. Filling a glass, she rushed into her bedroom to put on the dark lace under which she could hide.

"Here." She offered him the glass of water, and he drank it all in one long gulp. He smiled and handed it back to her and she could see by the way he rocked on his heels that he wasn't in his right mind. "Have you been drinking?" For some reason, it didn't occur to her that he'd come all the way inside, and wasn't waiting at the door as she'd asked.

"Not much," he said, shaking his head. "Just a couple sloe gin fizzes down at the Speakeasy with Pepper Pollock and some other fellas." He raised his eyebrows and blinked a few times. "Maybe three." He reached down for the armrest of the couch where he'd sat in her polite company the previous autumn. "Mind if I sit down?" he asked, not waiting for permission as he sank onto the cushions.

"What if I do?" She stood in front of him, holding the empty glass, uncertain of what to do next.

He patted the couch. "Come on and sit a minute." She took a breath, and shifted her weight. "Aw, come on, I'm not gonna bite you," he said, and smiled. The thoughtful way he looked at her was more than she could bear.

The lamp flickered behind him and cast a thick glow in Myrthen's direction. John propped his head against his fist, leaned back into the corner, and looked at her. She sat down at the other end and stared intently at her mother's sewing basket. They stayed that way for several minutes. The chill that had kept her company earlier, she noted, was gone.

"It's actually nice sitting here with you, quiet like this," he said.

In her mind, she heard herself begging her mother, *I can sit quietly with you.* Her mother saying no. Always no. It was a torment, not being wanted. She looked up at John.

"You know, you shouldn't wear that thing all the time. Nobody can see your face that way." His voice was gentle, soft.

"That's the idea," she said, not unkindly.

"Can I see your eyes?" he said. "I just mean so we can talk. It feels like I'm in the confessional with your face all covered up like that."

She didn't move, but neither did she decline. Instead, she tried to recall if anyone had ever asked her to remove her veil. She'd been wearing it in public for years. Her mother may have chided her in the beginning, but that wasn't the same thing.

John slid closer to her, slowly, either because he was drunk or because he didn't want to startle her. When she didn't move away, he reached out and lifted the black lace off her face, and draped it back over the top of her dark hair. "That's much better," he said, whispering. Then he moved back away, and watched her profile. After a moment and without looking up, she spoke.

"Why did you come here?"

He shrugged. "I don't honestly know. I know you don't want to go out with me. But me and the fellas, well, we were sitting around and talking and of course the talk gets a little silly sometimes, about girls and such, and it just felt cheap after a while. And then I started thinking about you, and never mind that you're so pretty, but I was just wondering…oh, I don't know. I guess I thought maybe I'd just come and talk to you, like friends."

She had no friends, she who was too different, who wanted things nobody else did. Over the years, the gap between her and everyone else had grown wider and wider. She was nine-teen years old but felt like she was ninety, and was fairly certain that, by now, even if she put forth the effort, no one wanted to be around her except, perhaps, Father Timothy. Not other girls, not her mother. Instead, she had the Church, and her one-sided talks with her dead twin, and the abiding desire to enter monastic life as a Carmelite nun, which Father Timothy had promised to help her accomplish after her twentieth birthday. Exactly five months and twenty-five days from today. For the first time, the idea struck her as a lonely one.

"We could be friends, couldn't we?" he said.

She stared at the empty glass in her hands, and thought of her mother in the sickroom of someone else's daughter. *Ava needs comforting. I don't think you can help.* A knot formed at the base of her throat and she felt a sting behind her eyes. Before she could stop them, tears spilled down her cheeks.

"Oh no, don't cry," John said. "I didn't mean anything—" He moved next to her, and she lifted a hand to cover her face. "Oh, please. I'm sorry. Don't cry." He took the glass from her and set it down on the table. Immediately, she brought her other hand up and curled her body forward.

John reached into his pocket for a handkerchief and handed it to her. But her eyes were closed, and she didn't see it, so he moved closer, touched her lightly on the wrist, and when she didn't jerk away, he brought first one hand and then the other away from her face. With the gentlest of dabs, he pressed away her tears. She couldn't remember such tenderness.

When he finished, he offered her the handkerchief. She took it, fingering the damp white cloth, the raised embroidery. Someone cared enough about him to stitch a monogram onto a rag, and she responded to it with a surge of longing. For her mother, for Ruth. For anyone. She'd been huddled inside herself for so long she hadn't realized until then how alone she really was. She wondered whether she'd ever feel anything but empty, even if she got everything she prayed for.

Myrthen looked up at him and smiled, weakly. "Yes," she said. "We can be friends."

He smiled back, and in that moment, something passed between them, a mutual understanding or curiosity or simple desire. She forgot about everything else — her mother and the Carmelites and Ruth and even God — and when John leaned in, she met him with parted lips.

He slipped her veil gently off her head, and threaded his fingers into her hair. Had there ever been anything so exquisite? Her mouth was dry but she didn't want to move it from his and her heart pounded so loudly in her ears she couldn't have heard the voice of God even if He had chosen in that moment, finally, to speak to her. No, no, this couldn't happen. She was devoted to God, to the memory of Ruth. There was no place for this, no room for the mole or the crinkled smile. *Please, God.* There was a flutter at her throat — his hands, trembling also — working at the buttons on her black dress, the wool that felt irreconcilably suffocating, and so she helped him — she *helped* him — to free herself from it. And then they unbuttoned his shirt together, quickly, fumbling, then his pants and then they were both naked, John and Myrthen, and they were not ashamed.

John laid her back on the couch, tossing the polite throw pillows onto the floor to make room, and began the hasty process of exploring her. She unfurled inside herself, stretching and yawning, awakened for the first time. If there were a prayer to recite, she wouldn't have known it. John might have stopped to ask, before he entered her, if she was certain, but there seemed to be no doubt in the way she gave herself over to him. He buried his face against her neck, kissing her there as he moved on top of her and spread one of her legs aside with his knee as though shooing a kitten. "Oh," she said.

"Am I hurting you?"

"No," she said, breathless. "No." And she tipped her head and arched her back and made room for him, if not in her heart, at least inside her body.

They gave no thought to consequences, or the passage of time, or the idea of privacy. Their bodies had captured their minds, and so they couldn't have imagined that anything would interrupt them: like Ava's fever breaking, or Myrthen's mother coming home once Ava was peacefully asleep. So when the steps up to the front porch creaked, they weren't listening—and couldn't have heard it over their own panting breaths—and when the door opened, they didn't notice. In fact, they didn't even stop when Rachel was upon them, standing with her mouth set and her arm raised. Only her fist landing with a thud against John's back broke their trance. At once they scrambled to untwine themselves from each other, grabbing at discarded clothes and pillows to cover themselves, Rachel striking at John the entire time.

"Mama, stop!"

Rachel's eyes flew open and her face turned red. She brought her hand up once more, and with all her apparent might, slapped her daughter's face so hard it hurt them both.

"*Du bure!*" she screamed in a voice that Myrthen, in all the years to come, would never forget.

You whore.

There was no forgiveness. Rachel and Otto called on John's parents early the following morning, and they sat gape-mouthed on their couch as Rachel lavished the sordid details of their children's ruination. She was prepared to threaten a public attack on John's character, but in the end it was unnecessary;

his parents agreed with Rachel that the two should be married as soon as possible. Both good Catholic families and all.

"Mama, no, please, no!" The brief spell of seduction forever over, the attraction to John irrevocably spoiled. Myrthen dropped to her knees and desperately clutched at Rachel's skirts. "I'm begging you, don't make me marry him! I'll leave Verra, I'll do anything, but please! I can't marry him. I can't marry anybody!"

"Quiet!" Rachel hissed, snatching the fistful of skirt out of Myrthen's sweating hands. Then she bent down and grabbed her by the chin and peered closely into her eyes so that there would be no mistake in her meaning. "You have ruined yourself. And you have brought shame upon this family. Did we raise you to become a whore? Is that what nuns do? No, I think not. They do not want whores living among them." She let go of her daughter's chin, and her hands fell to her sides. "What do you want people to think, that we brought disgrace with us from Germany to this country? What other choice do we have but for you to marry this boy?"

"No! I won't do it! I'll run away!"

"You can run away, but your God will know your disgrace no matter where you are," she said in a voice made all the more menacing by its absence of passion. "He will never forgive you if you run away from your family and your duty."

Myrthen buried her face in her hands and wailed. "All I've ever wanted is to be a Sister."

"We all must learn to live with suffering, Myrthen," she said. "We have all had things taken away from us that we hold most dear. You of all people should know this." Then she turned on her heel. Walking away from Myrthen, she said over her shoulder, "I am going now to speak to Father Timothy. I will choose a wedding date that is far enough not to make gossip, but close enough to hide your shame if you are carrying a child."

And she left Myrthen sobbing on the floor, a butterfly in a cocoon of black wool, her life so abruptly inverted that when she finally emerged from the shock, she would metamorphose into a caterpillar.

June 6, 1930

The morning before the day Myrthen was to marry John Esposito, her mother handed her a pair of gardening shears. Myrthen crossed her arms slowly, refusing them.

"Mama, I've told you," she said in a tired voice, pinched off so that it wouldn't break. A month and a half after she'd been caught with John, she still couldn't bring herself to believe a wedding would actually take place. "I don't want to wear a wreath."

"Myrthen," her mother said. "I learned English when I came to this country. I unwound my braids. I gave up many things to be here with your father." Rachel lowered the shears, then lifted her chin and stiffened her slender back. She was still a young woman herself, only thirty-six years old, but her blonde hair had gone mostly gray. The eyes that had long ago reflected the sparkling blue-green of the ocean now looked more like the sky clouded by fine coal dust. "I gave up many things. But I carried this myrtle from your grandmother's garden in Germany. I used some of it for my own wedding wreath. I planted it here, and it took root, just as your father promised."

Myrthen uncrossed her arms and clasped her hands into a prayerful knot. She closed her eyes and reminded herself, silent and slow and calm, *Honor thy father and thy mother.*

"Myrthen, stop it. Look at me." Rachel was anxious to have the wreath made so she could attach the veil, the final step. But tradition held that the bride must cut the branches herself.

Rachel pointed the shears at her. The kettle top began to rattle above the water's boil, and a moist heat filled the small kitchen. Myrthen reached up and took them, grasping the sharp ends safely with the hand that would be her own for only one more day.

As she stomped out into the garden, she glanced once over her shoulder at the house. Her mother stood at the open window, polishing her daughter's white Mary Janes for a second time. Through the glass, Rachel frowned and made a "go on" gesture with both hands, one of which was holding a rag and the other, a shoe.

Myrthen turned away without expression, crouched down, and gathered her heavy skirt around her legs. She fingered the even-shaped, waxy myrtle leaves, then pushed her clasped hands into the folds of wool on her lap and closed her eyes.

Almighty Father, please don't make me do this. I was wrong to give in to lust. It's my fault that I was weak. I swear to you I'll never give in to such impurity again. Please don't make me marry him. I don't love him; I love You. How can I convince You? I'll give up anything, I'll do anything. I'll pray harder and—

"Myrthen!" her mother called from the window.

Myrthen turned her head slightly. "Amen," she said, and paused a moment, letting the prayer take flight into the clear blue. Then she reached into the web of branches, grabbed the first two she felt, and hacked each off with a hard squeeze of the shears. She tossed them onto the ground and sheared off two more.

"There," she said, dropping the branches onto the kitchen table.

"I'll tell you how to weave it," her mother said, putting aside the gleaming wedding shoes. "Sit."

Myrthen put the shears down on the table, hard. "I cut the branches. But I'm not going to weave it."

"You have to, Myrthen. It will bring good luck to your marriage."

"I don't need luck," she said. "I need to go. I need to speak to Father Timothy."

"What have you done since yesterday, Myrthen, that you could possibly need to confess?"

She lifted her chin and raised an eyebrow. "That's between God and me."

Rachel sighed. "At least let me measure your head." She reached out and pulled Myrthen into a chair. She selected one of the branches and held the thick end in one hand. The she made a loop around her daughter's head and pinched it where it fit.

"Ouch!"

"I'm sorry, Myrthen."

"You pulled my hair."

"Of course I didn't mean to," Rachel said, then lifted the loop off Myrthen's head and overlapped the large end, weaving it around the branch circle. Holding the wreath with one hand, she continued to weave the branch in and out and around the beginning circle. When she reached the end, she took the next branch and began to weave the next vine, starting at a different spot from the first, wrapping it in and out and around, in the opposite direction.

Rachel glanced up from her work. "You may go," she said without stopping. "Give my regards to Father Timothy. Tell him we'll be there sharp at nine-thirty in the morning."

Myrthen dipped the middle finger of her right hand into the holy water basin and crossed herself.

"Good morning, child," Father Timothy called out to her from the tiny sacristy closet. She was often the only parishioner there during the day, so even without turning around, he knew it was she who had entered.

"Good morning, Father."

Father Timothy emerged, wiped his hands on a towel. "Myrthen, tomorrow is your big day. You don't need to clean today."

"I always clean on Fridays, Father." But rather than move to gather her polishing cloth and lemon oil, the dustpan and broom, she stayed where she was with her chin nearly resting on her chest.

Father Timothy sighed. "It's not necessary. You cleaned yesterday. And your mother-in-law has delivered the flowers already." He pointed toward the altar. "Orange blossoms and hydrangea. Lovely, aren't they? And tea roses from her garden." He clasped his hands. "You are a fortunate young woman indeed, Myrthen."

"She's not my mother-in-law."

"Mother-in-law-*elect*, then." He smiled.

She pulled her mantilla lower over her face, then pressed her cheek against her shoulder. "Father, will you please hear my confession?"

"Now, child?"

"I've examined my conscience and told God of my sorrow as you suggested," she said. "Please."

"Yes," he said, taking a breath. "Of course."

She followed him to the rear of the small nave, and after he entered his compartment in the confessional, she went into the other. When she had knelt on the prie-dieu, Father Timothy slid open the screen between them.

Myrthen made the sign of the cross and said, "In the name of the Father, and of the Son, and of the Holy Spirit. My last confession was two days ago." She confessed regularly—all her minor sins, in order to make up for the very big ones that she could not bring herself to admit even to Father Timothy. That she had wanted John to touch her.

That she hadn't wanted to share her birthday doll with Ruth.

"Yes, child."

"Father, tomorrow is supposed to be my wedding day." She paused.

"Yes."

"I still don't want to get married."

"It's natural for a bride to experience some uncertainty. Did you pray the novena, as I suggested?"

"I did, Father. And I know God wants me to heed my calling to a religious life. My parents..."

Privately, Rachel had told Father Timothy the truth behind the wedding, as well as about John's earlier courtship. In the end, Father Timothy agreed with Rachel that the shame of Myrthen's actions could be resolved only by marriage. Knowing her daughter, Rachel had told him that Myrthen would have cold feet, and would Father Timothy be so good as to counsel her on the correctness of fulfilling her duty?

Myrthen could hear a shifting of cloth from behind the mesh screen. An audible sigh. "Myrthen," he said. "Your parents are good, God-fearing people."

"Yes."

"They want you to marry John Esposito."

"Yes, but only because they need me to stay close by. They need me to take care of them when they're old."

"I understand their concerns," he said. "And you, as their only daughter, have a duty to care for them if that is their need. Remember the fourth Commandment."

"Yes, Father. Of course I do."

"And you have given your heart to your fiancé." He paused for effect, leaning back in his chair on his side of the screen, the side of authority, the side of God. "So you now also have a duty to him."

She brushed the lace mantilla off her face, sticky with sweat, and moved closer to the hard edge of her small seat. "But, Father, you said you would help me find my place at one of the convents," she said anxiously. "When I was the right age."

"Myrthen, I've known you since you were a young girl, have I not?"

"Yes, Father."

"And I know, though it pains me to admit it, that you are unable to hear God's voice. His message. Though of course you have been diligent in trying."

Myrthen hung her head lower. Even now, at what felt like a sentencing, she could not muster a defense. After spending so many hours each day for so many years in her company, Father Timothy knew her far too well. She answered in a tiny voice: "No."

"I have prayed for you, Myrthen. I have asked the Holy Spirit for His divine intervention. I received the reply."

She moved to the edge of her seat. "You did?"

"God rent the heavens and came down, Myrthen," he said. Was he going to release her from her bondage? "He told me that you must comply faithfully with the duties of your state, carry your cross most patiently, and endeavor to accomplish His divine will with the utmost perfection."

Yes! she thought. *Thy will be done.* "What did the Lord tell you, Father?" she whispered close to the grill, then leaned forward, curling around the space that would soon be filled with his answer.

"That you will marry John Esposito tomorrow."

"No!" She jerked up so quickly the wooden confessional quivered where she kicked it.

"Child. It was made clear to me even if it is not clear to you."

"No," she said again, but quieter; she was shrinking already.

"It is God's will."

She plunged her face into her hands. Had she not been faithful enough? Penitent enough? Had she not proved her heart, even in spite of falling prey to John Esposito's seduction that one and only terrible time? After a moment of sobbing, she whispered, "I am sorry for these and all the sins of my past."

"Say your act of contrition."

She cried as she did so, sniffing and gasping between the words.

"Go home, now. Get ready for tomorrow. It will be a big day for you and your family. A blessed day."

Myrthen left the church reluctantly, dipping her finger into the holy water and making again the sign of the cross; then she began the walk from the rugged heights of Whisper Hollow to her home, where her mother would be laying out sauerbraten and schnitzel. Her bridal wreath of myrtle branches would no doubt be completed and waiting.

Myrthen passed the cemetery without stopping. Into the mercilessly bright sky she whispered, "My God, my God, why have you forsaken me?"

June 7, 1930

On the morning of her wedding to Walter Pulaski, Alta carried an armload of foliage from her mother's garden up Whisper Hollow to St. Michael's Church. She hadn't the benefit of a mother to plan the ceremony, nor the means for flowers. But she had her mother's garden, which she'd tended alone for the four years since she died, and the ivy that grew along the fence.

Wedding ivy, it was called. It symbolized fidelity, faithfulness, and marriage. When her mother died, it symbolized something else, although she didn't have the vocabulary for it then. That variegated green that grew wild surrounded her shattered and mended home and was like protection from the outside world. Something that meant she belonged within the space it enclosed. So, on the occasion of her wedding to the gentle, unromantic man who'd asked her father for her hand during their lunch break, she thought it appropriate to adorn the altar and the first two rows of pews with these treasured-up vines. These barriers might become a path to something more encompassing as she moved into this strange new union.

Her ceremony was to take place at high noon, immediately following that of another couple whose identity she didn't know.

She expected few guests: her brothers, of course; her uncles and aunts. Punk and Maggie had sent a telegram with the promise of a visit and a gift later; they were in Paris on holiday. Her father would give her away — reluctantly, she hoped. She would still cook many of her father's meals, although from this point forward they would be served from her own kitchen.

Would Walter, whose mother had been a wonderful cook, like the *kluski*? And the fried chicken, green beans, sauerkraut, mashed potatoes, and rolls? She'd been up since 3:00 a.m. to set the dough for the desserts and by 7:00 had already prepared most of the meal. On this warm Saturday, she was to be many things: daughter, sister, bride. And since she had no women to prepare her trousseau or lay her banquet or set forth the bread and salt and wine that would ensure her health and happiness as a married woman, she would also take the role of the cook and the hostess and the server. Her future, therefore, would have to hang on her own inexpert skills.

When, she allowed herself to wonder for a tiny moment as she wound the wedding ivy around the kneeler at the pew, when would she ever be simply Alta?

From the far right of the sanctuary came a quiet sob.

She turned and looked. A girl, a bride wearing a fine ivory silk gown, knelt in front of the small side altar of the Virgin Mary, hands clutched in prayer. Her hair was done in two braids, a symbol, Alta knew, of a girl about to become a wife. But her voice, oh her voice, was not that of a young woman on the joyful path to wifedom. It was that of Charlotte Corday on her way to the guillotine, guilty of murder, or of Mary Easty at the gallows, condemned as a witch. In all Alta's life and with all the books she'd read, it was as shrill a plea as she had ever heard:

"Oh holy Virgin! Mother Mary! You know more than any-one what it's like to lose something. Your own son, sacrificed and in agony. I beg you to look down on me with your compassionate heart."

This girl, this bride, rocked forward on her knees, grinding her gloves into the silk across her thighs as she spoke, louder and louder:

"Oh Mother of Mercy, I have no one to turn to but you. Please please please hear my humble prayer. Take pity on me, I beg you. I cannot marry anyone other than your son, my Savior. I am devoted to Him and no one else. In His name I beg you."

She stopped and took a breath; then she released the gloves from their vice and set them down neatly on her lap. She wiped her eyes and spoke again, more softly:

"If I am forced to take this man as my husband, so be it. I will accept it as God's will. But my true heart will always be reserved for my Lord and only Him."

Alta quietly placed the unwrapped end of ivy on the floor, wiped her hands across her cotton trousers, and moved to where the girl knelt in misery. She hesitated, then reached out and touched her on the shoulder.

Myrthen whipped her head around and glared at her. Alta took a startled step backward and brushed against the hard edge of the first pew. "I'm sorry," she said. "I didn't mean—"

But Myrthen had already turned back to the altar and gotten back in position, bowing her head toward the Virgin Mary. She shot her right arm out behind her and made a flicking go-away movement with her fingers. Then she turned toward the cross in the center of the sanctuary and said in barely a whisper, "Heavenly Father, if it is Your will, please take this burden away from me before it's too late."

Alta retreated quietly, and knelt to complete her work. She wondered with pity about the man who would meet his grieving bride at this same altar only two hours before her own husband-elect would meet her. Did the other groom know how unwelcome he was? Had he imagined broadly enough his future with this mournful soul?

As she completed what now seemed like the silly task of decorating the church for her own—and this other unwitting bride's—wedding ceremony, she wondered:

What would become of them all?

June 7, 1930

By the time Myrthen was forced—by the clock, by her mother, by Father Timothy—to suspend her supplications to the Virgin and the Holy Father, she had run out of tears. Her face was streaked and splotched when Rachel snatched her by the arm and nearly dragged her down the length of the sanctuary, hissing, "*Was ist mit Dir los?* You're being married in forty-five minutes." She looked around. "I am glad your new in-laws aren't yet here to see you behave so badly. Again."

At the narthex, the girl who'd been decorating the pews, Alta, stood, open-mouthed and carrying her basket of tulle and twine. As Rachel, muttering in German, dabbed a spat-upon handkerchief across Myrthen's face, she stared back at Alta with shiny, lifeless eyes. Myrthen's gaze wasn't searching or curious. It was as though she'd picked Alta at random, a blank spot on a wall, something to anchor herself as she swayed rigidly under her mother's merciless swabbing.

"Perk up, Myrthen. What will your groom think of seeing you like this? It's almost time. People will be arriving any minute. Where is your wreath?"

Myrthen, still looking through Alta, raised a finger and pointed to where it lay on the pew closest to the door.

"I'll get it," said Rachel.

Myrthen was yanked from her stupor. "No!" she said, jarring them all with the sharp edge of her voice. She released Alta from her immobilizing stare and spun around. In almost no time, Myrthen overtook her mother and lunged toward the wreath.

"*Was soll das?*" Rachel's hands flew up by her shoulders, palms out, as Myrthen passed.

Myrthen quickly bundled the braided myrtle branches inside the attached veil and clutched it to her chest. "Nothing," she said, bending her head. "It's nothing." She didn't want Rachel to know that the day before, when she'd sent Myrthen to collect the myrtle branches, Myrthen had also picked some roses for her crown. But it wasn't the blossoms she wanted. She pulled those off, and later, after her mother had gone to bed, she added the thorny stems to the inside of the wreath.

Rachel recovered her composure. "Well, then. You should put it on. It's nearly time." She reached out as though to take the wreath from her. "I'll help you."

"No," Myrthen said again, but more quietly this time. She turned away, out of Rachel's reach. "It's all right, Mama. I can put it on."

"Go. Use the mirror in Father Timothy's lavatory."

When she had left to do so, Rachel turned to Alta. "Thank you for putting the ivy," she said, looking at her with the same intensity her daughter had, and only slightly more interest. "I hope you and your husband walk together in the happy ways of love."

Alta stared back until she recalled her manners. "Thank you." Then she turned and yanked open the door. "I wish her well, too," she said. Then she slipped outside and was gone.

The wedding day and evening were spent dancing and drinking and eating at Myrthen's parents' house. Myrthen wore the wreath for the duration of the event. Only a few guests showed up, but nonetheless, Rachel had rolled up the living room rugs and engaged their neighbor's brothers to play the accordion and clarinet while Myrthen dutifully, though unhappily, danced with the male guests. Each one paid a dollar a turn, a gift to the newlyweds. But if they counted the gifts against the cost to entertain, the deficit would have been staggering. Passage to the New World was a bargain compared with the price of a dress and ceremony for their only child.

"Your mama and I were married on the ship coming to America," her father said to her at the end of the night. "No money, no church. I said to myself, in America, it will be better. There I will make money enough to give proper weddings for all the daughters I will have." He patted her hand and looked at her with seeping rheumy-gray eyes that hadn't seemed happy in as long as she could remember. "But I only have one daughter, *Liebchen*. So I don't mind spending extra for yours."

At long last, the guests retired. John took his bride by the hand, and he bid farewell to her parents and his while she stared at the floor. A friend of his had offered to drive them to their new home, a company house that had been recently vacated.

A week before the wedding, in a rare moment of lightness, Rachel had used some savings to buy two sets of lingerie. "Perhaps some good would come of this coupling after all," she'd said. "Grandchildren, at least."

But when John's friend dropped the couple off at their front step in the middle of the night, Myrthen had only one hope: that her unwelcome husband had had too much to drink and might possibly abandon any intent to consummate the marriage.

John — who'd drunk only enough to overlook his wife's obvious unhappiness — unpacked her trousseau. He found the lingerie that Rachel had bought: a sheer yellow nightgown, and a peach-colored silk negligee. "Which will it be?" he teased, dancing into the living room and holding them both up for her to see.

"Excuse me," she said. She picked up her small valise and passed him, allowing a wide berth, and shut the bedroom door behind her. With slow, deliberate care — much more than was due the gown she detested — she disrobed. She hung her wedding dress on a hanger and suspended it from one of the three hooks on the wall. Later, she would put it away where she wouldn't have to see it. On the tiny nightstand, she laid her wreath, its veil floating down.

Minutes passed. A half hour. Finally, John knocked on the bedroom door. "Myrthen?" She didn't answer. "Myrthen?" he said again, singsong, pressing his mouth against the jamb. When there was no reply, he turned the knob and pushed the door. The room was dark but for the starlight. He blinked to adjust.

She was in bed, with the coverlet up to her chin. Her eyes were closed.

"Myrthen?" He tiptoed to the edge of the bed and leaned over. Then he pulled his loosened tie off, unbuttoned his shirt and dropped it onto the floor. He undid his belt and pants and wriggled out of them. Underwear. Socks. Once naked, he stretched and yawned, loud, extending it into the "aaarwwh!" of a coal car passing by the station without stopping.

Myrthen opened her eyes and beheld her husband and that part of him that only weeks before had ruined her life. "You don't want this any more than I do," she said, her voice a low growl. "We don't need to play our roles now. Nobody's watching." She closed her eyes again and shifted onto her side for sleep.

John pulled back the sheets, and she rolled unwittingly toward the center of the weak mattress when he climbed into the bed. He moved toward her and reached out to touch her face. As he looked at her, she noticed the way his eyes crinkled when his mouth spread into a slow smile. That mole on his cheek. For a moment, just a flickering moment, she remembered the pleasure that had passed briefly between them. Then she turned her face away. She had slipped that night, let herself indulge a low desire, and look where it led her. Never again.

"We're married now," he said. "We might as well make the best of it." He touched her neck. "What do you say?" Sliding his hand down her throat, he felt a thick flannel ruffle at the hollow there. "You're all covered up."

He moved his hand farther down, brushing her breasts. Instantly, like a flinch, her arms flew up to protect herself. As they did, she elbowed him in the jaw.

"Damn!"

"Sorry," she said, although she wasn't, not entirely.

He reached over and pulled her toward him by the shoulder. "You don't have to be sorry. Just come over here. I won't hurt you."

She lay still, staring at the wreath on the table.

"Come on, Myrthen." He pulled, and she snatched herself back.

John heaved himself up and yanked back the covers and lifted her a few inches to move her to the center of the bed. Then he straddled her and leaned down into her face. She squeezed her eyes against the sight of him, the smell of Prohibition liquor on his breath. Her parents, who never touched it as far as she knew, had procured it for the celebration. Rough and forbidden, it wasn't something people knew instinctively how to hold.

He fumbled with the thousands of buttons down the front of her warm, dull nightgown, the one she'd worn every night for the past several years, regardless of the season. She pushed at him briefly but realized it was futile, so instead she rolled her face away and looked at the wreath and the veil, and her eyes went blank as a doll's.

"You liked it before. I know you did," he said, pressing himself against her.

She knew then that she would never let herself enjoy intimacy with him again. Or let herself slide into some banal form of domestic bliss. No, she would save herself for God.

He reached down behind and between his strong legs and grabbed the hem of her gown, working it up from her ankles to her knees, her dead weight no aid, and then past her white thighs that made him gasp in the moonlight, and up higher. Then he reversed the direction with her undergarments, exposing a triangle of dark against the pale skin. She lay, unmoving, white and cool and passive as a corpse as he pulled her underthings off and tossed them on the hardwood floor with a whispery thud.

His weight on her was like the weight of sin, and she felt the loneliness and sense of abandonment that sin always produces. He bent down and tried to kiss her, but she pressed her face farther into the pillow. Below, something feathery and savage was taking place. It was different now that she didn't want it. She thought of the roosters her mother kept in the henhouse to defend the flock. How they chased down and violated the hens they were meant to protect.

My God, my God, why have you forsaken me?

Back and forth, back and forth, like a ship rocking over unknown seas. Against her will, she began to enjoy the sensation.

But she forced herself, as she thereafter would, not to, and to think of God instead, to keep her thoughts, if not her body, pure. She reached out with her left hand and grasped the wreath that lay nearby. John saw her. "What are you doing with that?"

"Just get it over with," Myrthen muttered.

While her husband chiseled drunkenly at her, she lifted her head and placed the wreath around it, then let her head fall back against the pillow. She pulled the veil down over her face, and closed her eyes.

Thy will be done, God. If this is what you want for me, then I will endure it.

Back and forth, the weight of sin ruthlessly crushed crushed crushed her into the bed and soon the thorns dug into her temples and she began to bleed.

December 12, 1931

Alta paced the bottom floor of her small house with a new gait: a cross between a skip and a trot that instinct told her would calm the screaming baby. Without her own mother to help her navigate these early days, instinct was the only thing she had.

Instinct, and a dog-eared copy of *Infant Care* put out by the Children's Bureau that Renata had lent her. Alta had read it cover to cover during one of the almost-sleepless nights, while Abel slept against her, snug in the curve of her arm, wrapped in a blanket she'd crocheted for him before he was born. The book emphasized the "absolute regularity and consistency in the formation of habits," and suggested the mother create a strict schedule for the baby's daily program and habit training. But her heart ached and her breasts leaked and her instinct admonished her whenever she put him down for a nap just because the grandfather clock at the base of the stairs told her it was time to do so.

So instead she held him, and rocked him, and nursed him whenever he wanted, which was nearly all the time. When he fell into that warm sleep that only babies can, she cradled him in her arms, breathing in his milky scent, watching his rosebud mouth pantomime a suckle. Tired as she was, she sometimes refused sleep just so she could stare at him and wonder at the depth of love that had been discovered deep within her.

It was at times like these that she longed for her mother the most.

One midmorning toward the end of winter in 1926, two months after Alta's fourteenth birthday, her mother put down her dishtowel and took off the apron that she'd worn from dawn to dusk every day that Alta could remember. She pressed her hands against the kitchen sink and dropped her head. Alta looked up from the piecrust she was rolling out on the kitchen table.

"Mama?"

A tiny, almost imperceptible shake of her head.

"Mama!"

Alta dropped her rolling pin and rushed to her mother. Her mother's back felt as if she'd been standing too close to the Glenwood C stove. "Help me lie down, Alta," she said. "My head hurts something awful."

Her mother lay in bed for a full day with fever and chills before the real illness set in. The company doctor was called. He examined her while she shivered in her nightgown, and jotted her symptoms down in a notebook: flush, photophobia, conjunctivitis, diffuse pharyngitis. He diagnosed influenza, rinsed her sinuses with Ringer's solution, and told her to rest. Then he said to Alta, "Young lady, you'll take care of your father and brothers so your mama can get well, now, hear?" She nodded. She'd already helped cook and clean for years.

Her mother died in her bed eight days later.

Then her grandmother, crumpled by then to a ninety-degree angle, died a little over a month later. From that point on, even surrounded as she was by the men in her family and all the responsibilities that her mother had left behind, Alta felt utterly invisible. Utterly alone.

Now, five years later, with her own child nestled against her for nourishment and comfort, she began to feel again a sense of deep connection to another human being. She whispered lullabies to her sleeping Abel, kissed him gently on his velvet cheeks. She loved him like she'd never loved anyone, not even her mother. Nor her father or brothers. Nor Walter Pulaski, her hardworking husband of one fragile year.

Abel finally released a loud burp and fell asleep after several patting, bouncing laps around the house. Placing him carefully in the kitchen cradle her uncle had made, Alta tucked his blanket in around him. She would have liked to lie down for a rest herself, but the breakfast dishes hadn't yet been done, nor the washing, and she needed to start thinking about dinner.

She tied an apron around her waist, which she noticed was steadily shrinking back down to normal size, then rolled up her sleeves and filled the sink with soap and water. As she scrubbed, she watched a gray-eared rabbit hopping along the fenced-off garden, which she could see from her kitchen window. She wondered if it was a mama rabbit, looking for food for her babies. Knowing now how exhausting it was to care for a newborn, Alta had an urge to go pull up some arugula and kale and offer it to her.

She was so tired and lost in thought, she didn't hear Walter, who was quiet anyway in spite of his bulk, come in through the back screen door.

He saw her there at the kitchen sink, her strong, graceful hands working in the soapy water. Seeing the curve of her hips and the swell of her full breasts moved him. She looked beautiful, ethereal in that mysterious way of hers that made him wish he were a man of words so he could tell her what he saw, but his ineloquence made him shy. He stepped up behind her, wanting only to be closer to her, to understand his unnamable desire—not just to be intimate with her but to know her. Her thoughts, her secrets. Underneath her plain beauty and dutiful habits, he could sense that something far more passionate coursed through her veins. He reached out and placed one hand on her waist.

Immediately, her hands stopped moving through the dirty water. Her back straightened into a rigid posture, startled, caught. As though she were that mama rabbit snatched up from her gathering. She took a deep breath, wiped her hands on her apron, and turned slowly around. He let his hand, calloused and coal-stained no matter how hard he washed, drop to his side. Then he lifted the other to show her his prize from his morning hunt. A gray rabbit, already stiff, that he held aloft by the ears.

"Thought we could have him for dinner," he said.

"Oh."

"I'll save the skin if you want."

She stared at it a moment, then shook her head.

"All right then."

He stood there, looking at her in that pleading way he had. She sighed, tired and now inexplicably sad. "The baby's asleep," she said, looking down at the tiny figure wrapped in blue wool.

"All right."

She interpreted this as a request, and so without a word, she reached out and took his free hand. He put the dead rabbit down next to the clean dishes and let himself be led upstairs to their bedroom.

Walter seemed embarrassed whenever he reached for her, and that cautious fumbling in turn embarrassed her. His movements were awkward, his enormous hands like paws. He didn't know how to seduce or please her, how to be graceful or patient. She didn't know if it was something she had to ask for, but she sensed that it would hurt his feelings if she did. So even after more than a year of marriage, they retained their early, sheepish habits. About this misfortune, neither of them ever spoke.

As he moved over and into her, she glanced at him briefly, smiled in a vague, polite way, then turned her head to the side and closed her eyes. Then, when he rolled himself off her, he saw her staring with a blank expression out the window.

"You can just rest here a bit if you want," he said in a hushed, low voice.

She sighed and nodded.

"I'll let you know when Abel wakes up."

"Thank you," she said.

That night, she served him a lavish meal of rabbit cooked with mushrooms, stale kaiser rolls, onions, and eggs seasoned with paprika and nutmeg. She garnished it with strips of bacon, potato wedges, jarred tomatoes, and green onions, then she poured them each a small glass of wine and even lit a pair of candles.

"What's all this?" he asked.

"You're a good man."

Serving him a heaping plate of food, she bent her head as he said a short prayer of thanks. She wasn't a believer, but she thought her thanks anyway: for Abel, for Walter. He wasn't whom she'd wanted, but he didn't deserve to know that.

"Ain't you having anything?" he asked.

Alta shook her head. After she came downstairs, she'd watched through the window as Walter gutted the rabbit, sliding the skin off and removing the entrails. There'd been babies in the rabbit's belly.

"I'm not hungry," she said. "But you go on. I'll stay here with you, keep you company."

He nodded, picking up his utensils. When he shoved a heaping forkful of the rabbit into his mouth, Alta felt her stomach lurch, and turned her face discreetly away to watch as dusk began to settle, inevitably, outside the window.

February 13, 1934

When Myrthen woke up that Tuesday morning as she always did, hours after her husband had packed his own dinner bucket and trudged off to work the first shift as electrician at Number Seventeen, she felt the sticky damp between her upper thighs that meant her womb would remain barren — at least for another month — as she always knew it should. Before she even opened her eyes, she gave thanks.

Myrthen crossed herself and flung back the covers, then swung her legs to the floor and looked back over her shoulder, pleased at the bloody mess on her marital bed. Nearly four years after their wedding, she still had not forgiven John for seducing her.

John felt that punishment in as many ways as she could think to inflict it. Not just the lack of a child — that miracle, she knew, was proof that God regretted not fulfilling her betrothal to His son and a monthly reminder of His remorse — but in the steady decline of standards about the house, irregular meals and mealtimes, unstocked cupboards, and general lack of cleanliness.

She knew from that first night, when John robbed her of her virginity — her only treasure — in his vile way, a common thief stealing chattel in the dark, that she would never love him. Would never honor nor obey. He was a decent man, she granted him that, but any kindness or concession she gave merely out of reluctance to waste a breath that could be better spent in prayer.

The issue of sex, however, was more complicated.

Once her purity was gone, she decided, it was gone. So she used her beauty to exact revenge. She quickly learned that the delicate curve of her breast, slightly revealed, widened her husband's eyes. The sight of her untying her apron — slowly, from behind — whetted his appetite for more undressing. Sometimes she threw him a long, straight look — though she never said an inviting word, never beckoned him to bed — knowing his shameless lower half would strain in response. He was still a man, after all, even if she treated him without tenderness.

When his desire was at its most distracting, she would change behind the screen, then kneel by the bed with her rosary beads, meditating on the fifteen Mysteries, praying ten Hail Marys on the beads and one Our Father and the Glory Be at each mystery. Only then would she climb into the bed and allow him to lift her nightdress. But instead of letting him caress her breasts or encircle the tantalizing circumference of her waist with his coal-stained hands, she allowed him only to mount and enter her as best as he could, touching nothing with his hands, and never kissing.

She prayed the entire time, usually aloud.

When he finished, she would push him off with a strange satisfaction and go to clean herself. She always waited until he was asleep before she returned, and by then, the victory of ruining his pleasure was replaced with the kind of guilt reserved for drunkards after a binge. She was meant to be the bride of Christ, and so she felt like an adulteress whenever she lay with her husband.

That morning, she stripped off her bloody nightgown and dressed in her usual habit: a dark wool jumper with a white Peter Pan collar, dark stockings and shoes. She pulled her hair back into a low bun and secured it tightly with pins, not bothering to check her appearance in the mirror. It didn't matter. She had nobody to impress but God.

Stopping at the cemetery on her way to the church, she knelt and spoke in warm tones to her sister's headstone. "I'm saved again, Ruthie," she whispered, and winked at the tiny cross at the top. She pressed on her thighs to stand and walked behind the headstone, then stood looking down at the two newer stones to the left of her sister's.

"Hello, Papa. Mama. I pray you're at peace." Her voice was condescending, even though she was slightly envious of their reunion with Ruth. But it was not yet her time. The Lord would call her home when He was ready. That was not her choice to make, even though she'd thought about it more than once. She would not—could not—risk eternal damnation, eternal separation from her twin soul, for the greed of wanting to be with Ruth before the Lord decided it was time.

He'd taken her father within the first year of her marriage, his blackened lungs finally collapsed into ash. Her mother died the following year, bereft of any grandchildren. Rachel never failed to remind Myrthen of that fact, or of the suspicion that her daughter had refused to consummate her wedding vows to John.

"I'll practice the Reproaches on the organ today," Myrthen said to their headstones, "so if you can strain your ears, you'll hear how well my inheritance was spent."

Indeed, when her mother died, Myrthen was the sole heir to a humble fortune: a generous savings account and the small house that her father had bought from Blackstone Coal. It hadn't been easy. Otto had only his scrip and money from modest investments in American products, chosen out of grati-tude for the opportunities he found when he'd gotten there. Chevrolet and Lucky Strikes and Kellogg and William Waltke & Company, maker of Lava soap — the only detergent that could ever eliminate all but the deepest-embedded coal dust from the cracks and cuticles of his hands. While other men jumped out of New York City skyscrapers after the stock market crash in 1929, Otto remained underground with his pickax, loyal to his adopted country and faithful to the companies that made it great. When he died in early 1931, he left behind more assets than Rachel could use, and when Rachel died, they all went to Myrthen.

And Myrthen spent it all on a secondhand organ she had brought all the way from Philadelphia to St. Michael's by train.

Just over a year earlier, on a January morning, Myrthen had arrived at the church and heard powerful music coming from Father Timothy's small office. She knocked on the door and, when he didn't answer, allowed herself in. There he sat in his chair, head dropped back and hands clasped in front of him as if in prayer but thrusting gently in the air along with the music as though he were directing each of the notes to their appointed place. His eyes were closed and a rhapsodic expression soothed away the lines on his forehead. Father Timothy was only forty-four, but he carried the girth and slump of a much older man. He didn't hear her enter.

When the music stopped and the arm lifted off the record, Father Timothy mouthed a short prayer of thanks and crossed himself. He opened his eyes, gasped at the sight of Myrthen standing in the doorway, and flung his hand to his heart. "Child, I didn't know you were there."

"What was that music, Father?"

He took a deep breath and closed his eyes again, savoring the grandeur of the sound. "That was the sound of angels singing. One single instrument that imitates the sounds of an entire orchestra." He looked back at her. "I don't believe you've ever seen an organ, have you? No, certainly not." On a scrap of paper, he began to draw a box with three rows of what looked like piano keys, stair-stepped on top of one another. Behind that he quickly drew several rows of pipes of various heights. "This is only a rough sketch, of course. You see these?" He pointed. "They're just like the piano keyboard you play with your hands, which you're of course quite familiar with. Underneath, there's sometimes another row of keys you play with your feet, but they don't work the way piano pedals do. Then there are knobs called stops"—he drew several tiny circles—"that admit the passage of air into these pipes."

His round face flushed pink, and he stood up with a quickness that defied his appearance, touching his thumb and fingers to either side of his throat. "The pipes are like vocal cords. Air goes through them and makes a range of sounds, deep to very high, just like the human voice. But the organ is the voice of not just one, but a hundred or even a thousand faithful, all lifting up together in praise. That's why organs are used in connection with liturgy."

He clasped his forearms, slipping his hands inside the sleeves of his robe. He had a habit of pacing in small ovals when he was talking. Myrthen watched him follow his own path round and round, visible now in the wood floor after fourteen years of circumscription.

"Oh, how I wish we could install such a holy instrument here. It would uplift the parishioners. And it would impart splendor and strength to our prayers. Surely prayers accompanied by an organ would leave a deeper and more lasting impression, when skillfully employed. The strength of a thousand prayers at once, all inspired and controlled by one."

At this, Myrthen discovered a personal interest in the idea. "Who would play an organ here?"

Father Timothy became solemn again. He stopped pacing and wilted back into his chair. "Herein lies the problem. We have no organ, no organist, and no money to pay for either. Perhaps we could petition a subscription from the parishioners. Though in such troublesome times, who would have sums like that to spare?"

After a few weeks of searching, Myrthen found such an instrument through an advertisement in the *Philadelphia Inquirer*:

> *Moravian Unity Church — To be sold by the Church-Wardens, the Organ in the Moravian Unity Church. The Instrument is modest but very neatly adorned. It consists of 1 manual and 8 stops (including a Terzian), 2 original double-fold wedge bellows and 486 pipes. (Scattered mouse and rat damage to the wooden rank of pipes and pine case have been repaired.) It may be inspected; will be sold cheap, and the Purchaser may remove it immediately, (another being expected from England this Autumn) but if it is not disposed of, is, on the Arrival of the new Organ, intended to be shipt to England.*

Without consulting Father Timothy or her husband, Myrthen liquidated her savings. She arranged for the organ's purchase and enlisted the son of a known Moravian organ builder to oversee its transport by train, reassemble and voice the instrument, then teach her as much as she needed to know so that she could assume the role of liturgical organist in addition to her position as church secretary. Her mother and, later, her aunt Agnes had taught her to play German waltzes and polkas on the piano when she was a little girl—happy tunes that never quite settled into her soul—a musical skill that could, she correctly believed, be translated to the organ. Her palms grew damp at the idea of playing on such a powerful instrument the hymns and dirges that would accompany her contemplation of the Savior and amplify the strength of her prayers to God.

Father Timothy, when she told him of the impending arrival of her gift to the church, hit his knees. Her husband, as she predicted, hit the roof.

From the moment the organ arrived at St. Michael's in March 1933, she devoted nearly all her time to it. Her husband rarely saw her. He never needed to ask where she'd been when she finally crawled reluctantly into bed with him at the end of the day; he could smell the moldy spoor of old wood and incense on her clothes.

The day before their third Valentine's Day together, John came home from work after his shift in the Number Seventeen mine ended at three o'clock, as he always did, to a house full of dust and empty dishes. Once again he'd planned to paint her a small gift — a winged Cupid or a tree with their initials carved in the trunk — something that might finally penetrate the icy back-country of her heart.

But when he went into the bedroom to collect his paints and brushes, he saw the mess on their bed. Sheets flung back, almost proud, the bloodstains dried to nearly black. There would be no baby again, a fact that tightened his heart into a fist beneath his work shirt. If there were someone to carry on his name, he'd thought, he might finally feel a sense of purpose. And if he could make her into a mother, she might be different. She would love the child, and maybe, finally, love him, too.

He balled the sheet and, if there hadn't been twenty families within earshot, he would have emptied his lungs of all the disappointment and anger he'd accumulated during their marriage. How he would have yelled until it hurt: at the bed, at the blood, and even at God. But instead he squeezed his eyes and pressed his fingers against his temples until his head pounded. Why bother? Even if there were a God, He wouldn't hear the scream of a lone half-believer. He couldn't. Not when the half-believer's pious wife, with her incessant prayers and incantations and organ playing, was taking up all of His time.

August 14, 1936

Alta, Walter, and four-year-old Abel stood on the platform at the train station, withering under the afternoon sun. Walter was wearing his Sunday clothes. Even though it was nearly four o'clock on a Friday, Alta had insisted.

"They don't care what I look like," he'd said.

"Please, Walter," she'd replied, more with panic than with admonition. "They're used to seeing people dressed up." He groused under his breath, but did as she had asked.

Meanwhile, she'd stood at the door of their small closet in her bra and slip, biting at a hangnail and fretting over her limited options. She tried on her housedress with the tiny rosebud print, but it felt too ordinary. Slacks were too casual. She had a pair of shorts, but they might look silly to her worldly aunt Maggie. Fashion arrived slowly to Verra; she wasn't even certain what would be considered stylish beyond the ridges that separated them from the rest of the world. She tried on each of her seven dresses, but in the end went back to the one with the rosebuds, because at least it fit nicely with the trim waistline and matching belt. And she wore her best shoes, polished to gleaming. There would be no mud crusting between her barefoot toes this time. She wanted to show Maggie how she'd grown up in the eleven years since the first and last time they'd met, now that she was a wife, a mother. If not exactly sophisticated, she was worthy.

The train was late. Walter tugged at his tie. Alta dabbed at her forehead with a handkerchief, fingered the limp curls she'd spent an hour coiling into place, and held tightly on to Abel's hand to keep him from running off to throw rocks onto the tracks. Finally, they heard the familiar rumble of the passenger train coming around the bend.

"Here they come!" Alta said, touching her hair again. Then she reached down and adjusted Abel's collar, licked her fingers, and passed them over his hair. "Stand up straight," she said. She took a deep breath and did the same.

The train heaved toward them, all steel and steam. The first few passengers descended with their jaunty hats and valises. Out-of-towners, for certain. Then Mrs. Colby, with her one inflated leg, coming from a specialist in Philadelphia, limping down the steps with the help of the conductor. And then her uncle, who stepped out first so that he could turn and extend his hand to her aunt.

Maggie, at thirty-two, was no less stunning than she had been the first time Alta saw her. She wore a navy-blue rayon dress with tiny raised polka dots and puffed sleeves that contrasted with her tiny, belted waist. The two buttons at her neck and chest, made from rabbit-fur pom-poms, were unnecessary and divine. Glossy, dark curls framed her felt beret and set off her flushed cheeks. At an age when most of the hardworking women in Verra began to look like their grandmothers, Maggie still sparkled like a girl.

She looked around, apparently delighted at the rustic tableau, and when she found Alta, who'd gone suddenly rigid, she put her hands on her hips and shook her head slowly, smiling, as if to say, *Well, look at you.*

Just then Abel, who couldn't resist a close inspection of any train, wrested free of his mother's grip and ran toward the engine. Alta, who'd hoped to impress her glamorous aunt with her feigned composure, sprinted after him. She caught him by the back of his shirt just before he was about to step onto the tracks, and came to a breathless, windblown stop in front of Maggie.

"Well, he's a live one, isn't he!" Maggie said.

Alta smiled weakly back at her, trying to smooth her dress and her hair while still holding on to Abel. "He is," she said, then to him, "Abel, say hello to your great-aunt Maggie."

"Hello," he said, looking down.

"Great-aunt! Now doesn't that make me sound simply ancient! Oh, but you're looking lovely, Alta. Simply lovely. And all grown up!" She rested a hand against her heart. "Why, it was just yesterday, and now look at all of you." She turned then toward the two men, who'd just introduced themselves, and said, "You must be Walter." He shook her hand awkwardly. To Alta, it looked as if he might crush her, his solid, coal-stained paw girding her dainty fingers.

"Pleased to meet you," he said, nodding and solemn.

"How do you do," she said.

Punk, still swift as a hummingbird and dapper in his shiny banker's shoes, gave Alta a one-armed hug. "You're looking fine, Alta girl. Just fine. And what a nice family you got yourself. Your mama'd be so proud." He squeezed her again. "Now, how about we get this show on the road? Can't have my bride melting out here in this infernal heat, now can I?" He looked over at Maggie and winked, his smile reaching all the way up to the graying hair at his temples.

The circumstance that drew them away from their Upper West Side apartment for a weekend visit to Verra and not, say, to the Hamptons or Nantucket Island was the twenty-fifth wedding anniversary of Punk's older brother. Alta tried not to think too hard about where Punk and Maggie might have been, so many years ago, on the occasion of her wedding to Walter or, more recently, during Abel's baptism, or on any of his four birthdays. They'd always sent a small gift along with their apologies, and often mailed postcards from their many trips — Canada, Cuba, Europe — but this was the first time they'd actually come back. Alta watched Punk fuss over Maggie's suitcases and the way she lightly touched him every so often on the arm or the cheek. Then she looked at Walter as he plodded along ahead of them, a suitcase in each hand and all the thoughts to which she had no access billeted in his squared-off head. Walking behind them all, she reached down for Abel's hand and gave it a gentle squeeze.

Punk's brother's house had no room for extra guests, since older relatives lived with them, so Punk and Maggie spent the weekend at Alta's. That news came first as a thrill — Aunt Maggie so close by; think of all the time they'd have together — later usurped by distress. Alta looked around their modest house. What would Maggie think of it, so plain, so unoriginal? There was no time — and no money, quite frankly — to do anything about the house, but at least she could present it well. She'd spent the better part of the day before, and then that morning, scrubbing and washing, making her bed with clean sheets — Alta would sleep with Abel and Walter would take the couch — and she gave Abel the job of picking flowers for a bedside bouquet. When it was all done, Alta stood back and tried to imagine what it would be like to see her home for the first time, but she couldn't. To do so, she'd have to possess a memory of something different to compare it with. But she'd never been to Canada or Cuba. She'd never even been past the borders of West Virginia. Everything she'd ever known looked exactly as she expected.

Because it was Friday, she made *pstragi* sauté for dinner: fried brook trout that Walter and Abel caught that morning, cooked with the head and tail and served with thin slices of onion, and a few sprigs of mountain cress for a garnish.

Any time she'd spent worrying about Maggie's reaction had been wasted, because her aunt had nothing but kind — even effusive — words for the meal, the house, the comfortable bed. She even expressed regret for having to take it over (but didn't offer another arrangement). "Won't this be cozy?" she said to Punk, leaning against him and threading her arm into his. Abel, usually as quiet as his father, warmed to Maggie so much that he volunteered that it was he who'd picked the flowers. She bent down and cupped his chin and said, "They really are the most beautiful flowers I've ever seen."

After dinner, Alta cleaned the dishes and put Abel to bed while the adults retired to the living room to smoke and drink the scotch whiskey Punk had brought. When she came back downstairs, she encountered a tableau vivant: Walter sitting uneasily in his easy chair, pressed back against the cushion as though he were being held there, both feet on the floor rather than one draped over his knee the way he usually sat when he was relaxing at home, and holding his glass of whiskey as though it were a dead animal; Punk sitting at the end of the couch, comfortable as though it were his own, one arm on the rest, the other draped over the back. Sitting very close beside him, but still maintaining an independent and dignified air, was Maggie, who held a cigarette and whiskey in one hand while trailing her fingers up and down Punk's trouser leg with the other.

Alta slipped quietly in while Punk talked, took the chair next to Walter's, and picked up the glass someone had filled for her.

"Have you been following the Olympics in Berlin?" Punk asked. Walter and Alta both shook their heads.

"Oh, you should, really. The games are simply wonderful," Maggie said. "We've been practically addicted to checking the scores, haven't we?" She looked up at Punk, who nodded confirmation of this shared experience.

"That's the first thing we go for when we read the *Times* over breakfast," he said. "So you didn't hear what happened to that Negro runner from Pennsylvania? John Woodruff?"

They shook their heads again, and Alta felt a heaviness settle across her shoulders. Maggie, on the other hand, smiling at her husband, flush-faced and elegant, seemed to be levitating.

"It was remarkable, really," Punk said. "Two weeks ago, the eight-hundred-meter dash, this Long John Woodruff they call him on account of his terrific height, he was what?" He turned to Maggie.

"Six feet three inches tall! Can you imagine?"

"So one of the other runners, a Canadian, I believe, started off at a slow pace and somehow or another all the other runners ended up boxing Woodruff in. So what does he do? He stops! Literally, right there, three hundred meters into the race, he comes to a dead stop."

"Why'd he do that?" Alta asked.

"He might've earned a disqualification if he were to push his way through, if he spiked another runner to get ahead," Punk said. "But the thing of it is, he won! He stopped dead and then moved out into the third lane and took off again, and he won the gold medal." He slapped his thigh. "Can you believe it?"

"One minute, fifty-two-point-nine seconds," Maggie said. "It'll go down in history, just you watch. If only we could've been there in person to see it."

"We'll catch the next Olympics in 1940, I promise," Punk said. "Say, maybe we could all go. I don't know where it'll be, but if it's in Europe again, we could sail across the Atlantic on the *Queen Mary*."

"The *Queen Mary*?" Alta asked.

"The British ocean liner," Maggie said. "She made her maiden voyage just this May. I hear she's simply divine. Oh, we must go. We must!"

Alta tried to smile and stole a glance at Walter, who had taken an interest in his whiskey. Bankers might sail to Europe on ocean liners, but coal miners did not. She picked up her glass and, in her mind, clinked it gently against Walter's. Then she took a sip, as though it were merely water, and it burned going down. When she tried to suppress a reaction, it made the sting worse, and in spite of her embarrassment, she stood and let go a salvo of heaving coughs.

"Oh dear!" Maggie said, and nearly leapt off the couch. "Punk, honey, a glass of water!"

Maggie patted Alta on the back, reaching up in order to do so; Punk scurried to the kitchen; and finally, Walter stood up, though he could think of nothing to do to help. After she had stopped coughing, and the spills had been dabbed off the rug, and apologies had been offered back and forth — *Oh, dear, I should've warned you*; *Oh, no, it was silly of me* — Alta said she was going to go check on the baby, and bid them all goodnight. Punk and Maggie agreed that it was indeed late, and they climbed up the stairs hand in hand, leaving Walter to make himself a bed of the couch alone.

On Sunday evening, after the aunt and uncle's anniversary had been celebrated, the family went back down to the train station with Maggie and Punk to see them off. Abel gave Maggie a sheet of scribbled-on paper as a farewell gift, and Punk presented Alta with an unopened bottle of I. W. Harper whiskey.

"Drink it slow, now, hear?" he said with a wink. He shook hands with Walter while Maggie gave Alta a hug. "Do think about traveling with us sometime, won't you? If not the *Queen Mary*, then perhaps someplace else. I've always wanted to see the Pyramids, haven't you?"

The whistle blew and Punk gently herded Maggie and her suitcases toward the train. "We'll see each other soon!" she called, and blew a kiss over her shoulder. When the train finally pulled away from the platform, the three of them, Alta, Walter, and Abel, stood still and mute until they could no longer see even a lock of smoke in the sky.

"Let's go on home then," Walter said.

That night, after Abel was long asleep, and Alta and Walter had gone to bed, Alta lay awake, watching the moonlight through the open window and listening to the crickets call. Next to her, the bouquet of wildflowers wilted. The silence that had overtaken the house again, now that Punk and Maggie had gone, rang in her ears. She thought about Long John Woodruff and the *Queen Mary* and the Pyramids. She thought of Punk and Maggie, the way they touched each other constantly, as though reminding each other of their presence, of their passion. Walter hadn't touched her at all since Abel was a baby. She wasn't even sure why. It was another thing about which they didn't speak, but maybe it was time.

She rolled onto her side away from the window, tucked one hand beneath her head. Walter lay on his back, as he always did, unmoving, as though practicing for the coffin. Slowly, she reached out across the span of bed, like the *Queen Mary* crossing the Atlantic, and let her hand rest on his chest, feeling his breath and the beat of his heart, slow and steady as a clock. She moved her hand higher up toward his neck, a gentle caress that inspired no reaction. She reversed the direction, dragging her palm over the button-front of his pajama top, over the crest of belly, and down the other side. When she reached the elastic waistband, and slipped the tips of her fingers just inside, he stirred.

She moved her hand deeper inside his pajama pants and Walter's breathing changed. He closed his mouth, awake now, and reached down for her hand. Gently, so gently, he withdrew it from behind the elastic and set it back down on the mattress. Then he patted her twice on the forearm, tenderly as a grandmother would, and rolled the other way.

"Goodnight, Alta," he whispered.

She tried to imagine him fawning over her the way Punk did Maggie. She tried to imagine herself crushed against him on the couch, talking about how a man who came to a dead stop could win a footrace. She tried to imagine them laughing together at something funny, something shared. But she couldn't. Perhaps some things were meant to be just exactly as expected.

"Goodnight, Walter," she said.

July 4, 1944

Eleven years John spent toiling underground without even the reward of a smile or an embrace from his wife at the end of his long, dark shifts. Myrthen would most likely be at the church, or else dropped to her knees somewhere in the shadows. No children awaited his return at the end of each day. Most evenings, there wasn't even a hot meal. He'd long ago given up hope for either, and instead crept like a stranger into his own house and tried as best he could to make himself at home.

When John heard—as all Americans did—of the Japanese air raid on Pearl Harbor on December 7, 1941, and specifically of the sinking of the dreadnought USS *West Virginia*, John felt the stirrings of renewed purpose. Fate presented him with new options, the chance to trade his scrap life for something else. It wasn't patriotism that fed his slow awakening, nor even a longing for excitement, but simply an excuse to bring an end to the meaningless, trenchant back-and-forth between the black bowels of the mountain and the gray solitude aboveground.

When he woke up the morning of December 24, he left Myrthen a note, even though he didn't expect her to be home at

all that holy day, and drove up to the post office in Charleston
to consign himself to the United States Army.

Gone on an errand. Merry Christmas Eve.

~J

After the holidays, he submitted his formal resignation to
Blackstone and said goodbye to his parents, who'd already
lost one son to the war effort. His mother dabbed her eyes
and reached for him once, twice, and then once more before he
finally stepped off their porch. His father clapped him on the
back with his one arm; his son had finally become a man.

At home, he packed a suitcase while Myrthen watched,
unmoved, from the bedroom threshold. It might have been
awkward that he would leave Myrthen, daughter of German
parents, and ship out to another continent to bludgeon the
descendants of her ancestors. But the truth was, John Esposito
could imagine nothing better. She stepped aside to allow him to
pass, and he stopped in front of her, aware that he felt not even
a jot of regret nor doubt nor nostalgia. He bent down to kiss her
dry cheek. "Take care of yourself," he said.

"May the Lord be with you," she said. She neglected to
express a wish for his safe return.

At the train station, he stood alone on the snow-covered
platform and stared down at his boots. When he looked up,
he nodded silently to the town of Verra and to the mountains
around it. He didn't think he would ever see any of them again.
As the train chuffed around the bend, he met it with a smile.

John spent the next ten weeks training at Fort Benning,
Georgia, then took a train to New Jersey and a ferryboat to
New York Harbor, where he boarded a troop ship that sloshed
across a storm-tossed sea for thirteen days before landing at
Liverpool, England, on a cold and fog-damp afternoon in early

April. The soldiers were sent to a camp in the southeastern part of the country, in Winchester. Though they were allowed to visit a Gothic cathedral in the city, by that time he had no desire to ever step foot in a church again. John had never been very religious to begin with; he found more peace inside the Quonset huts they bunkered in, with their exposed dirt floors and drafts that licked at the coal stoves they used for warmth, and the shed latrines made of five-gallon buckets that were emptied each morning by an old farmer and his dirty-looking wife.

While on leave, John traveled north by train to London. He and a few friends from his company went to Covent Garden in search of a pub one night, and there he met Siobhán McCutcheon, a French-Irish street violinist who parlayed her hawk-nosed, freckled beauty into nights of drama and music and haphazard friendships with expatriate artists. That night, she played Mendelssohn's Violin Concerto alongside a mime in whiteface, the force of her bow against the strings rocking her violently to and fro with frenzied energy. The sheen of perspiration on her forehead made her glow. He couldn't remember ever seeing a woman so vibrant, so self-assured. Lost in a reverie, he watched her until someone punched him in the arm and made him spill beer onto his army-issued boots.

Meanwhile, Siobhán took a deep bow and slunk into the pub so that the glove puppets Punch and Judy could take over with their strife encounters against the forces of law and order. *Huzzah, huzzah! I've killed the Devil!*

John had to catch her before she left. He elbowed between the multitude of drunks and made his way to where Siobhán was packing up her violin. "That was...wonderful," he said.

"Cheers," she said, without looking up, and toggled her bow into the case.

"Can I buy you a drink?"

She snapped her case closed and stood up to her full height of just over five feet. With her free hand on one curvaceous hip, she looked him up and down and then finally met his gaze with such level intensity that John had to look away. "C'mere, I didn't mean to scare ya." She laughed, a rich, coppery sound that made him smile. After another long look, she jutted her chin up at him. "You're real, aren't ya? You don't seem like the rest of those blow-ins." She handed him her case and nodded as though to confirm an arrangement. "Come with me then," she said, and he followed her through the dark, short streets to her tiny flat two floors above a butcher's shop. He made such grateful love to her that afterward he cried a decade's worth of unshed tears into her ginger-colored hair.

She told him that night that although she would never offer him either monogamy or fidelity, she would gladly share her bed and her meals with him when she was free. It wasn't uncommon for him to arrive for a weekend stay, unannounced, and find her apartment filled with other people: musicians and photographers, writers and painters, all of them representing a myriad of countries and talents. How they found Siobhán—or she found them—he never knew. She was generous with her friends and her libations and her body, but not with much else. He didn't mind. Instead, he accepted and even grew fond of the unusual boundaries of their relationship. He was accustomed, he supposed, to sharing his wife with God, so the idea of sharing his lover with her secrets and other men was not so difficult to grasp. Only once was he turned away from her doorstep. She didn't offer an explanation, just winked at him as she tied the sash of her silk robe and said it wasn't a good time but would he come back the next time he was on leave. He did.

Siobhán satisfied his physical passions—finally, voraciously—and her friends satisfied his artistic ones. Through her he met the gritty and brooding Spanish photographer

Raimundo Marqués, sent to the front lines to photograph the war up close, and the Bulgarian watercolorist Hercules Vidin, who almost exclusively featured prostitutes waiting for their clients. Hercules willingly shared with John many of the drawing techniques he'd learned at the Académie Colarossi in Paris and, after seeing him improve, even told him that he could be a "serious artist if he didn't get his head blown off by the Krauts first." He listened to the Portuguese-American poet Francisco Pousão read from his collection-in-progress, his richly accented English heavy in the smoke- and candlelight-filled room. John was taught how to do the fox-trot by a famous French prima ballerina, and how to play the bongos from an exiled Cuban who would reveal only his first name: Ulysses.

He had never in his life been as happy as he was during his time at war. John's hometown and wife—who didn't write him a single letter in twenty-six months—seemed long ago and far away, and, unlike the men of his company eager to return to America, he gave little thought to any end to his semi-patriotic expatriate adventure. That is, until he found himself standing alongside his photographer friend Marqués, who had embedded himself in John's company, churning across the English Channel at low tide and under a full moon. It was the early morning of June 6, 1944, the day before John's fourteenth wedding anniversary. The troops watched, stunned and steeled, as the Normandy coast grew larger on the horizon. Cold, rough spray stung their faces, and many of them vomited over the side, from either seasickness or fear. A thousand yards offshore, they started taking mortar shells and artillery, and then there was nothing but bombs and blood and screaming, crying, shooting, and chaos as the landing ship ramps were lowered and troops poured into the sea. Countless lives ended before they even reached the sand.

John ran forward onto the beach, leaderless, and somehow made it: through the small arms artillery and the litter of used

K-ration cartons, tin cans, empty cartridge casings, and dead
Allies, all the way to the bluffs. He had no idea about the passage of time, or how he ended up in an Army Ranger battalion
at the Pointe du Hoc cliff. And he couldn't recall how far up
the hundred-foot cliff he'd scaled before he took a round to his
left kneecap, which blew it to splinters inside his herringbone
pants.

John woke up in a hospital in London with a Purple Heart
and a Bronze Star and a shattered knee that would bother him
for the rest of his life. The army had no further use for him.
They were going to let him heal, then send him back home,
honorably discharged. He lay in his scratchy cot and stared at
the ceiling, dulled. The color drained out of his dreams, and
now when he closed his eyes, he saw black: slick, wet coal, the
underbelly of Trist Mountain, coal dust under his fingernails,
Myrthen's ankle-length wardrobe, her opaque soul.

On Independence Day, after nearly a month in the hospital,
he was finally able to sit up without pain in his back. He asked
one of the nurses for some stationery and a pen. He wrote two
letters. The first was to his parents, to let them know he was
alive and coming home. The other was to his wife:

Dear Myrthen,

*It's been more than two years since I left. I'm not sure if you got any
of my letters, because I never got anything from you. My mother
wrote and said she'd checked in on you from time to time, and saw
you at church, so I was at least glad to know you were doing okay.*

*I took some enemy fire about a month ago and am laid up for
a little while longer, but they say I'm going to be discharged in a
couple of weeks. They're sending me home.*

*But you know I got thinking, and I'm not really sure what
"home" is anymore. I know you didn't want to marry me, Myrthen.
I know you haven't been happy being my wife all these long years. If*

I'm being honest, I admit it hasn't much resembled what I'd hoped for when I said "I do."

I met someone here in London. I should have told you about her when it started. It wasn't very serious, but it was fun. She liked me a whole lot, and treated me better than she probably should have. I probably won't ever see her again, or even write to her, but before I come home, I needed to tell you. I'd be lying if I tried to say I'm sorry for what I did. Truth is, I'm glad, because now I know that I was really missing something before, and I hope I'll have the chance to find it again.

Myrthen, I'm asking you for a divorce. I didn't want to wait until I got home and spring it on you. I wanted to give you fair warning, so you'll have time to think about it before you see me again. We can do it quietly, and I'll make sure you're all set up. Believe me, I wouldn't have thought of this if I didn't know in my heart that you've probably been wishing for it all along.

See you in a few weeks.
~John

August 19, 1944

The day Myrthen received John's letter asking for a divorce, she fell to her knees in a protracted and tearful prayer of thanks. For the years after her parents died, she'd been waiting for the day when she would no longer be yoked to her husband: the mountain would swallow him up during a shift, he would run off with another woman, or he wouldn't come home from the war. She'd prayed desperately for severance of their marital bond, in whatever form it would take. She knew, of course, that Catholics were forbidden to divorce, but she'd spent enough time in Father Timothy's small library, reading books on canon law by Schulte and Fournier and Donne, to learn that if she could show that one of the elements of her sacramental marriage contract was missing, she could apply for an annulment. She didn't have enough cause before John sent his letter. But with his admission of infidelity and his desire to end their marriage, all she had to do was ask Father Timothy to help her prepare the paperwork and send it to the Diocesan Tribunal.

She was so certain of the events that would unfold and so eager to begin her new life as a contemplative nun that she didn't bother to write back to her soon-to-be ex-husband, or share her plans just yet with Father Timothy, who would no doubt object to her leaving St. Michael's. (Who would take over as secretary? Who would play the organ?) No, she kept her plans to herself. Her future was finally hers and Ruth's and God's alone.

Monday, July 24, 1944

Reverend Mother Mary-Joseph
The Carmel of St. Isabel
Bussie, Ohio

Dear Reverend Mother,

Praise be to the God and Father of our Lord Jesus Christ, who has blessed us in the heavenly realms with every spiritual blessing in Christ. For He chose us in Him before the creation of the world to be holy and blameless in His sight.

I am writing to petition your consideration. When I was nine years old, I first heard our Lord Jesus calling me to be His Bride. That was when I first learned about Sister Isabel of Lisieux and the Carmelite Order. I have spent the years between then and now in the pursuit of union with God, in imitation of Mary, who first showed us how to love and serve the Son of God, our Lord and Savior Jesus Christ, Who is the Way, the Truth, and the Life. I am finally free of all of the obligations that prevented me from following the Vocation which He has destined for me. I am now able to live a life of humble obedience, perfect chastity, and complete poverty. I wish for a life of intense prayer, hidden in Christ, my Divine Spouse, belonging only to Him, and with Him as my great and only reward.

I believe God, for whom my soul thirsts, has led me to your monastery to live in the community of the sisters there. Although I have consecrated nearly all my days and most of my evenings to St.

Michael's in service as Secretary and organist, I hope you will help me to answer God's call. May God bless you.

Yours in Him,
Myrthen Bergmann

———

Monday, August 7, 1944

Dear Miss Bergmann,

Praise be to Jesus! I received your letter dated July 24th in which you asked for information regarding the process of entering our monastery to become a Carmelite nun. There are many parts to this process, and I am enclosing a paper outlining the steps. Understandably, the application process is rigorous. We need to discern whether you are spiritually, physically, and psychologically healthy for the spiritual ascent of Mount Carmel. We want to make sure you have the potential to be formed into a good Carmelite who can live a life of prayer and sacrifice for the sanctification of priests and the salvation of souls. You must be at least twenty years of age, in good physical health, of sound mental standing, and free of outstanding debts and obligations, all of which, apparently, you are. Please, if you will, cable to arrange a time when we can meet face to face.

Yours in Christ,
Sister Mary-Joseph, Prioress

On the third Friday in August, Myrthen packed the same upholstery bag her mother had carried across the Atlantic from Saxony to West Virginia more than three decades before. Now moth-eaten and holding only a clean pair of underwear, a toothbrush, and her Bible, it suited Myrthen's own hopeful occasion as an expression of poverty and humility.

She was ready to live a life of monastic chastity, prayer, solitude, and guided Godliness. She'd always been ready.

The train took her north and west, through the verdancy of the state, through Phico and Kitchen, Fry and Leet and the Big Ugly Public Hunting Area, then to where West Virginia and Kentucky and Ohio connected themselves together along the banks of the Ohio River like distant cousins, and beyond to Coal Grove and Ironton and Garden City, and up along the winding river that led all the way around Shawnee State Forest to the tiny enclave of Bussie, Ohio. In the gloaming sunlit distance, she looked upon it as a new and everlasting home.

Sister Mary Margaret, an extern whose job it was to greet outsiders, met Myrthen at the monastery gates. Myrthen stood, transfixed. She'd never before seen an actual nun. Stirred by Sister Mary Margaret's attire, which was as alluring to her as immodest clothing was to men, Myrthen desperately wanted to reach out and feel the fabric of the wimple. It encircled Mary Margaret's lovely oval face like a swallow-tailed flag. For the first time in longer than she could remember, Myrthen smiled.

She was shown to the guest cottage by way of a broad vegetable and flower garden. A stone-faced Saint Joseph stood amid the blue phlox and wild ginger with the infant Jesus in the crook of an arm. Several nuns knelt along the rows, weeding. They looked up and smiled at her as she passed, but none of them spoke. It was to Myrthen's ears the most pleasing of any potential greeting. The cottage was no larger than a garden shed, with a plain door and two windows, one facing south to let in the sun in winter, and the other facing east to illuminate dawn prayers. The bed was a cot with a thin mattress and a brown coverlet pulled neatly up. A crucifix hung above it and, next to that, a framed rendering of the Virgin Mother, her sacred heart exposed aflame. Otherwise, the whitewashed walls were bare, and the only other piece of furniture was a straight-backed chair upon which was draped a rosary.

Sister Mary Margaret showed her the outhouse, and pointed out the public entrance to the main chapel. If Myrthen liked, she could sit that evening—behind the grille that separated the cloistered nuns from the outside world—and listen to them chant the Divine Office. Sister Mary Margaret would herself bring a meal to Myrthen at the cottage before Vespers.

Left alone in the joyful austerity of the room, Myrthen sank to her knees on the planked floor, crossed herself, and began to pray. But she was too excited by the prospect of living amid these dark-veiled brides in peaceful solitude and contemplation to continue the Rosary. Her mind wandered to Ruth.

"I can feel you so closely now, Ruthie. I knew I would be able to! All my life I've been waiting, and now here I am. It will almost be like we're together again," she whispered. "I wonder if they have an organ, and if I'll be allowed to play."

The next morning, Myrthen woke up at five o'clock and attended early Mass. She rejoiced at the sight of those black-and-white figures with their heads bowed in the pews, felt the body of Christ on her tongue as though for the first time. She didn't touch the breakfast that Sister Mary Margaret brought for her, not wanting to dilute the unleavened memory of the wafer in her mouth. When it was time, she was lead to the speakroom, where she would meet the Mother Prioress.

A large iron grille bisected the room like a screen on an open window. When the Prioress finally entered from her side of the grille, Myrthen bowed her head and held her hands, palms up, right over left, seeking her blessing. The Prioress gave it, and Myrthen would have kissed her hand were it not for the grille between them. Instead she simply stood.

"Please, child, sit down." The Prioress was small and round as she was tall. Her cheeks were squeezed plump by her wimple, which also covered every strand of her hair. It was difficult to guess how old she was, how many years she might have knelt in the choir, how long she'd followed her own path from cell to chapel. There were wrinkles about her mouth and eyes, however, and she used glasses to peer at the piece of paper she held in her hands. Ah, there they were, the liver spots and crêpe-like skin that matched the peacefully deep voice of advancing age.

The Prioress looked up from the paper she held—Myrthen's original letter of inquiry—and smiled. "What a blessing it is to have you come and visit us. Have you enjoyed your stay thus far?"

"Oh yes, very much. It's beautiful here, really. Sister Mary Margaret has been so gracious, and the nuns...oh, everyone has been very cheerful...I found myself enchanted by the sounds of their voices together last night during prayer. Praise be to God!"

"Praise be to God, indeed." The Prioress folded her hands atop the letter in her lap. "Now, Miss Bergmann, as I told you in my letter, the formation of a nun is a lengthy process, starting with our introduction. If that goes well, we will ask that you spend some time to seriously discern if God may be calling you to the religious life—"

"Oh, but I've already spent so much time! I'm certain that I've been called. I've known it all my life!"

The Prioress nodded for a moment, then said, "All right then, why don't you start by telling me about your life?"

"What...what would you like to know?"

"Tell me about when you were a girl. Did you like athletics? Did you join clubs at school? Did you have many friends?"

"I spent much of my time at home. My father was often ill. He was a coal miner. And my mother...my mother needed my help. And when I wasn't at home, I spent time at our parish, Saint Michael's." She wondered for the first time if her singular devotion was an asset in the eyes of the Prioress. How could it not be?

"What about your siblings?"

"I had a twin. Ruth. She died when we were almost six. She was helping our mother carry jars to the cellar and slipped and fell down the stairs." Myrthen dropped her head.

"I'm sorry, child. Surely she is with our Lord, in His care."

Myrthen nodded. That half-remembered memory left her cold whenever she got too close to it. The crash, the scream. Her mother, crying. *It's not your fault*, Father Timothy had said. *Everything is God's will, you must pray.*

After an appropriate pause, the Prioress continued. "What about suitors? Did you have boyfriends? Dates?"

"Not…boyfriends, exactly."

"No?" The Prioress looked at her over the top of her glasses. "Did you have dates?"

She thought of the night with John on her parents' couch. "I didn't have dates, not the traditional way." Now she was concerned about the flow of information, how it weighed in the Mother's mind. Was it good or bad for nuns to have been on dates at some point in their lives?

"I see. Nontraditional dates, then?"

"Well, yes. One boy would come sit with me and my parents, but I never went out with him anywhere. When I was nineteen years old, we married. Not by choice, mind you. I didn't want to be married to anyone other than God. But I had to, for the sake of my parents. They wouldn't hear of me joining a convent. They needed me near. My father was ill, as I said, and my mother. Well, I couldn't abandon my mother. So I did it, for their sakes. But it's ended, fortunately."

"Has he passed on, then?"

Myrthen looked down. "No. He's still living. But it's being nullified. He's asked for a divorce, which of course I won't grant him. It's being done properly." She looked up, hubris glinting in her eyes. "I'd have done it as soon as my parents died if I'd had the reason. But finally I did: he committed the sin of adultery. And more than that, he asked for a divorce."

"You know, of course, that a divorce is only a civil procedure."

Myrthen nodded.

"So you've been granted an annulment of the union?"

"Well..." Myrthen cleared her throat. "It hasn't been granted yet."

"Have you heard from the marriage tribunal? Where does it stand?"

"Well...I haven't actually...begun the process."

The Prioress folded up Myrthen's letter and set it to the side. "My dear, I must speak to you now from the point of view of canon law. Frankly, I'm surprised your pastor would send you all the way here without explaining it to you first."

Myrthen leaned forward, a line of sweat beading on her lip. "Whatever do you mean? I haven't been sent. I didn't even tell Father Timothy that I was coming."

The Prioress nodded. "You would have had to, eventually. All candidates must provide letters of recommendation from their pastors. Nevertheless, that's not what's important now," she said. "There are certain clear signs that entering the religious life is not your vocation."

Myrthen held her breath.

"You were married in the Church."

She nodded.

"It mystifies people, the nature of marriage." The Prioress twisted the gold band she wore that symbolized her union with God. "In the secular world, it is a contract between a man and a woman. But when two Christians are joined in marriage, it becomes a sacramental contract that is nearly impossible to break."

Silence.

"It's very rare — *very* rare — for an annulment to be granted. The circumstances must be extenuating, dear. Far beyond the straying of a spouse. You would have to prove that the marriage was null at the time of the ceremony. It would likely have to go all the way to the Vatican, and it could take years, and even then, your petition would most probably be refused." She paused for a moment and then looked Myrthen directly in the eyes. "I'm afraid that in the eyes of the Church, you are still married, Mrs...."

"Esposito."

"The canon law relating to admission to the novitiate clearly states that a spouse — while the marriage lasts — is ineligible. I'm very sorry."

"Ineligible?" Myrthen shrieked. "You're saying he has to die first? I have to wait for him to die?"

"There, there." The Prioress looked genuinely concerned. "Is there any way I can help you? Would you like to stay a few more days in the guest cottage and pray?"

Myrthen put her face in her hands and began to cry.

"There are secular Carmelites who live in the world as laypersons but follow Carmelite spirituality, blended with works of the apostolate. Perhaps you could seek out possibilities with them? Serve God and His community as an educator, perhaps, or a health care provider."

"No!" Myrthen yanked her hands away from her face and glared at the Prioress. She saw the Prioress's eyes widen and her back press against the rest of her chair. "No," she repeated, but more softly. "I don't want to live as a layperson. I want to be cloistered. I want to...I want to be with the Sisters and belong only to God."

The Prioress pulled a tissue from some hidden compartment in her habit and waved it, a white flag, through one of the big squares in the grille. Myrthen reached up to take it, and the

Mother let it go before their fingers could touch. "The law is clear, child. As long as your spouse is still living, and unless you are able to nullify it, you will remain married in the eyes of God."

Myrthen blew her nose and tucked the soiled tissue into her own pocket. She stood up to leave.

As long as your spouse is still living.

She lifted her chin. She would find a way. She wouldn't stand and be fired at by canon law.

"Thank you for your time, Reverend Mother," said Myrthen. "May the Lord bless you."

"And may He bless you, Mrs. Esposito."

After Myrthen had closed the door behind her, the Prioress sank down heavily into her wooden chair. It was a shame, really. There were fewer and fewer girls every year who expressed a sincere interest in beginning the process of formation. She slipped Myrthen's letter back into its envelope. She would take it to her filing cabinet in the rectory. But she didn't imagine she would be hearing from Myrthen Esposito again; at almost thirty-four, the girl was nearing the upper limit of the age requirement, and unless something happened very soon, her eligibility would expire before her marriage did. The Prioress put the letter into her pocket. A shame, but perhaps it was just as well.

There was something rather unsettling about her.

November 11, 1944

Alta Pulaski covered her husband and son's dinner of *halushki* and *rogale* with a dishtowel and set it on the kitchen table with a note: *Gone up the hill for a bit.* Walter was at work underground, and thirteen-year-old Abel—who was already as tall as a man and ready to be one—was going rabbit hunting with his friends. She tied a green woolen scarf around her pinned hair, still short while other women had started to let theirs grow longer to contrast with the war rationing and the somber mood of the day. Gathering up her metal paint box and an empty Ball jar, Alta set off on her quarter-mile hike.

All the way up she thought of her painting. She'd started it already, rendering individual leaves on dampened paper—red and yellow sassafras, scarlet-orange hornbeam, bright yellow witch hazel, rust and crimson oaks—translating the scents and colors into textures. Dry brush, stippling, a dash of salt from her kitchen, a scratch of veins into wet paint with a bobby pin pulled from against her temple. To make it seem more real, Alta used water from the mountain brook near her secluded perch. Used dry leaves from the ground for blotting.

Her mind had long forgotten those girlhood fantasies of the forest beyond the southern coalfields of West Virginia. Instead, she focused on the trees.

She was so absorbed in creative thought that the sounds around her — the crunch of leaves, the prattle of the creek — blended into a cool-white rush of noise. It lulled her into that part of herself that was neither dutiful wife nor artist, but essential to both. Preoccupied as she was, she didn't notice the heavy footsteps that stopped a maple tree shadow's length behind her.

John Esposito trudged up the mountain, his mind occupied by the burden of bachelorhood, and with a rocking chair slung across his shoulders. Going home to Myrthen wasn't like going home at all, so he had decided to find someplace else to call his own — a place where he could escape and paint and, possibly soon, a place where he could live.

His uncle, long dead now, had built a double-barrel shotgun shack out of white pine on a hill in Whisper Hollow, shortly after the Eighteenth Amendment forbade the sale of liquor. The same uncle had happily abandoned his pickax and crept into the forest, making a three-stage still out of sheets of copper, putting up corn mash, and running whiskey until he died. For a long time, the cabin and its add-on porch stunk of moonshine, but the years and the wind had blown that nearly all away. Now it suited John just fine.

It loomed in the near distance. John looked up, checking his path, and there, just in front of him, sat a woman on a maple stump.

Alta's back was to him, lithe and strong and bent over her paper. A tray of paint lay on the ground next to her. John held his breath and watched her dip her brush into the jar of mountain water and scrub it into the picture emerging on her lap.

She looked familiar, but without being able to see her face, he didn't know why. Her long arms and neck, the elegant and sure way she moved, the graceful stillness she possessed was vaguely reminiscent. He'd seen women like her lounging in bistro chairs at outdoor cafés or strolling along the Thames and the Seine and the streets of Montmartre in the evenings. But he'd seen none of them hunched over a stretch of paper, imitating life in art the way he, himself, would.

Alta put down her brush and straightened up. Then she angled her face to the wind and—he imagined—closed her eyes. Pulling her shoulder blades back like a butterfly flexing its wings, she moved her head from side to side. Then Alta untied the scarf from underneath her chin, balled it, and wiped it across her brow.

Recognition stretched into knowing. Within that infinite moment that she tossed the sweaty scarf onto the ground and picked up her brush, he knew his life would be forever changed.

Eyes still on her back, John let the chair slide slowly down one shoulder and drop to the ground. The thump it made blew behind him on the wind, and Alta showed no sign that she'd heard it—she bent back over her painting and appeared from behind to be completely absorbed in her work. John didn't want to disturb her, nor did he want to leave, so he eased himself down into the chair and leaned back to watch.

A cool breeze blew into his face, lingering like a kiss, and he relaxed into the rocking chair. He closed his eyes, and when he opened them again, he saw the figure of Alta, still bent forward, her hand moving with the tiny strokes of her brush. Seeing her brought him an inexplicable comfort. He tried it again. Closing his eyes against the breeze, longer this time, he allowed himself to breathe, listening to the faint rush of the stream in the distance, the leaves. Then he opened them, and there she was, still, again. He smiled. When he closed his eyes once more, he kept them closed even longer, rocking and listening and absorbing and enjoying and relaxing until everything he'd been carrying—both on his shoulders and in his mind—tumbled down onto the downy, leaf-covered mountain and left him to fall into a deep and peaceful sleep.

When he awoke, smacking away the stickiness in his mouth and opening first one eye and then the other, he blinked quickly, remembering what his eyes sought upon opening, and saw the tree stump on which she'd been sitting. But she wasn't there. *No!* He sat up straight, toward the edge of the seat, gripping the arms of the rocking chair. There was the impulse to run after her, but his sleep-washed mind was slow to decide in which direction. Then, from his right, he heard her voice:

"You sound like a bear when you sleep."

She was sitting with her legs crossed and her palms pressed onto the ground behind her, her head tilted to one side in a reflective way. "I heard this terrible roar and turned around. I thought it was a bear. But it was just a man, asleep in a rocking chair in the middle of the woods."

She was beautiful.

"How long have I been out?"

"Well, I've been watching you for about six minutes," she said, looking at her watch. "No telling how long you were out before that."

"I tend to fall asleep quickly."

"And snore like an animal."

"Will that bother you?"

Her eyes widened and her eyebrows lifted. A second passed, and she let them slide back down into place, biting her lower lip to hide a smile. "No."

They looked at each other like that for a long moment, strangers locked in recognition, approaching this immediate familiarity from opposite directions. The wind blew at them, cooler now, and she turned her head toward it, tucking a short piece of her light brown hair behind her ear. Finally he spoke.

"I know you," he said.

She smiled again. "Yes," she said. "You do."

Leaning forward off her hands, she dusted them together and extended the right one toward him. "I'm Alta," she said. "How do you do?" He leaned toward her from the edge of the chair and slid his hand against hers.

"I know," he said. "And I'm John."

A slow smile. "I know."

Finally, she let his hand go and looked up the hill toward the abandoned cabin, the direction in which he'd been going. "That cabin yours now?"

He nodded.

"That chair will be nice on the porch. Faces the sunset. Are you moving in?"

"In a sense," he said. "I'm a painter, too." It was the first time he'd ever called himself one aloud, although he'd been doing it for two decades. Because his painting had forever been a secret, he kept his stash of drawings and paintings in a flat box beneath his bed. Neither his father nor his wife had seen any purpose in such an idle distraction. Myrthen was given to heavy sighs whenever he spread out his oil paints across the kitchen table to work.

Alta tilted her head again, as if to regard him from another perspective. Then she stood up and dusted off the seat of her wool trousers.

"I need to go. My husband's waiting."

"Wait," he said. But she had started already toward the tree stump. He stood up and followed, watched her empty the water from the jar, shake out her brush, and place it back into the metal box. Watched as she touched the surface of her painting lightly, testing. Watched as, satisfied, she rolled it into a loose tube. Then she picked up her scarf and, despite the chill that had come down the mountain and settled around them, tucked it along with the paint box under her arm.

"Come see me," he said when she turned back toward him.

"What about your wife? You're still married, I suppose?"

"Barely."

"Myrthen is her name, I recall."

"She won't know," he said. "Wouldn't care anyways."

"I'm married," she said. "I have a son. He's almost thirteen."

"I'm sure we'll get along famously." A spray of fine lines fanned out from the corners of his eyes when he smiled. "How about you just come and paint? I'll even get another chair."

She bit her lip again. "I wish I could," she said.

"Someday," he countered.

She smiled again, faintly. Then she turned and began the short hike down the mountain, back to her husband and son.

December 1, 1944

When Myrthen came home from the convent in Ohio, she was resolute. She decided she would move back to her childhood home, which she'd kept even after liquidating the rest of her inheritance to buy the organ for St. Michael's, as soon as the essential repairs could be done. She didn't wait a moment longer than necessary to inform her husband of her plans.

The day John arrived home from Europe with a faint limp and a drawn face, she met him at the door and said, "In the eyes of the Church, we can't divorce, but we can separate. You may consider yourself free to do as you please. Not that you needed my permission before. I plan to have this marriage annulled." And she stood with one eyebrow arched, allowing time for the information to settle, before opening the door to allow him in.

During the following months, John went back underground and Myrthen resumed her dirge-filled days at the church. They shared a bed, but never their bodies nor any words that weren't fundamentally necessary. Then the Friday came when her parents' house was ready and she packed the bags she'd come with fourteen years before. When he returned home from his shift that ended at three o'clock, she told him, "I'm leaving."

"Do you need anything?" he asked.

"Nothing but my freedom."

"I won't stand in your way," he said, after she'd already gone down the steps. But then he called to her. "Myrthen," he said.

She stopped and sighed, then turned around.

"I'm sorry. For everything."

She looked at him, his graying hair, his sad and tender face. "No need to apologize," she said, straightening her back. "It was all part of God's plan."

Myrthen put down her bags and breathed in the new scents of sawed wood and paint. The workmen had bolstered the sagging porch, installed an indoor toilet and bath, replaced the fragile roof, and repaired the waterlogged walls of the house that anybody else would have considered past saving. She didn't bother with the paint. Improving the façade was not the point; in God's eyes, everything was beautiful. She merely required function.

Myrthen walked around the house. It was much smaller than she'd remembered, but she liked it all the more for its modesty. Here was the sitting room and the couch where she'd been led into temptation. She would get rid of it immediately. Here was the room that had belonged to her parents, which still contained their iron bed. The mattress had been thrown out after her mother's body had been discovered, nearly a week after her passing. She looked around and then closed the door. Her mother had had no need for her, not after Ruth died. Now Myrthen had no need for her mother, or any of her things.

Here was the room she'd shared with Ruth, the small bed and chair. Even after her twin had died, Myrthen made a point of taking up no more than half of that small bed that had been theirs. She walked over and touched the faded drawing behind the door, which she had explicitly told the workmen to leave alone. Ruth had drawn—directly on the wall—two stick figures holding hands. Myrthen remembered the day she'd done it: their mother had scolded Myrthen for fidgeting at Mass, and sent her to their room without lunch. Then Ruth had refused to eat and so she had been sent off, too. She closed the door with only a little bit of a slam, and went to Myrthen and gave her hand a squeeze. Then she drew the two of them there on the wall, and whispered, "Don't tell Mama." They giggled into their palms until Rachel came in to shush them.

Now, as though nothing had changed, the stick sisters stood side by side, holding hands. "I miss you, Ruthie," Myrthen whispered.

Here was the kitchen, the wood stove and sink, the table and chairs her father had made. She stepped up to the window and looked out at the unruly thatch where long ago, Rachel had tended her tidy rows of roots and greens, rosebushes and zinnias. Now the garden was overgrown and full of wild things, as though the woods behind the old shack were sneaking up to reclaim it. The workmen had offered to clear it out for her, but she declined. The only thing she allowed them to cut down was the transplanted myrtle tree that had been growing there for thirty-five years. She told them to chop it into kindling.

And here was the new indoor bathroom. It was very small, but with room enough for a toilet and a sink and a bathtub. It was directly off the kitchen, on a built-up floor where the door to the cellar steps had once been. The workmen had tried to talk her out of it, suggesting she convert one of the small bedrooms instead of going to all the trouble of filling up and sealing off the cellar. Wouldn't she need access to it? Where would she store her preserves?

There would be no preserves, she told them. There was nothing that needed storing except her memories of Ruth. Those, if possible, she would prefer to keep out of the cellar.

That very afternoon, before the house was plunged into darkness, Myrthen sat down at the old kitchen table where she had spent the first nineteen years of her life, and began her first of many letters to the Tribunal of the Diocese of Wheeling. She wanted to prove that her marriage was invalid and that she should, therefore, be unbound from it. Praying to the Virgin and vowing to Ruth, she would provide as many statements, depositions, documents, and reports as would be necessary to obtain an annulment. She would do whatever it took to be rid of John Esposito for good, even if it took years. Even if it took everything.

March 18, 1945

Alta sat on a stool in front of the cabin window, stretched paper on her lap. A glass jar of cloudy water rested on the sill. Another one, empty, held her brushes. She was naked.

"What's the color of happy?" she asked.

John was on the edge of the bed, his paints spread out on the rumpled sheets, his canvas on the easel he'd dragged in front of the nightstand. The cabin was filled with the scent of linseed and soup and the beginning of spring. He'd turned in the key to the company house he'd shared with Myrthen and moved the few things he wanted to keep up to the cabin, where he now lived full-time. Pushing his glasses up on top of his head, he scratched his beard. Then he tucked the paintbrush behind his ear.

"Purple," he said after a moment.

She smiled. "Why?"

He looked up at the ceiling, the exposed beams overhead. The sun filtered in, backlighting the dust. "Because purple is when blue and red take a holiday and meet in the middle," he said. "Even if it's only for a little while."

She nodded, and looked at him lying naked on his side, his long legs dangling off the end of the bed. She couldn't see the canvas he was working on. They weren't going to reveal them to each other until they were finished.

"Maybe we should paint the cabin purple then," she said, teasing, still watching him. It had been four months and seven days since they'd first met in the woods.

"Or your self-portrait," he said. He raised himself up and held up his canvas, its backside to her. "I think I might be winning."

She tossed a rag at him, damp with runny rainbows. "Who said it was a race?"

He caught it and tossed it back. "Shhhh," he said. "I'm working."

The rag landed at her feet and she bent down to pick it up. They shared a glance when she looked back up, one he broke by removing the brush from behind his ear and picking up his palette once more. They painted that way for a while, naked and nearby, until the sun had set so low they needed lamplight to continue. During that stolen time with the man who'd become her lover, her senses were heightened; her yearnings, finally, satisfied. It was also the only time she felt a reprieve from her guilt.

"Finished," he said. He reached down and set his palette on the floor, then tightened the caps on his many tubes of oil paints.

"I'm not," she said.

"Show me."

"You first."

He smiled and slowly turned his easel out to face her.

It was a portrait of Alta, sitting with one leg tucked underneath the other on her chair by the window. Her watercolor was on her lap, and her face was turned back to him with a mysterious smile.

"Baby, it's beautiful," she said. She put down her things and walked over to him, sat on the bed. She took his bearded cheeks in her hands and kissed him. With her mouth still on his, she said, "But it's not a self-portrait."

"It is," he said. He cupped the side of her angular face with one hand. "I see myself when I look at you. Because you've shown me who I am." She kissed him again.

"When you turn to me and smile," he said, "I remember the girl I wish I'd known. And I see the old woman I someday will. And then I just feel lucky I get to be with you now."

She looked at the portrait with a faraway gaze.

Finally he said, "Show me yours."

"It's not finished."

"I don't care."

She got up and walked over to where she'd left her painting. Sitting down next to him, she handed it to him, placing it carefully on his open palms.

It was a picture of the cabin, the foliage full of spring and blooming beyond the porch. The door was open and from within, a purple light glowed. In the center, just above the threshold, a multicolored butterfly floated inside. An abandoned cocoon lay on the middle step that led up to the porch.

He put his finger near the butterfly, wanting to touch it, but knowing better. Instead he reached out and took her hand, his eyes transfixed on the watercolored wings.

"That's me," she said. "Because of you."

July 7, 1945

Saturdays in 1945, while the world warred on another continent, the Blackstone Coal Company hosted dances at the recreation center just up the hill from the center of town. Since the war had thinned the ranks at the mine, and the work was even harder and the pay still low, the bosses felt the dances would do the job of maintaining the company spirit. The bosses' wives, dressed up in their homemade versions of the latest fashions and wearing husband-ordered smiles, served oatmeal cookies and Coca-Colas that boosted morale and brought different cultures—those that wouldn't typically mix—together. A six-piece band played polkas and waltzes. Children sweated in circles on the dance floor, unaware of politics or destitution, and for a couple of hours at least, the adults could forget about them, too.

It was the first time Alta and Walter had attended. He'd been encouraged, strongly, to make an appearance. The bosses wanted the foremen to set a good example. He'd spent almost his whole life stooped over in a hole underground, and now they wanted him to play the host as well. How was that going to make the men feel better about their hollowed-out lives? Alta, wearing trousers and a handmade sweater, stood awkwardly against the wall next to her even-more-uncomfortable husband. Their son, Abel, huddled with a group of boys who were eyeing a group of girls giggling nearby.

Alta found herself swaying to the music, holding an uneaten cookie in one hand and a paper napkin in the other. Glancing around, she watched the other couples and thought about John. Then, as though she'd conjured him out of her imagination, she spotted him across the room, his hands — oh, those hands — jammed into his trouser pockets. She flushed and looked quickly away, but not before she caught the slow smile she knew was meant only for her. Had Walter noticed? No, he was watching other things from behind his same, dulled eyes. She knew he'd already be asleep in his easy chair, a newspaper folded across his knee, if they'd been allowed to remain at home.

Alta and John faced each other as the musical harmony pressed them together and apart. She had never seen her lover of eight months and her husband speak face-to-face. Never, that is, until now.

John kicked off the wall, and moved toward Alta and Walter through the throng of dancers. "Evening, Walter," he said.

Walter, who'd been watching the band, turned toward him to look, taking a moment to adjust to the strange familiarity. Then he nodded and extended his hand. "John," he said, low and sincere. "Good to see you."

John turned to Alta. "You must be Walter's wife. John Esposito." He offered her his hand and she had no choice, no choice at all, but to slip her palm against his. Their webs met and spun into a silky tangle, warm and flashing damp. She forced herself to look him in the eye and smile modestly, then to say, "Yes, I'm Alta. How do you do." But the extra fraction of time — a second, a year — made her blush, and she glanced away before letting his hand go. She had to be sure that nobody had noticed how deeply his eyes had penetrated her. "The band is wonderful, don't you think? Walter? Aren't they simply wonderful?"

"Not bad," Walter said. "Not bad at all."

"Why don't the two of you cut a rug then?" John said, his eyes flicking to her like a tease.

She was sure her husband could feel the heat coming off them, standing as they were so dangerously close to one another. Taking a half step back, she said, "Yes, Walter, let's do." She reached over and touched her husband on the arm.

Walter put his hands in his pockets. "Oh no," he said. "Not me. You know I'm not one for dancing."

"Just one," she said, somewhat pleading. She wasn't one for dancing either.

"You want to dance, I bet John here would." Walter tipped his broad, flat chin in John's direction. "He swings a mean ax in the pit. Probably not a shabby dancer."

Alta's breath snagged. There's no way Walter could know about them. They'd been nothing but discreet ever since they'd met the November before. And she didn't do anything unusual at home, no updating of her wardrobe, no curling her hair. "Oh, I'm sure John would rather dance with his wife." She flared her eyes at him, turning them into round O's like a stop sign.

"My wife happens to be at church." They weren't divorced yet, but would be soon. He smiled again at her and lifted one eyebrow, then held out his hand once more, this time palm up, and waited.

Alta looked at her husband, who shrugged and gave a sort of half smile, relieved of the duty.

"I'm not a very good dancer," she said.

"We'll see." John pushed his hand a little closer to hers.

She looked down at her own and took a breath. She handed the cookie she'd been holding to Walter, who took a bite right off, then she let John lead her away.

The band had just struck up another song. John positioned her in front of him, and she placed her left hand on his right shoulder. Draping his arm around her waist, he clasped her other hand, and they began moving to the music.

"You nearly made me break out in hives," she whispered.

"Not weak in the knees?"

She allowed herself a tiny smile. "Always," she said.

"I had to be near you," he said.

"But doesn't it look strange?"

"What, me saying hello to someone I've been working in the pit with for the past decade?"

"You've never socialized before. It looks odd."

"No time like the present. War does that to people. Brings everyone closer together." He smiled at her. "Besides, we hide right out in the open. Doesn't look quite as suspicious that way."

"You're mad."

"Mad about you is all," he said, and he pulled her ever so slightly closer and turned her in a gentle spin. She sought Walter as she went around, worried that she seemed too relaxed in the arms of another man, but he was looking in the other direction. Still, she increased the distance between herself and John by an inch or two.

He responded by moving his thumbs slowly up and down, one at her waist, the other against her uplifted palm. A caress so slight that nobody would notice, even if they were looking, but deliberate enough that it caused a rush of blood both upward and down. The room was too busy, too full.

"I love you, Alta."

Her heart pounded. She made a strict effort to keep her face from melting into bliss. She looked again for Walter—he was watching his own feet—then let herself look John directly in the eye, just for a moment, just long enough.

"I love you, too."

"Do you think," he said after a moment, "we could ever not hide?"

But before she could think of an answer, the song ended and John had no choice but to let go of her. He bent over in a formal bow, and she almost laughed, but caught herself in time. He walked her back to where her husband stood and handed her off to Walter. Both of them flushed from their first profession of love, the dance, the thrill, and — at least in her case — more than a little guilt.

"Think I'll be heading home," John said. "Don't think I could find a better dance partner, and it wouldn't be right to claim you for the whole evening." He made a tiny bow in her direction. "Thank you for the dance." Then turned to Walter. "Thanks to you, too." Walter solemnly shook the extended hand, his broad, expressionless face a blunt contrast to John's animated one, and Alta had to look away, the shamelessness too disgraceful to watch.

"See you next shift," Walter said.

John nodded and turned to go. He walked, tall and straight-backed, through the crowd, and Alta felt pulled to follow. She watched him, everything about him familiar now, except for the sight of him walking away. It had always been she who left first.

Next to her, Walter watched John, too. He'd been stealing glances ever since they'd said hello. He'd seen the looks that passed between them. The way Alta smiled broke his heart twice: because it was so lovely, and because it was meant for someone else.

"Would you like to dance, Walter?" she asked, after John had gone.

He'd been focused on his shoes, the scuff marks he'd never noticed before. The wear. Now he looked into her face as though for the first time. He searched her plain prettiness for the expression she'd had for John as they'd danced, for that flicker of light that he'd seen from across the room, bright as a star.

It wasn't there. There was kindness; there was concern. There was even love, but it wasn't the kind that made a woman's face sparkle.

His eyes slid down again to his feet, and he shook his head. "I don't think so," he said. "If you don't mind, I think I'd rather just go on home."

January 26, 1946

It was Alta's birthday, a day her husband recognized with a chaste kiss on the cheek. She picked up her French easel — a gift from John she credited to her truant aunt Maggie — and patted Walter on the shoulder where he sat reading the paper and chain smoking. He nodded in reply without lifting his eyes.

After more than fifteen years of marriage, they treated each other with a kind of elderly respect and vague affection, but beyond the absolutely necessary exchange of information — the shifts to be worked, the few social obligations to be met, the bills to be paid — they hadn't much to say to each other. Walter stopped asking things like where she'd been while he and Abel ate the meals she'd prepared and left for them to serve themselves, or what had taken so long in town, or why she insisted on going all the way up to Whisper Hollow to paint. He never asked to see the work she created, which was a good thing. Not only could she not have produced the copious oeuvre that would match the number of days she'd supposedly gone up the hill to paint, but she also couldn't explain without guile the reason her subject matter had changed so dramatically over the past year. If Walter were to investigate her collection now, he would see watercolor pillows and sheets stained with human love and warmth; a bed in the middle of the woods spread with starlight; a fully-furnished tree house lifted into heaven; a flagrant portrait of herself as a butterfly, utterly changed. All difficult to explain to someone who didn't understand what it meant to be absolutely, completely in love.

Instead, Walter eventually began to wash his own dishes after dinner. To go to bed before she got home. If he suspected anything, he never revealed it. Alta sometimes wondered if he had some of his own secrets to keep.

Which was why it was so easy for Alta to slip away without excuse that Monday afternoon. She smiled as she hiked through the snow, thinking of how she would translate the sharp-edged season onto the stretch of paper that awaited her, and of the fresh palette of watercolors she'd bought herself—a color for each of her thirty-four years—and of the man with whom she spent her happiest days.

When she rounded the corner of the cabin and stepped up to the covered porch, she saw that something had changed on the south side. Where before a thin copse of trees had stood, there was now a clearing of about one hundred square feet. Four wood stakes marked the corners, and what looked like ten trenches had been carved into the snow in perfect parallel across the space.

Surprised by the grid in front of the cabin, she didn't hear John open the front door and come up behind her. She jumped when he slid one arm around her waist and pressed his chest against her back.

"Happy birthday," he whispered. He kissed her neck, which made her eyes drift closed from the sheer pleasure, the sense of peace. She wondered if anyone else had ever felt so rescued. Then he moved his other hand in front of her and when she opened her eyes again, she saw he was holding a bouquet of sorts, a bundle of something that looked like dirty tentacles.

"For me?"

He turned her around and gave her a long, slow kiss on the mouth. "Yes," he said, his lips against hers.

"You shouldn't have." She kissed him back.

He pulled away and smiled. "You mean you don't know what these are?"

"Flowers?"

"They don't last long enough."

She leaned forward and kissed him again. "What are they then?"

"Asparagus. Crowns and roots. For your new garden," he said. "*Our* garden."

She bit her lip and smiled, then kissed him again. "Is that what you've been doing all weekend?"

He nodded and laughed. "So now we have enough firewood to last a while, too."

She wrapped her arms around him and buried her face in his neck. When she inhaled, she could smell the clean scent of Ivory soap and aftershave and cold and sunlight and earth. "Thank you so much."

"You're welcome," he said quietly, into her hair. "But I have to be honest, it's as much for me as for you."

She straightened up and pressed the edge of her sweater sleeve against her eyes. "I know," she said. "I love it."

"So...asparagus," he said.

She laughed. "Yes?"

"The thing about asparagus," he said, looking at the two-year-old plants in his hand, "is that it takes patience. Commitment."

She reached over and fingered the tops of the roots, their hairy offshoots. "How so?"

"We plant them about a month before the last frost. But it takes a long time for them to produce. We can't harvest them until the third year."

"That's a long time to wait for a vegetable."

"Yes, but during that time, the root system is establishing itself. It grows wide and deep, and gets tangled up into the ground so much that you can't divide it once it's really in there. I mean, you could, but it wouldn't be easy. The plants would likely die."

His tone had grown serious, and her smile began to fade. She encircled him in her arms. "Then we won't divide them."

"That's the idea," he said, and smiled. "They're perennial. They'll last a couple of decades if they're well cared for. Hopefully more."

"You'll have to show me how to do it."

"We'll figure it out together."

She reached out and took the bundle of roots from him. "I've always wanted someone to garden with," she said. Walter had never shown an interest in cultivating anything.

"Me too." He kissed the frown off her face and as they stood there, it began to snow. Soon, the trenches he'd dug would be filled in again, until all that remained of them was the hopeful promise of spring.

October 5, 1948

Tribunal Diocesanum Vhelingensis

Nullitatis Matrimonii
Bergmann-Esposito
Prot. no. 1944/08

NOTIFICATION
of
DEFINITIVE SENTENCE

Enclosed, pursuant to the provisions of Can. 1719; 1877; Art. 205, is the Definitive Sentence of the Tribunal pronounced in the above-captioned case by the Rt. Rev. Msgr. Hugh Wishlinske, P.A. J.C.D., Officialis, and the Vy. Rev. Msgrs. Lawrence Brey, J.U.D, and Conrad J. Altenbach, J.C.D., Synodal Judges.

The dispositive part of the Sentence begins at page 10, paragraph 3, and may be rendered into English as follows:

"Having seriously considered and weighed all the foregoing issues of both law and fact, invoking the name of Christ, we the undersigned judges, constituting the collegial Tribunal in this case, sitting in judgment, having God alone before our eyes, discern, declare and pronounce Definitive Sentence in response to the question proposed:

"In the negative, that is, the nullity of the marriage is not proven in the case. (*Negative, seu non constare de matrimonii nullitate in casu.*)"

You have a ten-day period from the receipt of this letter to lodge an appeal from this Sentence of the first instance.

> Rev. Anthony Kiefer, S.T.D., J.C.D.
> Notary
> October 5, 1948

Myrthen Bergmann
c/o St. Michael's Catholic Church
Verra, West Virginia

by Registered Mail

November 21, 1949

"Hi, baby," John said when Alta stepped inside the cabin. Their paintings hung all over the walls. He was lying in their bed with the newspaper spread out beside him, writing something on a sketchpad.

"Hi, my love." Without pretense, she crossed her arms and lifted her sweater off. She kept her eyes on his as she reached behind and unhooked her bra.

He slid his reading glasses down.

She gave him a teasing smile and unbuttoned her slacks.

He flung back the sheets.

She dropped her clothes and strutted to the bed and climbed in, unencumbered, uninhibited.

Five years of ecstasy. Five years of agony: stealing away several times each week to find her true self and her true love waiting like an unfinished painting, hidden away in a secluded moonshiner's cabin in the woods. They'd harvested their first tender crop of asparagus that June.

"Marry me," he whispered as he pulled her in.

"I will."

"Now."

She opened herself and held on to his back. "Someday."

After they made love, they rested, sheet-tangled and sweating in the fire glow.

"What were you writing down when I got here?" she asked.

"A poem."

She raised her eyebrows and smiled. "What about?"

"You. And me."

"So?"

"So what?" Rolling onto his side, facing her, he propped his head on his open palm. She noted the few new silvery threads of his thick hair at his temples, the smile lines that had gone deeper near his eyes.

Laughing, she pushed him off his elbow onto his back and stretched over him to grab the pad off the bedside table. He reached out for it, but she touched her index finger to his lips and blew a kiss. Then she moved off him and flopped onto her stomach. Flipping the pad open, she read the title aloud: " '*You Are My Always.*' "

"Stop!" he said, grabbing it and laughing in embarrassment. "I just remembered, I'm a terrible poet."

"Come on, let me have it," she said, trying to take it back.

"It's silly. Anyway, I don't need to write a poem for you to know how I feel." He brushed his fingers down her back.

"No," she said, pressing against him and resting her head against his chest. "You don't." They lay like that for a while, quiet, in their way. When he finally spoke, his voice was serious enough to surprise her.

"Leave him."

"What?"

"You heard me. Leave him."

"Baby," she said. "Please. Not now."

"Yes now. I want to be with you now. Not someday."

She grabbed the quilt and wrapped it tightly around herself. It was a vulnerable feeling—and not a good one—that was creeping over her. "I thought we'd talked about this. I want to, you know I do, but I can't."

"I'm tired of sharing you."

"You're not. Not this way," she said, indicating their naked proximity. "I love you, but I have Abel to think about. And Walter. I made it clear from the start this is all I can give you right now. I thought it was enough."

"How can it be enough?" he asked, his voice rising. He flung back the covers and got out of bed.

"Don't do this, John." Her eyes welled up and looked at him with a pleading expression. "Don't force me to make a choice right now."

He knew what she meant: that she wouldn't, if she had to, choose him. And he couldn't bear the idea of not having her at all. It made him miserable sometimes, how much he loved her. Finally his expression softened, though not entirely, and he simply said, "You're right. I'm sorry." He climbed back into bed and pulled her to him, relaxing as she let herself be drawn back, fitting herself against him the only way she could.

September 16, 1950

Father Timothy heard confession for thirty minutes before Mass on Sundays, for an hour on the first Thursday of every month, and for two hours every Saturday afternoon. Those Saturday Sacraments of Penance were Myrthen's favorites. The church was quiet, the glide of penitents as steady as a stream. She was always the first in line to unburden herself of her sins, after which she would dip one knee in a graceful genuflection at the first pew, then slide onto the well-worn kneeler to pray.

Hers was an unremitting attendance, as moored and unmoving and silent as the statue of the blessed Virgin in the sanctuary. When those seeking absolution entered the thin-walled confessional booth behind her, they didn't bother to whisper. They trusted that her piety was as immutable as her presence. "Bless me, Father, for I have sinned," they would begin. And Myrthen would lean her bowed head, ever slightly, to better overhear the confessor's opulent array of sins. Most often, they would start with something small — the profane use of God's name, for example, or a lack of Christ-like respect toward others — and gradually empty themselves like a turned-out pocket of all the rest:

"I's lookin' out the window and saw that pretty gal next door gettin' undressed through her window—I won't mention her name, save her the shame of that at least—and I didn't look away. Figured then she might've wanted the audience, seeing as how she'd left her curtains open all the way and was just as close to the glass as I am to you right here. But I thought about it later, recognized it as shameful, her not bein' my wife, me being pretty much best buddies with her husband..."

"I was doing the weekly shopping downtown, buying what I could afford to, and used up near all the cash we had on hand, and well, Mr. Cantor was counting me back my change and he made a mistake—I don't think I even realized it until later—and I ended up with $6.74 instead of just the $1.74 and, well, I just kept it."

"I cussed a blue streak at the children, Devil must've had hold of my tongue."

"I found myself lookin' at...certain pages...in the Sears catalog. Women's underthings and such. Brassieres and whatnot. You know what I'm sayin'?"

Unfulfilled contracts, gambling, impure thoughts, petty theft, impatience, pride, envy. The salacious trespasses of the young, and the minor, indelible vices of the old. Myrthen heard them all with her eyes closed and her fingers clasped, committing them to memory, measuring the distance between the penitents and their Savior by their particular pageant of shame.

She was not often surprised, having heard so much for so long. Along the way, she'd developed a certain desensitization to the revelations of the sorrowful. But when she heard the weak and familiar voice of her first cousin, Liam, she shrugged off her languor with new interest.

As a child, Liam always seemed to be slipping in and out of the shadows, occupied by some mischief or other, hiding from his father, Ian, until the old man drank himself to death. His mother, her aunt Agnes, had dropped him once when Liam was only five months old—accidentally and at a disturbing angle. Ian called Agnes stupid and careless, and blamed her for nearly everything that went wrong, even his starting to drink again. When he was fired from the uranium mine, Ian told Agnes to pack: they were going to America.

They landed at Ellis Island in 1912, when Liam was three and Myrthen and Ruth, the twin nieces they'd yet to meet, were two. Agnes, wide-eyed and slightly seasick, held on to Liam with one hand and a bag with the other. In it was the sugar bowl that matched the creamer her sister, Rachel, had taken two years before; a few items of clothing; and a letter from her sister with the postal address: Mr. and Mrs. Otto Bergmann, Trist Mountain, Verra, West Virginia.

They lived with the Bergmanns until Otto got Ian a job at Blackstone Coal, then they moved into a nearly identical company house in the same row. Ian, resentful of his son for stealing his wife's affection, was more miserable than ever. He took refuge in the still he made behind the company house, but he found no joy in it. Instead, the moonshine just made him angrier in those critical years of Liam's youth, and so Liam learned the art of disappearing very early on. That suited Myrthen, who found his reptilian countenance disturbing. He always seemed to be dirty, always watching her with those shifty green eyes. Once, when they were young, she'd caught him masturbating behind her outhouse, and he refused to stop until he finished. Later, after she'd admonished him for committing the sin of Onan, he just laughed and told her it was her fault for being so pretty.

He'd enlisted in the United States Army Air Forces eight years ago, in 1942, and was sent to Fort Benning in Georgia to work as an electrician. She'd gotten a few letters from him while he was there, in which he'd talked mostly of his job, the weather, the training— *Them parachuters get drawn up a tower two* hundred fifty feet high, then get dropped down, jerking this way and that. Me, I like it better going that far underground instead of up. And he always ended with a wishful-sounding close—*Ruth may be dead and gone, but you always got me* or *I bet you're missing me being so far away* or *Someday I'll come back and maybe you and me can share a place like we did when we were young.*

She never wrote him back.

Subsequent letters indicated that after the United States declared war, Liam was reassigned to England. He worked on B-17s at a military base in Upper Heyford, and after the war ended, he went to a military complex in Heidelberg, Germany. She'd hoped that he—along with John—would've been swallowed up by the fighting, leaving her to her fragile peace. She knew he'd returned to Verra, but she'd been careful to avoid him. Even though the town was small, its inhabitants were divided into mostly separate communities according to ethnicity and faith. People could keep to themselves fairly easily that way.

"It's fourteen, fifteen years since my last confession," Liam said in a croaking, wheezing voice. "I accuse myself of the following sins." He went quiet for a moment, and Myrthen leaned in, straining her piety slightly. "I got passed over again," he finally said. "Again. Can you believe it?" He stopped.

"Go on," said Father Timothy. His voice never fluctuated or faltered through that crucifix-mesh lattice screen. He never assumed an apocalyptic tone, no matter how grave, how deplorable the sins. He'd told Myrthen once that he had vowed never to make someone suffer further along their righteous path toward reconciliation.

"I come back from serving this country and take up again with Blackstone. They're lucky to have me, I'll tell you. I been underground since I was, what, thirteen? Daddy'd get too drunk and so I'd go on down with his dinner bucket and pickax. Couldn't let my mother starve, could I? And all these years since—all these years!—before I left off for the war and then coming back these few months, I ain't ever been moved up. I ought to be fire boss by now. I know just as much as any of them others. How to check underground for dangers, particularly the explosive kind. They need someone like me. Don't they know that?" Myrthen righted herself, as it was no longer difficult to overhear what her cousin was saying, loud and sharp. Father Timothy said nothing.

"Those shirts don't seem to understand..." Liam laughed, a dry peal that sounded like dead leaves crunched underfoot and ended in a coughing spell. "Those guys ought to know how *easy* it would be for somebody like me—electrician with, what, twenty-three years' experience?—to blow their damn mine straight out of the mountain. They oughta be afraid. *Really* afraid." He coughed again until he wheezed. "I been thinkin' about doing somethin' about it, Father. I been feelin' awful nervous about it, too. Like I really could imagine myself doin' it."

A moment of silence. "How long has this been on your mind, my son?" Father Timothy said. Only Myrthen, who had heard him channel God's forgiveness thousands of times, noticed the vaguely sheared edge in his voice.

"Well, for a while now, but especially since I just got passed over again here recently. I thought it all through. You know, how I'd do it."

Father Timothy waited a beat, then continued. "Have you considered the effects of such an action? The miners whose lives would surely be lost? The grief and sorrow it would cause their families? Not to mention, you could lose your own life in the process."

"No, I guess I haven't really thought that part all the way through."

"My son, we do not have independent dominion over human life. God has granted us the right to use life, and placed us in charge of protecting and preserving the substance of it. Only He has dominion over your life and the lives of others. To do something like that would have consequences far beyond what your mind is capable of seeing. You need to think about those things, and pray. You must ask God to heal you, and lead you out of this temptation."

"I didn't have anybody else to tell it to except you, Father."

"I'm glad you did," Father Timothy said, restored to confidence. "God is a merciful God. Pray for forgiveness, and I will pray for you. Do you have any other sins to confess?"

Liam's voice returned to the raspy whisper with which he began his confession. "I sometimes touch myself when I'm underground, on my break. Sometimes when I'm alone in quiet places. The woods. The cemetery, oncet."

"That particular sin is made worse by defiling someone's final resting place. Now let me absolve you of all your sins, and especially this one."

As Father Timothy prayed, Myrthen's heartbeat quickened and her mind encircled a scheme, something she'd never thought of until now. Before Liam exited the confessional, she moved to the end of the pew, crossed herself, and nearly ran, light and brisk as though she were just a girl and not a nearly forty-year-old woman, down the aisle to the door. She burst headlong into the failing late-summer light, ran thirty paces down the path, and stopped. Then she took a breath, turned around, and with windless aplomb and the genesis of a savage idea, began a slow walk back to the half-opened door of St. Michael's, for a chance encounter with her cousin.

"Liam," Myrthen said, feigning surprise. "You're back."

"Hello there, cousin." His voice scraped against her. "I am. Few months now."

She straightened her mantilla down over her collar. "How have you been?"

He narrowed his eyes. "You just askin' to be polite? Or do you really give a damn?"

"Liam!"

He held his hands at his sides and looked down. "I ain't had a letter from you since I left." She could tell he was hurt by the way his voice softened to the pout of a little boy, just the way he used to sound after a beating from his daddy.

"Well," she said, shrugging. "I guess I'm not much for writing letters."

" 'Spose not."

"I'm surprised to see you here. You didn't often come to our parish."

Liam cleared his throat. "No," he said, and kicked at the wet dirt that met the bottom step of St. Michael's. "Not often."

"What brings you?"

"Nothing," he said.

"Nothing?"

"A troubled heart, maybe. Nothing much."

"A troubled heart?"

"No," he said. "It's nothing." He glanced up at her, then looked down. Looked up once again, up under her black lace, as if trying to peek under her skirt.

...Thy kingdom come, Thy will be done...

"Surely something must be troubling you if you've come all the way up the Hollow," she said, smiling. It was such an awkward use of her jaw. She brought her hand up to her mouth, testing it, as though it might break. Then she pressed her fingers to the inverted curve of lips. A blind woman reading her own facial expression.

Liam kicked the dirt again. "Been a long time since I seen you," he repeated.

"I'm here most days. I play the organ every Mass. And practice as much as I can." She looked over her cousin's ungroomed red hair at the cross that stood like a phallus atop the pitched roof of the church. "I should thank you again for your years of service. I'm sure the army was proud to have you," she said, her mind working, spinning sticky silk into an elaborate web.

"It weren't nothing."

She made her voice sound coy. "It was to me."

He looked up again. "I'd a done anything for you, you know that."

Myrthen nodded, adjusted her mantilla. She closed her eyes, languorous and brief—thinking, thinking—then flared them open and looked directly into his. "I need to speak to you, cousin. It's something of an urgent matter."

He leaned back, away from her sharp tone. "What is it?"

She reached out and took his hand....*Forgive us our trespasses*...She pulled him off the path, led him to a flat rock, and sat him down....*And lead us not into temptation*..."During my prayers," Myrthen said, solemn and downcast, "God has spoken to me."

Liam turned and stared at her. He hadn't been this close to her since they were children. The only other times she'd spoken to him as an adult were at her parents' funerals. And now here she was, holding on to his hand, looking mostly into his face. Her voice could have been that of an angel, speaking on behalf of the Lord.

"God has told me about your situation. He told me to help you, cousin. He told me, I'm the only one who can."...*But deliver us from evil*...

It was true, wasn't it? Why else would God let her hear the crimes of the sinners if not to help guide them on their path to righteousness? She took note of his slack expression and continued. "God has been trying to speak to you directly for some time, but evidently you haven't been paying attention. Do you know what I'm talking about, Liam?"

"I ain't got any idea what you're talking about. What do you mean, God speaks to you?"

"Well, of course."

"What makes you think it's God talking?"

"I don't *think*, I *know*." She admired her own conviction. "Do you need proof to bolster your weakened faith?"

He shrugged.

Closing her eyes and clasping her hands, she moved her lips in prayer. ...*Penetrate my being so utterly that all my life may only be a radiance of Yours*...She looked up. "God wants you to cease your masturbation in the cemetery. It offends Him."

Liam's eyes flew wide, one hand—unwitting—to his crotch. It wasn't too bad confessing it to the priest, he was a man, too, but hearing it come back at him, again, through his cousin's comely mouth now humiliated him. He panted a few dry breaths until he could steady his mind enough to speak.

"How did you know that?" he croaked.

She lifted one shoulder. "I didn't. God told me. When God's chosen won't listen, He sends another to translate for Him. For Jonah, it was a fish. For you," she said, opening her hands, "it seems to be me."

"You're lying."

"You remember the story of the prophet Samuel, don't you? Of course you do. I believe I was the one who read it to you when we were children." Her stare was unrelenting. He wiped his brow. "Twice Samuel heard the voice of the Lord speaking to him at night, but didn't recognize Him. He had to be told, 'That is your Lord speaking to you. Listen and do what He tells you.' God told me to tell you, Liam. He's been trying to talk and you're not listening. Now, you said you've got a troubled heart. That, cousin, comes from not listening when the Lord is trying to tell you something."

He shook his head, muttered something in the direction of his lap.

"What's that?" Oh, how clear and sharp her voice was.

"I said what's got me troubled ain't anything God would be sayin'."

"And how do you know that?"

"Because things I've been thinkin' about don't sound like nothin' would ever come out of God's mouth. Besides, God might be talkin' to you, but why would He be talkin' to me?"

"You're special, Liam. Like Samuel. But it's not for us to ask why God chooses to speak to those of us whom He does. We are only meant to listen and heed."

Liam pulled a pack of Pall Malls out of his pants pocket. They were supposed to guard against throat-scratch better than other brands. He set one between his lips after he stopped coughing again, then he struck a match on the rock and cupped a shaky hand around the flame.

Myrthen moved a few inches away from him. "Why don't you tell me about it, cousin? God told me I'd be able to help you."

He exhaled downwind, hard like a sigh, and coughed. Picking a bit of tobacco off his lip, he relented. "I been thinkin' some crazy thoughts. They fly up in my head like motion pictures. Realistic. I can just close my eyes and see it all like it's already happened."

"Like *what* has happened?"

Liam jutted his chin vaguely westward. "The mine. Blown up. Those assholes at Blackstone standing there watching, all their money falling out of holes in their pockets, till there's nothing but scrip, and then that's gone, too. Smoke pouring out from the pit, entrances sealed up. Them thinkin', *We should've raised up old Liam 'stead of passing him over like we did. He'd a prevented something like this happening. We shoulda listened to him. Now look what we got.*" He stared across the thin woods, through the Hollow and toward the tipple.

Myrthen watched him, ruthless, her placid countenance inversely proportional to his agitation. She tucked away the creep of a smile into a bitten fold of cheek.... *Make us worthy of the glory of thy Son, O dearest and most clement Virgin Mother...*"Liam, I want you to know," she said, virtuous, bewitching, "that I've been keeping up with you. Even though we don't see each other often, I'm interested in your well-being."

So what if she had to make up a bit of a story to help deliver the message? The thoughts that entered her head weren't entirely hers, were they? God had a say in the words that came out of her mouth. Everything under the heavens was unfolding according to His great plan, was it not? If that was so, then whatever she said must be grounded in truth, even if it didn't actually happen.

He looked up at her the way a dog awaits a treat, his bitterness momentarily forgotten. "You been keepin' up with me?"

She nodded. "You may not be aware of this, but John and I are no longer living together as man and wife. Even so, I spoke to him not very long ago on your behalf. I asked him why you haven't been promoted in spite of all your years of faithful service."

He narrowed his eyes at her. "I thought you said you didn't know I was back home."

"I didn't want to appear overeager." She smiled again, then opened her hands. "I'm sorry. I was unable to convince my former husband to take up your cause. And in fact, I'm deeply ashamed to say, I think he might in fact be one of those who have prevented your rise." She looked down and then back up from beneath her eyelashes. "Perhaps it's partly because he's jealous of you. He may know, on some level, that I've always had a deep…affection…for you. Perhaps that's even why he asked me for a divorce."

Liam's mouth fell open, but it was a moment before he spoke. "You have…affection…for me?"

Myrthen straightened her back. No need to take it too far. "Liam, do you realize that God is revealing to you His judgment upon Blackstone Coal Company?"

He cocked his head slightly. "God's revealing what?"

"Liam!" She slapped the rock with the palm of her hand. "Pay attention. I'm telling you! God has chosen you. He has chosen both of us. Who are you to question Him?"

He scoured his cigarette onto the rock. "So what are you saying? I'm supposed to go blow up the mine?"

She shifted away from him to hide the pounding of her heart through her clothes. "If that is what God wants you to do, then what choice do you have?" A hint of a smile. He looked away.

"It don't sound like a good thing. I don't understand. I mean, I wanted to do it. I…I want to do it. Serve those bastards right. But what if somebody got hurt? Somebody innocent? Guys I worked with, what, fifteen, twenty years? Good guys, some of them. I wouldn't want them to get hurt. Except maybe them who's been keeping me down."

"You don't know who is innocent and who is not. That's for God to know. And God will protect the innocent. Remember the story about the three men King Nebuchadnezzar tosses into a furnace for refusing to bow to him? No? Well, when he looks into the fire, he sees not three but four men, and none of them burning. The fourth was God's angel, sent to protect them because they were righteous before the Lord. And God will protect the innocent, Liam. You don't need to worry."

Slowly, he began to bob his head. His eyes searched the ground, looked left and right, a sign he was thinking things through. Myrthen watched her idea, like a minnow on a hook, sink itself into the soft contours of his mind.

Just like that, she could be rid of them both. *Thank You, Lord.*

After some time, Liam stopped his unconscious nodding. "Okay," he said. "Okay. Maybe you're right."

She patted him on the hand. "Sometimes there is evil inside people that you can't see. It's like a coal seam buried deep underground. You don't see it, but God sees it. He knows. And he wants them to be punished. You're doing the right thing, listening to God," she said. "Go now, and pray. Come back and meet me here on Wednesday evening. Father Timothy makes house calls then. I'll help you, Liam. I'll help you make a plan. I told God I would."

The voice of God, yes, he could hear it now. How had he mistaken it for anything else all this time? His mind was swirling with penance-turned-permission, his cousin's impossibly delicate skin, being chosen, being seen, those Blackstone bastards with money running out of their trousers like the liquid wrath of angry bowels.

He hadn't thought to wonder if there was something in it for her.

She stood up, their meeting adjourned, and smoothed her skirt in a practiced sweep. "Don't tell anybody else about this. God chose you and only you. Other people might not understand. You hear?"

"Yes," he said, then dipped his head and added, "I always had affection for you, too."

"Wednesday. Seven sharp. We'll make a plan." She walked a few steps up the path toward the doors of St. Michael's, then turned. "And one more thing," she said, straightening her back. "Stay out of the cemetery."

October 6, 1950

Three weeks later, John and the rest of the crew on the Number Seventeen's day shift spilled out of the cold darkness of the pit into an October afternoon so clear and bright their voices trilled off the exposed mountain face.

"Hold up, Gibby!" said a middle-aged half-Polish, half-Italian miner named Mooska. "My old lady's goin' to visit her mother this weekend," he said when he caught up with him. "So poker night at my place tonight." Mooska nodded at two others, Willit and Bullseye, who'd turned around while they were walking. "You're in, right?" They both nodded. One of them said, "I'll call up Jonesey. I think he's got a honey-do list but maybe he can get out of it." They chuckled, happy the workweek was done, a weekend of liquor and cards ahead, their smiles like cracks in dried mud on their dirty faces.

John Esposito walked past them with a long stride and a wide smile. "Hey, Johnny," said Mooska with a tip of his chin. "Poker night. You in?"

"No thanks, boys," John said with a smile. "I got other plans."

"You and your other plans," said a guy who'd been called Sugar so long that even his wife of two decades didn't know his real name. "One of these days we're gonna figure out who 'Other Plans' is."

The day crew collected around the mine office, their sooty faces tipped, grateful, toward the sun, lighting and dragging on cigarettes and talking before they went inside the small shower shack to clean up before heading home. At the same time, the miners going onto the second shift drifted in with dinner buckets swinging. In the changing room adjacent to the office, they each had a wire basket that hung from a cable, where they stored their clean clothes while they were underground and left their belts and hats when the shift was over. The two crews overlapped — those on the way out taking off their filthy overalls and steel-toed, mud-slung boots, and those going in putting theirs on. Eventually, all the wire baskets would be raised to the ceiling, where they'd remain untouched for at least the next eight hours.

Most of the men ended up with nicknames while they were still rookies wearing red hard hats. Going underground with a crew of colorfully named brethren gave them a sense of camaraderie, belonging, a feeling of comfort in a dangerous place. But there was one miner whose nickname never stuck: Walter Pulaski, strong and serious, with a neck that seemed to push his lower jaw forward and turn his mouth into a muzzle. When he first went into the mines, some cheeky upstart gave him the name Tiny. Walter was genial enough about it, but whenever someone tried to use it, it slid off and landed in the dirt. Eventually, they simply called him Walter.

He was among the men coming on for the second shift that day. Walter had been an electrician for the first half of his career, then promoted to foreman a decade ago. He'd demonstrated he was good at running things smoothly underground: initiating swift and decisive action, bearing pressure without complaint, influencing the men without persuasion.

Abel, Walter's eighteen-year-old son, was there, too. He was still a red hat, a bright young man and quiet like his father. Because Walter liked to keep watch over him, they always worked the same shifts. From the time Abel was a small child, Alta had spoken to him of what she knew of the world beyond Verra's blue ridges. She told him stories of her aunt Maggie and uncle Punk, conjured their elegant life in New York City and their travels to exotic locations such as Paris and London, California and Texas. It all sounded vaguely frightening to him, especially when his mother's expression grew tense and animated in the telling. Instead of inspiring Abel to consider his other options, his mother's stories only served to tether him closer to the confines of home. He knew all along that he'd follow his father underground, and come home black-faced and tired—God willing—each evening to his own small family of three or maybe four. To her credit, his mother never voiced disappointment in his choice if she ever felt any.

Stanley Kielar, a twenty-seven-year-old electrician, came into the changing room just as the rest of the second-shift crew were rolling their clothes and hoisting them into the wire baskets. His dinner bucket dangled at his side and his shoulders slumped forward. Ever since his son, Eagan, had fallen ill several months before, Stanley hadn't been the same. His robust frame looked slighter, his hair thinned. The skin around his eyes bagged like an old man's. It was obvious he was lacking in sleep, had been for months. But today, there was a different kind of restlessness in his demeanor. A weight-shifting sag to his gait. He pulled on the string to lower his basket of work clothes without so much as a hello.

Walter walked over to him. "How's your boy doing?" he asked.

"They say he won't get much better," Stanley said, staring at the coal-dusted floor. "Thanks for asking."

Walter nodded and put one hand on his shoulder. There wasn't much more he could say. "See you outside."

"Got some extra work needs doing this weekend, boys," Walter said to the commingled crews. "Need to lay track, set up some more stoppings. Anybody wants overtime, shift foreman for tomorrow needs ten, eleven men."

Walter held a clipboard and the stub of a pencil, nodding in response to each of the men who raised their hands: Babe Scardava, Stinky Lipersick, Piggy Kochran, Duck Luleck, Bones Krempeley, Pie Eye Del Vecchio, Cross Newcomb, Prairie Slack, Trout Palumbo, Fossil Zulcowski, Pops Langloss, Gibby Governsky, and finally, without looking Walter in the eye, John Esposito.

Standing just outside the loose knot of men was the electrician on Walter's shift, a red-haired and nervous man named Liam Magee whom they called Sparky. When Liam saw John raise his hand for the next day's dead work shift, he chuckled out a black lungful of smoke.

Walter counted the names. "Thanks, boys. Be safe tomorrow." He went inside the small office and laid the clipboard on the desk for the mine foreman. Then he picked up his carbide headlamp, his gas tester, and his dinner bucket. He tipped his head toward the mine and said to Abel and the others going in, "Let's go."

Willit, Mooska, Gibby, Sugar, John, and the other day-shift crew nodded their goodbyes and set off down the mountain.

Liam lagged behind the others as they headed underground. Stopping just outside the mine entrance, which was only eight feet tall and opened into the side of the mountain like the gaping maw of a sleeping giant, he finished his smoke. He watched the crew start to climb aboard the mantrip that would take them more than a mile into the mountain to the face where they'd be working. Above their heads hung a hand-painted message: A GOOD SAFETY RECORD MEANS HAPPINESS FOR ALL, SO KEEP UP THE GOOD WORK, MEN. BE CAREFUL.

Liam squinted at the sign through a final hard draw on his cigarette. Then he chuckled to himself once more, flicking the butt, still smoldering, to the ground.

Walter's production crew in the Number Seventeen worked hard that night, trying to haul out as much coal as they could. That slick and filthy stuff upon which their lives depended—made from the dead flora of peat bogs buried under three hundred million years of pressure and decay—ran through the mountains of West Virginia like the veins inside the miners themselves. Some of those men were on fixed salaries of sixteen dollars for an eight-hour shift, but most were paid by the ton loaded. An extra ton of that clotted mountain blood could mean an extra pair of shoes for a growing child, an extra pound of meat for a crowded dinner table.

Battler, who yelled because he was nearly deaf, worked up front. He was the miners' favorite machine man because he was best at cutting the coal, making it easier and faster for the men shoveling it up. There was an art to running the machine that gnawed away at the bottom part of a seam of coal with its sharp-toothed cutting chain, and sheared away a space between the seeping wet floor and the rest of the face. Then working-men like Suds and Dixie came in. They bored holes and tamped in the powder that would explode the overhanging coal into chunks like fist-sized diamonds, never letting themselves think too hard about the fact that the entire mountain was pressing down almost upon them. They'd shovel it up as fast as they could, loading it into a waiting coal car. When the car was full, one of them would drop in his check—a round piece of metal that identified the loader so he'd get credit for the work once it was weighed. Hawk, the brakeman, would couple up the cars into a small train, and Petey, the motorman, would drive it out fast as a river through the cool, dank shafts, past the power station that electrified the whole operation, all the way to the tipple, where it was weighed and washed and driven away by steam engine to power factories and plants and homes all over the Mountain State and beyond.

Walter checked his watch. Tipping his turtle-shaped headlamp up—never higher than chin height, so as not to blind a man in the darkness with sudden light—he shouted out to the men. "Shift's over. Let's go." Then he lifted his lamp toward the golden door.

Cramped and bent from eight hours of stooping labor, they climbed into the mantrip that had whooshed them to the mine and now spilled them back out into the dark night.

Liam said aloud, as he'd practiced, "Damn it all. Tomorrow's dead work, ain't it?" Dead shifts were for maintenance, not for mining.

Walter turned. "Yeah. What'sa matter?"

Liam made a show of sucking on his fresh-lit cigarette, then tossing it to the ground and stamping on it. "I forgot to put the batteries on. They're gonna lay track, they're gonna need 'em charged up in the morning."

Walter nodded. "You go on. I'll do it."

Liam raised his small-fingered hand. "My mistake. I'll take care of it. 'Sides, you got a wife waitin' for you home in bed. My whiskey ain't frisky, she can wait a while." He chuckled low.

Walter shrugged. "All right. Want me to drive you back in?"

"Naw, you go on." He turned and raised a hand without looking over his shoulder.

Walter nodded. He *was* tired. All of them were. Seamlessly, they'd moved from the darkness of the pit into the dark of night.

Cracking jokes and ass-slapping on the way to the changing room, they then drifted out and ambled down the hill toward their waiting wives and sleeping children, work clothes balled into rolls under their arms, swinging empty dinner buckets. Nothing visible but the fiery ends of their cigarettes burning like red stars in the night.

Liam turned and re-entered the mine.

October 7, 1950

At 6:00 a.m. the phone sounded like a siren coming from the kitchen. Alta was already up but was in the bedroom changing from her nightclothes to her slacks and sweater, wrapping her short hair in a cloth, preparing for the work of morning. She ran downstairs to answer it.

"Hello?"

Static, for a second. Then silence. "Morning, baby."

She turned quickly toward the window, cupped her hand over her mouth, and hushed her voice to a whisper. "John. Why are you calling me here? What's wrong? What's the matter?"

"Nothing, nothing. I need to talk to Walter. Is he up?"

"He's moving around. What's the matter? What are you going to say?"

"Nothing, baby. Nothing. It's work. Lemme talk to him. It's work is all."

"You sure? You're not going to say anything." The weight of their argument from the previous night was still heavy on her mind.

"No, no. Course not. Just work stuff."

"You promise." She took a deep breath, straightened her already straight shoulders.

"I promise."

She stood, tense as a sentry, wearing her worry on her forehead. "All right then. Hold the phone a minute. I'll get him."

"Alta," John said.

"What."

"Alta, I'm sorry about last night. I'm sorry I said those things I did. I swore to myself after last time I'd never bring it up again, but…" His voice trailed off. She could hear the morning song of a bird through the phone line. "Alta—"

"Hold the line. I'll get Walter for you."

She cradled the phone and called out, trembling, to her husband.

A moment later, Walter picked up the phone. "Hello?" he said, wiping the cream off his shaven face.

"Walter, it's Johnny. Sorry to bother you this time of day, so late in the morning."

"It's only six."

"I hate to ask a favor, but I gotta skip out of this morning's shift. I know Soup's scheduled for foreman, but I can't raise him by phone so I called you. They're gonna need an electrician. I can't do it, I'm sick as a dog. All night."

Walter shifted his weight onto one leg, leaned against the counter. The smell of bacon grease and eggs filled the kitchen. Kinking the phone against one shoulder, he pulled up one strap of his overalls and hooked them to the breast. "I'm not on today, it's Soup's crew."

Alta's hands shook slightly as she shoveled scrambled eggs onto his plate. Bacon. Biscuits she'd made earlier. She called aloud to Abel, low and loud as she could without disturbing Walter's conversation. Adding more to Walter's already-full plate, she topped off his short glass of orange juice. She didn't roam more than three feet away from the telephone pressed against her husband's ear.

A beat of silence and static on the line. "I realize it. I'm calling because I was thinking you might be able to take my shift. They're gonna need somebody but there's no way I can make it down. I know you worked second shift yesterday and I hate to ask it but I just can't do it. I've got to send somebody in my place."

Walter didn't sigh. He didn't complain. There was no sense of irony when he said to John, "I'll go. I'll get Abel to go on with me. We could use the extra pay." Then he looked down at his heaping plate and added, "I'll ask Alta to take you up some biscuits and such. Keep your strength."

"I thank you, Walter. And, uh, no need to trouble your wife with anything. I'll be fine. Back down on Monday for certain," he said, nerves riding to the end of his voice. "Sorry again to ask the favor."

"No trouble. You go on and get yourself feeling better, hear?"

"Thank you, Walter. Safe down there today."

They hung up and Walter leaned against the counter. "Guess you heard, I'm taking John Esposito's shift. I'd call up Liam Magee and see if he could take it, but knowing him, he's likely facedown drunk somewhere," he said. He clapped his hands once and rubbed them together, as though to mark his decision. Then he called up to Abel, "We're going on dead work, son. Get dressed and eat up."

Her hands still shaking, Alta filled her son's plate. "I'll put the biscuits in your buckets," she said, as she did every day. "Eat what you can now. I'll pack extra."

Alta always packed their dinner buckets full to brimming. The bottom half was filled with water, and then on top was a drop section for dry food. Walter never ate a full meal, despite his bulk, and instead offered what she packed to the miners whose wives came up short. Times were lean—again, still—and some men lived on little more than pinto beans and corn bread and wild ramps fried in bacon grease. Every shift some hungry man shyly accepted what Walter claimed he couldn't possibly finish.

When they were dressed and fed and full, she leaned across the chasm between them to kiss her husband goodbye, her lips barely touching his cheek, and handed him his bucket. Then she took her son into a full embrace until he wriggled gently away. He kissed her, then, and took his lunch.

Alta's heart had just started to settle back to a normal pace when Walter turned at the door and said, "You might want to run some dinner up to John, if you've got some time. He's been sick all night he says. He doesn't have a woman at home anymore, so he probably could use a decent meal."

Alta clenched the embroidered towel Walter had used to wipe his face. Giving a slight nod in response, she lifted her hand slowly in a gesture of goodbye a moment too late—their backs were already turned. Then, with a bang, the screen door closed behind them and they were gone.

It was a few minutes past seven o'clock when Walter and Abel arrived at the entrance of the mine. Everyone else was there, drinking coffee and smoking, grousing about the earliness of the Saturday, laughing occasionally, flicking cigarette butts, talking about their women and money or lack thereof. Bones snuck up on Pie Eye—who looked a little drunk, as usual, from the night before—and grabbed his pack of Lucky Strikes out of his back pocket.

"Hey! Hand it over!" Pie Eye slurred. "You gonna owe me sixteen cents, you don't give it." He lunged toward Bones, who laughed and made a show of staggering out of the way.

"All right, men," Walter said with one hand aloft, as though raising the flag. Though Soup Piontkowski was technically supposed to be running the shift, he leaned against the wall of the mine office with a mild, sleepy smile, watching the guys cut up.

The men let their laughter dissolve into chuckles, then huffs, then reverberating silence. They dragged on their cigarettes as if they were taking their final breaths, then stamped them into the soot. After they all assembled together, Soup finally said, "Let's load up. We'll be adding track into Three West and setting up stoppings along Two East." He pointed to a pile of concrete blocks and eight-foot cedar ties, steel spikes, and tools. "Pile in those blocks and timbers, then we'll get going."

Grumbling again, they began hauling equipment into the empty coal cars all coupled up and hooked to the flat-headed electric engine that would pull them underground. It was only about waist-high, a miniature of the trains that leave the tipple full of processed coal, then thunder through and beyond the mountain to parts unknown. The mine itself, just over five feet at its highest point, forced most of the men to crouch. Piggy was the only one who could stand up to his full height for those eight long hours.

When they'd loaded everything, the men slowly climbed in, too. They all took a last glance at the lightening sky, then Fossil turned on the motor and fed them all to the hungry, hallowed mountain.

John said goodbye and hung up, glad to be free of Walter's plainspoken kindness. Relieved, too, that he'd be taking his shift. The only sickness he'd felt since Alta stormed out of the cabin the night before was heartache. Watching her gather up her clothes and hold them to her chest as though suddenly embarrassed—for the first time in six years—to be naked in front of him.

"You've got no right to keep demanding it of me, John. I've loved you since I first saw you sleeping in that damned rocker in the middle of the woods. Before that, even. And I knew I always would. But you've no right to keep asking me to walk away from my husband and my son. Not until I'm ready."

He leaned forward, the covers falling away. "Loving you gives me the right! How do you expect me to go on like this, never knowing if you're going to leave him? How am I supposed to love you like I do and think there's a chance you'll end up spending your whole life under his roof, in his bed? How am I supposed to live every day with that, Alta?"

She twisted and stamped her foot into her soggy boot. Ran her fingers through her bed-mussed hair. They were farther apart than they'd ever been. "Someday, he'll…pass on. And then, I can marry you. But not before," she said. "I couldn't live with myself if I broke Walter's heart. He's a good man, a good father. He lost his mother young and if I left him, too…" She shook her head. "My heart belongs to you, but I can't do it. It would be too cruel."

John sprang from the bed. "Damn it, Alta! Why's it all right for you to be cruel to *me*? Wait till he's dead? That's what you want me to do? Well, I don't know if I can wait that long!" Then he picked up the rocking chair that he'd fallen asleep on — fallen in love with her on — raised it above his head, and hurled it down with such force that it didn't even send splinters in all directions. It just collapsed into itself right there on the floor.

With her hand on the yanked-open door, she looked at him with her lips parted as though she were about to say something else, but thought better of it. Then she just walked away, letting the door groan to a close behind her.

He'd been stunned at them both, too stunned to move until she was long gone, but by the time he realized he wanted to run after her, beg her forgiveness until she agreed to come back, it was too late. She would be already too far down the well-worn path through Whisper Hollow and across the creek and up toward the home she shared with her family. He had to let her go, couldn't risk raised voices or any ado that might inform any gossips on witness this late at night. There'd be no explaining such a scene. So he spent the rest of the night lying awake on her side of the bed, thinking about how to make it up to her.

Asking Walter to take his shift was the first part of his plan, because it would mean she'd be left home alone. Walter had said he'd take Abel on the shift with him, a bonus, so he knew there'd be no disturbing them. He could paint the picture of her morning routine in his mind. Even though he'd never eaten a meal in her kitchen, never partaken of her domesticity, he knew Alta as well as he knew himself—unlike Myrthen, who had remained an unsolved mystery for the fourteen years they were married. Alta always stayed home in the mornings, he knew, to roll out dough for the next meal, tend her garden, clean and set her home to right, do the wash. Only after her chores were done, her house and husband and son taken care of, would she allow herself some time to take a walk, or paint, or—at least three times a week while Walter and Abel worked the second shift—slip out her back door and make her stealthy way up the mountain to the cabin where John lived alone and which he considered theirs equally.

John quickly shaved and dressed, and almost ran down the hill toward the Polish bakery on Main Street. There was a chance that he'd be seen, and his sudden return to health might get back to Walter, but the odds were slight, and anyway, it was worth the risk. *She* was worth it. The long night had assured him of one thing: he would wait for her as long as he had to.

The scent of hot-oven yeast collided into him at the door. The butler's bell rang above his head and Callie Kaminsky, the dimpled wife of the second-best Polish baker in town, as she would say of her husband, met him at the counter, wiping her hands on her apron. No doubt she'd been up since the wee hours making walnut tortes and gingerbread with candied orange peels, potato and cheese pierogies, thick spinach quiches. It smelled so good that he smiled in spite of the night that splayed out behind him like a cooling corpse.

He asked for a half dozen of Alta's favorite pastries — *rogale świętomarcińskie* — rolls filled with white poppy seeds, walnuts, and cream that were available throughout autumn and winter but were traditionally eaten on November 11, St. Martin's Day. November 11, 1944, was the day they'd met in the woods, just shy of six years ago. Maybe the fresh Martinmas rolls, if not the pleading apology he'd rehearsed, would warm her heart to him again.

"*Dziękuję!*" he said to Callie when she handed him a folded paper sack filled with the rolls. He and Alta had traded their second-generation knowledge of their parents' native languages over a bottle of wine one night shortly after they'd first started meeting with predictable regularity at the cabin. Callie laughed out loud at his thanks, pleased by his effort and entertained by his mispronunciation.

John laughed along, too, feeling optimistic. The butter from the rolls had already stained the brown paper sack, which, even though folded, could not contain its yeasty steam. He imagined Alta in her kitchen with her hair pulled back in a kerchief, chopping carrots and onions, peeling potatoes. He would pick some wildflowers on the way, he decided. She loved blue vervain and aster, evening primrose and moss pink and wild live-forever. There were plenty of places between downtown and Alta's house to pick a handful. He imagined himself stealing through her garden, glancing left and right for the watch of female neighbors. She would accept his gifts, place the flowers into a jar or a vase, then pull out a chair at her table. He would insist that she be the one to sit down in it while he found the plates, the napkins and forks. She'd laugh at his fumbling in the kitchen, would lean forward with her chin resting on threaded fingers, waiting. Her smile would herald his second chance.

Nodding goodbye to Callie on his way out, he closed the door behind him. The sun was already coming up orange-pink behind the ridges of Trist Mountain. All the world was quiet and calm, except for somebody's dry-heaving cough. John looked over and saw Pudge Bellini slumped against the door of the barbershop. Pudge's bald, inflated head rested on his chest at what looked like an uncomfortable angle, and his thick legs were splayed wide apart out in front of him. The back of one hand rested on the pavement, and the other clutched a bottle inside a wet paper bag.

"Pudge," John said in a low voice. He didn't want to disturb the peace of the day rising around them. "Pudge!" John shoved lightly at his thigh with the side of his shoe. "Pudge, wake up." Nothing. John knelt down and lifted Pudge's chin.

His eyebrows lifted but his eyelids did not. "Wha."

"Pudge, you gotta get up. You can't be sittin' here like this. It doesn't look right. People will be coming soon. You gotta get out of here."

Pudge lifted one brow high enough to open the corresponding eye, then the other, and tried to focus. "Dat you, Johnny?"

"Yeah, it's me." He extended a hand. "Come on, you gotta get up. Let's get you up."

"Who's comin'?"

John leaned down and picked up a limp, meaty hand. "People. Doesn't matter who. Come on, let's get you up."

"God?"

"What?"

" 'S God who's comin'?"

"Hell, Pudge, you must've had some kind of drink." John unfolded the bag of *rogale* and put one in Pudge's unmoving, upturned palm. "Eat something, you'll feel better." Pudge smacked his lips and closed his eyes again. "Come on, Pudge, you can't just lie here like this. Mr. Campbell ain't gonna want to come open up his shop and see you lying here all spread out on his stoop like this."

Pudge rolled his head and squinted at John. "Didn't think they'd have no barbers up in Heaven."

John bent down and put his hands under Pudge's arms and tried to heave him up.

"How'd I die?"

"What in foolishness are you talking about?" John's strength was no match for Pudge's drunken weight.

Pudge looked around, blinking. He tried to push himself into a straighter sitting position against the barbershop door. "Heaven ain't no better-looking than Verra. What kind of joke is that? Live your life in a dump and then spend all eternity in it, too." He widened and then narrowed his eyes again. "So, how'd I die?"

"Pudge, you are a half-cut fool if I ever saw one. You're not dead. You're just drunk. As usual," John said. "Now get up."

"I musta died falling down or something. I can't get up."

"That's cause you're fat and soused and you're not listening to me. I told you, you're not dead and you're sure as hell not in Heaven. Why are you talking like that?"

" 'Cause if you're dead, then I must be dead, too," Pudge said, looking at him for the first time with steady eyes.

"I'm not dead."

"You sure as hell are."

John sighed. "Stop this infernal bullshit, Pudge. What makes you think I'm dead?"

"Sparky said so. Told me last night." Pudge bobbed his round head. "Said you was gonna die underground today. So I figure, you're dead and I'm talking to you, so I must be dead, too."

John straightened up and looked down at Pudge's body, which spilled onto the sidewalk at too many slovenly angles. "What exactly did Sparky say?"

"Said you and some others was going down today, work a dead shift or something. I don't know what that means, never did go underground myself. Swore to my mommy I wouldn't after my daddy died from black lung back in twenty-four. I's only twelve years old at the time—"

"Pudge, what do you mean, Sparky said I was going to die today?"

"Hey now, that kind of tone don't seem too heavenly, you ask me."

John reached down and grabbed him by the arm. He could barely get his hand around all that flesh. "I'm not kidding you now, Bellini. What did Magee say to you?"

Pudge tried to wrench his arm out of John's grip. "Now you don't mind letting me go, I'll tell you." John released his arm and Pudge rubbed the aching spot. "I can't say I remember 'xactly. Just something that today some people were gonna meet their maker underground. Something about bein' passed up for a promotion a while back. And his girlfriend...wait, maybe that's his cousin or his sister, I can't remember which...anyway, she said God spoke up to her recently and said it was His will or some such that Sparky clear up the mess that those Blackstone bosses had gone and made."

"You mean Myrthen?"

"Myrthen. Myrthen, yeah, that's her. Funny name. Kraut, I think. Nice-lookin', though. Oh wait, shit. She's your wife, ain't she?" He swatted at a fly near his face. "Well, think of that."

John let his arms drop to his sides. He'd barely spoken to Myrthen since she moved out six years before. Hadn't spoken much to her at all before then. Not ever, really.

"And Magee said I was going to die today?"

"Yep. He said he rigged it up last night. He's pretty proud of himself for it. Had it all figured out. Came and got me afterwards, brought a couple jugs with him. Don't know where he went off to. Think he's dead, too?"

"We're not dead, goddamn it!"

"Your shift ain't started, then. Supposed to go boom sometime right after you get underground, according to what Sparky said."

John felt a rush of ice through his veins and he shuddered. "Where's Magee now?"

"Dead, too, I guess." He looked round again. "Ain't so bad, seems like. Got any more of them rolls?"

John looked at his watch. It was 7:14 a.m. Walter. Abel. He hurled the butter-soaked sack of rolls at Pudge and took off running before it even landed.

The mantrip carried them all in, Fossil up ahead, and darkness swallowed them whole. It was steadily cool underground, always around fifty-five degrees. The electric engine lit up the track only a few feet at a time and rumbled and rocked through the shafts of the mine, deeper and deeper into the dark. Their voices bounced oddly off the slick rock walls as they passed through.

It might seem logical that there would be silence underground, so far away from the cacophony and euphony of the surface world. But there was always an eerie jangle of noises. The hum of the enormous ventilation fan that pulled clean air from the main entrance through the working areas and diluted the odorless but dangerous buildup of methane gas. The heavy, clanging machinery that clawed out and scooped up and loaded the coal. Then there were the sounds of the mountain itself, what being inside the body of a very old man might be like: creaking joints and groaning shifts of position, something trying to get comfortable even while being methodically eviscerated in three eight-hour shifts every day.

Fossil stopped the mantrip at the power station to let Walter off. As the fire boss on this shift, he was responsible for running the electricity that charged the batteries and controlled the machinery, the lights, the phones. He took his jacket and dinner bucket and climbed off the car. "I'll be up to do the track with you, just a minute here, after I power up," Walter said to Abel and patted him on the shoulder. Abel nodded. The mantrip pulled away again, heading to the end of the line a dozen breaks away, where they would unload the equipment and begin the hard work that lay ahead.

In the distance behind him, Walter thought he could hear a voice above the underground din. A shout from somewhere, he couldn't tell where. Then another. It sounded urgent, but indistinct, and traveled through the chambers and shafts of the section indirectly, one shout sounding vague and far away, the next as though the caller were no more than a few feet from him.

Walter turned around, trying to orient himself. "Who's that?" he called.

"...got to get...don't..." The voice traveled closer. The mountain yawned around them, its cavernous gullet grinding the speaker's words.

"What?" Walter shouted back, spinning around again. "I can't hear you!"

"...have to...come on!" It went faint again.

"What!" He heard running, but couldn't tell from where it came. It must have been one of the guys on crew.

"…the switch!"

"All right!" He walked over to the lever that electrified the lights and machinery. Guys must be needing extra light to unload the equipment. Walter grabbed the throttle in his fist, then John appeared, wildness in his eyes, rushing toward him with his hands outstretched.

"No!" John yelled, lunging at Walter, who reacted by jerking the throttle into the upright position.

In an instant, there was a sense of all the air being sucked backward through the shaft, a holding of breath, a swell of something unspeakable. And then…

BOOM.

It sounded like the old man mountain falling down and breaking a hip. No, worse. Like a shotgun had blown off his head and the bits of bone and flesh were falling down inside his own body, splinter and dust. The power of it knocked Walter and John together to the ground, Walter hitting the floor first and softening the landing for John.

A few seconds later, a second blast concussed through the waffle cone maze of rooms and pillars, shafts and tunnels. The walls, those brittle bones, began to collapse under the force, rolling in on themselves, claiming timber supports and machinery and rail cars and track…and men. A giant slate slab ripped away from the other strata and fell down upon them, the same slate that had only moments before been suspended by the grace of God above Walter and John. The only things that spared them then were the enormous batteries housed at the power station, four-foot-high things big and strong enough to catch the slab at just the right angle so that it didn't crush them where they lay in a blind heap on the floor. Instead, it canted to one side and formed a triangular space about as large as a kitchen pantry.

Walter, who always spoke in a low, even tone, let out a shriek as loud and shrill as a woman in labor, and from the depth where there were no words, no thoughts, just air-stealing, mind-numbing pain.

The air was smoke-filled and dark. Their helmets with carbide lamps had been knocked off, so nothing lit the black coal dust suspended all around them. Walter went still and silent after the one scream. John, without moving much, reached tentatively up to feel for a pulse. It was there, and fast.

"Walter?"

No answer. John, whose heart was also pounding hard, did a check of his own body. He moved slowly, wiggling his ankles, testing his knees and hips, shoulders and elbows, tightening his stomach muscles. All this while lying sprawled across Walter's unmoving body, gently, lest he cause more damage to the other man. He didn't want to hurt him, hadn't wanted to hurt him. Alta, he knew, in spite of her love for John, loved her husband. And so no matter how badly he wanted her for his own, after seeing the pleading in her eyes and hearing it in her voice the night before, he couldn't bear now to cause her the pain of losing anything—or anyone, even his rival—that she loved.

"Abel!" John shouted at the darkness. "Anybody!"

The mountain groaned in reply. His own voice rang out too loud in the tiny space that pinned them. He groped around to find the helmet he'd slapped onto his head just before he dove underground only, what, hours, minutes, seconds before? Finding it, he felt for the light switch. It was like driving through thick mountain fog, the edges of the road and the horizon all but gone. He shined it around, taking stock. The space they were in was maybe eight feet wide by ten or eleven feet long, the two triangular ends sealed with smoking piles of coal, packed all the way up the pitch of the slab. It was impossible for John to measure how much of the mountain was pressing down upon their lean-to shelter. Then he felt a stab of panic. The air, he realized, unless he could move those rocks, and maybe even then, was in limited supply.

John shifted his focus to Walter. He shined the light on his face, which was cut across the forehead and bleeding. Pushing himself carefully off, he rolled to the side and sat up against the warm face of the battery. His thigh hurt when he moved it, but not miserably. He inspected the rest of Walter's body, moving the light quickly up and down — nothing was bent or bleeding too badly — then more slowly, looking for the source of his pain. He wondered if it was internal — his heart, maybe, or some other organ. Then he followed his light down the length of Walter's left arm. It ended at his wrist. The slab had fallen just there and either buried or severed his hand. John swallowed hard at that, the coppery undertones of nausea instantly rising.

"Anybody!" He waited in the settling, swirling dust, the sound of his own voice hurting his ears. "Who's out there? Anybody?"

Walter stirred next to him, groaned as though rising up from a troubled sleep.

"Walter? Walter, you're gonna be okay, hear?" John moved to pat him on the shoulder, in an expression of comfort or solidarity, but then he froze. Lord knew he had no such right to touch him. Instead he scooted over a foot or so toward one end of their space and began pulling at a hunk of coal that stuck out far enough to grab it. Then he yanked it free and fell backward from the sudden give. But rather than revealing a hole, a hope, the empty spot filled again with fallen clots that had been lying above the one he removed. Walter moaned again.

John had never been trapped inside a collapsed mine before. There'd been some small cave-ins in his experience, worked-out sections fallen in after the last pillars supporting the roof were mined. But there'd never been an explosion he knew of personally, never any lives lost. It happened all the time, of course — that was the risk of going underground. Though it hadn't happened in Verra, he'd heard that any explosion or cave-in would be felt aboveground. That the entrances would work like chimneys and dump smoke into the sky. That people on the surface would see the smoke that signaled disaster, feel the mountain moving. Help would soon come running.

John heard Walter try to speak and shined the lamp on his face. Walter squeezed his eyes against the brightness and licked coal dust off his lips.

"Abel?" he said.

"Don't know. Can't hear anything. You okay, Walter? Are you feeling anything?" John didn't want to draw attention to his left hand, gone under a crush of slab.

"Head hurts."

John nodded, shining the light around again, sweeping the space for Walter's dinner bucket. No small miracle that it was trapped with them. John lifted the lid and pulled out biscuits wrapped in a cloth napkin, two lengths of kielbasa, a pear, and a pat of garlic cream cheese. He felt an oddly timed sting at that, this small act of treason, this particular food preparation, customized for Walter's tastes. If she'd ever had the chance, Alta would never have put that particular combination into a bucket for him. Here was a symbol of the life she lived when he wasn't making love to her in their cabin in the woods. This man he lay trapped with had no idea the luck he had, the loyal bit of love Alta saved for him. John may have had her heart, her body, but Walter had this: their history, their son, this thoughtful dinner bucket filled with Polish food and a folded napkin. Lifting the tin that held it all, John placed it on the ground. They might, if they lasted, get hungry for it.

Meantime, he leaned forward and scooped Walter's head into his hand and lifted it up. Then he held the bucket to Walter's lips and let the water fill his mouth, careful not to pour too quickly. Still, Walter coughed and winced, then tried to lift his head forward, wanting a little bit more. Frowning at the flow,

John lifted his head up again. He was thirsty, too, he realized. But then, John didn't have a hand cut off at the wrist. He'd save all the dinner bucket water for Walter.

"Wha happen."

"Something. An explosion. I'm not sure how, but I think it was planned. Where are the other guys?"

Walter opened then closed his eyes. "Abel."

"I know. I know he's here."

Walter let his head fall back and his eyes close.

"Walter, Abel got out," John said. "I was calling and he heard me. He made it out. I passed him on my way in." John's voice grew louder, confident. "He wanted to come back in for you, but I told him no. Said I'd come in. He wanted to come for you, he did. He's all right. He's safe."

Walter pressed his eyes closed and nodded. "Thank..." He nodded, very slightly, again.

"He's all right," John said, and nodded, too.

"Why're you down here? Ain't you...sick?" Walter asked in a strained voice. Then he raised his head and pressed against the floor with his good hand. "Need to sit up."

John glanced again at Walter's wrist. "Best you stay where you are," he said. "Space's tight. Not much room for sitting up." He scrunched himself down lower as he spoke, took a breath that came up short. What time was it? Theirs were the only voices he'd heard.

"Gotta get them," Walter said. "They're up...at the face." He took a breath and waited. "Laying track. Must be 'bout lunchtime."

John's head started to thump in the center of his forehead. "Long about," he said. "Don't worry. They'll take a break when they need one."

Walter rolled his head slowly toward John and fixed his stare. "I know," he said.

John nodded. "They'll be getting along...fine."

"Not that," he said. "I know...about you...and Alta."

Were his head not pounding, John might have had a different reaction. But feeling the cool, tight air turning into poison, making it harder and harder to breathe, knowing the lack of human sound around them meant their time was counted, he just said, simply, "I'm sorry."

Walter shook his head. "No." He paused. "She was only happy 'cause of you." He took a labored breath. "I couldn't ever make her happy...as she deserved to be...you did, though." He breathed. "An' I'm grateful for it...believe it or not."

John dropped his head into his hand, then turned the light away from the both of them.

"Air's thick."

John nodded.

"Something's wrong with my arm."

"I think there might be."

"You get outta here, you give her a message for me, will you?"

"Truth said I think my fuse is...pretty short, too," John said. "I'm not sure I'm getting out if...you don't."

"Then...let me...I want to leave her a letter, tell her something," Walter said, quiet. "Abel, too."

With this, John could see their end. Rivals crumpled up together inside the mountain, voices and wants and futures muted. Their mutual love for Alta, revealed at this last moment, seemed almost conspiratorial. John had a violent urge to confess everything to Walter. But he restrained himself and instead patted down his own pockets in search of a pencil and paper.

"Notepad...in...my pocket," Walter said.

John leaned slowly in, as though he were swimming upstream in New Creek, and dug into Walter's front pocket, never minding the oddness of the act. He pulled out a short ballpoint pen and small leather-bound pad of paper. Peeling back the cover and the first dozen or so pages of notes — when they'd tested for methane gas and where, how many buggies had gone out on the production shifts — he found a blank. He handed it to Walter.

"Can't. Something's wrong…with my arm. Can't…feel it…at all." He stopped and took a labored breath. "You gotta write it for me. I'll tell you…what to say."

So John took a dictation, sloppily spoken and sloppily translated, from the dying husband of the only woman he'd ever loved. It was longer than he'd thought, and harder to write, but he owed it to him, considering. When he was finished, John tore out the pages and folded them in half.

"Put 'em…in my bucket," Walter said. "Bottom half. Least she might…get that…if we burn up down here."

John hadn't thought of the possibility of a fire. But of course, it was there. They were surrounded by methane gas and coal dust, ready for ignition.

He was about to say something to Walter, he didn't know what — his thinking was starting to become a little unhinged — but when he looked down, he saw that Walter's eyes were closed again, but in a different way. Less determined, somehow. And his mouth had gone slack.

He'd have reached out to shake him, but he was afraid there wouldn't be any response. So instead he peeled back the pages of the pad again and began to write a note of his own. He started to think about Liam, why he'd planned this, if he should give him up, but it was too confusing. He didn't have enough energy to sort it through. Instead he thought of Alta, the source of his greatest comfort. He could barely think of what it would feel like for her, finding those two notes stashed together in the emptied-out bottom of her husband's dinner bucket, any more than he could imagine himself and Walter dying together, alone, three miles underground. Nonetheless, he felt the walls folding in, the air seeping out, and time squandering itself into unclaimable scraps.

John finished his own note to Alta, folding it up unnecessarily small. He poured out the rest of the water and put his note on top of Walter's at the bottom of the bucket. Then he emptied the top portion of its thoughtful, wasted meal, and set it down inside. Walter remained still. Wax-like. Then John set the lid and pressed it down with all his remaining might and leaned back against the filthy coffin wall.

The last thought he had, before his entire, unfinished life passed before his eyes, was of Alta. She was lying on the white sheets of their bed in the woods, looking at him. She was smiling.

October 13, 1950

Nearly a week had passed with the entire town slogging through the days. Those who'd lost only their sense of security brought food to those who'd lost their husbands, fathers, sons. People greeted one another with nods and grim hellos, but they took extra care to help one another carry bags and cross streets, aware of the precariousness of daily life. The Number Seventeen was shut down, under investigation; the Blackstone Coal officials, panicked; thirteen miners, gone.

"Behold, I tell you a mystery," Father Timothy read to the congregants gathered that Friday night at St. Michael's. The pews were full of mourners, lapsed and faithful both, there to honor the passing of the six dead Catholics. The Methodist and Presbyterian churches were likewise full, remembering their own. "We shall all indeed rise again: but we shall not all be changed."

The caskets were open. Six of them lined up, each with candles at both ends. At Abel's head, his baptismal candle; only he was young enough for his mother to still have his to use. They were all laid out, hands crossed, in their Sunday clothes. Except for Walter, whose left hand couldn't be put back together respectfully enough. Instead, his right hand rested across his still heart.

Myrthen sat at the organ, upright and chaste, watching the mourners. She wouldn't look at the gray, blank faces lying in their coffins; they threatened to remind her of all the things she wanted to bury. When she saw Alta lean so far down into the last coffin, her hand resting on her son's, Myrthen turned her back to them. She had suffered her own litany of inconceivable losses, she reasoned; it was God's way of keeping things in balance.

"Let us pray," said Father Timothy, vested in his alb and stole, once the bereaved had all passed their loved ones. "Be mindful of our brothers who have fallen asleep in the peace of Christ. Lead them to the fullness of the resurrection and gladden them with the light of your face. Amen."

After a moment, they all looked up at Father Timothy and he nodded at Myrthen. She hadn't yet paid her respects as the others had, because, as the parish's honorary music minister, it was her role to console and uplift the mourners. She was to create, through the music of the organ, a spirit of hope in Christ's victory over death. It was a role she usually relished, but tonight she stared at her own fingers as she played dirge after dirge, slow and somber.

After so long, she was finally free. But even as she breathed the deeply fusty, divine love she'd so long held, she couldn't breathe easily.

Myrthen lifted her hands from the organ keys in a floating movement, then let them drift back down to her lap and interlace themselves into their familiar clasp. She remained seated at her bench as one after another stood and shuffled to the lectern to share their memories of their dead. Stinky, whose given name was Elmer, was eulogized by his twin brother, Homer, who scrubbed at his tears with his fist and wished to God he'd taken on that fated dead shift in his brother's place. Bones's son, Jacob, stood next, in from Philadelphia, where he was going to dental school. He told a story about how his daddy had taken him down the mine when he was seven years old and made him lie flat on his face and hold his breath until he was gasping. That was what it was like working underground, his daddy had said. Bones saved every bit of scrip he could and forced Jacob to do extra homework, even on the weekends, so he could earn a different kind of living. Cross's wife, Betty, went up, carrying their four-month-old son, their sixth child, and meant to say something poignant and meaningful her five elder children could remember, but all she could do was cry. Father Timothy took her arm and walked her back down to the pew.

Nobody moved to eulogize the other three men. John's parents were both gone by then, as was his brother, lost to war. Myrthen made no move to speak, and nobody encouraged her to do so. Walter and Abel loomed too large for the congregation, a respected foreman and his quiet son, and when Alta remained blanched and silent, nobody dared take her place. Not even her brothers, who'd returned to Verra from their scattered homes to be with her.

When the prayers had been said and the candles had dripped down to their holders, it was time for them to go. People flowed out through the aisles and peacefully into the night, Myrthen accompanying them on her organ with a dirge entitled "Though the Mountains May Fall." Father Timothy shook the mourners' hands as they left the narthex, giving details about the Requiem Mass and burials scheduled for the following day. After a quarter hour or so, everyone was gone, the church empty but for its low light and ancient incense smell, and the laments bursting gravely from the organ.

Only one person stopped to offer condolences to Myrthen.

"I'm sorry…," Alta said from behind her.

Myrthen went rigid, her back, her fingers. She took a deep breath in and held it. Alta.

"For your loss —"

Myrthen flung up her right hand, quickly, to stop her. She didn't want anyone, especially Alta, to intrude on her narrowed thinking. She had prayed very hard, bruised her knees and squeezed her eyes so intently until she no longer saw or even thought of the periphery of her actions. If there were credit or blame to be assigned, it all would go to God.

"I'm sorry for your loss, too," she said without emotion. "Now, if you'll excuse me."

Alta turned as if to go, but then stopped. "They say it was your cousin who was responsible," she said, her voice trembling.

Myrthen paused. It wasn't the first time in the past week she'd been asked. "So they say."

"Do you believe it?"

"It's possible," she said to the organ keys.

"But why? *Why* would he do such a thing?"

"It's not our place to understand God's will."

"God's will?" Alta cried. "*God's* will? You think God wanted my child to die? Our husbands? You think God wanted Liam to take everything away from us?" Alta stamped her foot and Myrthen jumped at her stool. "Turn around, for chrissakes! Look me in the eye and tell me that God wants me to be a childless mother!" Alta cried out. "You sit there like a statue. Like we haven't lost anything." Her voice shook. "You have no idea — no *idea* — what I've lost."

Myrthen turned slowly around and pressed her shoulders back against the guilt and fear until they were nearly smothered. "We have all suffered, and none so greatly as the Lord Himself. He lost His one and only son —"

"I lost my one and only son!" Alta screamed at her. "Do you hear me? My one and only son!" With each word, she banged her heart with her fist. "You can have your God," she said. "I want no part of it."

Myrthen looked around, hoping Father Timothy would come in to hush Alta, to take her away. The rawness of her was beginning to take effect.

"You can only know God's grace if you have faith in Him," Myrthen whispered, looking down at the worn planks of the church floor.

She forced herself to forget her part in it, to believe her own words. Then she turned back to the organ and began, again, to play.

November 9, 1950

Alta sat at her kitchen table, her long hands cupping a mug of hot coffee. Next to her sat a soggy, three-day-old *Charleston Sentinel*. Her bowl and spoon had been washed and set to dry on a linen towel spread by the sink. The counters cleaned. The stove quiet. The only sound was the clock in the living room, ticking away the minutes.

She looked beyond the steam rising from her cup and out the window. It had just started to rain again, fat drops, slow and even. She'd been staring through that window daily since the day they came to tell her that everyone she loved had died.

She'd only just seared the pork tenderloin for that night's dinner when Sonny Schumann knocked on her screen door. He still had on his turtleback hat. When she opened the door and stood before him, he took it off and held it at his waist.

"Mrs. Pulaski?"

"Morning, Sonny. What brings you by so early?" She hadn't heard the thunder and lightning coming up from underground. Other townsfolk had. They'd come trotting up to the mine entrance, gathered around, watched the black smoke billowing out, growing tense, waiting.

"It's the mine," he said. "Mr. Pulaski—your husband—was working Number Seventeen this morning, wasn't he?"

"He was working, yes."

"There was...an accident."

"No," she said. She took a step backward.

Sonny paused, then wiped his brow and said at last, "Your husband and your son were underground." He waited a moment for her to absorb his words, seeking her eyes for the moment of recognition.

"There was an explosion."

"No."

He looked down at his hat, the expression on her face too much to bear. "I'm sorry," he said.

"An explosion?"

"I'm sorry, Mrs. Pulaski. It was an explosion. They got rescue teams going down. But your husband...your son...they both been found. I'm sorry."

Alta swallowed hard. Abel's and Walter's dishes were drying beneath a shaft of sunlight on the kitchen counter. The ironing board wore one of Walter's shirts, the empty sleeve dangling loose in the open air.

"Found?"

"The mine collapsed around 'em, Mrs. Pulaski. I was sent to tell you. Walter—Mr. Pulaski—was found in the power station with Mr. Esposito, don't know if you know him, and your son—Abel—was with the other men closer up the face. The investigators are coming in, but it appears to be caused by methane. Weren't nobody found alive."

Alta, her month-ago self, lowered her head and let the door fall closed on Sonny Schumann. Now at her breakfast table with yet another cup of tepid coffee and a windowful of rain-smashed memories, she looked and looked outside but saw nothing. All the ticked-away minutes adding up to nothing. Just the world traveling its slow way around the sun.

For all anyone knew, Alta mourned only two lost miners — more than anyone ever should — her son most of all. Her love for John was private, and her grief would be, too. Nobody would ever know the fathomless depths of her loss or the crushing weight of her guilt.

Well, I don't know if I can wait that long. John's last words to her in person. "Did you do it?" she asked the empty room. All she knew was that he had asked Walter — the obstacle that stood in his way — to take his shift. Then they were dead, and nobody knew why.

The town called John a hero. Eyewitness accounts saw him running toward the mine after the others had already gone inside. They all thought he'd intended to save everyone, but died instead. But the townsfolk didn't know how he stood to profit from their loss. That she was the fallen woman who'd driven him to such madness. She'd told him she'd marry him when her husband was gone. Didn't she, therefore, deserve some of the blame?

You are my always.

Maybe he didn't do it. After all, even the investigators hadn't yet figured it out for certain. In need of someone to blame, everyone seemed to agree that it had been planned by the missing renegade named Sparky Magee.

The rain abated. The windows were streaked and steamed; the coffee, cold; the silence, sterile. There was nobody home. No clothes to wash and iron, no meals to cook and warm on the stove while she stole away. No one to steal away to.

She wondered about the asparagus. If weeds grew on the graves of her three lost loves. Whether she would survive.

Alta looked down at the paper. The front page announced that President Truman was heading to Key West for a vacation in the sunshine. She'd never been to Florida, or anywhere but where she was right then, in a lackluster coal-mining town with mountains like arms around her, always squeezing. Every day of all her thirty-eight years had been spent in a town that, at its greatest density, contained only a little more than seven thousand people. She used to imagine traveling to some glamorous place, maybe even moving. Folding the *Sentinel*, she pushed it deep into the potato peels in the trash.

Then she thought of her lost aunt Maggie and how abundant with pleasures her life had seemed. How elegant she'd looked that first time Alta saw her, just off the train from New York, standing in her flapper dress smoking a cigarette. That was the day she'd first encountered John, too. Both of them, Maggie and John, mesmerizing and mythical in her thirteen-year-old mind. And even as Alta aged, even after Maggie disappointed her and, many years later, John fell in love with her, both of them retained in her mind some of that dazzling, inaugural splendor.

Alta pushed herself away from the table. She went into her bedroom and knelt beside the cedar hope chest her father had made her. Underneath her wedding dress and Abel's christening gown and a quilt that had belonged to her grandmother, next to her mother's Bible and the first watercolor she'd painted—a small brown mouse asleep on a bed of lettuce—was the *Motion Picture* magazine with Colleen Moore on the cover that Maggie had given her in 1925. She looked at the starlet's porcelain skin, her rosebud mouth, the faded orange-and-maroon cover. Alta pressed it against her chest, just as she'd done more than a quarter century earlier, and carried it back to the kitchen table.

Listen, do you like motion pictures? Maggie's effervescent voice bubbled in her memory. *I'll take you to one sometime, you and me, okay?*

Flipping open the magazine, she read the articles and film novelizations, gazed for minutes apiece at the photos and advertisements, until she found the cigarette that Maggie had given her with a wink and a promise: *Don't smoke it yet. I'll teach you how sometime.* Alta peeled it carefully off the page and held it between her fingertips. Maybe she should go now, to Florida or Paris or someplace even farther away. Distract herself with beaches or art galleries or foreign languages. What did she have to keep her here? What left did she have to lose?

She found a box of matches in a drawer and sat back down, put one end between her lips and struck the match. She lit the flattened cigarette and inhaled until her lungs filled all too quickly with hot smoke and stale tar, then slapped her free hand against her chest in protest. A few seconds later, she'd coughed it all out and she held the burning thing out away from her and wondered how that kind of suffocation could become a habit. She stood at the sink while a month's worth — a lifetime's worth — of hot tears ran down her face. Everyone she loved was gone.

No, she decided, she wouldn't go anywhere else. There was no point in it. She would stay where her memories were buried, a weed growing on their graves.

Opening the tap, she ran water over the cigarette until it disintegrated into nothing and fell down the drain.

~ PART TWO ~

March 19, 1964

Lidia Kielar slid into the booth across from her friend Peggy. This was only their second time taking part in the pep rallies. Every Thursday night in the spring, after baseball season started, the high school kids gathered at the school's front steps and did cheers along with the cheerleaders. When it got too dark, or too cold, they moved to the Sugar Bowl, drinking Cokes with peanuts, and listening to music by Frank Sinatra and Ricky Nelson. It was 1964, but the old Wurlitzer didn't have songs by the Beatles or the Supremes or the Four Seasons or the Beach Boys yet. Lidia and Peggy didn't care. They were happy just to be there.

Peggy shrugged off her overcoat and shoved it down in the seat next to her. Bouncing a little in the seat, she smiled as she looked around, proud of the way she filled out her mohair sweater. She knew it was like honey to the Verra Bears.

"Isn't this great?" she whispered, leaning forward. Lidia could see a player elbow his friend as Peggy's chest pressed against the Formica table.

Nodding, Lidia shrugged out of her brother's hand-me-down jacket and hung it on the rack beside the booth. She finger-combed her dark blonde hair, and settled herself in her seat. It was rare for her to be out socializing at night, needed as she was at home. But she'd done her homework and fixed her father's dinner right after school, covered it and left it on the kitchen table. Her brother, who would turn eighteen in a week, was already doing an eight-hour shift in the mines: the third shift, which meant he'd be asleep until after she got home. He started at eleven at night — the hoot-owl shift — but because it was the easiest shift, it was safer for him.

"How do you think you did on the math quiz?" Peggy asked. Before Lidia could answer, Peggy began to hum along with Paul Anka on the jukebox. Her eyes drifted around the diner and landed on the new boy in school, Danny Pollock. "Hey there, lonely boy...," she sang under her breath, flashing a coquettish smile in his direction. She dropped her gaze and looked back to Lidia.

"Did you see who's over there?" Peggy asked, leaning forward again and tilting her head with eyebrows lifted.

Lidia looked over her shoulder and saw him standing at the counter, holding a Coke. From the corner of his eye, he stared back at her, his face nearly expressionless. Inside, Lidia felt herself give way. Her eyes dropped to her lap, her hands suddenly damp.

"Danny Pollock," Peggy said, flashing a quick smile at him. "I heard he's a really good second baseman." She giggled. "I bet I could get him to prove it."

Lidia smiled and kicked her lightly under the table. "You're awful."

"No, I'm not." She winked. "I'm terrific. Or at least I will be." They both laughed at that. Peggy took the straw out of her drink, then tipped it back to drain the last bit. It was shocking, the way Peggy wiggled her tongue around the inside of the glass, her plucky disregard for the manners her mother would slap her for ignoring.

As Peggy set down her glass, her mouth full of soggy peanuts, Danny Pollock slid into the seat next to her. Peggy turned and looked at him with wide eyes, mute but for the sound of frantic swallowing.

"Ladies," he said, nodding first at Peggy and then at Lidia. "Buy you a Coke?"

"Well, isn't that sweet of you, Danny?" Peggy said, recovering. She kicked Lidia under the table.

Lidia shot her a smile, then looked down at the tiny flowers on her skirt.

"My friend here is a quiet little bird sometimes," Peggy said.

Danny propped his head on one palm, threading his fingers into the sandy-colored hair above his ear. Lidia could feel his curiosity before she saw it, and when she looked back up at him, she couldn't stop.

"I've never seen a girl as pretty as you," he said to Lidia.

She blushed.

"I mean it," he said. "You must get that all the time."

Peggy swiveled toward him with her eyebrows pinched together. "No, actually, she doesn't," she said in a petulant tone.

"I don't believe that for a second," Danny said.

"It's true," Lidia said, looking at Peggy.

Peggy cleared her throat and bounced once in her seat, as though to change the subject. "Oh, I'm just teasing, aren't I?" She reached over the table with her hand open, and offered Lidia a smile that wasn't quite synchronized with her eyes.

Lidia played it off, bringing her hand up and placing it near Peggy's. Peggy squeezed it once, then let go. "So, Danny," she said, moving slightly closer to him. "How do you like Verra so far?"

Danny hauled his gaze from Lidia and turned his head slightly toward her friend. "Um, I like it fine. I like the team. I didn't get to play as much back home as I do here."

"But you're really good!" Lidia said.

Danny smiled and she reddened. "Thanks," he said. "But a lot of fellas were good back in Jersey. Verra's a smaller pond. So I'm a bigger fish."

"Are you going to stay here after you graduate?" Peggy asked, swirling the few bits of ice left in her glass with her straw. "You only have another year."

"I wasn't planning to. Don't know if you know it or not, but my mama and I came here because my grandfather needed the help. He's getting on in years. And since Daddy died, Mama said there wasn't really much sense in refusing to come." He shrugged. "I was thinking about going back to Jersey for college, though. Or maybe New York. I want to be a lawyer." Then he looked at Lidia with an expression she couldn't read. "But you never know."

Then, as though pulled back from a distant memory, he glanced at his watch. "Look at the time. It's a school night, ladies. Can I give you a lift home?"

"You have a car?" Peggy asked.

Danny nodded. "My daddy's. Okay, well, technically now it's Mama's. But she let me drive it all the way here from Jersey." He reached over and picked up Lidia's unfinished Coke and took a sip. Then he held it out to her and she smiled, downed the last of it in one gulp. As she reached for her jacket, Danny jumped up, taking it before she did. He held it for her, waiting for her to slip first one slender arm, then the other into the sleeves. Nobody had ever helped her on with her coat before.

"Let's go then," Lidia said.

"Ahem," Peggy said, glancing down at the crushed overcoat on the seat behind her.

Danny huffed a short laugh through his nose. "Sure," he said, and reached down to help her into it.

There was a brief pause at the passenger door of the 1955 Dodge Coronet. "Lucky me," Peggy said. "Lidia lives closer, so you'll have to drop her first. I'll ride in the back and then switch to shotgun after."

Danny looked at Lidia but she only smiled and said, "It's okay. I don't mind." He opened the door and Peggy bounced into the backseat. Then he took Lidia's hand and helped her in, an unnecessary gesture she happily accepted.

They pulled up to Lidia's house, and she noticed through the window of Danny's shiny car that the wooden porch seemed to sag. The paint was beginning to chip around the doorframe. She did what she could to keep the house and garden neat, but since her mother had died nearly two years before, her father had started taking on extra shifts. The time he once spent fixing and mending and building around the house was now spent underground. He said it was for the extra money, but she knew different. They never spoke about such things, but she knew.

She looked too much like her mother. And her brother was such an unfathomable disappointment. Even though it wasn't his fault.

"Thanks for the ride," Lidia said.

"Jump out, honey," Peggy said from the back. "It's my turn up front!"

Lidia climbed out, pulling the seat forward for Peggy; then she stood on the patch of yard amid tiny green stalks of rye grass pushing up through the dirt into spring. Danny leaned in front of Peggy toward the open window. "Goodnight, Lidia."

Peggy waved at her and said, "Toodles, Lid! See you tomorrow!" Lidia thought she could see Peggy arch her back and push her mohair sweater closer to Danny's cheek.

Lidia waved back at both of them and watched the car pull slowly away, until the taillights disappeared around the bend of the road. Once the dust settled back down along the curb, she turned and walked up the porch steps. But with her hand hooked into the pull of the screen door, she paused. She took a slow, deep breath and turned around. It was late, nearly ten, and she needed to pack her brother's dinner bucket and then wake him, a challenging, tiresome process even when her mind was focused. But tonight, her mind was wandering.

To the Sugar Bowl. To the cool leather seat of Danny Pollock's daddy's car. To his sixteen years and deep brown eyes and easy smile. To Peggy and her sweater and second base.

She sank down on the top step of her family's buckling porch and stared up through the clear, dark night at the countless stars. Seeking Orion, the hunter, she leaned back to watch him make his stealthy, patient way across the sky. He'd traveled some distance by the time she saw a pair of headlights glowing at the far bend of the road. They moved slowly and then came to a stop in front of her house. In the same spot as before, but facing the other direction. Danny stepped out, closing the door quietly behind him.

"I really wanted to take you home second," he said when he got to the base of the porch.

She smiled. "Me too."

He climbed the first step. "Did you know I'd come back?"

She thought for a moment, looked up at Orion. "No," she said. "But I hoped."

He took the last two steps and held out his hand. She stood, not knowing what he wanted, but deciding right then she'd give it. He was handsome, but in an unremarkable way. His interest in her — to her amazement — was obvious, but unthreatening. And she wasn't so much excited by him as she was soothed. She put her hand into his.

He brought it to his lips and kissed it, light as a breeze, then walked backward back to his daddy's car. "I'll see you tomorrow, Lidia."

"Tomorrow," she said. And to her own infinite surprise, she kissed the tips of her fingers and blew it in his direction, a line drive to second base.

He laughed at that, reaching up fast to catch the kiss coming at him, straight out of the air.

January 5, 1965

Three hundred and thirty feet into a section just twenty feet below the surface of the earth, inside a glistening cavity worked out from between layers of slatestone, somebody laughed.

"Eagan, you can waste your day off if you want to, but there's no sense in you registering. The United States Army ain't gonna send no retards to Vietnam."

Somebody else shoved the speaker hard enough to make him drop his pickax, but a round of low snickering spread among the men nonetheless.

Eagan Kielar turned red and dropped his chin. He didn't care for people pointing out his defects. But he didn't know what to say to them once they did.

"Shut up, Sam. He can't help it he's retarded. Just get back to work."

It was still dark when Eagan's shift ended that early-January morning. Inside his nostrils, the air was dry and sharp, and he drew it in with great heaving breaths. Each time his lungs inflated to capacity, he exhaled a steaming mouthful with an audible huff. He sounded like an agitated bull, and with the bulk bundled into his padded jacket, he looked like one, too. Charging into the wind, he walked past neighbors' houses with their Christmas lights still twinkling around porch posts. He paid no attention to the small group of boys on bicycles who rode toward him on their way to school, then halved, then regrouped once they'd passed him, like a school of striped rainbow trout in New Creek. He didn't hear the random bark of a dog, or the gritty rumble of a pickup truck engine, or the shouts of mothers calling goodbye to their children.

When he got to his own house, Eagan pulled open the screen and pushed open the door, which he then forgot to shut behind him. The screen crashed shut against the frame and he stood there inside it, his hands hanging thick and heavy against his thighs. He glanced around at the familiar room: the polished grandfather clock, the yellow tweed couch with worn armrests, the floral wallpaper. The smell of bacon and cabbage that clung to everything. He felt better here.

"Eagan, you can't leave the door open like that," Lidia said as she walked into the living room, wiping her hands on her apron. She pulled him farther inside, then closed the door with an efficient push. "Here, take off your jacket. Your breakfast's almost ready." Reaching up, not quite on tiptoe but almost, she tried to help him. "Let's get you into your bath."

He remained still, not responding to her familiar, gentle, busy movements, her small hands on his shoulders trying to work off his coat. He stared at the grandfather clock against the wall next to the faded picture of his parents from their high school prom, which listed slightly to one side.

"Come on, Eagan, help me. Get this off and go upstairs. What's the matter with you?"

The edge in her voice pulled him out of his thoughts, and he twisted his upper body quickly, a bull shrugging off a fly.

"Nothing'sa matter with me," he said. His voice sounded too small for his bearded mouth. His eyes looked too weary for his youthful face.

"Okay, then. Come on."

Dutifully he followed her up the carpeted stairs that creaked under his weight with each step. She was already bent over the edge of the claw-foot bathtub, plugging in the stopper and filling it with hot water when he made it to the bathroom. She stood up and blew a few strands of hair off her face and wiped her hands again on her apron, a practiced move for someone so young. At the sight of him standing limp in the doorway, she put her hands on her hips.

"Eagan, take off your jacket, please, and get into the bath."

"Sam called me a retard."

"What?" she asked, only mildly surprised. She stepped forward to help him undress. "When did he say that?"

"Today. Underground. He said I was too stupid to join the army."

"Oh, Eagan. I'm sure he didn't mean it." She lifted his left arm and pulled it out of his sleeve, then his right, then folded the jacket in half and laid it over the edge of the sink.

"He did. He said I was stupid."

"You're not stupid." Starting at the top, she unbuttoned his flannel shirt. "You're just…different." She patted him on the chest, then knelt down to check the water temperature. Too cold. She twisted the tap with the H on its porcelain button and dragged her hand through the tub in figure eights to blend the rush of hot water. He was silent as he finally stripped off his coal-stained work clothes, dropping them item by item in a heap on the floor.

"Get in."

Stepping inside, he shuffled one foot, watched the wake it created. She sighed at the pile of clothes, then gathered it up.

He was barely audible over the water. "I don't want to be different."

"There's nothing wrong with being different," she said in a matter-of-fact tone. With her free hand, she pulled a clean towel off the hook by the door and laid it across the toilet seat. "I'm going to get your breakfast ready so don't dilly-dally up here. I have to get going or I'm going to be late."

He kicked once at the water, sending an arc of it out of the tub and onto the tile grid of the floor. "I can get my own breakfast. I'm not a baby. You don't have to treat me like a baby. I'm a grown-up man."

"Yes, Eagan, I know you're a grown man. Now I'm going on downstairs. Hurry up."

"Don't tell me what to do!" The pitch of his voice went up. "I'm a grown-up man! You don't believe me? Look." He pointed to his exposed male parts, as if she hadn't seen them a thousand times before, and kicked another spray of water onto the floor.

"Eagan, stop it! Look what you're doing!" Lidia grabbed the towel off the seat and was about to toss it down to absorb the puddle when Eagan reached out to take it from her. But being twice her size and standing at an even greater height inside the bathtub, he pulled her off balance and sent her sprawling backward instead. She landed on her backside, her feet splayed, her apron and the nightgown she still had on underneath it hiked up. She stared at him with her mouth open like a doll propped up by rigid arms.

"You don't think I'm a man!" His normally docile face went red and wrinkled with anger, his big hands clenching into white-edged fists, his chest heaving up and down with every breath.

Lidia remained where she fell, mouth still open and eyes wide, until she saw the undeniable and increasing evidence of Eagan's manhood. Pointing first at the floor in front of her, it quickly aimed itself like an accusing finger up her uncovered legs and her lap and then at her own heaving chest.

"Eagan, no." She kept her eyes on his, pushed herself a foot or so backward toward the door. A hot rip of pain across her tailbone made her cry out. "No!"

He stepped out of the tub and moved toward her, but there was no compassion in his approach. His eyes went black, sharp and dull at the same time. He lunged down, collapsing on her as she fell back again under his weight.

"Stop! Stop!" But he did not. He grabbed the top hem of her white panties and yanked them down, not all the way, but far enough, the tiny pink satin bow mashed into her thigh. She kicked and twisted under him, but he was too big and too angry. "No!"

"I'm not a baby! I'm a man and I'll show you I'm a man, and you'll never call me a retard again. You'll never call me stupid ever ever again." He shoved her down, kicking her legs apart and clamping them to the slippery tile floor with his own. He pushed himself into her. In that searing moment, she became still. Too shocked even to cry, she lay in submission for those few eternal seconds until he finished.

Another few seconds passed while he lay unmoving on top of her. She looked at the pipe snaking out from beneath the sink and entering the wall behind it. It seemed to be leaking. A sour-looking stain sweated through the wallpaper. She would have to call the plumber.

Eagan pushed himself off her. He brought his hands to his mouth and she could see that the ebony glaze in his hazel eyes was gone. Now it was his turn to stare wide-eyed at her as his face rearranged itself. He let go a piercing yelp, the sound a puppy would make if its tail had been crushed, and he bit into the back of one hand. His eyes filled with tears and he shook his head.

"I'm sorry. I'm sorry," he said, his voice quaking. He scrambled backward across the wet floor, dragging his limp-again weapon like a tail, and wedged himself in the too-small space between the bathtub and the toilet. He began to rock back and forth, back and forth, hitting the wall each time. "I'm sorry, Lidie. Please don't tell? Please don't tell?"

Lidia sat up, wincing at the pain from her initial fall and at the burning sensation between her legs. While Eagan begged her forgiveness, she peeled the ripped panties off and balled them up. She stood weakly but calmly up, and straightened her nightgown and the apron over it, the paisley one that had been her mother's. Pushing her hair off her expressionless face, she looked down at the slick floor and saw a runnel of blood flowing to meet the spilled bathwater. Eagan's plea was a run-on susurration: "Please don't tell please don't tell please don't tell…"

"I won't tell."

He looked up, his eyes pleading. "Do you still love me?"

She looked down at him. "Yes, I love you," she said, the weight of her whole short life pushing down on her.

"You do?"

"Of course I love you," she said in a whisper.

"No matter what?"

"I'll always love you, Eagan," she said. "You're my brother."

Then she stuffed the wad of panties deep into the front pocket of her apron, took a deep breath, and said in her soft, clear voice, "Now dry yourself off. I'll go down and get your breakfast."

January 30, 1965

Lidia knew how girls got pregnant. Her mother had told her not long before she died, unexpectedly, just two weeks shy of Lidia's fourteenth birthday. Girls grew up early in Verra. Her mother knew that fourteen was not too tender an age for that kind of information, and she didn't want Lidia to have to find out about it on her own. From partially informed girls whispering behind cupped hands on the playground. From the steel-haired and disapproving physical education teacher at the school. From poorly written books. Her mother, from experience, knew that some of the most important facts were often omitted during that particularly delicate transfer of knowledge. But what her mother hadn't known — could never have imagined — was how young her daughter would be when she would have to draw upon that education. When her cycle hadn't started two weeks after her brother raped her, Lidia knew that what kept her from wanting to crawl out of bed wasn't merely shame.

Her bleeding, like the rest of her, was regular from the very start. She'd never had to run to the school nurse in the middle of the day as Peggy sometimes did, her face as red as the spot on her skirt. Peggy had eventually started keeping a change of clothes with her. Of course none of the girls would comment if she returned from a restroom break wearing a different skirt, but more than once the boys did, in their boorish, ignorant way. "What's with the costume change, Peggy? You got so many outfits you have to wear two a day?" While they snickered and elbowed one another, she'd put her hand on one blooming hip and retort with a smile, "Oh I just wanted to give you a variety of things to look at, since you can't seem to keep your eyes off me." Then she'd saunter off as the other boys turned their laughter toward her flush-faced victim.

Every twenty-eight days for the past two years, Lidia had put on a Kotex pad and belt under her clothes. If she was going to school or into town, she put an extra into her purse. Usually by lunchtime it would have started. But this week, after nine straight days of wearing pads that never needed changing, she woke up from a dream in which she'd been trying to save a newborn bird that had fallen from its nest. She knew, even before she was fully awake, there would be no time-of-the-month in January.

After school that Friday, Danny met her as usual on the front steps to walk or drive her home. "Want to see *My Fair Lady* tomorrow night?" he asked as they shuffled down Main Street through the powder dusting of snow.

"Really? You want to see that again?"

"I don't mind. I know you liked it."

She had liked it. Danny had driven her all the way to Charleston to see it in the big theater there the week of Christmas break. She'd been enchanted by Audrey Hepburn as Eliza Doolittle, a poor East End flower girl with a Cockney accent, and found herself later trying to mimic the upper-class accent Eliza had acquired in the movie. "The rain in Spain stays mainly in the plain," she'd said to herself over and over, with elongated vowels.

That had been just a month—and a lifetime—ago.

"It's just you seem a little down in the dumps lately," Danny continued. "Thought it might perk you up. We don't have to go, though. I don't really care what we do, long as we're together." He reached over and held her mittened hand.

She looked at him and smiled. Under the wool, she could feel his class ring press into her middle and pinkie fingers. When he'd given it to her at the end of that previous summer, she'd wrapped it in adhesive tape until it fit. At night, after she lay down to sleep—Eagan gone for his hoot-owl shift—she would twist it around her wedding finger in the dark, imagining their future. They'd leave Verra and move to Charleston, or someplace else close enough to visit but far enough away to start a life of their own. Danny would become a lawyer like he wanted. Maybe she'd even go to law school, too.

"That sounds nice. Yes. I'd like to see it again."

Danny held open the movie theater door and then skipped ahead of her on the pavement singing, "I'm getting married in the morning. Ding dong! The bells are gonna chime. Punch me and jail me, stamp me and mail me. But get me to the church on time!" His breath steamed into the cold air. He twirled and laughed as only a seventeen-year-old senior boy with a letter jacket and an infallible throwing arm could. Even in her distracted state of mind, Lidia laughed as he swung himself around a lamppost and tried to emulate Alfred Doolittle's march-dance with knees and elbows akimbo.

When he grabbed her around the waist and picked her up, she stopped laughing. The baby.

"Down!"

"I'm just joshing you, silly."

She put her thumb beneath her waistband and gave it a tiny tug. It would be months before she would need the slack, she knew. But the idea of him — in two days she'd already begun to think of it as *him* — being crushed made her uncomfortable. Protective.

Then she relaxed again. "I know," she said. "I'm just cold. Let's get to the car."

It was more than an hour's drive back to Verra. The interstate was quick, but the road up into the mountains was steep and tedious. They listened to the radio station until the static took over, then Danny reached over and snapped it off. For the next five or ten miles, they rode in comfortable silence, until Lidia pointed ahead to a scenic overview and said, "Pull off up there."

"There? Why?"

"Just pull off."

"It's cold out. Can you wait? We'll be home in a quarter hour."

"I don't need the restroom."

He glanced at her. "Okay."

On a wide lip of the mountain face, he slowed to a gravelly stop. If they were standing outside, they'd have had an unrestrained view of a river hundreds of feet below. He put the car in park.

"Cut the engine," she said.

He did. Lidia closed her eyes to adjust to the blackness of the new moon, then looked up through the window. Snow fell from trillions of winking stars.

"You all right?"

She reached out with her left hand and felt for his, then pressed his ring, secure on her finger, into his large, warm hand, and exhaled. Peggy, with her womanly figure and cheeky bravado, acted like she knew so much. But Lidia knew that she'd only ever been kissed—and only once at that—by the younger brother of a classmate during a basement game of spin the bottle. Peggy had never had a steady, barely even went on dates. Before she got home after school, she wiped her lipstick off so her daddy wouldn't see. Her mother wouldn't notice her wearing makeup even if she hadn't started drinking by then, but Peggy wouldn't risk her daddy's wrath.

And certainly, Peggy had never pulled off the side of the road on a makeshift lovers' lane in the dead cold of winter.

Lidia squeezed Danny's hand, and then turned to face him. She moved slowly to the center of the bench seat, until she was so close she could feel his heartbeat quicken. Then she moved closer.

During the countless kisses before this, she'd always closed her eyes. She never knew what Danny's face looked like when their lips touched, because it always seemed natural to keep them closed. Tonight, she kept them open. Tonight, she kissed him with more purpose than longing.

She put her hand inside his collar, and felt the warmth of his neck. Without moving her lips from his, she twisted her body so that she was facing him, sliding between his lap and the steering wheel, moving astride.

"Whoa," he said, breaking contact. "What's gotten into you, Lid?"

"I think it's time."

"Time for what?"

"To go all the way."

He blinked several times in the darkness. "No."

"Yes."

"We said we were going to wait."

She held up her ring finger. "We're going to get married eventually, aren't we?"

"Jeez, Lid. I haven't even asked for your hand."

"It's obvious, isn't it? How things are going? Even Daddy knows your intentions."

Danny pressed himself back into the leather seat. "Yes, but..."

"But, nothing," she said. "I'm here, I love you. Why wait?"

"You ain't never said 'I love you' before."

"It's not an easy thing to say."

"I love you, Liddie."

She nodded.

"Are you sure you want to?" he asked.

She answered by taking his hand and holding it firm as she climbed over the bench into the backseat. He hesitated.

"Come here," she said.

He swung one long, muscular leg over the top of the seat and then the other, holding himself up by straight-arming the front and back seats. Lidia scooted down until she was horizontal, resting her head on the armrest in the door. She moved her hair away from the ashtray embedded there. "Come here," she said again.

"Lid, I don't know about this."

"I do."

"I...I've never done it before."

She closed her eyes. Then she inhaled deeply, filling her chest with air and pressing her tiny breasts upward. "I haven't either."

In the darkness, he couldn't see her. Couldn't see if her expression matched her voice. By then, as she pulled him down on top of her, kissing his neck and untucking his button-down shirt from his slacks, he was losing his ability to discern anything, anyway.

They fumbled in the narrow span of seat, bumping into the backrest and armrest and window. Took turns apologizing and sighing. Danny moaned as he found his tentative way inside her. Lidia, pretending virginity, cried out when he first entered her. This time, at least, she was ready. Nonetheless, her tears were real.

He finished quickly, and immediately apologized. "Are you all right? Did I hurt you?"

"No." She shook her head. "No."

He moved to sitting, and shimmied his slacks up from around his ankles. "Do you feel okay? Do you need anything?" Danny buckled his belt, slid the rawhide leather into the loop.

She shook her head. "I'm fine."

"I love you."

"I love you, too."

Before he climbed into the driver's seat, he looked at her, bewildered and happy. He held out his hand for her to follow, and she did.

Soon he had started the engine, flipped on the headlights, and backed away from the mountain edge. He looked at her again just before he pulled back onto the hairpin road that would take them into Verra. "You may have just made me the happiest guy on the planet."

She smiled back. "I hope so," she said, then buttoned her blouse and climbed back into his letterman sweater. She ran her hand across her belly once more, under the cloak of starlit darkness, and thought of a name: Gabriel. Archangel, spirit of truth. It wasn't his fault his origins would be a lie.

As they descended the long stretch of snow-covered mountain road into their hometown, Lidia began to sing in a voice so low it was nearly a whisper: "I'm getting married in the morning. Ding dong! The bells are gonna chime. Punch me and jail me, stamp me and mail me. But get me to the church on time."

March 13, 1965

From the kitchen, Lidia could hear the creak of the screen door opening, then a knock on the door behind it. She put the lid back on the pot, rinsed her hands, and went to the living room. Before she opened the door, she took a deep breath and tried to calm her flared nerves. But when she saw Danny standing there with his hands buried in his pockets, and that broad smile he always had for her, she relaxed.

"Hi," he said.

She reached out for his arm. "Come in. It's cold. Dinner's almost ready."

He stepped into the warmth and looked around. "Nobody's home?"

"Daddy took Eagan to Charleston to see a different doctor. He hasn't...he hasn't been feeling very well lately."

"You sure you don't want to go to the dance?" he asked, removing his coat and following her into the kitchen.

"I'm sure."

"The whole school's gonna be there."

"I'd rather be with just you."

"Me too," he said, and caught her with a fast kiss as she moved past him. "How long you think they'll be gone?"

She swatted him with a dishtowel. "Not long enough for that."

"You can't blame a guy for asking, can you?"

Since that first time, hovering inside his car somewhere between a river-rushed mountain and a starlit sky, they'd made love only three more times. Emboldened, Danny would have liked more opportunities to discover this new pleasure and improve their technique, but the last few times they'd had the opportunity, Lidia suffered from a certain nausea that made bending into strange backseat positions too uncomfortable to enjoy.

He walked over and took the dishtowel she'd slung over her shoulder, dragging it slowly down her chest with a wink. Balling it, he used it to lift the pot lid, which released a draft of steam. "That smells great."

"Kielbasa," she said. "Your favorite." She'd cooked all the family's meals since her mother died, but this was the first time she'd cooked for Danny. Lidia opened a drawer and pulled out her mother's wedding silverware, then tore off two pieces of paper towel and folded them, precisely, into triangles — an arrangement that seemed slightly more formal than the plain rectangular one she usually made — then set them into two places at the small kitchen table.

"Did you talk to my mama or something?" He picked up a wooden spoon and bent into the mist to stir. "What else is in here?"

She laughed. "You don't think I know how to make kielbasa? Let's see. Potatoes, carrots, peppers, onions, beans, cabbage." She counted them off on six fingers, squinting at the ceiling to remember. "Oh, and salt and pepper." She took the spoon from him, then the pot lid. "Satisfied?"

"Completely." He backed against the counter and heaved himself up.

From the refrigerator she pulled out a bottle of Budweiser, popped off the cap with the wall-mounted opener, and handed it to him. "Cheers," she said.

"Where's yours?"

She took a glass from the cupboard and filled it with tap water, then walked over and touched it to his bottle.

"You ain't havin' a beer with me? Nothing goes better with kielbasa stew."

She wrinkled her nose. "Not tonight."

He looked at her out of the corners of his eyes. "You feeling okay, Lid? No dance, no beer?" Sweeping his arm through the steam, he said. "You going to all this trouble."

She put down her glass and walked over to where he sat, then stood between his legs and put her hands on his knees. "I have something to tell you," she said in a voice both bold and hushed.

"Okay."

The grandfather clock chimed the half hour in the front room; the steam rose from the pot of stew. He looked for the smile he expected on her face. Waited for her to say something. Anything.

He dropped his hands from around her neck to her arms, then to his lap, then, intuiting that he might need something to hold on to, to the edge of the counter.

"I'm pregnant."

The words took a moment to travel from her mouth to his mind, a pop fly arching into a bright sky and then landing into a mitt with a solid thwack. He closed his eyes after he caught it and let out the breath he'd been holding.

When he opened his eyes again and found hers, wide and waiting, a smile crept up the edges of his mouth until his entire face was lifted. "What a relief," he said.

She blinked at him and let her hands drop from his knees to her sides. "What?"

"I thought you were gonna break up with me or something!" He jumped off the counter in front of her and kissed her on the mouth. Then he held her by the shoulders and shouted, "Hell's bells! We're having a baby!" He picked her up and spun her around, then stopped abruptly with a stricken look. "Did I hurt you? Or it?"

It. The image that occasionally interrupted her sleep. Indistinct, but unsettling. She'd had just enough biology, theology, and instinct to worry about what was growing inside her. And more than a little guilt that she was incriminating not her brother, but the boy she truly loved.

"No," she said. "We're not hurt." Then she smiled, shy, and offered the only compensation she could: "And it's not an *it*. It's a *him*, I'm sure of it."

"A boy? Oh, Lid."

"I didn't know…how you'd feel about it. Us being so young. And you're wanting to go on to college…"

He shook his head. "I decided that night," he said, and raised his eyebrows to indicate the night he meant, "I ain't going anywhere without you. Ever."

She leaned into him, her cheek landing against his chest. Quietly, she began to cry tears that took her by surprise. Cried out of guilt and grief, happiness and hope. Cried for the loss of her mother and her innocence and her childhood. Cried, too, because she believed him when he said he'd never leave her.

He pushed her hair back off her face and held her at arm's length while he calculated. "Did you know in six days it'll be a year since the night we met at the Sugar Bowl?" Then, smacked with an idea, he let her go and moved around the kitchen, looking for something. He opened drawers and scanned the countertops. At the sight of the white trash can by the refrigerator, he said, "Ah!" and leaned down into it to retrieve something, which he wiped on his pants, then concealed in his fist.

Standing in front of her, he took her hand in his. Slowly, he dropped to one knee.

"Lidia Kielar, will you marry me?"

She nodded, fighting more tears.

Opening her hand, he placed into her palm the Budweiser bottle cap she'd pried off and thrown into the trash. "At least it's round. And shiny." He shrugged and she laughed.

"I love it."

"I'll get you a real one."

"I like this fine."

He smiled. "I'll still get you a real one. So you will?"

"Yes," she said. "I will."

September 7, 1965

Lidia and Danny moved into his mother's house after they were married that July, less than two weeks after she turned seventeen. Her young belly might have concealed the reason behind their hastiness early on, but now, mired in the deep wet heat of early September, it pushed as flagrantly forward as a late-summer sunflower seeking the sky. Not that modesty mattered with her best friend, Peggy, around. From a crowd of girls that Lidia hardly knew, Peggy had organized a combination bridal and baby shower the week before her wedding, which preempted any notion of secrecy. Of course, Danny's mother, Geraldine, had known from the start.

With her husband gone and no other children, Geraldine had welcomed Lidia as though she were a daughter. She liked seeing Danny happy again, and liked Lidia for making him so. Yes, they were young, but she recognized that grateful, homecoming feeling that comes with finding a true match.

Growing up in Verra, Geraldine had been neither exceptionally pretty nor bright, but was smart enough to know that her options were limited. When she was just eighteen, she met the visiting distant cousin of her best girlfriend, a twenty-year-old recent engineering graduate from Rutgers. He was tall and so reed thin it stirred in her a heretofore-unexplored desire to bake. His feet were long and narrow and required a relationship with a personal cobbler. His hair was unkempt and his fly perpetually abandoned in the open position — thoughts of the dynamic loads of waves or traffic or air pressure took precedence over such banal considerations as personal hygiene or dress. But behind his glasses, his eyes were gentle and unflinching. They belonged to a man who would never stray, never yell, never leave. During their first date, he spoke to her of cantilevered beams, gusset plates and trusses, the miraculously strong and inexplicably beautiful structure of a dome (a Platonic shape of ideal perfection, he'd said with a sigh). She rested her chin in the cup of her palm and never took her eyes off his, and was actually fascinated to learn that the roof of Santa Maria del Fiore had been erected without a scaffold by Brunelleschi in 1420. He'd accepted a position with an engineering firm in New Jersey. Would she, had she, ever considered leaving West Virginia? They were pronounced Mr. and Mrs. William Pollock the following month, both of them disbelieving their extraordinary luck.

When Danny and Lidia came to Geraldine with the news of their engagement and the impending birth of a child, she recovered quickly from her mild surprise. Then she spent a weekend clearing the attic room of boxes and cobwebs and dust, heaving her own mother's things out of trunks, shaking them out, and examining them piece by piece, wondering at the disintegrating memories that could've belonged to anyone — the christening gowns and baby shoes and unfettered locks of hair. Neither she nor her parents had been good storytellers, and so the things they carried stayed unnamed. But shouldn't there be some binding tie? A sense of place and purpose? Something to wend one generation unto the other? With a grandchild of her own on the way, she resolved to give their family a sense of tradition.

That balmy July, Geraldine cleared the space in her home and her heart, and on her son's wedding night, she unveiled the attic bedroom that she hoped was comfortable enough to keep them. Just before she left for a three-day trip to visit her aunt in Ohio, she pressed a newly cut key into her daughter-in-law's hand.

Lidia wished her father had been as gracious, but he took the news like he would a slap. Rearing back, then angry. Hadn't he raised her better than that? Now what would he do? Upon whom would he now rely to look after home and hearth, as she had done since Anna died? And who would be home to care for her brother?

Her brother.

Her child's father.

For Lidia, the next few months passed slowly. It wasn't being swollen to the immobile size of a fat tick in summer, or the incessant cravings, or the way her meals repeated on her that wrenched Lidia into torment.

It was the dreams.

They began in her sixth month, as she lay nightly next to her husband, who slept the deep, uncomplicated sleep of the tranquil unenlightened, unaware of Lidia's restlessness. She held his hand and forced herself to imagine a happy ever after in which her child would be loved by the father and family upon whom she'd shamefully bestowed it. Sometimes, out of desperation, she prayed.

But when she finally fell asleep, a child-insect swelled in her dreams, six-legged and blood-feeding, spreading typhus from her abdomen into her mind. She and the baby both growing feeble-minded like her brother. Worse.

Then one night in early September, a voice thundered in her sleep. It was an unfamiliar one, a deep whisper that came from everywhere at once. It could've been her father's, or God's. It might even have been that of her brother, Eagan, impossibly lucid.

Greetings, you who are highly favored! The Lord is with you.

A quick, seizing pang. She awoke in a sweat.

Lidia reached out and grasped Danny's arm, but he groaned in his sleep and turned his back to her, still unaccustomed to sharing his childhood bed.

She gripped the warm spot of sheet he'd abandoned. After a minute or so, another freehold vise overtook her insides. No internal distress had ever measured up against this pain.

"Danny," she whispered into the dark.

No response, just deep, even breathing beside her. Outside, a windstorm howled through the maples. She took a deep breath and blinked, drowsy, at the white grid of the ceiling. It must have been a dream.

Another grip. Lidia felt like she was being squeezed from one dream into another. From childhood into old age. Her eyes grew wide and took in the entire length of ceiling, stunningly bright in the dark, until the vise released her again.

The next time, she yelled outright: "No!" She grabbed her belly and pushed against the pain. Danny shot upright.

"What'sa matter?"

Lidia pressed harder against her belly and pushed her head against the pillow, closing her eyes tight. It was only early September. She was two weeks early — or six weeks early, according to the lie she'd told. Geraldine had said it would be the end of October before the baby came.

"Mama!" Danny yelled toward the door. "Mama!"

"No," hissed Lidia. She felt Danny lean over her, smelled his sour, pre-morning breath, and turned her face away. "No," she whispered. "It's too soon."

But who was she to be disobedient to the wisdom of the righteous?

"Mama!"

Geraldine appeared at the doorway, her gray hair rolled and tied in rags, clutching her chenille robe at her throat. "What? What is it?"

From the far edge of the bed, Danny pointed, wide-eyed, at his swollen, writhing bride. Geraldine rushed in.

"Lidia, sweetheart. You're having contractions?"

From within a moan, Lidia nodded. She'd asked Geraldine once how she would know when her time had come, and Geraldine had smiled and patted her hand and said, "You'll know." *But how*, she'd insisted. *What does it feel like?* Geraldine had turned toward the window, through which she could see her son hammering away at the teeter-totter he was building out of scrap wood. "It feels like the worst and best pain you could ever imagine. There's nothing to compare it to, because there's nothing else like it. Nothing at all."

When she'd gone into town one afternoon to meet Peggy for a Coke at the Sugar Bowl, she told her what Geraldine had said. Peggy shook her head and with her straw still between her teeth, said, "Oh no thanks. Not me. My cousin Mabel told me it was absolutely horrid. Sorry to be the bearer of bad news, Lid, but you're in for some serious what-for. If and when I ever have to push some watermelon out — and I mean *if* — I want the ether right off. Mabel says it starts bad and ends worse." Then she laughed, prematurely rueful. "And *that's* just the beginning."

Now as she lay twisted in the sheets, Lidia wondered how much worse it would get. Not that it mattered. She wouldn't let herself be anesthetized against it. Regardless of the pain, she would stay awake and alert until the end. She refused the possibility of being the last to know what came out of her.

"Sweetheart, do you know how fast they're coming?" Geraldine's hand on her forehead was tender and cool. Lidia felt the mattress sink next to her with her mother-in-law's generous weight. She shook her head.

"Danny, honey, get me your grandfather's watch. We need to time the contractions." He bolted out of the room, grateful for a job, and returned with it an instant later.

Geraldine turned on the lamp and used Lidia's expression to time the intervals. Two minutes, almost exactly, between the closed-eyed winces. "You're going fast," she said. "Danny, call Doctor Bartlett. We don't have time to get Lidia to him. He needs to come here." The tone of her voice had changed, revealing a metallic hint of alarm that sent Danny rushing off without even saying goodbye, but then was calm again for Lidia.

"The doctor will be here soon, sweetheart," Geraldine said. "Just keep breathing."

Lidia refused offers of water and walking and anything else Geraldine could think to give. Minutes that felt like hours passed. The languid moon had moved across the window and was gone again. The sheets were tangled and damp. There was no time for the doctor.

Lidia repeated to herself: *The best pain. The best pain ever.*

"He must have something to tell the world," Geraldine said with a smile. "Don't worry, everything will be fine." But there was a crop of sweat on her brow.

Lidia only cringed. "I need to push," she whispered.

Geraldine lifted the sheet that draped Lidia's lower half. Long ago, Geraldine had nearly completed her nurse's training when she found out she was pregnant with Danny. She'd wanted to become a midwife. This, as it turned out, was to be her only chance. She guided Lidia's hands to her knees and told her to hold them. When her face contorted with the next contraction, Geraldine said, "Push!"

Lidia did and Geraldine pressed on her belly. "Breathe!" Lidia let out a whoof at the end, and let her head fall back. She felt something leap in her belly.

"Doctor Bartlett will be here soon. He'll give you something for the pain."

Lidia shook her head. "I don't want anything."

"There's no shame in it, sweetheart. No reason to suffer unnecessarily."

Lidia opened her eyes and caught Geraldine's. Her face was soft and straight and kind. That's when she knew this child would be welcome whatever it was, human or insect, or something in between.

She took a fierce breath and grasped her knees again and bore down. Geraldine whispered, "Push, Lidia, push."

This went on for minutes, days, years, lifetimes. Excruciating pain. Cymbals and pounding and lightning and thunder. Dark clouds and black night and sleet. Every contraction made her feel as if she were ripping, slow-motion, into shreds. She was grateful that there was no doctor, no Danny to watch this graceless evisceration. This was between herself and God. And Geraldine.

"Push, Lidia. You can do it. I can see the head. I can see the hair!"

And then, from within that torn cocoon, her child's head crowning between her legs, came nothing but:

Light.

Silence.

Wonder.

Lidia unhinged her neck, let herself fall back, and landed as though on a bed of clouds. She closed her eyes against the blinding white. Only pressure, no pain. The pain was gone. Completely.

And then, laughing.

It sounded far away at first, laughing amid such torture. She wondered if perhaps she'd died. From behind closed eyes, she sought her mother's face among the clouds. But then her arms were filled with something thrust gently against her. She opened her eyes and saw not the face of her mother, but that of a different kind of angel.

"You have a son," Geraldine whispered.

Lidia swallowed.

"A son! He's bigger than I expected. But then Danny was a big boy, too. He takes after his father already."

Lidia looked down at the tiny face. He didn't cry, but he was breathing, soft and even. His eyes were open, squinting at her. Lidia yanked back the towel that Geraldine had wrapped around him. How many arms and legs? How many fingers and toes? They exchanged a long look, this child-tick and its mother. Without his swaddling, she could see him for what he was.

He was perfect. Two arms. Two legs. Ten each fingers and toes. Eyes as dark and calm as bedrock.

As they lay, staring at each other, Danny burst into the room ahead of the doctor. Geraldine spread her arm across her son's chest to stop his approach. They stood, astonished and reverent, in the doorway.

October 21, 1965

Lidia was standing at Gabriel's crib, her chin resting on crossed arms, watching him sleep, when she heard a knock at the door. She pulled on her robe and checked the clock on the bedside table. She wasn't used to receiving visitors.

"I brought you this," Stanley said when Lidia opened the door. He stood on her mother-in-law's porch like a peasant begging for something, carrying a ragged yellow blanket rolled up like a loaf of bread.

"Come in, Daddy."

He wiped his feet more than was necessary on the welcome mat before he stepped hesitantly in, then glanced around the living room, a reverse carbon copy of his own. The fireplace was on the left here. The staircase on the right. How did Lidia negotiate this backward life?

"I'll get you some coffee."

"I had some already."

"Cake then. Or *kołacz*. We had apricots. Your favorite."

He waved her off. "No, nothing. Don't trouble yourself."

"It's okay, Daddy."

"All right then, a little of the *kołacz*."

She cut him a slice and put it on one of Geraldine's dessert plates, then set it down on the round kitchen table with a fork and a folded paper napkin.

Stanley hunched over it with a forearm flanking each side, a gesture leftover from his childhood. He was the youngest of five hungry, greedy brothers, always protective of what was his, even if he didn't really want it.

He took a bite and nodded. "Good." Then he licked the fork and set it on the edge of the plate and pushed the plate away. Reaching down for the blanket, he placed it on the table and put his hand over it, briefly, like a blessing.

"I don't remember if it was yours or your brother's. Your mother made it, I know that." He took a deep breath and bent his head. "She loved you. Both of you."

When Eagan was almost four, he'd come down with a fever. A week later, Eagan lay stiff and confused and wetting the bed, and they were told it was bacterial meningitis, that the extra white blood cells trying to fight it had flooded his brain, which swelled and pushed against his skull and damaged his frontal lobe. The effects revealed themselves more slowly in the weeks and months that followed: hearing loss, headaches, mood swings, temper tantrums. When he was six and had started school, he lagged behind the other children. He couldn't remember his letters, even though their mother, Anna, sang the alphabet to him over and over again, the upbeat swing of her voice not quite hiding her growing concern.

Then he began to grow. His height and brawn seemed inversely proportional to his slow speech, his poor memory, his undeveloped intellect. When he became frustrated at the other second-graders for taunting him—"Retard! Retard! Eagan is a retard!"—his occasional violent outbursts against them were unlike anything any of them knew.

The school superintendent spoke to Stanley directly. Both of them were company men, higher up than most. Something like this had to be handled, see, or else it was going to create problems all around. Can't have an eight-year-old who looks like he's twelve and acts like he's three going around roughing up the other miners' sons. Couldn't Stanley beat some sense into him?

When Anna heard that, she was outraged. "He'll never step foot in that school again!" she said. And he did not. She kept him home and did her best to teach him herself.

But Eagan couldn't stay focused when Anna wrote sentences on the chalkboard she set up in the kitchen, even though he tried. When she asked him how to spell "cat," he would answer "six" or "z" or "I can't remember." She was patient, though, and gentle, and it soothed him to be with her. He rarely threw a fit when his mother was around.

The following September it came time for Lidia to go to school, but Anna was hesitant. She would have liked to keep her little girl home as well, would have enjoyed the continued happiness of having both her babies with her in the kitchen, doing lessons after breakfast and making cookies after lunch. The three of them were always together and almost always alone. Ever since Stanley had been promoted to foreman after the big mine explosion—not long after Lidia's second birthday—he spent little time at home. He was busy working to earn their living and staying clear of his damaged son, who had been so smart before the illness took hold. He couldn't bear to be reminded of his own failure.

———————

Lidia looked at the tattered blanket in front of her father, and then at him. The pouches under his eyes seemed to sag more than the last time she saw him, a few weeks ago. His cheeks looked sunken, making his stubbled chin jut even more prominently forward.

"Your mother had a way with your brother," Stanley said. He kept his hands folded in his lap, his eyes downcast.

Your brother. She hadn't seen him since Gabriel was born. She pointed to Stanley's plate, wanting to change the subject. "You didn't like the *kołacz?*"

Stanley pulled the delicate wedding china plate back toward himself a few inches with the half forefinger left over from an accident involving a horse-drawn hay mower in 1939. He picked his fork back up and poked at an apricot. "Where's Danny's mother?"

"She went downtown."

"Oh."

"You sure you don't want some coffee?"

Stanley shook his head.

"The baby'll be up soon. You wanted to see him?"

Stanley stabbed a bit of pastry and put it into his mouth. Moments later, when he finished chewing, he said, "I wanted to talk to you about your brother." He took a slow breath and said, "He hasn't been the same since January."

Lidia swallowed.

"He told me what happened that night."

Lidia sucked in a breath of air and stood up, abruptly, and moved to the sink. She filled the kettle and set it on the stove, then lit the fire, fingers trembling. "What...what did he say?" she asked, without looking at him.

"He told me what the guys said to him. About him wanting to enlist. About him being retarded..." Stanley shook his head. "He still won't go back into the pit."

She let out the breath she'd been holding. Stanley dragged the fraying yellow blanket across the ironed tablecloth and against his chest.

"Since you been away…I been trying," he said. "But he won't go back." He wrung his hands around the blanket. "I don't know what to do with him now you've moved on…"

Stanley took a deep breath. "I can't take care of him, Lid."

The clock on the wall ticked off the seconds. Eight thousand miles away, the United States special army was fighting North Vietnamese troops. Lidia wondered what Eagan would do if he were there. Eagan in jungle trousers and lace-up boots and helmet. Would he understand how to be part of a platoon? Would he know what to do with a grenade? With a submachine gun? Would he know how to fill his own canteen?

"I was thinking…maybe you could…" In her life, Lidia had never heard her father sound so watered down. "You have a way with him."

She thought back to the days and weeks following the incident in the bathroom. How she'd fed him his dinner that night, and every night for the next six months, up until the day she moved into Danny's grandfather's house. How she'd cooked his breakfast and packed his lunch, which he ate in his room because he refused to go to work. How she'd washed and mended his clothes. How she'd cut his hair and cleaned his room. Although he'd hardly spoken at all since that night, whenever he began to rock and moan and glaze his eyes against whatever daylight demons stalked him, she would rub small circles onto his broad back between his shoulder blades and hum one of the two lullabies she could remember her mother singing before she died.

Although she didn't treat him any differently, Eagan seemed to know that he had taken something from his sister. What he didn't know was that he had given her something, too.

The roundness that strained her clothes and plumped her face had kept her from becoming hard-edged or prematurely withered. And her fear kept her from telling anyone the truth about the secret that had grown inside her, even though it haunted her like a ghost. Thank God their father was ignorant of the begets of the seven-week-old baby sleeping in the other room. It would probably kill him if he knew.

"Gabriel's up," she said, soft.

"Okay."

"You want to see him?"

Stanley pushed his plate away again and studied the imaginary crumbs in front of him. Then he dusted them off with a slow swipe of his hand and placed the blanket on the table. He closed his eyes and nodded slowly.

"Sure," he said.

March 28, 1967

He was forever moving. Even when he suckled at her breast, Gabriel pawed at the air like an animal. And he never crawled; he walked upright without assistance at nine months. Everything he did seemed rehearsed. Eating, walking, playing with blocks, the way he looked so seriously at everything.

Lidia had been around kids all of her nearly nineteen years. Younger siblings of her friends, miners' children. And every kid she'd ever known had made toys out of chunks of coal. It spilled off the train cars as they rumbled down the tracks. It came home in the pockets and cuffs of their fathers' work clothes after they crawled out of the grave at the end of every shift. They threw it at one another in the streets and skipped it into the creek and kicked it along the endless stretch of rail that hauled the coal from the mines and out into the world beyond theirs. To anyone living in a coal-mining town like Verra, it was as common and necessary and plentiful and miraculous as mother's milk. But the first time his daddy offered Gabriel a hunk of black diamond, when he was only fifteen months old, he snatched his fat baby hands away and made a face.

"It's coal, Gabe," Danny said, holding it out again. "It's all right. You can touch it."

Gabriel backed away and clutched his hands against his round bare belly.

"It's nothing," Danny said, and then he laughed and tossed it up and down as easily as he would have a baseball just a couple of years before. "Well, I guess it's more than nothing. It's more like everything. Here, take a hold of it."

Gabriel looked him dead in the eye. "No," he said. "Hurt you."

Occasionally, when he would lie in her arms as she rocked him to sleep, he would gaze off at indistinct points around the room. Lidia watched him narrow his eyes, and turned her own head to see what he was focused on. Nothing. A calendar. A curtain. A bare spot of wall where the paint had chipped. Once, she thought he might have been watching a mosquito. But his eyes moved the way they would if he were looking intently at someone's face. Sometimes, he would let go of the yellow blanket that he called "Bobby" and lift a chubby hand and point.

Other times, he smiled at the nothing in the distance.

"You looking at angels again, baby boy?" she would whisper in the twilit room. She would tuck Bobby back under his chin and pat him on the back, then begin to chew on a hangnail to calm the panic that rose inside her. Danny boasted constantly that Gabriel was so smart, walking and talking so early. He pointed it out, proudly and with amazement, even to her, who was with him all day long.

Was he smart? Was that all this was? Or was it something else? She peered into the sleepy hazel eyes blinking languorously back at her.

He did look an awful lot like Eagan.

September 13, 1967

For the past six days, since receiving a fishing pole for his second birthday, Gabriel had refused to take a nap. Instead, he insisted that Lidia walk him across the tracks and up the mountain to the little stream that came down from Whisper Hollow and fed the big creek that ran through the town of Verra.

On Gabriel's birthday, Danny was working the hoot owl shift, so he had the day off. Lidia packed a picnic of baloney sandwiches and potato salad and an apple pie. She tucked in some napkins and a change of clothes and the long, thin gift she'd wrapped in brown paper and tied off with a blue bow. Then they took Gabriel up to the stream and spread out a blanket and ate their lunch. As they picnicked, they talked quietly to him about the leaves and birds and the random creaking buzz of cicadas in the oaks and maples. After a while, Lidia put three candles into the pie — two for his age and one to grow on — and they sang "Happy Birthday" and told him to make a wish and blow out the flames.

As he did so, Lidia, with her eyes open, made one, too. *Keep it secret. Keep him safe.*

Gabriel pulled at the bow and ripped off the paper, but there was no delight on his face when he saw the two halves of the pole. He reached out and touched the reel. "What is it?" he asked.

Danny laughed. "It's a fishing pole. Just your size," he said. "I'm gonna teach you how to catch a fish just like my daddy taught me when I was little." He opened the margarine container he'd filled with dirt and night crawlers dug from the dew-soaked garden that morning. Then he showed Gabriel how to thread a squirming worm onto a hook and how to cast his line into the stream in the quiet spots near the bank where the trout would likely be. And how to hold on to the little cork handle and bounce the worm and watch for the bobber to get tugged under the water's surface.

The first time he got a strike, Gabriel was so surprised he lost his balance and slipped into the stream before Danny could catch him. The trout got away, but Gabriel didn't let go of the pole. "That's my boy!" Danny said, and scooped him out of the water. Lidia used the picnic blanket to dry him off and changed his clothes for the spare set she'd brought.

Raising her older brother had taught her about being prepared for accidents.

Once he was dry and the stun had faded, Gabriel walked back to the bank and picked up his pole. He handed it to his father and said, "Again."

And every morning since, he'd told Lidia, "I no need a nap. Take me fishing." After a couple of days of resisting and insisting that he lie down, that they could go later after they'd both had a rest, Lidia finally gave up. She helped him dig up the night crawlers and bait his hook, and helped him cast his line, and stood behind him so she could take over when he got a strike to keep him from falling in.

They'd had rainbow trout for dinner three times that week already.

"Gabriel, baby," Lidia said on Wednesday. "Let's please not go fishing today."

"I no need a nap."

"Well, you might not, but I do."

"Take me fishing. Please?"

It melted her, the way he looked up with those saucer eyes so full of hope. The way he used the word "please" correctly and, if she was being honest, manipulatively.

She sighed, balling the dishtowel, and tossed it onto the counter. "Fine," she said, shaking her head and smiling with her tired eyes. "Go get your worms."

They repeated their adventure identically. Picnic, worms, casting, waiting. The only difference was that today was Wednesday and the sun remained hidden beyond a blanket of clouds. A cool breeze blew off the mountain, whipping a few early-turned leaves off their stems. Lidia could smell the ascent of fall.

"Gabe, come lie down here with me a minute." She lay back on a bed of leaves and patted her shoulder. Gabriel, who wasn't tired, complied. He put down his pole and snuggled his over-alled little body and Johnson & Johnson–scented head against her, and she wrapped her arm around him. For a moment, the sun poked from the clouds and radiated heat at them. Lidia closed her eyes.

Minutes or hours later, when she woke, she felt no heat against her face. Or her shoulder. The clouds were thick again; the sky revealed no sense of time.

She sat up quickly, smacking the stale taste off her lips. She looked around. The gagging sound of stream on rocks. The belly-up float of fallen leaves. A wavering V of geese against a pewter sky. How long had she slept? Where was Gabriel? She stood up, leaves sticking to her hand-knit sweater.

Lidia ran toward the stream, scanned the bank for any sign of him.

"Gabriel?"

Without hesitation she picked her way straight out into the middle, hoping to see his pole sticking out from somewhere along the bank nearby.

"Gabriel?" Louder now.

She sprinted from the stream and back to where they'd last been lying. His pole and worms were gone.

Standing, frantic and paralyzed, Lidia wanted to run but was unsure which way to go. Upstream? Down? Into the wood? How far would he go? What if he'd fallen in the stream and been carried away?

"Gabriel!"

Somewhere to her right, there was a rustling in the brush. She couldn't see if it was him, but it was enough to catapult her from her bewilderedness. "Gabriel! Gabriel!" She launched forward, screaming his name over and over as she ran into the wild.

Lidia crashed across fallen branches and ducked under low boughs, coming to the place where she thought she'd heard something, but found nothing there. Dizzy with fear and panic, she turned around. The next time she called his name, it came out garbled.

There were stories she'd heard all her life of mountain people who lived out in the woods in tar-paper shacks. Vagrants and crazies and moonshiners and all manner of nearly feral beings who refused to live in a civilized community. What if the stories were true? What if one of them had—

"Gabriel!"

Another rustling nearby. She sprinted to a pair of red maples and yanked back a handful of scrub brush, already imagining her serious little boy, crouched down and peering at some interesting creature.

She was partially right. Four or five speckled brown cottontail rabbits burrowed together, their long ears touching. The sight of them was so unexpected that for a second she forgot herself. She felt the urge to reach out and stroke their fat little backs, their little white tails. *Gabe, look at this!* she wanted to say. But Gabriel wasn't there.

Panic rushed back in and she let go of the brush, which snapped into place over the sleeping rabbits. She looked this way and that, trying to decide. Then she saw his fishing pole lying in the dirt just a few feet away from where she stood. It was unbaited and unbroken, just tossed aside as if forgotten. Gabriel had wanted his pole next to his bed at night. He wouldn't have thrown it down like that. The worms had been dropped too; the lid on the margarine container had come off at impact, and a small mound of dirt spilled out. The night crawlers were gone, either fished away or already digging under unfamiliar earth.

As she scanned the ground for clues — which way, how long ago — she realized that a path had been cut into the sedge and clover. She decided that Gabriel would go up and not down the mountain, so she took off running, calling his name as she ran.

It wasn't long before she crested an incline and saw a garden and a cabin next to it. Even from within her adrenaline-fueled hysteria, she noted the neat rows of vegetables, the lack of weeds, the tended dirt. A line of smoke threaded toward the sky and blended into it. An odd comfort. She slowed down and could smell something cooking. Familiar and fragrant, like a meal her mother might have made once upon a time. She moved steadily forward, but as she approached, she began to wonder if she was moving backward instead.

Mama? she thought. But her mouth said, "Gabriel?"

She walked around the southern border of the garden toward the front of the cabin. The windows were open. Amid the smell of food, she could also smell paint.

"Gabriel?" she called.

"Mama?" His voice was muffled. She sprinted around to the front porch.

"Gabriel!"

There he was, sitting cross-legged on the porch, his mouth full, a half-eaten cookie in his hand. "Mama!" he cried, and smiled wide. "Look!" As he pointed to something in the near distance, she cleared the steps without even touching them. When she got to where he sat, she scooped him up, burying her face in his neck that smelled of baby shampoo and stream water, loamy dirt and sugar cookies. She burst into sobs.

After a moment, she pulled her face away and peered into his. "Are you all right?" His eyes were bright and fine. "You're not hurt?" He shook his head and smiled. "Why did you run off like that? I didn't know where you were! Don't ever do that again, Gabriel! You hear me?" Then she yanked him through her anger to hold him close again.

"He only got up here about ten minutes before you did." Alta's voice behind her was calm and warm.

Lidia jerked her head up. She'd only had eyes for her son; she didn't notice anyone else was there.

"He was chasing after this little rabbit here." She held up the tiny thing. It looked just like the ones Lidia saw back near the stream. "I gave him a cookie, and was trying to get him to tell me where he lived. I was just about to take him down to town to see if we could find his parents."

"I'm his parent."

"So it seems." Alta smiled. "You look a mess. Must have been frantic. Come sit up here and I'll get you a cup of coffee." She patted one of the two rocking chairs moving on its own in the September breeze. Then Lidia carried Gabriel over and sat down and leaned back into the slats. She could have been a little girl again curled up in someone's lap for how comfortable it was. Gabriel wriggled in her arms and she let him down.

"Can I see the rabbit?" he said.

Alta put it down in front of him. "Remember what I said. He's little and probably scared." She glanced at Lidia. "Kind of like your mama is right now. So you be gentle."

Gabriel offered the rabbit a bite of his cookie and it stretched out its neck and twitched its nose before declining. It turned away and hopped on long feet a few steps across the porch. Gabriel giggled and clasped his hands over his mouth.

The other rocking chair was halfway painted a cherry-blossom red and resting upside down on a flapping issue of *The New York Times*. A few drops of paint splattered the headline: "U.S. Encouraged by Vietnam Vote." The pungent paint smell mixed with the food — cabbage soup, perhaps — and fresh coffee made Lidia want to cry again. It was as if she'd gone back to the home her mother had made, or someplace even better.

Then Alta was standing next to her with a handkerchief and a steaming mug. "I'm Alta Pulaski. Gabriel already told me his name. What about you?"

"Lidia Kielar. I mean, Pollock. Lidia Pollock."

"Stanley Kielar's girl?" Lidia nodded and Alta smiled. "How long you been married?"

"Just over two years."

"Takes a while to make the name stick." She nodded, searching Lidia's tired eyes. "I can understand that."

Lidia looked down at the coffee. Smoke came off the top in a veil, as if it were trying to hide something underneath. She had a sudden desire to tell this stranger everything she couldn't tell anyone else.

"I fell asleep. We were having a picnic. I didn't think…" Fat tears rolled down her cheeks. "I'm sorry." She laughed once, a hiccup, and settled back into the crying.

"Shhh, now." Alta stepped closer and patted her on the arm.

"I've just been so tired is all."

"It's hard," Alta said, still patting her in long, gentle strokes, the way she had the cottontail rabbit. "Being a wife and a mother. And you so young. I know it's hard."

"I shouldn't have fallen asleep, though. Something could have happened to him."

"Something's always going to happen to people. Good and bad. You're trying your best, I can see that. But you can't always keep things from happening. Sometimes they just do."

Lidia tipped her head up, slow enough not to discourage Alta's motherly hand. Now that even her mother-in-law was gone—died the year before of heart failure—this stranger was the closest thing she had. She sniffed and used the handkerchief to wipe her eyes. Then she took a long sip of coffee. "Do you know what time it is?"

Alta turned her wrist and checked her watch. "It's almost three o'clock." She glanced at the sky. "Hard to tell on a day like this."

Lidia gasped. "I didn't mean to be out so long. I have to go get dinner started. I haven't done a thing."

Alta laughed. "I remember feeling like that back when. Always having to be on somebody else's time."

She shook her head. "Danny doesn't demand anything. He's good to me."

Alta looked at her with a sad sort of smile. "I believe it." Then she stood up straight and took a deep breath. "Does Danny like cabbage rolls?" Before Lidia could answer, Alta winked and lifted an index finger, then disappeared behind the slam of the screen door.

Gabriel chased the little rabbit around the porch, crouching down each time it stopped, mimicking its twitching nose and occasionally reaching out to stroke its fur. Lidia watched from the rocking chair and felt both very old and very young. She couldn't decide if she should get down and play with

Gabriel, or let herself into the cabin and offer to help this utter stranger. Her kitchen clanging and tapping clearly meant that she was dividing her dinner to send with Lidia back down the mountain.

Alta returned a few minutes later with a full sack. "I always make too much food. Old habits. It's nice to be able to share it."

Lidia stood. "How can I thank you for this?" She lifted her palm toward her son. "For..." She closed her eyes and shook her head.

"You just come back for a visit, that's how. I don't get a lot of visitors and I'd be happy to have some company."

Lidia nodded and tried to smile.

"You've had a time of it today," Alta said. "There's cabbage rolls here, and some asparagus from my garden. Now where exactly did you leave your picnic things? I'll walk you back and help you get situated."

Lidia reached out to take the sack, but Alta waved her off. "You take the baby. I'll carry this."

"Gabriel, it's time to go," Lidia said. Gabriel must have heard the reluctance in her voice, for he didn't even lift his head in response. Lidia and Alta stood side by side, looking down at him. Neither of them seemed too hurried to force the issue either. After a moment, she leaned toward Gabriel and said, "You know, I think I might set that rabbit up here for a pet if it'll have me. Then you'll have something to play with when your mama brings you up the hollow to see us."

Gabriel looked up at her and said, "I'll come back."

"I know you will, sweet boy."

They gathered themselves and their things and set off down the path toward the stream. Without ado, Alta stopped and picked up the margarine container and tapped out the last bit of earth into the dirt. She lidded it and put it into the sack and then found Gabriel's pole and gathered it as well.

Lidia led her silently to the blanket and basket and Alta lost no time in setting things to right. As she transferred the covered dishes from the sack to Lidia's empty basket, she said, "This asparagus in here. I've been growing it now almost twenty years. It's fresh cut so you just steam it and add some butter. You've never tasted anything so good. These cabbage rolls just need some reheating."

Lidia turned to Alta in the falling light. "Thank you," she said. And Alta, who hadn't had a human embrace in longer than she cared to remember, brought her close and said, "You bring that gorgeous boy back to see me, hear?"

And Lidia nodded against Alta's shoulder. "I will."

Then she took Gabriel's hand in one of hers and the full basket in the other and gave Alta a smile, bigger than any she'd managed all day, and turned down mountain toward the unbeaten path.

December 15, 1967

Lidia did return to Alta's cabin with Gabriel, tentatively and with a fistful of wild onions and calico asters the first time, then again and again until their visits were frequent enough for Alta to pull down some of Abel's childhood toys and keep them in the living room for Gabriel to play with.

On this cold day, Lidia bundled Gabriel into his warmest clothes and wrapped his head with a soft wool scarf that had belonged to her mother-in-law, until only his eyes and nose were uncovered. Then she walked him, hand in hand, down their street and across the tracks and up the hill toward Whisper Hollow, where Alta would welcome them with mugs of hot chocolate and tea.

"Oh, it's a cold one!" Alta swung the door wide in spite of it, allowing a flurry of snow to enter along with Lidia and Gabriel. She bent at the waist and pushed Gabriel's scarf back and pressed her cheek to his. "You're like an icicle! Come get warm." He wrapped his arms around her, mid-thigh.

"Hi, Mimi," he said. He'd given her the name on their second visit, when they'd reintroduced themselves with polite details of belonging and heritage. "Mrs. Pulaski" was hard even for an articulate two-year-old like Gabriel to say, so he mispronounced it a few frustrating times until he resigned himself to a mightily abbreviated version that brought Alta nearly to tears and ruined any pretense of formality among them.

Meanwhile, Lidia slipped off her boots and, once Gabriel let Alta go, went to find his box of toys. She gave Alta a quick hug and then hotfooted it over to the couch across from the fireplace, where she spread an afghan over her legs. "Don't make a mess, Gabe," she said.

Alta called out a second later from the kitchen, "No, you go on ahead and make one, Gabriel. Your mother knows I don't mind." She came back into the room with a wink at Lidia and two full cups. Setting them both down on the coffee table, she turned the handles out so that each of them—Lidia and Gabriel—could easily reach over and pick their own up.

"Thank you," Lidia said with chattering teeth. "How'd you do that so fast?"

"I heard you all coming a mile away. Voices carry better when it's snowing. Like church bells at Christmas."

Lidia blew the steam off her tea. Alta always put in a tiny bit of nutmeg and milk, and it was the only way Lidia would drink it now.

"Lidia, you don't mind me telling you," Alta said, sitting down. "But that child doesn't need as much worry as you give him."

"What do you mean?"

"I mean I can hear you clear down the mountain telling him to watch his step and to be careful of this or that. I know you had a scare, but you don't need to fuss all over him. He's a smart boy. He'll do fine."

Lidia took a sip of tea and set it down on the table. Then she sighed and slumped down into the seam of the couch and pulled the afghan up higher. Gabriel was dumping pieces from two different puzzles out on the braided rug next to her.

"I can't help it."

Alta reached over and patted her on the shin. "You're a good mother. I know how much you love him. How much you want to protect him."

Lidia rested her eyes on her son and slowly nodded.

"My Abel was a smart boy, too," she said. "Much as I loved him—love him—he was nothing like Gabriel. The way his mind works, the way he talks." She jutted her sharp chin toward Gabriel. "That one's really special."

"I've been thinking about what you said before," Lidia said. "But I don't know. I don't know if I can send him to that early school. My mama kept us home. She taught us herself as long as she could."

Alta nodded. "It's hard to let your babies go."

"No," Lidia said. "I mean, yes. That would be hard. But I don't mean so much that as…" She lifted a finger to her teeth to work a hangnail. "I mean, it's because he's so…" She lowered her voice. "Different."

Alta glanced at Gabriel, who was picking pieces out of a jumble and building a picture of a Union Pacific train coming around a mountain bend, without the benefit of a picture to go by. If he was aware of them talking about him, he made no indication.

"I won't deny it," Alta finally said.

"So what should I do?"

"You've got some time yet," she said. "You'll know."

The snow fell, the fire burned, the tea cooled, the shiny black diesel locomotive materialized on the rug. Lidia breathed deeply and roamed her eyes around the now-familiar cabin. They lighted upon a small watercolor in a corner that she hadn't noticed before.

It was of a willow tree bending toward a stream. Its bark was thick and even, its tendriled branches like yellow hair. It looked strong but somehow defeated, the way it dropped its leaves into the water, as though it was being pushed too hard by the wind and succumbing to the earth and stream below.

"Did you paint that?" Lidia asked after staring at it for a full minute or longer.

Alta nodded. "Seventeen years ago. Not long after I lost...my love." She looked at the painting with a slight squint, as though wincing. "I don't mind telling you," she said. "That's the best self-portrait I ever did."

Lidia looked at her, expectant.

"Willows grow strong and fast, and can absorb standing water like other trees can't. But when they begin to die, they decay from the inside out. Looking at one, you can't even tell if it's gone to rot." She shook her head and looked back at the painting.

Lidia said nothing but just sat alongside Alta in the comfortable quiet that followed, wondering what memories played behind her closed eyes, inexplicably certain that someday she would know. She had the sudden urge to confess to her the truth about Gabriel and Eagan and her constant, lonesome worry—of discovery, of her son's monstrous conception, of his unsettling seriousness and mysterious commentaries—that manifested as a blend of nightmares and insomnia, leaving circles too dark for her young eyes.

She knew right then that if—*if*—she ever decided to tell anyone, she could tell Alta. But in the silent meantime, she tucked her legs up, closed her eyes, and waited.

October 27, 1968

Gabriel crouched on fat legs to help Lidia wrap tinfoil around a box that would be his Lunar Orbiter 5 costume.

"I'll crash on the moon."

"Of course you will."

"I saw the moon before."

"You did?"

Gabriel nodded.

"When did you see the moon?"

He grinned. "Yesterday night."

Lidia let out a breath. Such questions asked of or by her three-year-old weren't always so easily answered. Where he came from, why the sky was blue, who made up the alphabet, how fast someone can run, why people blink, how ducks can fly...They were endless, the questions. Lidia realized how little she knew, even though she'd been a diligent student — excellent, they'd called her. The simplest questions were forgotten amid the complex. How to hide the biologic manifestation of an incestuous rape, what to do with a feeble older brother, what to say to an awkward widower father, how to hide from her child-husband the somnambulistic terrors that sent her mind reeling back to the tile floor of her childhood bathroom.

They were endless, the questions.

"Can I be a astronaut?"

"Yes," Lidia said, taping down the corners of the foil. "Of course you can. And you can soar through the blue sky and into the dark and see the moon and the stars."

Gabriel's face grew serious and he put his tiny fat hand on her shoulder as she worked. "Because I don't want to be a miner like Daddy."

Lidia looked up. "Why?"

"I don't want to go to the mine."

She spread the piece of tape into place and then rocked back onto her seat and sat down cross-legged.

"Why don't you want to go to the mine?"

"It's dark there. And there's rocks. I saw it."

"When did you see it?" She sat down and pulled him into her lap. "Did Daddy take you there?"

Gabriel wadded a bit of foil and furrowed his brow. "No. I went there."

"Where, exactly?"

"Where we go in. Remember?"

Lidia breathed deeply. This wasn't the first time she'd heard Gabriel tell of something she didn't remember. "No, I don't remember," she said.

Gabriel picked up one of the pipe cleaners Lidia was going to use to represent a telescope that would photograph the far side of the moon. "I don't ever want to go to that place again." He climbed off her lap and turned to her. His face was grave, his hazel eyes dark.

She reached out and took the pipe cleaner from him. "Why not?" she asked, slow and without looking up, ignoring the use of "again."

"I don't want to fall again."

"Tell me what happened."

"It was dark like in the sky," he said. "We were running and then I fell."

"Oh no." Lidia searched her memory for some forgotten event, a walk Danny might have taken him on, a time they'd gone out in the dark. But the only thing she could remember that seemed remotely relevant were the stories she'd heard about the mine explosion, what, seventeen years ago? Gabriel knew nothing of that. Hardly anybody ever discussed it anymore. Maybe he'd overheard one of the older men talking at the barbershop or the hardware store sometime.

"Remember that?" he asked.

"No," she shook her head. "I don't."

"Yeah. And I was in it."

"You were?"

"Remember?"

Lidia shook her head no.

"Yeah, and those people helped me, remember?"

Gabriel patted the tin against the box.

Lidia, with a knot in her stomach, asked, "What people?"

Gabriel reached out and took the roll of foil and unrolled a long stretch of it, which crumpled in his inexperienced hands. "The dead people."

She took a slow breath and handed him a piece of Scotch tape. "Do you know what 'dead' means?"

With the tip of his tongue poking out, he taped the foil down. Then he stood back and looked at it, and looked at his mother, and nodded.

Lidia took a pair of scissors and stabbed a hole into the rectangular head of the box. She twisted the blade until she had enough clearance to cut a small circle around the jab. When she was finished, she struck the blade once more into the box a few inches over and twisted and carved an identical orb. She lifted the foil-covered box and placed it on top of Gabriel's serious face. His dark eyes peered out of the holes at her.

"Do I look like a astronaut?"

"Yes," she said, quiet. "Exactly like one."

"I'll fall into the sky and see the moon and all the stars."

Lidia pressed the box down a tiny bit farther and made a few adjustments to the foil and pipe cleaners while he watched her through those two circles, quiet as an owl inside a tree hollow. Halloween was just four days away. She wanted to be certain his costume was just right.

November 6, 1968

Coming down the mountain from Alta's cabin, Gabriel had seen a duck peel away from the flock overhead. Their V-pattern of flapping white stood out against the bright blue and cloudless migratory path, and he had pointed upward and asked Lidia why they were flying that way. She was explaining that it was easier to fly one behind the other instead of flying alone, when one of them veered inexplicably off. "She's going away!" he said, "Get her, Mama! Tell her to go back!"

Lidia and Gabriel were close to the railroad tracks that ran the length of the town of Verra, parallel to New Creek. Theirs was a shortcut, away from the train station and shops, an alternate path from the camp houses up to Whisper Hollow, where Alta lived. Gabriel skittered down the last sloping bit onto the train tracks. "Gabriel!" Lidia shouted. "Be careful!" She'd told him a hundred times not to jump onto the tracks without holding her hand, in case a train came suddenly roaring down upon them. "But you can hear them coming, Mama," he always replied.

"You can hear anything if you're paying attention, Gabriel," she would answer. "But we're not always paying attention."

He ran the flat shoulder along the two sets of tracks without taking his eyes off the lone duck in the sky. "Tell her, Mama!" he called.

Lidia ran after him, picking her way over fallen rocks and flung bits of coal. She was slowed by her basket, heavy with produce from Alta's garden and another rolled-up watercolor of a rainbow trout Gabriel had painted for Danny. "Gabe! Slow down!"

Without looking back, Gabriel came to an abrupt stop ahead of her. He pointed at the sky. The duck had changed its trajectory and rejoined the formation. The other ducks shifted their positions to absorb it back into the flock. Lidia looked up to where Gabriel was pointing and, in so doing, lost her balance and tripped on a rail spike, which turned her ankle and sent her sprawling a few feet behind her son. She cried out at the lightning bolt of pain.

Gabriel turned at the sound of her falling and sprinted to her. "Mama!"

She slowly heaved herself to a sitting position, fighting the searing sensation in her ankle, her eyes wide with shock. When she tried to stand, she fell back from the pain. "I think it's twisted," Lidia said aloud, though not particularly to Gabriel, who crouched down and tried to tug her upward. "I can't walk on it."

Gabriel knew his mother to be wary. Even at just over three years old, he already had begun to push her constant pleas for caution into the background. *Slow down, be careful, watch out* became nothing more than lullabies. He had never been hurt by any of his own running or jumping or wandering, but, more significant, he had never seen *her* hurt. The sight of her crumpled on the tracks, betrayed by her unquestioned strength, was unprecedented. He panicked.

"Mama!" he screamed.

"Shhh, Gabriel. I'm right here. Just give me a minute." She closed her eyes and breathed slowly.

"The train!" Gabriel looked up and down the tracks. Nothing was upon them, but he knew, suddenly, that they had to move. He grabbed her arm with both hands and pulled. "Mama, come on!"

"Just a minute," she whispered. Her ankle was starting to turn an ugly shade of purple, dark like an eggplant, under the hiked-up hem of her pants.

Gabriel looked around for someone to help them. They were on the west side of town, out of view, although they could see other people crossing the tracks farther down. Kids, mostly. There wasn't much up Whisper Hollow besides St. Michael's, the cemetery, and a few residences, so there wasn't a lot of traffic going perpendicular to the rails.

"Lady!" Gabriel shouted. Lidia looked up and saw him running again, this time to an older woman bent inside a heavy wool dress who was walking across the tracks about thirty feet away. "Lady!" He went right up to her and pulled on her hand, tugging her toward his mother. The woman resisted, clearly confused by the child's sudden appearance, the alarm in his voice. Though she appeared not to want the bother of whatever was the matter, when she saw Lidia splayed against the tracks, she allowed Gabriel to lead her where he wanted her to go.

"Are you all right?" Myrthen asked when she got to Lidia. Gabriel dropped to his mother's side and took her hand in his.

"It's my ankle. I turned it."

"Can you walk?" Myrthen clasped her hands together as though in prayer, not being the type to reach out. Lidia thought she recognized her from somewhere, but had never seen her up close before. Though lined with age, her face, Lidia noted with surprise, looked astonishingly beautiful under her black shawl.

Lidia shook her head.

"Well, I can't carry you," she said with obvious impatience. "I'll have to find someone who can help you up. Do you live far?"

"Just up at Cinder Camp."

Myrthen nodded. "I'll get someone. You stay put." She turned and walked toward town but without any apparent quickness to her step. Struck into obedience by Myrthen's cold calm, Lidia watched her go.

Myrthen eventually returned with a strapping and bearded man they didn't know who introduced himself as Grizzly Wroblewski, a man who worked with Lidia's father. After inquiring about the injury and performing a quick examination of her ankle, he announced that he would first carry her home, then go back to town and send the doctor to her. Grizzly turned to Myrthen and asked if she wouldn't mind accompanying them, because he couldn't carry the girl and her basket and son all together. He needed an extra pair of hands, and besides, it wouldn't be appropriate for him to take Lidia home alone.

Myrthen sighed and nodded. Grizzly picked up Lidia's basket and hung it over his meaty forearm, then scooped her up and cradled her like a baby. Taking Gabriel reluctantly by the hand, Myrthen pulled her dark shawl close around her face and picked up an efficient pace behind Grizzly's giant strides.

They arrived at Lidia's house and Grizzly placed her on the couch with her feet propped up on pillows. He asked Myrthen to get ice from the freezer and make a compress for Lidia's ankle. It was swollen and bruised, but Grizzly didn't think it was broken. He said he'd go back and ask Doctor Bartlett to come around, and meantime would Myrthen be able to stay until Lidia's husband got home?

She looked at him flatly. "I've got to be back for five o'clock Mass." Reaching into a deep woolen pocket, she withdrew a watch face and her rosary beads. "I'll stay, but only for another twenty minutes." She turned to Lidia. "Will your husband be home by three-thirty?"

"His shift ends at three. He always comes straight home." Lidia recognized her now. She remembered her from St. Michael's, the few times she'd had to go. The woman played the organ.

"I'll wait then. You go on, Mr. Wroblewski. I'll tell Father Timothy of your kindness today."

Grizzly closed the door behind him, and Myrthen sat down on the edge of a chair. She looked around the living room, lighting her gaze like a fly on objects around the room: the floral couch, the lace curtains, the *Charleston Sentinel* opened to the sports section, the child-drawn watercolors taped to the wall, the framed death announcement propped up on top of the Magnavox. She didn't even realize that Gabriel was standing next to her until he reached out and touched the rosary beads she worked in her fingers.

"Gabriel!" Lidia hissed. "That's not polite!"

Myrthen jumped.

"What's that?" Gabriel asked.

She looked down at the beads as though she'd never seen them before, then pushed them into her pocket and sat back deeper into the chair.

"What is your name, little boy?"

"Gabriel."

Myrthen raised an eyebrow. "Angel of the Lord," she said. "Interpreter for Daniel the Prophet, bringer of the word of Truth."

Gabriel tilted his head to mirror hers and blinked his eyes. "The word of Ruth?" he asked in a languid voice, as though waking from a dream.

Myrthen gasped and shot forward in her chair, nearly colliding her face into his. "What did you say?"

Gabriel reeled backward several steps until he bumped into his mother's swollen ankle, which rested on the rolled edge of the couch. "Oh!" Lidia cried out.

"Sorry!" Gabriel said, first to his mother and then to Myrthen. "Sorry." He was so startled that he plunged himself against his mother, burying his face in her sweater and sobbing.

"It's all right. Shhhhh," Lidia said, and then looked at Myrthen. "He didn't mean anything."

Myrthen cleared her throat, adjusted herself on the chair. "I apologize. I thought he said..." She shook her head. "Never mind."

Gabriel lifted his head and looked up at Myrthen with pink-rimmed eyes. "I wasn't talking about that."

She blinked at him several times. Her face grew very pale. "About what?"

Lidia interrupted. "I'm sorry, Mrs.—?"

"It's Miss. Miss Myrthen Bergmann."

"I'm sorry, Miss Bergmann. Sometimes he says things that are...confusing. But he doesn't mean any harm by them."

Myrthen stood abruptly up. " 'Folly is bound up in the heart of a child, but the rod of discipline drives it far from him,' " she said. "Proverbs. Your family is Catholic, is it not?" She jutted her chin toward the crucifix on the eastern wall of the room.

"My husband's mother was. And my parents. Danny and I don't...attend services."

Myrthen raised one sharp eyebrow. "You owe it to your child to take him to church. You'll want to lead him to salvation. A child like this," she said, turning to look him over, "*especially* a child like this needs to learn communion with God." She turned back to Lidia. "And you should unburden yourself as an example." Myrthen glared at her, as though measuring the freight and strain of her sin.

Lidia pulled Gabriel closer.

"Father Timothy hears confession on Saturdays and also thirty minutes before Mass on Wednesdays and Sundays at St. Michael's," she said.

"I don't know."

"We are all of us sinners, child. You think your Lord doesn't know? Of course He does." Lidia's face burned as Myrthen spoke. "But the Heavenly Father can take away the sins of the world. Even those of which we cannot bear to speak. And you will be forgiven."

She thought of Gabriel's eyes, how they matched her brother's exactly. Of Danny, and how proud he was of this, his only and ill-begotten son. It was as though Myrthen had already heard the confession that screamed wordlessly, constantly, in her mind.

"What happened?" Danny slammed the door behind him and slid to where Lidia lay sprawled on the couch as though into home base.

Gabriel looked up from where he lay coloring on the floor, picked up his picture, and ran headlong into Danny, who tousled his hair and picked him up.

"She was trying to go to Heaven," Gabriel said.

"What's that, slugger? Who's going to Heaven?"

"Gabriel and I were walking home from Alta's. He was chasing a duck and I was trying to catch him," Lidia said.

"See?" Gabriel said, and pointed at his picture. A wavy Crayola vector of what looked like flattened-out 3s flew across the blue construction paper. A single one wilted off course, away from the others. "She was almost there."

"Is that right?" Danny asked, raising his eyebrows, but it came out more as an ending than as the beginning to a conversation. He roughed the boy's hair again, but more gently—almost reverently — as though not to disturb whatever was happening underneath.

"Anyway," Lidia said. "I tripped crossing the tracks and here we are."

Danny released Gabriel, who lay back down to finish coloring. "Grizzly Wroblewski met me on the way out of the pit. He was going to find Doc Bartlett. He should be here soon, I'd expect," Danny said, sitting down next to her. "I ran all the way."

Lidia looked up at her husband. "Thank you," she said. Coal dust darkened the lines on his face, making him look much older than twenty. She felt responsible for that.

"What do you need?" Danny asked her. "What can I do?"

"I'll be fine. It's just a little swollen. I'll be all right." She pushed herself upright, trying to hide the pain that strangled her ankle. "I'll be up to put dinner on in a bit."

"Oh no. You'll stay put." His face was grave.

"Funny. That's just what she said."

"Who?"

Lidia shook her head. "She said her name was Myrthen Bergmann. She was crossing the tracks after I fell. Gabriel found her and brought her and then she got Mr. Wroblewski and walked us home." She looked away. "She was quite strange."

"How so?" he asked.

She waved her hand in a gesture of dismissal. "No, that was rude of me. She was very kind to help us." Lidia shifted again.

"Myrthen Bergmann. That name sounds familiar. I think she's relatives with that no-account Liam Magee. You know, the electrician who caused that explosion back in 'fifty? In the Number Seventeen?"

Lidia nodded. Her own parents had taken in the widow and infant son of one of those fallen miners. Lidia was only a little more than two years old. The woman, whom Lidia's mother recalled over the years as being a child in grown-up clothes, was so bereft she just sat at their kitchen table clutching her baby so tight he cried, saying over and over, "It ain't so it ain't so it ain't so." Finally Lidia's mother made contact with the girl's people in Kentucky, and a long-faced aunt and uncle came within the week to collect them. Mining coal was like challenging the Reaper to a duel every shift. Most times, the miners won. But those times they didn't, the tragedy scythed a notch out of the town's soul. Nobody wanted to remember, but they never could forget. Lidia wondered now whatever became of that girl-mother and her pink and squalling baby. He'd be eighteen years old by now, if he were still alive.

"Nobody talks about it much except the old-timers," Danny said. "They mention it every once in a while, but quiet, like it's bad luck or something. I tried to ask your daddy about it once, but he didn't seem to be much in the know. Or else he didn't want to talk about it. He must have been around twenty-six, twenty-seven when it happened, and he got foreman when he was, what, thirtysomething? So he'd have known." He thought for a moment. " 'Course he'd have known." Danny scratched the top of his head, raked his hair back off his forehead. "Must've had his reasons not to want to talk about it, I guess."

Lidia watched as Danny considered the mine explosion as though for the first time.

Danny had slid into the midst of their ruin long after the wounds had reconciled into scars. He'd moved to Verra from New Jersey when he was sixteen, so he hadn't grown up with the rumors of conspiracy and blame that ended lifelong friendships, or the wringing, huddled fear that made the survivors age double-time, or the decay that had crept into the town and filled the gaps left when the prosperity and possibilities drained out.

Danny and his mother had come because of his grandfather, but they didn't intend to stay forever. He planned on college and then law school, and never meant to slip underground like the rest of them, but here he was, covered in dust, muscled from installing roof bolts that supported the mine's haulage ways, and nicknamed Timber, even though they hadn't used timber supports in the mine since the accident. After Lidia told him his fate that night three and a half years ago, Danny never spoke about becoming a lawyer again. Going underground was the easy decision for someone who now had people to provide for. "It's called a 'mine' for a reason," he'd said to her shortly after he'd proposed. " 'Cause everybody's working to support their own. I'll be working to support mine." He'd held both of her hands in his when he said this, giving them a single, gentle pump after he was finished that meant she shouldn't feel guilty about his becoming part of the town's crumbling history.

But how could she not feel guilty? She loved her husband, but was that enough to pardon her for making him a father to a child that wasn't even his? She turned her head away from him as he sat there trying to fathom it, the fate of those husbands and sons he'd never known and the crime that stole all their lives. Alta lost her husband in that accident. Her son. The course of her life irreversibly altered because of the selfishness of one man, that Sparky Magee.

And here was Danny, hers by love, yes, but also by entrapment. The course of his life irreversibly altered because of the selfishness of one woman. What might he have chosen, if she hadn't chosen for him?

"I'm so sorry, Danny," she said. Her eyes were still closed and her voice choked.

He looked up, startled from his contemplation, and moved quickly to her to wipe her misinterpreted tears. "Liddie, it's okay. You'll be fine. Doc'll be here any minute now, get you fixed right up. And anyway, it's not your fault. It was just an accident is all. Just an accident."

She thought of Gabriel. Of Eagan, who'd ended up in the army after all, after she refused to take him in, then died six months later from malaria-carrying mosquito bites in the marshes of South Vietnam. That was more than two years ago. She thought of Danny, who would cook their dinner tonight and then get up and go back underground in the morning. She thought of her father, alone at home, and her mother, six years gone.

It wasn't her fault. It was just an accident. But who besides herself could she blame?

March 15, 1969

Anyone else might have started thinking about adding to his brood of one by now. But Danny Pollock, in spite of his being a young and hardworking man with decent means, sincere ambition, a reasonable Catholic upbringing, and the love of his wife of not quite four years, found himself too fascinated by his three-and-a-half-year-old son to entertain such a greedy idea.

Danny didn't know much about other people's children. Even the other men close to his age, twenty going on old, whose nights were filled with diaper changes and teething and worried wives, whose days were spent on work and worry and the occasional—when they could afford one—drink, didn't speak out loud of their upended lives and the babies who'd turned them into men. But he noticed other kids his son's age, saw them sucking on their fingers and pulling on their mothers' skirts. Watched them stumble and trip, screech and bawl. Heard them crying and whining and begging in pidgin for whatever unmet needs they had.

Not Gabriel. Gabriel started speaking so early Danny couldn't recall a time when he didn't know exactly what his son was thinking in clear, concise speech. No made-up words and baby talk. Milk was milk. Tree was tree. Daddy was Daddy. The only thing that went by another name was his special blanket, that raggedy yellow one that had belonged to Eagan and then Lidia and had become for Gabriel, for some unknown reason, "Bobby."

Though he still took Gabriel up the hollow near Alta's cabin to fish for rainbow trout, more and more Danny liked taking him into town to show him off—though he wouldn't admit that was what he was doing. Danny taught him how to extend his hand when he met or greeted someone, to look them in the eye and say, "Nice to meet you." Or, when offered a soda or a piece of candy, "Thank you very much." It was charming, that straight-faced etiquette coming from such a little boy.

"That's a mighty fine son you got there," people would say. Gabriel withstood the rough hands tousling his hair, smiled politely, but always quickly retreated behind his father's legs when he'd had enough. Except when he got to go to the hardware store.

Charlie Stickley, who'd inherited the store from his father a decade ago, was tall and bearded with enormous hands that looked oddly like a child's. He loved his job, and he was good at it, gifted with the ability to identify the length of a board or a screw or a nail within millimeter accuracy just by looking at it. Charlie could build anything, fix anything, and was happy to advise anyone who needed help on how to do it themselves. If they still couldn't do it after he gave his laborious, detailed instructions, he'd likely end up at that person's home on a weekend or an evening to do the job himself. Men tended to congregate at the store, even if they didn't need anything, just to share the latest gossip or talk shop or pass an idle bit of time. Most often they ended up buying something anyway, perhaps to justify their having been too long away from home.

"Afternoon, Mr. Stickley," Danny said after the jingle on the door settled down.

Gabriel trailed behind his father, dragging his fingertips lightly across the display of tin buckets filled with nuts and bolts, nails and screws, until he arrived at the end of the counter, where Stickley was sharpening someone's knife on a long strap of leather.

"Afternoon," he said to Gabriel. "How's my favorite customer?"

"Fine," Gabriel said. "We came to buy spinners. We're going fishing tomorrow."

"Nothing like fishing with your daddy on a Sunday. You're going out in the morning?"

Danny nodded. "Gonna try shallow, then go deeper after the sun comes up."

"Trout, or smallmouth?"

"Brookies."

Stickley turned to Gabriel. "Brookies like the cold water, but you gotta move your bait real slow, make it easy for 'em to take it."

"Yessir."

"I got some nice size number-two Mepps back here. Want to come take a look? Pick a couple out?"

Gabriel nodded and followed Stickley around the organized maze of boxes of merchandise.

"You catch something, you let me know." Stickley winked at Danny, who lagged behind on purpose. "Better yet, you invite me to Sunday dinner and we'll eat 'em up together."

Gabriel took the tin of spinners and spoons that Stickley held out, and he began fingering through them. "You go on and pick a couple out, let me get back to that knife, hear?"

Gabriel nodded, taking the job of choosing the right equipment as one of solemn consequence. Meanwhile, Danny joined in the conversation among the other men. Toot and Bones sat across from each other at a folding card table that Stickley had set up. Frail and concave as his name suggested, Bones leaned forward on sharp elbows, folding and unfolding the corner of the *Charleston Sentinel*, talking out of the side of his mouth that wasn't affected by palsy. Toot leaned back in his chair with one muscular calf draped across the corner of the table and his arms crossed, making his usual snide remarks about things and people, even if they were standing within earshot.

"Anybody happen to see Jethro Kaveck last day or so?" Stickley asked.

They shook their heads no and Toot asked, "Why?"

Stickley shrugged. "He came in what, Monday? Needed some chain and bar lube for his chain saw. Clearing land, I think. He raises chickens, right? Anyway, he asked me how fast I could get some and I said I could have some by Friday but I'd have to special order it from Charleston and he said that was fine. Paid extra, too. Then he never showed up. He's a good customer, doesn't even use credit. Just strange is all, even to let it go a day, the way he was talking."

Gabriel came out from behind the counter then with twelve shiny spinners, more than they would need, but Danny hadn't specified a count. He laid them out on the counter side by side, adjusted the angles very slightly so they lay in a perfect row, like a stringer of trout on an imaginary line.

"Row, row, row your boat, gently down the stream...," Gabriel sang low, nearly under his breath as he moved the spinners again, by threes, as though down the treble clef. "Merrily, merrily, merrily, merrily..." And the first five he shifted again, like a stair step. "Life is but a dream."

He repeated the chorus, moving the spinners again as he did, slow but strict, matching the notes. "Row, row, row...," he sang, a whisper, the spinners becoming boats going merrily down the stream of wood, ending where Stickley had picked up a third knife and slap slap slapped it up and down the leather strop at exactly the same pace as the spinners moved along the clef.

"Life. Is. But. A. Dream."

Danny pulled out a thin fold of dollars from his front pocket to pay for the dozen spinners that would keep him and Gabriel waist-deep in Brookies for the next year. The door opened, bells jingling, and another one of the old-timers came in.

"Afternoon, boys," he said, raking from his bald head an imaginary plague of hair. "Guess you heard about old Jethro Kaveck?"

"Stickley here was just asking about him," Toot said. "What's going on there?"

"Evidently went up to Pleasant Lake bass fishing Thursday. Took along a cousin of his from somewhere up in Mineral County—Keyser, I think. Buddy somebody. Anyway, they's going after some old bass bastard named Ole Joe, and Jethro hooked him and they tussled out there, him standing up in the boat and Ole Joe wrestling himself away, and according to some bystanders out there but not near close enough, Jethro got himself tripped up on the edge of the boat and tumped it over, him and his cousin and all, and both of 'em drowned. Right there, in the middle of Pleasant Lake, hanging on to his rod and Ole Joe swimming away like some no-account. Can you imagine?"

Stickley shook his head and said, "Well ain't that the damnedest thing. Here we's just talking about him and now we find out he's gone to meet his Maker."

They sat quiet for a moment, except for Gabriel.

"Row, row, row your boat, gently down the stream...," he sang, then gathered the spinners one at a time until they were nothing but a thick stack of silver in his hand. All the men turned toward him.

"Thank you, Mr. Stickley," Danny said quickly, pocketing his change. "Let's go on now, Gabe. Mama'll be wanting us home for dinner."

Gabriel extended his hand and looked Stickley in the eye and smiled.

"...merrily, merrily, merrily, merrily...," he sang.

Stickley took Gabriel's hand without a word, just looked at him as though he'd never seen the little boy before.

"I'll catch us a big one," Gabriel said, still smiling. "Big as Ole Joe."

Stickley dropped his hand and looked at the other men, who only stared.

"Take care, Mr. Stickley," Danny said without looking at him, and led Gabriel by the hand out the door, which jingled its pentatonic chime.

"Life is but a dream."

March 24, 1969

Monday mornings were always busy for Lidia. It was the day she changed the sheets and mopped the floors, cooked a stew from Sunday leftovers if there were any, and drove downtown to the A&P to do the week's shopping.

She helped Gabriel put on his coat and gloves and led him to the Coronet, which no longer held a shine but was as sturdy and reliable as her husband. Gabriel bounced into the seat, and when she closed the door, he blew a squall of hot breath onto the window and got as far as G-A-B-R before the steam evaporated.

"Want to help me remember the list?" she said as she turned the ignition.

Gabriel nodded and smiled enough to show the dimple on his left cheek she could never resist poking.

"Pot roast," she said.

"Pot roast."

"Ground beef. Peanut butter. Spam."

Gabriel nodded. "More."

"Corn. Vienna sausages. Bread. Baby shampoo. Rice. Did you like the applesauce I made?"

"Yes!"

"Apples, then." The late-morning sun made diamonds out of shallow puddles of mostly melted snow along the curbs, but the road was dry and the temperature was headed toward sixty. Lidia cracked her window and let a rush of outside in, tipped her chin toward it. "What a beautiful day. Just downright beautiful. Bacon. Eggs. Butter. Corn Flakes."

"And a Hershey bar."

Lidia laughed out loud. It would be fifty-one cents over their budget, she knew. "And a Hershey bar."

They carried on like that for the five-minute drive, her thinking up all the things they needed to buy and him memorizing them. What started out as a teaching game had become useful in an unexpected way — it had been weeks since she'd written out a list.

She pulled into a parking spot and let Gabriel out. Inside, he picked a cart and climbed into it. He knew the A&P as well as she did, and so he sailed the cart through the aisles with the pirate-point of his index finger. Chocolate first, lest it be forgotten or decided against at the last minute. Then the butcher counter. Dairy. Dry goods. He announced all the items that she'd said she needed.

"I'm forgetting something," Lidia said after she'd filled their cart with as much as she could afford.

"Baby shampoo."

"Oh yes."

She wheeled the cart toward the aisle with baby goods. Just as she rounded the corner, Lidia collided carts with a woman named Susan Forrester, enormously pregnant — all the way up to her face — with her fourth child, and arrogantly observant of a certain formality she'd learned from reading too many works of romantic fiction.

"Well, hello there," Susan said with affected sweetness. "It's Lidia, isn't it?"

Lidia backed her cart up. "I'm sorry." Everyone was vaguely scared of Susan, even if they knew her only by reputation. Though she acted kind enough to people's faces, she possessed an ugly talent for gossip, especially when combined with her affinity for homemade wine.

"What a handsome fellow." She nodded her head toward Gabriel, who turned his head into Lidia's shoulder. "Shy, is he?"

"No. I mean, yes," Lidia said.

Susan was married to a miner whose buddies called him Chick when she wasn't around, because he was so mercilessly henpecked. "He's a handsome one," she said again. "What's his name?"

"Gabriel."

Susan nodded. "That's what I thought. Listen, I know we've only just met." Susan leaned forward, pressing her bulk against the handlebar of her cart. "But as someone who's active in the Church and in the community," she said, "I feel it's my Christian duty to tell you something. I'm sorry to have to say it in front of your boy."

Lidia pulled Gabriel closer, covered his exposed ear with her hand. "What's that?"

"Some scuttlebutt that's got to do with your boy here that's made certain folks uncomfortable," she said. "It's really not my place to talk about it, but I feel it's important that you know what people are saying."

Lidia glanced from side to side, feeling exposed. How could anybody know what Eagan did? He was gone, their secret buried with him. She'd never told anyone—not even Alta.

"I've heard tell," she said, "that your son has been...talking about things he shouldn't." She dropped her voice to a hiss. "Things he shouldn't *know*."

Lidia exhaled, but the relief she felt was complicated by confusion. "What are you talking about?"

"Evidently your son's been telling people things about themselves…about their people and such. You ask me, I'd say it's from a lack of godliness in his life." She patted her enormous belly, as though underneath that monsoon of flab she carried the Son of God himself.

Lidia gathered up all her dignity and folded it into the overpowering instinct to defend her child. The hand that wasn't covering Gabriel's ear gripped the handle of the cart, as though she might catapult it forward if she didn't hold it back. "There's nothing wrong with Gabriel."

Susan leaned forward and patted Gabriel's head. "No, no. Of course not," she said.

"Then I'm not sure what you're trying to say." Lidia backed her cart up a few inches and changed the angle to prevent Susan from reaching for Gabriel again.

"I understand you don't go to church."

Lidia thought of the conversation that had taken place a few months earlier, the day she'd sprained her ankle. The way Myrthen Bergmann had said in that strange, haunting way, "*Especially* a child like this needs to learn communion with God."

There was nothing wrong with Gabriel.

Was there?

And you should unburden yourself as an example.

"No, we don't go to church."

Susan frowned, making the row of lines around her mouth — unusually deep for someone of childbearing age — stand out like exclamation points. "This way he has of talking about things, it makes people nervous. It makes them wonder where he gets it. Now I, being a Christian woman, believe everyone should have a personal relationship with God, but what I'm saying to you is people are talking about your boy and I believe they'd all feel a lot better if he was attending Sunday services on a regular basis."

For her little family, Sundays were days of rest, and family time, and fishing, and helping Alta harvest vegetables from her garden, and chasing birds and butterflies. There was nothing wrong with that, nothing wrong with him. Nothing except that his uncle was also his father. Had the Devil somehow mixed his seed in along with Eagan's that awful night as she lay there on the bathroom floor?

"Thank you for your concern," Lidia said. "Now we need to be getting on home."

They looked at each other for a long moment over their carts that were filled with similar items that would feed their different lives. But how different were they, really? They were all stained by something. Everyone had something to hide.

"Oh yes, so do I. There's always so much to do, isn't there?" Her voice was syrup again, her second face arranged and smiling. "Especially now with another one on the way."

Lidia nodded and gave a sort of half smile and turned her cart to go.

Gabriel picked his head up and said in his soft, clear-bell voice, "Don't forget the baby shampoo."

"Oh!" said Susan. "And here that's exactly why I was in this aisle in the first place!" Then her eyes widened, first at Lidia and then at Gabriel. "But how did you know? How did he…how did he know I needed baby shampoo?"

"He didn't. He was talking to me. I need some, too." She tried to sound calm, but the alarm in Susan's high-pitched voice made her own sound unconvinced and, therefore, unconvincing.

"You see what I mean? That's just the kind of thing has everyone all worked up about your boy. How does he *know*? It's like he's reading people's minds. It's not *right*." She backed hastily up, bumping into a shelf of diapers, and wrestling the cart forward as though she could waste no time on a graceful exit. Over her shoulder she gave Lidia a stabbing but scared-stiff look. "You get that child to church, hear?"

And then she was gone.

"I'm sorry you had to hear all that nonsense," Lidia said to Gabriel. "She doesn't know what she's talking about." She leaned down and kissed him on the nose.

"And she forgot to get her shampoo."

Lidia watched him from beneath a furrowed brow as he fished among the groceries for his Hershey bar, found it, then held it with both hands in his lap. "Yes," Lidia said, and exhaled a deep sigh through her nose. "I suppose she did."

March 29, 1969

The day before Palm Sunday, Lidia went to St. Michael's for the first time since her mother's funeral nearly seven years before. She hadn't looked forward to it. Even up until that very morning, she thought she might still back out. She had no interest in God. But Susan Forrester's scolding over-the-shoulder command, *You get that child to church!* had bedeviled her day and night for a haunted, sleepless week.

Although her father refused to go, making excuses every Sunday that they needed him underground, her mother had always taken them to St. Michael's. She taught them how to make the sign of the cross, how to kneel and pray, how to sit until the Alleluia and rise to greet the Gospel. At seven, Lidia took her first Holy Communion. Eagan had to stay seated in the pew during the Communion rite. Her mother told them both, in her kind way, that maybe when he could understand things a little more clearly he would be able to make his first confession, and then work toward the next Sacrament. Lidia always felt guilty when she had to step past Eagan's bowed head, so much taller than her own, and stand in the slow-moving line to receive the Eucharist from Father Timothy's withered old hands. And she worried, too, because she'd learned in her classes that without this Sacrament, it would be difficult for someone to resist grave temptations and avoid grievous sin.

Then God took away her mother just two weeks before her fourteenth birthday, and left her nearly orphaned and responsible for raising her brain-damaged brother. She'd never gone back. She hadn't seen the point.

But as she lay awake that week in the black hole of night, her accused son asleep in the next room, she wondered if she should have continued in her mother's faithful footsteps. Whether she should have insisted that Eagan receive the sacraments of initiation. Whether she bore at least some of the blame for his sins because she had not. And whether, by continuing to renounce God, she would also bear responsibility for the sins of their son.

By noon that Saturday, she decided that she could handle the burden of sin, but if she could do something about it, she couldn't allow her child's reputation to suffer. So she told Danny that she was taking Gabriel to visit Alta, and set off on a walk up through Whisper Hollow to the carillon welcome of St. Michael's.

"Come on, Mama!" Gabriel called back at her from over his shoulder.

"I'm coming." She met him on the top step, then took a deep breath. She heaved open the door, and they stepped together inside the narthex.

That smell. That moldy scent of piety and dogma. It had been seven years. Seven years, but the smell, unlike her own small life, hadn't changed. The organist, her black-veiled back bent away from them, pounded a sonata by Giovanni Battista Cirri. Lidia recognized her: the imperious Myrthen Bergmann. She'd seemed as uncomfortable in Lidia and Danny's home that day as she seemed here to be at home. Sometimes we become our surroundings, Lidia thought. And sometimes our surroundings become us. Myrthen, with her sturdy shoes, draconian posture, pulled stops, and invigorating hymns, looked to have rooted herself into the bench upon which she sat.

Nobody sat in the pews; nobody lit candles. Holding Gabriel's hand, Lidia crept toward the confessional in the hall, quiet so as not to disturb the dust. Nonetheless, the organ playing stopped.

"I'll watch him for you while you celebrate the gift of reconciliation."

Lidia turned around, and Myrthen met her gaze from her organ bench.

"Father Timothy is inside. Your boy—Gabriel, isn't it?—can sit here with me in the pews while you confess your sins." When Myrthen smiled at Lidia, extending her palm-up hand toward Gabriel, it looked insincere and youthful, as though the canvas of her face had been stretched the wrong way. The few wrinkles on her face seemed not to come from a lifetime of smiles, but from some other expression.

Lidia hadn't thought about what she would do with Gabriel when she spoke to Father Timothy. The confessional, which had appeared so colossal and oppressive when she was a girl, looked small from where she stood. There wouldn't be room enough for the both of them, unless she held him on her lap. Then again, she didn't want him to hear what she had to say.

She looked down at Gabriel. "Would that be all right with you? To sit here with Miss Bergmann for just a couple minutes?"

Gabriel looked at Myrthen and then back at Lidia. "Does she live here?"

"No, no. She works here. She plays the organ."

"I'm also the secretary. But no, child, this is the house of the Lord. We come here to celebrate the presence of God in our lives. This is where we come to connect to the eternal love that binds us all together. This is why your mother brought you here. So that you, too, shall know the power of God's love."

Gabriel looked at her, level and sincere. "I think we're lost."

"So many of us are, child."

"We were going to Alta's house. We were going to plant things in her garden."

"Gabriel, why don't you sit here with Miss Bergmann? I'm just going to go speak to the priest in here a minute. You sit here." She patted the back of the pew. "You sit here and I'll just be a minute. Hear?"

Gabriel nodded.

"I'll be right in here. You need me, you just knock. I'll see you in a couple few minutes."

"All right, Mama."

Lidia turned and took a deep breath, then opened the tiny door.

"In the name of the Father, and of the Son, and of the Holy Spirit. It's been...seven years since my last confession."

"We have missed you, my child." Father Timothy had been in the parish since 1918, nearly fifty years. He'd known every parishioner, performed their baptisms, their confirmations, their communions, their marriages. His hair was now a paper-white tonsure, and his once-substantial heft had been eroded down to modest, feeble proportions. His hands shook when he lifted them to make the sign of the cross, but after all he'd seen, he still passed no judgment on his parishioners, even the lapsed ones.

"I...I've..." Lidia stopped. She looked down at her ragged nails, bitten to the quick over the past few days. "I'm..."

"How are you, child? Is something troubling you that's brought you back home?"

She sighed. "I don't know where to start. It's been so long. So many things...so many things have happened."

"God already knows."

Lidia stiffened. If God already knew, then why tell Father Timothy? Perhaps it was enough that she was here, in this familiar and foreign place. Perhaps just the sight of her, coming and going, would ease the troubled minds of the townsfolk who had enough spare time to care. Nobody would know what she said—or didn't say—to a priest who'd no doubt heard plenty before.

"Do you mind, Father...you mind if I just sit here quiet a minute?"

"Of course. I'll pray with you, child."

She could hear him murmuring behind the lattice screen. His voice, soft and low, sounded like a grandfather reciting a lullaby. She closed her eyes and thought of what she could not bring herself to speak aloud, not here, not yet. But it was tempting, the idea of releasing all that contrition she'd buried inside for so long. Letters and syllables tickled her tongue, assembled themselves into small groups, congregated into heretofore unspoken words. Her lips parted, dry and sticky. And what if those words came out of her mouth and adhered themselves to the porous wood of the confessional, layered thick already with decades' worth of unburdened sins? What would be one more?

Father Timothy's sonorous voice came to a gentle stop and he said to her, "Don't let your shame keep you from salvation. God is good."

And so she began, on a breath no louder than a whisper, to speak.

Outside the confessional, Gabriel sat next to Myrthen on the pew and swung his legs, growing impatient and uncomfortable as the minutes wore on. She was on her knees with her forehead pressed into her interlaced fingers and her ear attuned, as always, to the small wooden box. Lidia's voice was soft, and so Myrthen had to strain to overhear. Without lifting her head, she whipped her left hand out and grasped Gabriel's shoe mid-swing and hissed, "Don't kick the kneeler."

He stopped.

She went back to her interception and her eyes grew wide behind her veil. After a moment, she heard Gabriel sniffling. She tried to ignore him, thinking he would settle down, but he did not.

"What is it?" she said, lip curled.

"You're not very nice."

Myrthen ducked her head down to his level and glared at him. "You're not very nice either, now are you? You listen to me. You stop that infernal sniveling and you sit up and sit still. This is God's house and you need to learn how to behave. Your mother is in there trying to save your soul. And the good Lord knows you need it. And you should thank me for sitting here with you, because I'm not doing it for my own sake, I assure you."

Gabriel hung his head. He didn't speak or even sniff for the next few minutes. When Myrthen's ears had filled to brimming and she heard Lidia recite the memorized Act of Contrition, expressing her sorrow and desire to perform penance, she knew that the confession was nearly over.

"Quickly. Let's go outside. You clearly can't sit still. We'll wait for your mother out there."

Myrthen hurried out, crossing herself, and he followed. She stood outside on the path and tipped her chin up, breathing in the Heaven scent, and began to pray. Gabriel sank down onto the dirt path and constructed a small pile of stones. A few moments later, Lidia emerged, puffy-faced and smiling. Gabriel saw her and jumped up.

"Mama!"

Lidia kissed him on the forehead. Then she turned to Myrthen. "I hope he wasn't too much trouble."

Myrthen dipped her head in a pious nod. "No trouble at all. We were fine, weren't we, Gabriel?"

Gabriel didn't look at her, but instead bent back down to his rocks and began drawing with his finger on the ground. It looked like a bird in flight, a flattened-out number 3. Then apart from it, several more, flying in tight formation.

"It is good that you confessed your sins. I was praying for you, Lidia. Praying that you would be cleansed and healed by God's love. God will continue to forgive you, but only if you continue to confess."

Lidia looked down at Gabriel. He'd finished drawing and picked up a smooth, flat stone to examine it.

"You bring Gabriel here with you anytime. I'll be happy to watch him for you. It's nice weather now, we can even walk down to the creek." She turned to Gabriel. "You like playing with stones, do you?" She pointed to the stone he held. "You know how to skip them?"

Gabriel shook his head.

"Next time your mother comes to celebrate penance and reconciliation, we can go skip stones."

"I don't want to."

"Gabriel," Lidia whispered. "Be polite."

He looked up at Myrthen, who stared back down at him. "Okay," he said. Then without dropping his gaze, he let go of the rock he was holding and it landed with a dusty thud on the ground. "But you have to go first."

April 3, 1969

Lidia paced the length of her small kitchen, dinner already simmering on the stove even before Gabriel had woken up, and listened to the AM radio station out of Charleston. They were playing "Good Lovin' " by the Rascals, which seemed too fast and happy for the day, so she switched it off. A peal of thunder rattled the windowpanes. She hoped it would rouse Gabriel. She could use the company.

Three years ago today Eagan had died.

She always thought about her brother with a confusion of detachment and anger, longing and regret. He'd hurt her, yes, but he couldn't be blamed for the meningitis that had damaged his four-year-old brain and demoted him forever from older brother to younger. And Gabriel, now nearly the same age Eagan had been when he'd fallen sick. She couldn't imagine what it would be like to watch her son's precocious mind melt from fever into something altogether unfamiliar.

Abruptly she stopped her movement and sank down into the kitchen chair to cry, for the first time in years. She wept for the brother she lost once when he was rendered a permanent child, and again when he turned into a monster in the bathroom, and then forever after a mosquito in the Nine Dragon river delta in southwestern Vietnam infected him with parasites during a blood meal.

And she wept for her son, a brilliant, perfect lie.

Her crying, not the storm, finally woke him up. She didn't even realize it until she felt his tiny hand on her arm. He held out his tattered yellow blanket. "You can use this," he said.

She gathered him into her lap and held him tightly for a long moment. Finally, after the sadness abated, she whispered in his ear, "Hungry?" He nodded. "I'll make you some eggs, then when Daddy wakes up maybe he'll take you fishing, okay?"

After she fed them a Saturday banquet of fried eggs and fatty bacon and biscuits, and the rain stopped, they all trudged off together — the boys to go fishing and she to see Alta. She never needed an invitation or even a reason to cross the creek and hike the half mile up through Whisper Hollow to Alta's cabin, but today, she had one. She took a fresh-baked loaf of bread to go with it.

Alta could tell from the quiet footfalls on the damp earth a hundred yards out that Lidia was alone. She knew her well enough to recognize the slow, even steps, picking carefully around the fallen branches, an indication that something preyed on Lidia's mind. When she came to visit without Gabriel, it meant something was awry. Alta met her at the door with a smile tilted toward understanding, brought her into the cabin, and settled her on the couch. They sat across from one another in the stillness, each of them blowing the steam off her tea.

"Tell me," Alta said after a while.

"Oh, I'm fine. It's just —" She hesitated. "I've been thinking about my brother."

Alta nodded. It was a small town. She already knew the story. The public story, anyway, that Eagan Kielar had died in the war, his daddy, Stanley, so stricken with grief and guilt he didn't even want to hold a memorial service.

"I never really got to say goodbye," Lidia said. "After Gabriel was born, Eagan went to war and...and he didn't come back. There were...things...I never told him. And now I never can.

"It was my fault." Lidia looked down at her lap, tears coming again. "I couldn't take care of him, not once Gabe came along, and Daddy couldn't either. Daddy took him to Charleston and helped him sign up. Eagan was only over there a few months...then we got the telegram from the Pentagon saying he was dead. They circled the word 'son' on a form. 'We regret to inform you that your son was killed in action in Vietnam on April 3, 1966.' Daddy came to the house and he handed me the piece of paper and just stood there looking like he did when Mama died, and I knew I was supposed to break down and cry right there on the linoleum, that's what I should've done, but I didn't. I just sat down at the kitchen table and let out my breath that I felt like I'd been holding for more than a year. Daddy touched me on the shoulder and said, 'I'm sorry, Liddie,' and he left. We didn't even find out until later that he wasn't killed in action. He died of malaria. But the worst part is..." She closed her eyes and knitted her brow and shook her head gently. "I felt relieved."

Alta only nodded. She wasn't one to shush someone out of her pain.

"And Gabriel..." Lidia pressed her hand over her mouth and shook her head again. "Eagan never knew...I'm so ashamed. Alta, I'm so ashamed to tell you this...There were things I had to do..."

But here, Alta interrupted. She crossed the room and sat down next to her and took her hand. "Stop, now. Whatever it is, if it shames you to tell it, then just stop. You don't need to tell me anything."

"I've never told anybody."

"Then no need to start now."

"But it's awful! I tried to tell Father Timothy over at St. Michael's but I couldn't. I just couldn't make the words come out. But I just keep thinking: Shouldn't I tell somebody the truth?"

Alta held Lidia away from her with both hands and looked at her, this young girl, and thought of her own set of long-entombed truths, her own coal-covered burden of shame. They were as much a part of Alta now as anything else. To excavate them would do nothing but spread disgrace and cause discomfort. She doubted her burden would be lightened after that. Her voice came out soft. "What purpose would it serve?"

"What?" Lidia pulled back.

Alta sighed and dropped her hands into her lap. "Whatever truth it is you're talking about, what good would it do anyone to know it? You're a good girl. A good mother, wife. A good friend. Your family loves you." She smiled. "I love you. What's past is past. You start telling people things they don't really need to know, you'll just end up giving them fodder for gossip."

"But what if what happened was the truth?"

"People learn to live with their own versions of the truth," Alta said. "You have to ask yourself if what you say is going to help people, or hurt them."

Lidia's eyes were pleading. "But shouldn't we always be honest? Isn't that the right thing to do?"

Alta interlaced her fingers and met Lidia's eyes with a sad smile, then lifted one shoulder, just barely, a gesture that was not quite a question, but not quite an answer either.

April 23, 1969

"I heard he sees visions."

"Susan told me he can read minds."

"You think he sees ghosts? Marian said he can talk to ghosts."

"There's no such thing as ghosts."

"Sure there is, you damn old fool."

"Then I wonder if he can tell me where Daddy buried the money."

"Some say he's a prophet."

"More like the Devil. Ain't nobody supposed to be able to see into the future."

"Stop it now, all of you. What if he really is a prophet? Bible says 'I will put my words in his mouth, and he will tell them everything I command him.' What if it's the Lord's words coming out of that little boy's mouth?"

"I ain't never heard him say anything like outright prophesy."

"How do you know what's prophesy and what ain't? Modern-day prophets, like what's in the Bible, tell the truth about what's happening in morality and religion. They're truth-tellers, you'd say. Anybody heard that boy saying anything but what's truthful?"

"It just ain't natural, him knowing things. And the way he looks at folks, all plain-eyed and...calm, like he's grown."

"He's a beautiful child."

"That child ain't a child."

"Come on now, hear? He is a child. He's a sweet little baby. His mama goes over to the Catholic church least once a week. They's good people. Everybody knows her daddy, Stanley, since the earth cooled. Somebody just got their imagination all fired up and started all this fool talk. Ain't nothing to it."

"I don't know about all that. I know Stanley fine. He's an honorable man and a good worker. Took on the job of running the mine after the explosion in 'fifty. Lord knows that man's got ghosts aplenty without having to think about his own grandson seeing any. His son was touched and then he lost his wife. Then his boy died in 'Nam. Now people's talking about his grand-baby like he's the Devil and what's anybody supposed to think about that? People just need to mind their own, you ask me."

"Nobody asked you."

May 24, 1969

Danny could hear the phone ringing all the way from the back-yard, where he was repairing part of the fence that had gone to rot with all the spring rains. According to the guys over at the lumberyard, it was over seven inches last month alone. Gabriel helped by handing him nails while Lidia pulled weeds from the vegetable garden. The late-afternoon sun lit everything in a sultry, lambent gold. The cucumbers demanded attention, taking over the less aggressive tomatoes and bell peppers. Lidia had suggested installing a trellis so they could go up instead of out, which Danny promised to do as soon as he'd finished and repainted the fence. There would be plenty of time for such small repairs. The house was sound, the garden flourished, they were happy.

He tossed his hammer aside and wiped his forehead as he trotted into the kitchen, where he picked up the phone and stretched the cord to get a glass of water. "Hello?"

"Danny. Stanley here."

Danny put down his glass and wiped his mouth. He straightened his back without even realizing it. "Afternoon, Mr. Kielar. Hold the phone, I'll get Lidia for you."

"Wait. I'm not calling for Lidia. I'm calling...I'm wondering if you'd be able to come down to the the Shelter for a spell. I got something I need to talk to you about. Thinking maybe it's best said over a beer or two."

Danny shifted his weight, glanced out the window at his wife, her strong back bent over a thatch of green. "I guess that'd be all right. What time you thinking of going down?"

"Time is it now?"

Danny peered into the living room at the grandfather clock. "Not quite five."

"I suppose Lidia still feeds everybody early. You'll be done with supper by six-thirty, tops. See you down the Shelter around seven."

Danny heard the line click and return to that empty, low-frequency tone that sounded like a desperately lost insect. "See you then," he said into the hum.

An old Scot named Goudie ran the Shelter, a dark place with a long bar and a row of booth seats along the west wall. Some old chessboards that had belonged to somebody in Goudie's family got some fair play in the early evenings.

"Danny," Stanley said, nodding, when Danny slid into the bench seat across from him.

"Mr. Kielar."

"Stanley."

"Stanley."

"What'll you have?"

"Beer, I s'pose."

Stanley reached up to signal Goudie, who returned a moment later with a couple of Pabst Blue Ribbons and set them down on cardboard coasters.

After at least three long slugs, Danny finally broke the silence. "You wanted to talk to me about something?"

"I guess you know there's been some talk." He looked, eyebrows up, expectant. "About your boy."

Danny leaned back into the buttoned vinyl seat. "Yeah, I've heard things."

"What've you heard?"

"Small talk. Petty talk. About the way he speaks sometimes." He shrugged. "I don't give it a thought."

Patting his pocket for a pack of cigarettes, Stanley took a moment to tap one out and light it, drawing on the smoke as if he was waiting for something to happen.

"It's not nothing," Stanley said. "What people are thinking."

"It is nothing. Just small-town gossip. When we moved here from New Jersey, my mama warned me that small towns are like that. Everybody makes everything their own business. Mountains out of molehills, she always said."

"It's gone past gossip, Danny. Gossip's just idle talk. Women's talk. What folks are saying now has fear behind it. It's got some impact."

"I've heard it, Mr. Kielar. Stanley. People saying things about him being able to tell futures and such. That he knows certain things. He can see ghosts and tell things people don't want told."

"That's right. Like I said, that's not nothing."

"But it *is* nothing, hear? Because Gabe can't do any of that. He's just a little kid. He just says what's on his mind is all. Nothing more to it than that."

"I'm not saying what my grandson can do and what he can't. I'm just repeating what other folks been saying."

"He's three years old."

"Going on four."

"No difference, he's a baby. He doesn't know tomorrow from yesterday."

"Not according to a lot of townsfolk. They're talking about him like he's some kind of prophet. Or the Devil, depending on who's speaking. Lidia ain't told you about any of this? People coming by the house during the day, wanting their futures told, asking questions?"

"She told me. She hasn't let anybody talk to him, of course. If I'd been home I'd have seen to it they never came back. I told her, anybody ever comes by again like that, send for me and I'll break shift."

"It's not just people coming by the house." Stanley looked at him level and unflinching for several seconds, then blinked before taking a long draw on his cigarette. His fingers trembled enough to send ash floating to the table.

"What is it, then?" Danny crossed his arms and leaned back into his seat.

"Old Pops Larsen said he was going to see if Gabe could tell him what ever happened to Liam Magee," Stanley said, lowering his voice. "Said if he could find him, he'd want to string him up by the toenails and beat him until he told the truth about the mine accident in 'fifty. Lot of guys died in that explosion, you know. Everybody thinks it was Liam who did it, but since they never found him after, there's still plenty of folks who'd like to know exactly what happened. Even more who'd like to see him hang."

"How would Gabe know that?" Danny's voice was sharp.

"Hold it down, now. Nobody needs to be overhearing this," Stanley admonished, shushing him with his hand, a thread of cigarette smoke whipping between them. "Sissy Borasky evidently was looking after Gabe when Lidia was over there helping Peggy with something and Gabe told her there was something shiny under the hydrangea bushes alongside her house. He couldn't even see the bushes from where he was sitting, she said, but she went out anyway and didn't see anything so she went back inside. Said Gabe was insistent about there being something there. Curiosity got hold of her—she's heard the stories, too, of course—and so she dug up that whole row of hydrangeas that'd been growing there lord knows how long and damn if she didn't find a cigar box full of gold coins her daddy won in a poker game and buried to keep her mother from spending it. He died before he ever told them where it was. And so according to Sissy, it was Gabe who solved the mystery of it."

"He could have been talking about a shovel! Or a nail or a gum wrapper! Could have been anything."

"But it wasn't just anything, see?" Stanley took another drag.

"So are you saying you believe all this nonsense? You really think Gabriel…knows things?" he asked.

"I don't know if I believe it or not," Stanley said with a sigh, looking down at the space where his finger had once been. "But in case he does…" He looked back up. "Danny, you're a good man. You're a good worker and a good father and I appreciate you taking care of my Liddie like you have. But in case what they're saying about Gabe is true, you need to take him and Lidia and go." He took a long swig and set his mug down hard.

"Go? What are you talking about, go? Go where?"

"Go back to where your people are. New York or New Jersey or wherever. Anywhere. Kentucky. Ohio. Anywhere. But you need to take them away. Get them out of Verra for a bit, maybe a couple years, give him time to…grow out of it. Or for people's concerns to die down. I'm telling you," he said, shaking his head. "It's not good for you here right now."

Danny pushed his mug a few inches away. "Stanley, I have to tell you, you sound as crazy as the rest of them. Gabe's just a regular kid, normal as Lidia and me."

"I know things you don't know," Stanley said, in a voice husky and close to a whisper. He raised an eyebrow at the table, tapped the ash off his cigarette, then looked up at Danny.

"What things?"

"If there's a chance—just a tiny chance—that Gabriel knows...things, or can tell the future, or the past...then there's cause to protect him."

"So what if he can tell something that's already passed? Who cares about that?"

"Everybody," he said. "Everybody cares about what's passed. Everybody! Don't you want to know what happened before your daddy died? And your mama? Don't you want to know what guilt they owned? What secrets they took on with 'em to the grave? People always want to know the truth. They never rest completely without it."

"Well?" Danny shrugged. "What's wrong with knowing the truth? Not saying Gabe knows the truth about anything except the sun's going to come up in the morning. But so what if folks think he does?"

"So what?" Stanley said. "So what if the truth is something you don't want shared? What if the truth would change everybody's thinking about what's done and gone? People come to terms with things, then maybe somebody comes along and tells them something different and all of a sudden they have to change their view? And what if what really happened is a whole lot different than what people assumed? There's responsibility in that." Stanley looked down again. "That's asking a lot. Of everybody."

"And now you're asking a lot of me to take my family off to God-knows-where just because a few people are scared he might say something they don't want everybody to know. I mean, what could he say that would justify us leaving home? What's the worst that could happen? So what if somebody gets shamed by something? Maybe they'd deserve it."

"You don't get it."

Danny shrugged, then sat up straighter against the seat. "No, I s'pose I don't."

"Then let me tell you something that might make you see things a little clearer," Stanley said in a low voice that sounded like thunder and fear at the same time. He took another long swig of beer and set it down, quiet and precise.

"I never told anybody this," Stanley said. "I didn't intend to tell you now, but you don't seem budged by me pointing out the risks to you keeping my daughter and grandson here. There's something else…" He paused. "There's something that if it got out, it could get me hanged. Something I did. But nobody knew it was me who did it. I let somebody else take the blame for it, though, because in the end, it wasn't something I meant to do. It was an accident, really, even though it didn't start out that way." He shook his head and closed his eyes. "After it was done, I couldn't tell anybody what really happened. I kept it buried like a seam of coal all these years. Let the weight of time hold it down deep, and now, if it was to get dug up and hauled out into the light…" Stanley dropped his head back against the seat pad and looked dull-eyed at Danny. "If I was found out, people would want me gone or dead or both — and my family with me. They'd never want to lay eyes again on anyone related to Stanley Kielar by blood or marriage."

Danny leaned forward, his wide eyes reflecting the candlelight like a boy sitting by a campfire, equally scared and riveted by the ghost stories being told. "What'd you do?" he whispered.

"About five months after Eagan got sick with the meningitis, we knew he'd never be the same. I blamed myself, you know. One day I'd come home and my wife said he'd woken up from his nap irritable and lethargic. She worried about him enough to want to take him to the doctor, but I didn't. I checked on him, patted him on the head. He said to me, 'My neck hurts, Daddy,' but even then I figured he just had a regular fever, even though he'd had it a few days already. It'd been a long day, and I figured he'd be all right. Next day, though, the fever hadn't broken and Eagan acted confused, and if he tried to move his neck he cried, so we took him down to see Doc Bartlett, who said we needed to get him to the hospital in Charleston. Doc rode with us, sat in the back with Anna, holding Eagan across their laps while I drove. It took me twice as long as it would've otherwise because of a hailstorm." He stopped, letting his memory idle for a moment, helpless, next to his young son's hospital bed. He tried not to let his voice crack when he said, "I never did forgive myself for not taking him down the night before. I should've put my boots right back on that minute and carried him down. I found out later it might've turned out different if I had."

Danny wondered about the last time Gabriel had had a fever. He always deferred to Lidia in such cases; he tended to assume—right or wrong—things would work themselves out. "How could you have known?" he said, suddenly aware of how vulnerable they all were to the things they didn't know.

"I looked back on it and thought I should've, somehow. And then they told us he was most likely going to be retarded for the rest of his life, and the bills came, and Anna started worrying about how we were going to take care of him. So I came up with a plan. Which is the part that nobody knows. I was going to do something that would make sure Anna and Eagan and Lidia—who was only a year old at the time—would be set up with enough money so they could leave Verra and move someplace where Anna could get help for Eagan. Because all I know is mining coal. I didn't have any other ideas about how to get us all out of here together and into a city with a real hospital if Eagan needed one, or a special type of school. So this plan I had would take care of them, and also take care of me. It was supposed to deliver me from my guilt. But instead, it only made it worse."

Danny had always thought the reason Stanley acted so reserved and remote, serious and older than he should have been, was because of Eagan, but he didn't know exactly why. Now, watching him wrestle with the past, Danny wasn't sure he wanted to witness his father-in-law mine the depths of his own shameful history. He wasn't sure he wanted to know the reasons for all the lines on Stanley's face.

"Dead shift was coming up. We only did it three, four times a year. There's no hoot-owl on nights before a dead shift, you know, so I knew the mine would be empty for the eight hours after the second shift ended and dead shift started the next day. So I decided…" Stanley bought a minute more of solitude with his secret by lighting another cigarette. "I decided I was going to do something to make things better for Anna. That morning I got up when Anna and the kids did, early morning, which was unusual because I usually slept in to around ten o'clock. I ate breakfast with them, and Anna kept looking at me funny, but I just told her I wanted some time with them, and so I spent the whole morning with them, holding Lidia and trying to play with Eagan; all the while I was saying goodbye to them inside my mind, and to Anna, too. It took everything I had to keep from breaking down right there, but I kept telling myself they were going to be better off."

He stopped again, and Danny, alarmed but understanding the rhythm, waited.

"At the end of my shift that night, Walter Pulaski, who was foreman — you know Alta, right? Walter was her husband — he called the end of the shift and everyone got on the mantrip and went about their business getting changed and going home. I planned to say I'd forgotten my dinner bucket and go back down on my own, take care of what I needed to, but that's when I heard Liam Magee tell Walter he was going back in to put the batteries on charge. So I just hung by the side of the hole in the dark, hunkering down behind a rock. It was a crescent moon that night, but I could see pretty well, and I waited what seemed like a lifetime for Magee to come back out. Must have been a half hour or more, then he comes out and reaches up and slaps the safety sign like he always did. I saw him pull out a flask, but that was typical. Magee was a drunk just like his daddy."

Danny interrupted him. "I gotta tell you, Mr. Kielar — Stanley, I mean — I'm not following you exactly. When was this?"

"It was October 6, 1950. The night before the Number Seventeen exploded."

"So you're saying you saw him do something to cause it?"

Stanley slipped out of his seat and stood up. He heaved a sigh and walked with a heavy stride toward the front of the bar. Danny swung around to watch him, wondering if he would keep on going right through the door. But he didn't. He stood looking out the window a moment, then walked slowly back to their table and sat down.

"I'm not saying Magee did something," he said in a low voice full of ache. "I'm saying *I* did."

"What?" Danny said. "What do you mean, *you* did?"

"I mean I waited for Liam Magee to come back out and then I went back in." He sighed and looked down again. "I planned to rig the ventilation system, make it look accidental, open up some of the stoppings to change the air flow, you know, then let the methane build up in one of the drifts near the face, where I'd be waiting..."

"Waiting for what?"

"Waiting for the methane levels to get up to five, six percent of the atmosphere, not too high—I didn't want too big a blast. Nothing that would shut down production for any real length of time, but enough that they'd find my body next day when the dead shift crew came on. Like I was just in the wrong place at the wrong time."

"Your body? You mean..."

Stanley nodded.

"But why?"

"I told you, I wanted to set Anna up so she could take Eagan and Lidia out of Verra."

"But you're here. And Liam Magee's not. And all those guys died."

"I know it. And it's my fault."

"So why does everybody talk about it being Magee's fault? I heard he never turned up again after that day, and everyone seems to think it was because of something he did. Where'd he go after he left the mine that night?"

"Best guess is he came somewhere downtown. According to Pudge Bellini, he had more than a few, then said he had to be going. As for why they blamed him, it was because Pudge said he was talking about setting something up. Apparently, he was pissed off about being passed over for promotion. He'd been making a stink for months about the mine not being safe, heckling the Blackstone shirts to get us better safety protocol, better ventilation. They ignored him, of course, maybe passed him over because of it, but it would've worked to my advantage having everyone already thinking that maybe the conditions weren't as good as the company wanted us to believe. Anyway, Pudge said Magee was drinking with him and started bragging about having cut away part of the insulation on the trolley wire and setting something metal against it so it'd set off a spark when the dead crew powered up the power station.

Nobody knows for sure, of course. Magee never could be found to question and the investigators couldn't do more than guess what happened based on the explosion and what Pudge claimed Magee had said."

"Then I don't understand why you're saying it was your fault."

"Truth is I'm not a hundred percent sure it was. But I know I opened up plenty of the stoppings in the old works to screw up the ventilation corridor. I was underground awhile; couple, three hours at least. I just sat there holding that book of matches, waiting for the gas tester to tell me it was time to go. But then when it finally got built up enough, I couldn't do it. I kept thinking maybe there was a chance they'd tell Anna it was my fault, that I shouldn't have been underground past my shift, that if it was a normal shift the fire boss would have tested for gas buildup and evacuated the crew if the levels were too high. And if they didn't think it was their fault because of poor ventilation, they wouldn't pay anything out to Anna. Then where'd she be? I'd be dead for nothing. Couldn't even offer her and the kids what little I had. So I went back, closed up the stoppings again, then slipped back into my bed like it was a regular night. I recall Anna rolling over in her sleep, putting her arm across my chest. She didn't even know I'd been gone any longer than usual."

"Okay, but if you closed up the stoppings, then it wasn't your fault."

"Point is, it could've been. I might've forgotten a stopping or two. Or maybe the airflow had been compromised long enough to leave a buildup higher than usual. If Magee did do something, it could've been the combination. I don't know for certain, but there's a strong chance that what I did at least contributed to it, if not caused it altogether."

Danny pinched the bridge of his nose. He couldn't think of anything that would make him want to abandon Lidia and

Gabriel like that, even for a minute. But that's not something he could say to Stanley.

"So what do you think happened to Magee?"

Stanley shrugged and took a drink. "He must've thought he caused it, if that was his plan. He wouldn't want to stick around for what would happen if they caught him. Maybe he drank himself to death. Who knows? Point is, he was smart to stay away from Verra once people assumed it was him who did it. What the law would've done is nothing compared to what folks around here would do. Nobody messes with other peoples' livelihoods, their lives, takes away fathers and husbands and sons. People never will forgive Magee, and they'd be even less forgiving of me. Don't forget, Walter Pulaski and John Esposito were the senior electricians, and after them, Magee. So when they died and he took off, I was the next one in line. I got moved up because of it. I got a promotion and a pay raise when I should've been strung up by my toenails. Don't think folks wouldn't be happy to do it now. The taste for justice only gets stronger the more time goes by." Stanley took a long drag off his cigarette.

"So you can understand now, it's not just that I want to protect Lidia and Gabe and you. If Gabe knows about me, about what I did, and tells somebody...I can't take that risk, hear? You gotta take Gabe away from Verra. Maybe he'll forget about it, or if he says anything about it to folks in another town, they might just pass it off as something he made up, a dream or something. But if he said it to anyone who's ever lived on Trist Mountain, they'd come after me for sure."

Danny leaned forward and rested his head against his fists. "You're asking me to uproot my family because of something you did nearly twenty years ago that nobody blames you for and you ain't even sure you did. All because you think there's a chance my kid can tell people's secrets."

"There's a chance, according to the stories being told."

"I can't do it, Mr. Kielar. I can't take off like that. Just like you couldn't light that match. I'm telling you, there's nothing to all this nonsense about Gabe. He doesn't know any more about what happened underground in Number Seventeen than I did a half hour ago. Less, even. Your secret's safe with me. I ain't going to tell anybody what you told me."

"Least tell me you'll think about it."

Danny sighed and leaned back. "All right. I'll think about it. I can't make you any promises, though. Except that I won't tell what you said." He thought of Lidia picking at the weeds in their vegetable garden, the cucumbers that threatened to choke the peppers and tomatoes, and the trellis he needed to build. The fence that needed repair. Just a few hours ago he thought he had all the time in the world to get it done. Now he wasn't quite as sure.

May 27, 1969

Just before she entered St. Michael's that sun-soaked Tuesday afternoon, Lidia closed her eyes tightly for a few seconds, even as she pulled open the door and stepped inside. With her eyes shut, she could adjust more easily to the darkness.

Inside, the dank, incensed air was still. Not a whisper of prayer or confession, no elegiac organ music to disturb the silence. Nothing moved at all, except the faint flicker of a few vigil candles near the statue of Mary. That made it an ideal time to speak to Father Timothy.

Except that when she arrived at his office, he was asleep, his body slumped against the back slats of his chair, his cassock bunched and wrinkled, his mouth open. On his desk sat a record album cover—the Beatles' *Revolver*—and a half-empty bottle of Irish whiskey. His turntable crackled and hissed as the vinyl record spun round and round, finished for God knew how long. Lidia stood at the threshold, unmoved by his secrets, but wondering all the same if she should wake him up to bother him with hers.

Father Timothy began to snore, softly, then appeared to stop breathing altogether, until a long snort startled them both and he lifted his head enough to notice her standing there.

"Why," he said in a raggedy voice. "I didn't see you come in." He stood and grasped the edge of the desk to steady himself, and she stepped forward to help in case his whiskeyed legs couldn't hold him. She'd seen it happen to her father once or twice when she was younger, before her mother's death and the additional responsibility it levied forced him to stop drinking altogether.

"Are you all right?" she asked.

"Fine, fine. Must have just fallen asleep there for a moment." He glanced sideways at the record, the whiskey, his graying old face flushed pink as a girl's. "I was just having a little nip." He picked up the bottle and trembled a smile. "Helps with the...arthritis." He opened a drawer to put it away, then apparently changed his mind and held it out to her instead. "How thoughtless of me. Would you like some?"

"No. Thank you," she said, holding her hand up. "But you go on ahead. I didn't mean to interrupt. I just came by thinking maybe I could talk to you about some...things."

He motioned for her to sit and he did, too, lowering himself slowly back down. "Bless you, child," he said as he unscrewed the cap and poured three fingers' worth into his fingerprint-covered glass. The drink steadied his hands and sobered his expression almost immediately. "What is it you wanted to talk about?"

"It's about my son, Gabriel," Lidia said. She glanced at the crucifix hanging above Father Timothy's head. "Well, not so much about Gabriel, but about what other people are saying about him."

Father Timothy waited, accustomed to the time it took to develop enough courage to speak the unspeakable.

"Have you...have you heard anything?" she asked.

"I'm not God, child. I don't hear everything." He sighed and ran his fingers along the edge of his desk, touched the whiskey glass briefly, then clasped his hands in his lap. "But I'd be lying if I said I haven't heard a little something here and there. And I'll be honest, I've had a few parishioners come to me asking about Gabriel."

"What did they say?" she asked. "What did you tell them?"

Father Timothy couldn't resist the glass again. He picked it up and took a drink with his eyes closed as though it had been transubstantiated, then set it back down as gently as he would the Communion chalice onto the corporal.

"I said to them what I'll say to you now: that God gives special gifts to each of us. It's not always for us to know what those gifts are to be used for. Your son has done nothing that appears to be destructive, or blasphemous, or immoral, and even those who have concerns about him had to agree on that. We just need to be patient, and pray for God's guidance to understand and appreciate Gabriel for who he is."

Lidia's lower lip trembled with the crush of relief. "Thank you."

"You don't have to thank me. He's a good boy. People will see that and they'll come around. As Solomon said, 'This too shall pass.'"

Lidia ran her index finger quickly under either eye. "There's one more thing. One more person who...who's been telling me a few times when I've seen her that Gabriel ought to be considered for something called an exorcism."

Father Timothy sighed. "Oh dear Lord, hear us on behalf of Your servant who is thus troubled. We humbly beg the help of Your mercy so she may be restored to health and render her thanks to You."

"She? How did you know it was a she?"

"There's only one person who'd think to propose such a ritual. And I know who it is because I've known her all her life, and most of that life she's worked right here alongside me."

Lidia nodded. "She came by one afternoon last week. Two or three people had already come by asking to spend a minute or two of Gabriel's time, wanting certain questions answered. Some of them I'd never even seen on the street," she said. "Anyway, Miss Bergmann came by, said she wanted to know if I'd been to confession lately. She hadn't seen me, she said. Of course, you know I've been coming regularly, but I didn't think it her business to know my whereabouts with God. So I just told her Gabriel and Danny and I got along just fine, thanks for asking. But she was insistent. Said there was evidence that Gabriel was possessed by a demon. Some book called the Roman Ritual listed things that indicated demonic possession." She reached into her small satchel and pulled out a folded piece of lined paper, the kind children practiced their penmanship on at school. "I wrote it down: *Supernatural abilities or strength. Knowledge of hidden or remote things that the possessed have no way of knowing.* She made it sound like something I should be worried about."

"Lidia, child, I don't think you have anything to worry about. I told Miss Bergmann when she brought it up to me that the *Rituale Romanum* also indicated that blasphemy and sacrilege would have to be present as well to even begin to convince me, much less the bishop, that Gabriel suffered from demonic possession."

"She actually talked to you about it!"

"You might be surprised to know what gets spoken about within these walls."

"Well, did it satisfy her? Because she seemed hell-bent on getting me to agree to an exorcism."

"Myrthen has a mind of her own. I don't fully understand why she's taken such an interest in Gabriel. I'd think she'd find a little more compassion for someone who wasn't quite aligned with convention. But I do know this: she's strong-willed and doesn't always follow the rules exactly to the letter." He shook his head. "I wasn't a bit surprised when I got that letter from the Prioress at the convent where Myrthen had been doing her training. Even after eleven years cloistered, she just wouldn't be mollified or trained. They dismissed her before she could take her final vows."

"She was what?"

Father Timothy hiccupped and pressed his fingers to his lips. "Oh no." He held his hand in front of his face, eyes closed. "Forgive me. I shouldn't have said that. It's not my story to tell."

Lidia slid to the edge of her chair again. With a fluid movement that surprised her even as she did it, she picked up the bottle of whiskey and unscrewed the lid. "No," she said in a gentle, soothing tone. "It's fine." She poured another three fingers, paused, then poured one more. She pushed the glass slowly toward Father Timothy. "I don't mind you telling me." Myrthen Bergmann had been a baleful, admonishing figure in her life ever since the day Lidia twisted her ankle, more than six months before. Until that moment, she hadn't thought there might be a flaw in Myrthen's history that might render her less a menace to Lidia's peace of mind.

Father Timothy picked up the glass and held it toward her. "Chin-chin."

She lifted an imaginary tumbler. "*Na zdraví.*"

He took a drink.

"Miss Bergmann is so pious," Lidia said. "I heard she'd gone away to live in a convent. I don't know much about that sort of life, if someone can just come and go from it."

"No, child. Just like the Church forbids divorce, once someone takes solemn vows, there's no going from it. It's a permanent commitment, a marriage to Christ. But, of course, there's time to be sure it's the right step. Postulancy, novitiate, simple vows for a time, then a renewal of those. That can take a decade

or longer. And Myrthen did it. After her husband died underground in 'fifty, she joined the monastery in Maryland. Went
all the way through; then the Mother Superior and a council of
Sisters got together to decide if she was good material for solemn profession." He closed his eyes. "She was not."

Lidia let this information mingle with the impression she
had of Myrthen's irreproachable fervor, her unflappable zeal.
"Do you know why?" she asked.

"I had a telephone conversation with the Mother Superior
after I received the letter. I knew if Myrthen came home she'd
come back to St. Michael's, and I felt I needed to hear both
sides of the story. Not for any punitive reason, of course..." He
sighed. "I wanted to be able to support her if I could. She's had a
lot of...disappointment...in her life. So I thought if I knew what
had happened..." He opened his hands in a gesture of resignation. "The Mother Superior said it was mostly that Myrthen
didn't get along well with the other sisters, didn't seem suited
for community life. Apparently she had some trouble with her
pride, too. God wants us to take a certain contentment in our
abilities, but all our good qualities come from Him and must be
attributed to Him. Our faults and sins are our own." He smiled
at that and lifted his glass toward her, then took another drink.
"According to the Mother Superior, Myrthen had a tendency to
attribute all her good to herself and shift blame for her not-so-
good to everyone else. She seemed to have missed the spiritual
sense of peace she might have gotten if she'd been able to see
herself as small in the eyes of God."

Lidia nodded, but didn't really understand. She'd always
felt small in the eyes of God and nearly everybody else save her
husband and son, but she didn't have much peace to show for it.

"So they kicked her out?"

"Essentially, yes. It was a shock to me, I'll tell you. Being a
nun was all she ever wanted. She lost her twin when she was a

little girl—about Gabriel's age, in fact—and she had it in her mind that she wanted to become a sister again, in the monastic sense, and devote herself to God, probably to make up for not having Ruth. Didn't want to get married, even though that nice fellow seemed to be genuinely devoted to her at the time." He stared at something on the wall. "I can still see her standing next to him during the ceremony. Eyes glassy and red from crying, blank expression on her face. She went through all the motions, but…" He closed his eyes and shook his head. "Well, she was never the same afterward."

After a moment of reverie so still she wondered if he'd fallen asleep, he sighed and lifted his hands in submission and said, "But everything that's happened is according to God's will." Then he reached across the desk, past the empty glass and half-empty bottle, and put his cool, dry hand on her wrist. She could feel the slight tremor coming off his bones, like the rattle of a train cutting through the mountain. "Faith in God doesn't give us immunity from suffering. And the things that make us suffer in this fallen world don't always happen because we've done something wrong. You've done nothing wrong. Gabriel has done nothing wrong."

She had to look away. There were so many secrets, ill begotten and intertwined. Would Father Timothy still say she'd done nothing wrong if he knew them all?

"As for Myrthen, I'll have a word with her, ask her to show more grace where Gabriel's concerned," he said. "You just be strong in your love of God and patient with those whose fears or greed create trouble." Then he clasped his hands again and smiled.

June 3, 1969

"Want to go visit Mimi today?" Lidia asked. She glanced out the window at the steady pelt of rain. "It's awful wet, but we can wear our boots."

Gabriel spoke through a mouthful of pancakes. "Can we look for frogs?"

"Sure. I bet Alta's got a whole lot of them in her garden."

"If I find one, can I keep him?"

Lidia laughed. "You really want a frog for a pet?"

"Yes!" He clasped her cheeks between his palms.

She peeled his hands off and pressed one of them to her lips. "Okay, okay. But you'll have to take care of him, you know. Make a little nest for him, find him bugs and grass, fill a little dish with water."

His three-and-a-half-year-old face grew serious with the honor of responsibility. "I can do that."

After she cleaned up the breakfast dishes, they put on clothes and galoshes and raincoats and took off hand in hand up the hollow to Alta's. By the time they arrived the rain had all but stopped, and into the shiny, wet quiet that ensued, bull-frogs cacophonied about the weather and their need of a mate.

Alta, as usual, stood on her porch waiting for them. Gabriel ran up and hugged her around her long legs. Lidia kissed her on the cheek and handed her a towel-covered loaf of fresh bread to go with whatever soup Alta would have been cooking since early in the morning. "I can't believe you came out in this rain, but I'm glad you did. Always glad to see my two favorite people. Now come on in before you catch your death."

"Mimi, I'm going to find a frog in your garden. Mama says I can take him home."

Lidia shrugged. "He says he'll take care of it."

"Abel used to do the same thing. Catch frogs and put them into his daddy's dinner bucket." She laughed at the memory. "I can't tell you how many times I opened up the lid to pack Walter's lunch and found some pathetic little thing in there looking up at me like I was the Savior." She turned to Gabriel, who surveyed the asparagus leaves from the porch steps. "Go on then. Let us know if you find one. We'll be inside making you some lunch."

They'd hardly had time to slice the bread before they heard a little-boy voice above the brassy clacking of frogs. "Mimi! Mama! I found one!" Gabriel stood amid the tender shoots with both hands raised and wrapped around a gloomy-looking frog that must have weighed a pound at least.

"That sure is a big one!"

"Can I keep him, Mama? You said I could."

Lidia looked at Alta, who winked and nodded. She crossed her arms. "Come on then, bring him up here. Let's see what you got."

He high-stepped through the croaking and the bright green of the garden, squeezing that poor old frog all the way up the steps to where Alta and Lidia waited, then he thrust it out toward his mother and said, "I named him Henry Donner."

"Where'd you ever come up with a name like Henry Donner?"

"He was my friend," he said.

" 'Course he was." Lidia sighed and turned to Alta. "Do you have anything we can keep Henry Donner in?"

"I just threw out a box that would've been perfect. And I have a bucket, but it's full of manure for the garden. I could dump it out, but it might still stink a bit. Let me think." She looked around her tidy porch. "Well, what goes around...," she said, and lifted a finger. "I've got Walter's dinner bucket. Seems appropriate to house old Henry in that. No doubt some of his ancestors took up residence in it one time or another."

She went inside and opened a closet and pulled on the string for light. Then she stood on an unopened box and stretched high up to a shelf, moving aside the miscellany that she'd brought with her when she'd moved into John's cabin almost eighteen years before. Finally, she found the metal pail with a lid and wood handle and brought it down. She stood holding it with both hands, staring at it beneath the bulb light as though it were a time capsule or a present or a bomb. Then she blew off a coat of dust in a firm discharge of air and handed it to Lidia.

"I haven't looked at that thing in nearly twenty years. They brought it back to me after they died, along with their other personal belongings. I couldn't even bring myself to open it. Compartments are probably all rusted shut by now."

"You sure you want Gabriel to use it? Seems like something that special shouldn't be used to carry frogs around."

Alta smiled. "I can't think of a better use for it."

They walked back onto the porch and put the bucket down, and Lidia pried off the lid and handed it to Gabriel. "Here you go."

He looked at it. "It's like Daddy's."

Lidia nodded. "Sure is. It belonged to Alta's husband a long time ago. Here, you give me Henry Donner and I'll watch him while you take out that top compartment where the sandwiches go and put some water and leaves down at the bottom of it for him."

Alta and Lidia went into the kitchen to find something to keep him in until Gabriel got the bucket ready. When Gabriel sat down on the porch steps and carefully pried out the inset compartment, he discovered it wasn't empty.

He reached in and found two small folded scraps of paper. He unfolded the first one, which was smeared with too many words for him to read. Then the second one, which had only four. Those he could sound out, even if he didn't understand them.

"Mimi?" he said when Alta came back out carrying a soup pot with the frog inside.

"Humm?"

" 'You are my always.' "

Alta stopped so fast it was like she'd run into a glass wall. The pot slipped from her hands and clattered to the porch floor and the frog tumbled out and sat, stunned, where he landed. When she spoke, one hand across her chest, her voice was a hoarse, breathy whisper. "What did you say?"

Gabriel bowed his head, and shrunk just slightly, toward the floor. " 'You are my always'?" Then he handed her the folded papers. "This was inside. I didn't know how to read the other one."

With trembling hands, she took the papers from him. "You found these inside the dinner bucket?"

He nodded. "At the bottom."

All of a sudden, the pain of doubt and mystery and fear surrounding the explosion in 1950 felt like an old wound split open again, all the gangrenous viscera exposed anew.

She had never opened the dinner bucket. She had never thought to look inside.

A growl of thunder overhead silenced the chorus of frogs. Rain began again to fall. Lidia stepped quietly around and righted the soup pot to put Henry Donner in it. Then, without a word, she took Gabriel by the hand and led him into the house, leaving Alta standing next to the rain, stricken and clutching the decades-old notes.

Alta looked at the words written on the paper, the deliberate and masculine handwriting. She could hear John's voice as though he were standing right there, speaking those words he'd said to her so many times.

You are my always.

The title of that silly poem he'd written for her so long ago had become their endearment. They used it so much they finally shortened it, even signed their paintings that way: Alta was Always, and John, Forever.

"And you are my forever," she whispered.

She unfolded the other note, stiffer and more wrinkled than the first. It must have been on the bottom, with just enough water left in the bucket to run some of the words into a faint blue bloodstain on the paper. But she could get the gist:

I had to get John to write for me, my hand's not right. Not much time now but wanted to tell you I loved you all these years. I know it wasn't like what you had with him and it's okay. If he gets out of here, I want you to be happy with him. He tried to save us...I promised your daddy I'd get you out of Verra someday. I'm sorry about that. Sorry I didn't make you a happier life. You were a good wife to me. Love, Walter.

She folded the notes back to their creases and sank down into the rocking chair that John had carried over Trist Mountain that autumn day in 1944, the one he smashed the night before he died, the one she spent months rebuilding and restoring when she moved back to the cabin, once she had time and patience and distance from grief enough to do it.

Alta thought of her son, the pain of his loss ever present. Even now, when she saw a troop of miners after a shift, she couldn't help but feel some low-slung anticipation that Abel would be among them, hungry and coal-black and tired, heading home to her.

Then she thought of Walter, that good, distant man she loved like one of her brothers and with whom she shared a house and a son and nearly every meal for twenty years. Twenty years. He'd been gone now nearly as long as they'd been married, but still he held a post at the kitchen table. How long had he known the truth?

And she thought of John, remembered finding him asleep in the rocking chair she now breathed back and forth in, and his waking up with that sleepy smile that became as familiar as her own hands, as essential as air. He hadn't done it; he hadn't killed them.

The relief was overwhelming.

In all those years since they died, she'd wondered many things. Their last words, their final thoughts. Who'd been responsible, and why, and how. She'd had countless conversations with their ghosts, all of them unsatisfying and unfinished. There was so much she would've liked to ask of them all. So much she would've liked to say.

I love you.

You gave me purpose. And strength. You taught me what it means to love.

Did you do it? How could you?

How dare you?

I miss you.

Did I love you enough?

I love you still.

And now, at last, this.

When the rain stopped once again, and the frogs started up their dyspeptic trills, she remembered that Lidia and Gabriel and Henry Donner were still there; she could hear them inside. She knew Gabriel wanted to take the frog home and make a pet of him. But she decided that she wouldn't allow it. Who knew whom that frog had been looking for when Gabriel found him? Who knew who would miss him if he were gone?

Later, after she was alone again, she sat back down in the rocker. The sun sank with the weight of all that was still and silent, casting a heady glow on the rain that covered the ground. She thought of them all one by one, Walter and Abel and, finally, John, and she held the image of him in her mind until it was too dark to see anymore, running into the depths of the mountain, trying to save them all.

June 28, 1969

There'd been no peace for a month. People ringing the bell
at all hours, waking the neighbors' dogs, begging Lidia or
Danny to pass along a question to Gabriel, or to let them talk
to him directly. "Where did Daddy go after he left town?"
a middle-aged spinster wanted to know. The younger sister
of a Korean War veteran asked who'd killed her brother and
how. An older woman hoped to be reassured that her daughter had made it to heaven after flinging her brokenhearted
self from the top of Queen's Point. A young man who suffered
from claustrophobia and desperately wanted to avoid working in the mines asked whether he should bet everything he
had on a Thoroughbred racehorse named Arts and Letters in
the Belmont Stakes that month. Mothers wanted to know the
gender of their unborn babies. Wives wanted to know if their
husbands were stepping out. Some wanted simply to know
the most auspicious day to plant a garden or plan a wedding
or conceive a child.

The constant interruptions exhausted Lidia, the incessant
insistences that her son was either a prophet or a soothsayer or
an oracle — or worse, a son of the Devil. She stopped answering

the door, stopped going out unless someone went with her, preferably Alta, whose elusive calm and imposing height gave thoughtless intruders pause. If someone did dare approach Lidia with Alta at her side, they'd most often sidle off after she shrunk them with her pale, unflinching gaze and a single admonition: *You should be ashamed of yourself.*

"Why don't you go spend the evening with Peggy?" Danny suggested that morning. "Get away from all this nonsense for a while. Go into Charleston and see a movie. Somebody told me *True Grit* was a good one. Or anything. Just get your mind off all this for a night."

"But what about you? I hate leaving you here with nothing to do. Or worse, having to manage anyone coming around."

"Oh, now, don't you worry about that. First of all, traffic's gone down a lot since I put up that do-not-disturb sign on the door. And folks don't bother with me as much as they do you. I've been practicing my go-to-hell face. I think it might be working." He set his mouth into a hard line and flexed his eyebrows into two stern-looking ridges. Through a squint, he bore his eyes into hers until she began to squirm. Then he broke into a laugh. "See? It does work."

She allowed herself a half smile.

"Go on, call Peggy. Gabe and I'll do man stuff around here tonight. We'll work in the yard and wrestle and eat TV dinners and skip baths. He'll be fast asleep by the time you get home." Danny leaned over and kissed her, quick, then looked at her deeply tired eyes and kissed her once more, slower this time.

"Thank you," she said in her languid, sad voice, and placed her palm against his bearded cheek. "I don't deserve you."

"Yes you do," he whispered, his face only a few inches from hers. Then he straightened up and smiled and gave her a playful swat on her behind. "Now go call Peggy before she makes other plans."

"Oh, Daddy! I see one!" Gabriel squealed. "Oh! And another one!" He dashed around the freshly mowed lawn between their garden and the back door of the house, leaping and snatching fistfuls of night. The tiny strobes of light escaped each grab.

Danny set his beer bottle on the grass and pushed himself out of the lawn chair. Coming up behind Gabriel, he said in a soft voice, "Watch here for a second." Gabriel stopped and Danny crouched down beside him. "Keep your eyes peeled in one spot and wait for one to light up. Now, when you see it, don't go right after it. Watch to see what direction it's moving before it blinks off again. That's where you need to go, too. Then you hold your hands cupped together like this, and when he blinks on again, you can reach up and catch him."

Gabriel, solemn with the weight of instruction, did as Danny said.

"I can't! I missed him again!"

"Let me show you."

Gabriel watched his father as he stood still and followed the trajectory of a firefly, then cupped his hands over and under it—like catching a pop fly—the instant it flashed again. "Careful now. We don't want to squash him." He held his hands toward Gabriel. "Do you want to hold him?"

Gabriel shook his head, smiling in the glow of porchlight. "Let's put him in the jar."

"Oh, you must have done this before with Mama. And here I thought I was showing you something new."

"No, I didn't do it before." Straight-faced, serious.

"Well, how'd you know about putting fireflies in jars?" Gabriel shrugged.

Danny sighed and looked down at him, sweat-matted hair unmoving in the faint breeze, sturdy little arms and legs, grass clippings stuck to his bare ankles, faint mound of belly giving little-boy shape to his favorite blue T-shirt. Then he shrugged and smiled. "Well, let's go inside and find a jar for him then. You lead the way."

Gabriel turned and sprinted into the house while Danny followed, cupping the luminescent bug. The screen door banged shut and, from inside, Gabriel shouted, "Daaaaddy! The phone's ringing!"

"Hello?" Danny said, then whispered, "Gabe, look in there for a jar." He jutted his chin toward the cupboard he thought most likely to contain one.

Through the spiral phone cord, he heard an unusual din. Music in the background. A faint shout, laughter. "Hello? Is this the Pollock residence?"

"Yes," Danny said, sighing. He should have known, some drunk calling to ask for Gabriel's prophetic opinion or prediction. Still focused on the task at hand, he interrupted the caller's request to say to Gabriel, not bothering to whisper or even move the mouthpiece away: "That's a good one. Unscrew the lid for me."

"This here's Goudie calling from the Shelter. Pub downtown?"

"No sense in you bothering, Goudie. I'm not passing along any damn requests to my son." Danny shook his head and exhaled an indignant huff, then walked around the table to slam it back down on the cradle.

"Wait!" The voice came across faint, suspended as it was in midair between Danny and the hook, but adamant. "It's nothing like that."

Danny pressed the phone back to his ear. "Well, what is it then?" He carefully dropped the lightning bug into the jar and screwed the lid. Then he found the ice pick and tapped a few airholes through the metal.

"It's your father-in-law. Stanley? He's been in here two, three hours, getting pretty sauced. 'Fraid I didn't realize it until it was too late. Then he started in on some kind of crazy talk about needing to get his grandson away from town before the kid spilled his guts and got him strung up. Started in on how people don't want their skeletons dragged out of their closets. Then he started crying right there, just like a baby. Saying everything was his fault and he couldn't go on holding it all in anymore, just sitting around waiting for his own lynching. I tell you, I've tended bar twenty-three years and I've never heard such carrying on."

Danny handed the jar to Gabriel and put a finger to his lips, mouthed the words *Just a minute.* "All right, well, give him a cup of coffee and tell him to sit tight. I'll be down to pick him up."

"That's the thing. He ain't here. He left a few minutes ago, saying something about going to the cemetery. I'd have gone after him myself, but there's nobody here to hold the fort and the place is packed. I sent someone after him, but he already came back and said he lost track of him. I asked around and that's how I got your name. Looked you up in the phone book. State he was in, I think you'd better go get him. He's got no business trying to get all the way up the holler if that's where he's headed."

"I'll go," Danny said, remembering the wretched panic in Stanley's voice when he'd begged him to take Gabriel and Lidia away. "Thanks for letting me know."

He hung up the phone and turned to Gabriel. "Buddy, we've got to run an errand. Can you go get your shoes on?"

"An errand? But it's night." That face full of innocence, those wide, wise eyes.

"I know. Crazy, ain't it? But it's something we gotta do."

"Can I take my lightning bug? He'll light the way."

"Sure. That's a good idea," he said, brushing the hair off Gabriel's sticky face. "Now get your shoes on fast as you can, okay? We need to get moving."

Their street was lit by porchlight and lampposts and the single traffic light they encountered during their brisk walk toward Main Street. But once they passed the Shelter and the other shops downtown and crossed over the rickety bridge that suspended them over New Creek and the railroad tracks, nothing could guide them toward St. Michael's cemetery save the prisoner firefly, the light of the full moon, and the well-worn path of memory.

"Where are we going, Daddy?"

"Granddaddy's gone up to the cemetery. We have to go pick him up and take him home."

"But why?"

"Because he's…sick. And he needs some help getting home."

"That happens sometimes."

Danny reached down and smoothed Gabriel's hair, neither of them breaking stride. "I suppose it does."

Gabriel knew the route well, because it was the same one he and Lidia took whenever they went to visit Alta. Once Lidia had started going to confession several months before, Gabriel learned the landmarks that led them to St. Michael's: first the dirt path up from the bridge, then the crushed summer smell of sassafras and swamp azalea, then the willow tree whose branches dipped into the creek. Go straight as the creek flows, and they'd be headed toward Alta's, but veer left at the slow-rotting stump of a downed sugar maple tree, and that meant St. Michael's or the cemetery.

Walking confidently ahead of his father, Gabriel hummed a medley of lullabies, holding his punctured jar aloft so they could see where they were going. They heard the rise and fall of cicadas screaming, the crunch of each other's footfalls, the rush of creek, the occasional plaintive trill of a screech owl. But otherwise, they felt alone under the stars in the woods on an early Saturday night, everyone else either in town or at home.

Everyone, that is, except for Myrthen Bergmann, who was marching primly home from a day of prayer and cleaning and organ playing. It wasn't until they were only a dozen yards apart that Danny heard the footsteps on the soft, dry ground.

"Mr. Kielar? Is that you?" he called.

"Who's there?" Myrthen answered in a clipped, prideful tone. If she felt any fear at encountering a disembodied male voice in the wooded dark of night, it couldn't be detected over the bell-clear annoyance in her own.

"It's Danny Pollock," he said, softer now, their voices on a crash course.

"Lidia Pollock's husband?"

"One and the same," he said, and nodded at her as she came to a pert stop a few feet in front of him.

She looked down at Gabriel. "Whatever are you doing out so late with that child? I only hope you're going up to light a candle."

"No, no," he said, respectful. "But that's not a bad idea. Maybe we'll stop in on our way home."

Gabriel stepped quietly behind his father's legs, clutched a fistful of denim with his free hand. "Gabriel, say hello to Miss Bergmann," Danny said, reaching around and prodding his shoulder lightly.

He could feel Gabriel's head shake.

"Gabe, that's not polite."

"Daddy, let's go," Gabriel whispered.

"Sorry about that," Danny said to Myrthen. "He's anxious to see his grandfather. We're on our way to pick him up."

"Pick him up? Now? Here?"

Danny scratched his cheek and took a breath. "Well, seems he's got himself in a tight spot. I was told he was heading to the cemetery, and, well, I need to go help him get on home."

"Well, I'll say a cemetery at night is no place for a child. Why in Heaven's name did you bring him with you?"

"My wife—Lidia—she's spending the evening with a girl-friend. I didn't really have a choice but to bring him." Danny thought a moment about the icing of apology in his voice and he straightened up. "Listen, thanks for your concern, but we're doing fine. We need to be moving on now." He nodded again and slid his hand down to detach Gabriel from his pants. "Let's go, buddy."

"Here now, it won't do for you to take that boy with you. Especially if there's trouble waiting for you once you get there. Why don't you let me take him back to the church and let him wait for you there? Father Timothy's gone on to bed by now, I'm sure, but I have a key and I'll be happy to look after him."

Danny thought for a moment, then nodded. He hadn't had time to consider what scene Stanley might create once he got there—or what he may have already. It might not be a bad idea to keep Gabriel from seeing his own grandfather in whatever state he might be in. "I wouldn't want to ask you to change your plans. You must've been headed home."

"My home is where our Lord is, and He's with me every-where I go. Let me take Gabriel. He'll be safe with me."

"You don't mind?"

"Of course not," she said, and unfolded her hands to extend one to Gabriel. "Come along, son. I'll tell you a story along the way."

"No, Daddy," Gabriel whispered, inching even closer. "I want to stay with you."

Danny crouched down and held both of Gabriel's soft fore-arms gently. "Gabe, I need to go get Granddaddy, and it'd be better if you were with Miss Bergmann right now. It's hard to explain, but I need you to stay with her. Just for a little bit."

"I don't want to." It wasn't a whine. It was pleading, plaintive, desperate. His eyes opened wide as a screech owl's. "Please, Daddy, don't make me go."

Danny stood up. "Buddy, I have to. You'll be fine. Miss Bergmann said she'd tell you a story. How 'bout that, huh? And you can tell her all about how we caught your lightning bug. Okay? I won't be long, I promise."

Then Gabriel started to cry, dropping the jar so he'd have two free hands to fling around Danny's legs. Danny smiled weakly at Myrthen, who stood erect as a cross and arched a single brow. "I'm sorry," he said.

"Gabriel, you come along with me now. Your father needs to take care of some family business and you don't need to bear witness to it." She offered her hand once more, moonlit and pale, palm toward the ground.

Gabriel squeezed Danny's leg harder.

Harder than he meant to, Danny bent down and held Gabriel's forearms, gave him a tiny start, and spoke in a dark, deep voice. "Stop this right now. You have nothing to cry about. You're just going to go with her to the church and wait for me. Nothing's going to happen. I'll get Granddaddy and then come back and get you. Now you stand up. Straighten up." He let go of Gabriel's arms and picked up the jar and handed it to him. "Go on now. I won't be long."

Gabriel stopped the sobbing sounds, but the tears continued to stream down his face.

"Thank you, Miss Bergmann. I won't be too long."

"Never you mind," she said without turning back. "We'll be just fine."

"I love you, buddy," he called to Gabriel, who'd already begun his forced march into the moonlight. He didn't reply. Only the faint metallic sound of a lid being unscrewed and the soft thump of a jar hitting the mountain floor could be heard.

Danny watched his son trudge off into the dark until he couldn't see them anymore, hoping that Gabriel would turn back, just once, so he could wave, give him their private I-love-you sign. But he hadn't, and so Danny turned and continued up the path toward the cemetery.

Some years ago, somebody had pried a gap into the row of thin iron posts that circumscribed the cemetery. The posts were as old as the earliest graves, about six feet tall and set about six inches apart, most likely installed to keep out the deer. The cemetery had only one gate on the eastern side, so Danny assumed somebody thought there needed to be another entryway. The narrow slot required a body to turn sideways upon entering, but the footpath that led to it confirmed that visitors used it often. Danny could see it easily in the moonlight that dappled between the sugar maples. He slipped inside and disturbed a covey of nightjars nesting on the ground, sending them flying into the trees with a whoosh. Once they settled, Danny strained to hear human sounds above the rush of wooded silence.

In the distance, he thought he could hear a voice. He took a few steps in the direction where Lidia's mother lay buried. Another voice, a sob perhaps. He nodded to nothing in particular and hooked his thumbs into his jeans pockets and set off to find the source.

Danny found Stanley just where he thought he'd be, staggering around on the plot of grass between the graves of his wife and his son, mumbling. Staying a few yards away, in the shadow of a grave marker in the shape of an angel, he listened to his father-in-law's incoherent grumble. When Stanley fell to his knees on Eagan's grave and started clawing at the earth with his hands, yanking chunks of fescue and dry moss out by the roots and digging into the dirt like a dog, Danny came forward.

"Stop that, Mr. Kielar," he said, not unkindly. He reached down and put a firm hand on his arm. "Stop that, hear?"

Stanley jerked his arm away and nearly toppled over, then planted his hands on the ground to steady himself. Danny thought he'd settled down, but a moment later, he flung himself into another heat of frantic digging. This time Danny tackled him, wrapping both arms around the older man's chest and heaving him, not easily, off the grave. The two men fell between Anna and Eagan. Once Danny extricated himself, Stanley rolled onto his back and let his arms flop down at his sides. Danny considered pinning him down with a knee on his chest, but then Stanley began to weep. He lay there with his eyes closed and his mouth open, his torso shaking from silent sobs. After a moment, he dragged a dirty hand across his face and rubbed his eyes until he looked like he'd just finished a shift underground digging coal.

"What are you doing here, Mr. Kielar?" Danny asked.

Stanley blinked a few times and stared at the moon that hung full and glowing directly overhead. "Dreaming. I was dreaming. Last night. Eagan and Anna and all them miners coming to tell me what wrongs I'd done. So angry, all of 'em. Worst was my Anna. My beautiful Anna. Telling me things. And when I woke up, I couldn't tell if it was real. I had to come here to see if they really were dead. They were so real, all of them. Sittin' right there at my kitchen table, Anna pouring black coffee for everyone. Walter Pulaski. His boy, Abel. Piggy and Pie Eye. Fossil. Gibby and Cross. All the rest of them. And Eagan." He rolled his head from side to side on the grass, and new tears glinting in the moonlight. "Eagan wasn't retarded. He was wearing his army combat uniform and cap and he sounded just like my daddy, yelling at me for being weak. Said I was a sonofabitch for signing him up, said I was the stupid one, not him." A wrack of sob escaped him. "I never thought of him as being stupid. He was my boy. I loved him." He rolled over onto his side, tucked his knees up and his elbows inside them, tears flowing into the dirt by his right cheek.

Danny swallowed hard, and thought about Gabriel. That little body, back turned, trundling away into the dark of night. What must Stanley have felt like, knowing he'd never get to see his son alive again, thinking it would have been partly his fault for letting him go off to war. Or making him go. How do you move on from that?

Without changing his fetal position, Stanley spoke, clear and calm. "I'm having them dreams again. I don't know if my own grandson knows the truth, or whether he's going to tell it, and I think maybe I ought to just say it myself and get it over with. I don't know how much more of it I can take."

"Mr. Kielar," Danny started. "Stanley. I know when we talked a month or so ago, back at the Shelter, I said I couldn't just take my family and up and leave like that. But things haven't passed over as much as I assumed they would. It's been hard on Lidia. Been hard keeping it all from Gabe. All these people wanting things from him. It's nonsense, it is. I know he's real smart, but he's not what they're saying he is. Even Father Timothy said so. Lidia talked to him. Not that I give much mind to that either. But anyway, I've been thinking about what you said, getting away from Verra for a while. And, well, I once thought I'd like to go to law school. And, no offense, I really hate working the mines." He sat back and crossed his legs. "I sent away to the City University of New York for an application. I worked on it every night for a week and sent it off the first of June. 'Course there's no guarantee I'll get in. But I thought you'd be interested to know: I hear what you're saying, and I don't want any of this to affect my wife or my son, or you for that matter. So maybe that'll ease you up a bit."

Stanley dropped his face into his open palms. He sat like that for a moment and then spoke. "I'm losing everybody one by one," he whispered.

"But isn't that what you wanted me to do? You said so, plain as day."

Stanley reached out and grasped Danny's forearm without looking up. "I did. And I thank you. But you've got to know. I've already lost damn near everything. You three are the last I have." He pulled back his hand and sat up, taking a sober breath. "But it's good, it's a good idea. Get you above ground, save Lidia and Gabriel from the fear of losing you every shift."

"I'll make sure nobody—" Danny stopped short, craning his neck toward a shriek in the distance. "What was that?"

Stanley shrugged in slow motion, fatigue and alcohol dulling his motor skills. "One of them owls, I'd guess. On the hunt."

But Danny turned his ear toward it. It didn't sound like an owl on the hunt. It sounded like something that'd been hunted.

Myrthen led Gabriel down the worn path to the entrance of St. Michael's. The light of the full moon was so bright it cast shadows along their way.

"Come on now," Myrthen said without turning her head. "It's not much farther."

"I know how far it is," Gabriel said.

Myrthen raised an eyebrow but didn't respond. She wasn't used to children, impertinent or otherwise. Perhaps this was how all almost-four-year-olds were.

But she remembered Gabriel wasn't like all almost-four-year-olds. She slowed her step, fell back a bit, softened her voice. "How do you know so many things, Gabriel?" she asked, sidling to him and matching his gait.

The ground crunched beneath them, crickets called.

Silently, Myrthen prayed: *Lord, You are a true and faithful witness. Whether this be good or evil, I will obey Your voice.*

"I want to go home."

"You can't go home now, Gabriel. You heard your father. You'll stay with me until he returns for you."

Gabriel's shoes had come unlaced, and the aglets flopped like two trouts on a line.

"How long do I have to wait?"

Myrthen stopped and turned to him. "As long as you must." Then she resumed her walk, slow and steady and even.

Her thoughts turned to her cousin Liam—long gone and possibly buried—and her conversation with him nearly nineteen years ago. The voice of God she'd tried to convince him with, knowing all along it was only the deaf leading the blind. And she'd done it; she'd convinced him to play out his revenge such that she would benefit—at last a widow, finally able to fulfill her original pledge to love no one but Jesus. *In our weakness, you remain. When we're broken, you sustain.* And he had done according to her plan. He'd even stayed away all these years as she'd demanded, a miracle that suggested God was on her side. In her widowhood, she'd been freed. But not entirely.

The nightmares kept her captive to the past.

"Gabriel, do you know anything about the mines?"

Gabriel kicked the dirt ahead of each blue canvas shoe. "I don't want to talk about the mine."

Myrthen felt her heart quicken. She refused the temptation to look at him directly, remembering what she'd once been told about her particular unflinching blue stare, that it unnerved people.

Though God might allow the living to see ghosts on occasion, the Church forbade the initiation of occult contact with departed souls. Recourse to mediums, interpretation of omens, and conjuring of the dead were all practices to be rejected. Such divination represented a personal desire for power over time, history, and other people. It contradicted the loving fear man owes to God alone.

O my God, I am heartily sorry for having offended You and I detest all my sins, because I dread the loss of Heaven and the pains of Hell...Myrthen stared straight ahead into the darkness.

"Gabriel, has your daddy or anybody else ever told you about the accident that happened some years ago?"

"Where's my daddy?"

"He's gone to retrieve your grandfather, who is no doubt inebriated and in need of special attention. Nothing that a child like you should contend with," she said. "Quite frankly, I'm shocked he'd expose you to such debauchery."

"He needs my daddy to take him home."

The slap of footsteps on the dirt, a wavering hoot in the distance. She nodded. "Just like those miners in the accident I mentioned. Did those miners underground get to go home?" she asked.

"Yes."

"Yes?"

Gabriel stopped in his tracks and looked at her, the mantilla framing her face despite the June heat. "You know," he said.

Myrthen slowed to a stop just ahead of him and closed her eyes. She thought fleetingly of John. Over the years and especially since she'd moved back home to Verra after leaving the convent, she had dreams of John trapped underground, clawing at the dirt trying to escape. And in each of them, she served as the only witness. Somehow, she could look down at him as though she could see through the crust of earth that separated them. Through this looking glass—she from her safe, ventilated side of freedom, and he from his tomb—they locked eyes. And each time, again and again, she watched him die.

She always awoke from these dreams cold and sweating, and prayed as many Hail Marys and Our Fathers as it took to distract her back to sleep. Sometimes in the dream, however, John became her twin sister, and after one of these, she couldn't lull herself back to sleep. The vision of Ruth screaming and trying to climb out of the undercroft became far too realistic to fade into the drape of night.

"No, actually. I don't. I know some of them died underground, but..." She swallowed, hard. "But I don't know exactly why." She turned slowly back and reached out her hand to his. "Do you?"

Gabriel tucked his hand into his pocket and started walking again, watching the ground pass slowly, step by step, beneath him. The dwarf huckleberry shrubs meant a left turn up ahead to get to the church. Right, if he were to cross over to the cemetery. "*You* know," Gabriel said again. Then, a moment later: "I don't want to be here now. I want to find my daddy."

"Your people are running afoul of the cemetery where the dearly departed are resting!"

Gabriel looked at her, and sniffed once, hard. "My daddy's there," he said.

"And he said you'd stay with me."

"I don't want to stay with you," he said.

Myrthen grabbed Gabriel by the upper arm. "You have no choice!" She glared down at him then, ice-blue and insistent. His wide eyes blinked up at her a few times.

Then, in a single fluid movement, he wrenched away from her grasp and took off running.

He was fast, but the moon was bright and Myrthen was smart. She didn't bother calling his name; she knew he wouldn't stop even if she did, and besides, she knew where he was going. In an instant, she lifted the hem of her long skirt and went after him.

She could see his shadow bobbing on the mountain floor, could hear his footsteps crunching twigs and slapping the dirt.

Running behind him, she tried to close the gap, but it had been many years since she'd moved herself so quickly through space. Her joints ached at every pace; her lungs filled with fire. A small rut in the path nearly ended the race: she stumbled headlong in fast-motion with her hands outstretched, ready to fall. But she righted herself in time.

Animated with the utmost lively confidence, I come laden with the weight of my sins, to prostrate myself before You.

There. She found him in her sights again, a dozen yards in front of her, running along the perimeter of the cemetery's iron fence. He seemed to be slowing a bit, perhaps confused by his direction. Was he looking for the gap that she had long ago pried open with a crowbar from the shed behind St. Michael's, for want of easier access to her sister's grave? If so, he'd passed it already. Now he would have to run the length of the southern edge and turn up to enter through the proper gate. She didn't know if she could run that far. Perhaps she should just let him go.

But no, she couldn't. He knew something, and now that she'd started her line of questioning, she needed to know what it was. The image of John trying to escape the pit — hands bleeding, that panicked, transfixed stare — had her by the throat. She might not have another chance until she died to find out to whom God had assigned the blame.

"Daddy!" Gabriel yelled. "Daddy, where are you?" His voice was high and piercing. "Who-who!" a screech owl called in return. "Who-who!" He ran fast again, but the sugar maples along the path that stretched a hundred feet into the sky choked the moonlight. There came no answer from the cemetery, so he kept running, past the left turnoff to the gate. He must be lost, or else headed somewhere else. Myrthen fought to catch him — how dare he go so far, and now he had started toward the mine, of all places. John's old cabin was somewhere nearby, she realized, and the thought brought the dream of his exploded interment again to her mind. She quickened her pace, trying to ignore the burning in her chest, legs, feet.

And then she was nearly upon him. He ran headlong down a hill, straight for the highwall above the mine entrance that had been sheared away sixty years ago when Blackstone had first come in to excavate the pit. When those early workers had gouged out a notch in the mountain face, they'd created a man-made cliff above it. And if Gabriel didn't stop, he'd go straight off the edge.

"Gabriel, stop!" she screamed. Either the panicked tone or the mere closeness of her voice startled him, and he jumped midstride and glanced over his shoulder. She lunged forward with her hands outstretched, the downhill momentum pitching her forward, and he made a small, wounded sound like a yelp before he leapt away from her once more.

"Look down!" she screamed again. Something about that command made him obey. He slowed to a trot and must have realized where he stood, because his legs stuttered to a stop even while his torso moved forward, an imbalanced inertia that forced him to swim his arms wildly about in order to remain upright. In that moment of uncertainty, Myrthen skidded side-ways to a stop beside him and grabbed one of his forearms. A tiny landslide of pebbles rolled past their feet and off the edge of the sheer overburden of rock. A second later, they could hear them landing on the ground below, a faint and gentle sound, like falling rain.

She pumped his arm once, hard, and spoke through a pant. "Do you see what could've happened? You could've run right off this cliff. What foolishness got into your head, running down here like this?"

"Let me go!" Gabriel said, pulling his arm, and panting along with her. She gripped it like a hawk refusing to release its prey.

"Not until you settle down. And once you do, I want you to tell me what you know."

He tried to wrench his arm away, but she knew his tricks. She wasn't going to chase him all over Creation again. She squeezed his arm more tightly.

Gabriel glanced at the ground near his feet and then bent over to grab a stick. It was thicker than a fishing pole, but only as long as his forearm. He clutched one end and raised it above his head, clearly intending to bring it down upon her grasp, a plan that she—older, taller, more wicked, and less desperate—foresaw and intercepted with her free hand. There was an exchange of grips, a flurry of yanking, until somehow each of them ended up holding one end of the stick.

"I want my daddy!"

Myrthen had grown tired, the fight instinct that had earlier charged her system and fueled her chase now replaced by an awareness of the aches throughout her usually inactive body. Her sudden weakness made them a fair match, and they grunted back and forth, silent but for the shortness of breath, until Myrthen finally hissed through clenched teeth, "Your father isn't here. And instead of whining about that, you should be on your knees giving thanks to your Heavenly Father that I was here to save your life."

Whose life have you saved?

"What did you say?" she demanded. Gabriel stared at her.

You know what happened. You can't hide your secrets forever. You can't hide them from God.

Myrthen felt a white heat crawl over her scalp, felt something inside her go loose. She squinted at Gabriel, searching his face in the moonlight, trying to match the voice with his, but it didn't fit. What she heard was an angry girlish voice of someone more familiar, a voice that spoke only inside her own mind.

"What did you say?" she said again, whispering this time.
"I said let go, you meanie!" Gabriel said.

And with that, the calendar of her life flipped backward to almost the beginning, the clocks unwound, a lifetime of things undone, unsaid, and there, through the lens of memory, she held on to not a branch of a broken sugar maple tree, but a broken birthday doll handmade by her mother. And she wasn't yanking it away from Gabriel, but from her long-dead twin, who'd screamed those very words when Myrthen wouldn't let it go.

"She's *mine*. Mama gave her to *me*." The words rang in Myrthen's ears. She strained not to hear, but one can't avoid the truth once it's been spoken. *You don't understand the Word of God. You don't hear His voice. You have nothing and nobody, because you are mean. You are wicked. You are evil.*

You. Are.

Ruthless.

Myrthen's skin tingled as though she'd been plunged into an ice bath. She felt nothing, saw nothing. Just held on to the doll-stick that tethered her to the past. There was a tug, and she was pulled back into the present, past the brief bit of life she shared with Ruth, past the stretch of time that followed in which history had been reshaped, past John's brief and contemptible courtship and their wedding and those long and regrettable years of marriage, past Liam and the confessional, past the plot that blew up the mine and her husband along with it, past the disappointing years in the convent and the disappointing years since, past the organ dirges and prayers — oh, the prayers — that had been tossed up to God, countless confetti words that now rained back down upon her, disassembled into jibberish, as she stood on the precipice of time, doubled back, looking again at an angry angelic face before her that symbolized something of which she wanted no part, and with Gabriel's feet sliding in the scree at the edge of earth and her own shaking, aching self struck by horrified awareness, she let go.

In an eternal, screaming instant of damnation, the boy-shaped vision of Ruth stumbled backward, eyes wide. The stick rammed against his tiny chest from the unexpected release and launched him backward into the dark, and then he was gone.

Myrthen gasped through her mouth and blinked and then stepped forward, breathless, to see what she had done — then and now — and saw the bodies on the ground below. Both of them, one spectral and one bleeding.

And all at once the curtain she'd hung up inside herself that night so long ago was torn from top to bottom and she saw everything that she had hidden from herself, everything she had done that could never be undone. Ruth, broken on the cellar floor; Liam, manipulated and banished or dead; John and the other miners crushed and buried inside the belly of the mountain. All of it because of her.

June 28, 1969

Peggy sped toward Lidia's curb like an outlaw on the run, repeating her favorite lines from *True Grit*. Lidia had been gripping the door handle with one hand and the edge of the seat with the other, her heart pounding in her chest.

"It's so good seeing you, Liddie. Tell that sweet husband of yours thanks for sharing you for the night." Peggy beamed at her and reached over to give Lidia's hand a squeeze. Then she affected her best southern accent: "Come see a fat old man some time!" She threw her head back and laughed. "I just love that John Wayne."

"Thanks for getting me home safe, Peggy," Lidia said. "It was great to see you, too."

"Let me know if you want to go see it again. I can get a kitchen pass next weekend if you can."

"I'll let you know," Lidia said, and opened the door. She stepped onto the sidewalk and turned back. " 'Night!"

"Toodles! Oh, and happy belated birthday again! Twenty-one years old! Can you imagine?" Peggy waved and took off.

Lidia raised a hand, but Peggy was already gone, a cloud of dust and dross swirling in her wake. Lidia smiled and shook her head, then walked quickly up the steps back to the safety and comfort of home.

She turned the key quietly. It was after ten o'clock and no doubt Danny would be tired from running after Gabriel all evening. Closing and locking the door, she tiptoed through the living room, avoiding the creaky planks. The house was dark except for the kitchen.

"Danny?" she whispered, imagining him at the table, whittling something for Gabriel or reading the paper over a beer or a cup of coffee. Dropping her purse on the kitchen chair, she smiled at the quiet, thinking he must have left the light on for her and was probably asleep with his feet hanging off the end of Gabriel's bed, a book open on his chest. Probably *Mr. Pine's Purple House*, Gabriel's favorite.

Lidia walked softly down the hall and poked her head into Gabriel's bedroom, the light slicing through the darkness as she pushed open the door. But when the bed came into view, she was surprised to see it was made up, just as she'd left it. Of course. No matter how many times she insisted that Gabriel stay in his own room, lest it become an unbreakable habit, Danny couldn't say no when they felt the slap of yellow blanket on their covers that always preceded Gabriel's gymnastic climb onto their bed. No doubt he didn't bother waiting tonight for the stealth approach, but took Gabriel straight into their room to fall asleep there. She hoped Danny had remembered to put a night diaper on him.

But across the hall, her and Danny's room was filled only with moonlight and silence. The bed, like Gabriel's, still made. She stared at it for a moment, so unusual did it seem, so empty. There wasn't so much as an impression in the stretched-smooth quilt, where someone might have sat to tie his shoes, or lain down for an afternoon nap, or rolled around during a tickle fight. She turned her head and listened for something. Breathing?

Voices? Were they teasing her? Were they waiting to pounce out of a closet just as she got near?

"Danny?" she whispered again, louder this time. "Gabe?" Surely they wouldn't stay up so late just to play a silly trick.

"Danny?" Her voice rang clear and loud as she walked back into the hall. It echoed back at her from the quiet. "Gabriel!" She trotted back into Gabriel's room, and flipped on the overhead light. "Come out right this instant, both of you!" Yanking open the closet door, she saw his toys and clothes, a stack of puzzles he'd already outgrown. Then she bent over to peer underneath the bed, in spite of the improbability. It rose less than a foot off the ground.

"Answer me!" She jogged now, down the hall and into the few other rooms. Outside! Of course! Oh, the relief. She slowed her gait and closed her eyes, let that nameless panic that had erupted in her gut come to rest.

"Okay, you snipers, I'm home," she said into the yard. The cicada squall rushed loud in her ears. The moon stared down, unblinking, through the void.

"Danny?" She listened. "Gabe?"

Panic rose again. She ran the perimeter of the small yard, trampled through the garden, tripping on the long, ripe cucumbers, ruining them with the heels of her shoes. "Where are you?" she screamed.

And then, an answer. From within the house, the phone began to ring. She sprinted across the yard and into the kitchen and grabbed the handset before she'd had time to take a breath. "Danny? Where are you? Is everything okay?" Then, "Alta, what's the matter? Are you crying?"

Her heart beat wildly in her chest.

"What do you mean, fell? Where is he? Is he all right? Where's Danny?"

The second hand on the clock above the sink began to slow. "No," she whispered. "No, that can't be right. They're here somewhere, hiding. They're playing a trick on me." Her eyes darted around the room, seeking proof, and found it in the form of Gabriel's blanket draped across the seat of his chair. She stretched the cord to reach it. "See?" she said, lifting it up and holding it close to her. "I have Bobby here. Gabriel wouldn't ever go anywhere at night without Bobby."

She clutched it to her chest, knuckles going white as she listened to Alta. And then, the clock stopped ticking. The faucet stopped dripping. The cicadas stopped screaming. There was no noise, no heat, no light, no air. Nothing but the faint, urgent voice that came from the telephone receiver she'd dropped on the floor, "Lidia, stay where you are. I'm coming to get you."

June 28, 1969

Alta had been restless that night; there was something too stark in the way the moon hung so full and low outside her bedroom window. She tried rolling away from it, plumping and punching the pillows, but the shadows that swayed on the opposite wall felt just as disarming as the moon. Finally, she flung back the sheet, pulled her work pants on underneath her nightgown, stepped into her boots, and went outside to confront the sky.

Walking into the garden, Alta surveyed the asparagus ferns. The emerging spears shot up thin as pencils, which meant the end of that year's harvest. John had told her back then that the plants would last twenty years if they were well cared for. It had been twenty-three. She wondered how many more crops these plants would yield.

An owl screeched somewhere in the distance, loud. Then again. Alta was used to the sounds of owls defending their territories and seeking mates, but this one sounded not angry or amorous, but hurt. Desperate somehow. There it was again. Alta turned toward it and listened and when she heard it another time, it was clear: that was no owl.

Without a thought, she took off running, following the sound, hopping over the branches and brambles that lay in her path. In a few minutes, she knew from where the crying came. She'd worn a route between the cabin and the mine during those long, haunted years, those unfathomably dark nights with nothing but the owls and crickets and fallen leaves and snow and ghosts for company. It wasn't uncommon for her to pull on her pants and boots under her nightgown—dressed half for day and half for night, perfect for the half life she'd lived since then—and make her way down to the entrance of the mine, where she would sit and remember or beg or simply listen in case any of them would care to speak to her. But they never did, and so she played their parts in her mind, speaking for and with them, working out the details of their last hours over and over, always hoping that by some miracle of time or circumstance, they would come walking out from underground, all of them, coal-dusted but breathing, and she'd be there, waiting. To forgive and be forgiven.

A woman's voice twisted tightly, ululating, "No, no, no, no." It grew louder as she approached, but only slightly, as though the woman was growing weaker as Alta drew near.

Alta saw her: on her knees, her back curled forward, rocking. The hands, she could imagine, clasped together. She looked just as she did nearly forty years before, kneeling and sobbing at the foot of the Virgin on her wedding day.

She reached out and touched her lightly on the shoulder. "Myrthen," she whispered. "Myrthen, what's wrong?"

There came no answer except the ghost-owl screech of no-no-no-no, quieted now to merely a whisper. Alta, following Myrthen's blank stare, walked the few steps forward to the edge of the highwall and looked.

Then screamed.

She ran to the clearing that led down, not caring how steeply, grasping thistles and weeds and skidding on scree bottom-first and bumping down the two stories of shale, scraping and tearing, until she got to Gabriel. He lay with his arms and legs splayed out, one leg bent an odd way. One of his shoes had come off and his pale foot seemed to glow in the moonlight. He wasn't moving. She touched his face with both hands, then his chest and ribs, feeling for breath. He was still, but he was breathing. With a heady mix of panic and relief, she gathered him up into her arms, holding her breath and willing him to consciousness, until finally she was able to scream, "*HELP!*"

A sound so fierce and immediate, it silenced everything between them and the nearest pair of ears, which, after a short time and some repeated calls, came running. Of all people, it was Danny, followed staggeringly by his soon-to-be-sober father-in-law, Stanley.

Danny slid feet first into the dirt beside Alta and pulled Gabriel from her arms into his own. "Is he dead?" he screamed. "Is he dead?"

"He's breathing," Alta said. "But he's hurt. His leg. I think it's broken."

"What happened?" Stanley asked.

"He fell, I don't know. Myrthen Bergmann's up there, crying. I don't know."

"I left Gabe with her while I went looking for Mr. Kielar." His face turned ashen, and he looked up at her from a hollow place, like a scared little boy, not someone's father. "It's my fault."

Alta shook her head. "Where's Lidia?"

"Movies." Danny started to stand. "We gotta get him to the hospital." Gabriel lolled in his arms.

"Wait," Stanley said, forcing the slur from his words. "Lay him flat." He bent down and swiped at the ground with his rough hand, clearing it of rocks.

"You're drunk, Stanley. He needs a doctor!" Danny said.

"I know it. But look at his foot. It's turning blue." Stanley reached out and cupped Gabriel's foot. Blood ran down Gabriel's leg, and dripped off his heel onto the ground. "No pulse in his foot. Here," he said, pointing to the space he'd cleared. "Gentle now." Cupping Gabriel's head as Danny laid him on the dirt, he ran his hands gently over Gabriel's left leg, feeling the thigh where blood soaked his blue jeans. "Broken. We gotta set it." He stood up, wobbling a moment, then finding his balance. "Sticks."

"Can't we just get him downtown?" Danny said.

"Stanley's right," Alta said. "No pulse in his foot means the blood supply's kinked up."

Stanley returned with two branches from a fallen maple. He held first one and then the other against his thigh and broke them at the collar, stripped them of their thin offshoots. "Give her your shirt," he said to Danny, all hint of liquor drained from his voice. Then to Alta, "Tear it. Three strips. Now, Danny, you hold him under the arms while I pull." Danny, flustered, didn't move.

"Do it!" Stanley yelled.

Danny pulled off his shirt and flung it toward Alta, who started ripping it at the seams. Then Danny crouched down at Gabriel's head and leaned over him to get a firm grip at his armpits.

"Got him tight?" Stanley asked. Danny nodded. Stanley held on to Gabriel's ankle with both hands, then took a deep breath and seemed to say a short prayer. With a hard, controlled yank that produced a crunching sound like a truck stopping hard on a gravel road, he pulled Gabriel's leg straight. Danny let go of Gabriel's arms, turned away, and vomited in the dirt.

Alta blew out a hard breath and put her hand on Gabriel's forehead, grateful he wasn't awake to feel that pain. Holding Gabriel's foot, Stanley watched as the color started to return.

"Is it set?" Alta asked.

He nodded, then pressed the two maple branches against either side of Gabriel's leg and told Danny to hold them in place. He threaded the strips of cloth under the bundle and tied them as tight as he could without cutting off circulation again.

"Danny, you and me'll carry him down. Alta, you find Lidia and tell her to meet us at Doc Bartlett's." Stanley nodded at Danny, who bent down to lift Gabriel into his arms while Stanley took hold of the splinted leg.

"Go slow, hear?" Alta said. "Danny?"

"We got him." They started awkwardly down the mountain, Danny stepping blindly over stumps and rocks, Stanley walking sideways. Alta watched them for just a moment before she turned her attention back to the moaning coming from above.

When Alta climbed back up the slope, hurrying past the fatigue and the ache that was settling into her bones, she found Myrthen where she'd left her, kneeling on the rocky ground and mumbling. She reached down, not gently, grabbing Myrthen under her upper arm, feeling the flesh yield beneath the black wool.

"What happened?" She gave Myrthen's arm a firm shake. "Why did Gabriel fall?"

"Have mercy on me, O God, according to Your steadfast love—"

"Stop that, hear? Tell me what happened!"

"According to Your abundant mercy blot out my transgressions—"

Alta slapped Myrthen across the face, hard enough to leave a ghost-white impression of her hand before the blood rushed back and turned the handprint red. The praying stopped, but Myrthen didn't look at her. "Stand up," Alta said, and pulled.

"Danny said he left Gabriel with you. Why are you out here? Why did he fall?"

Myrthen looked up at her, still rocking. "He wanted his daddy," she whispered.

"And what? You brought him here?"

She dropped her head again and shook it, slowly, from side to side. "He was running. I went after him..."

"And what? What did you do?" Alta grabbed Myrthen's arm again. "What did you do?"

"I tried to stop him, I screamed, and she called me a meanie and said I didn't know how to play baby. But it was my birthday doll, *mine*." Myrthen began to sob. "Oh mighty God, forgive me..."

"Stand up!" Alta said. She hauled Myrthen's dead weight to her feet and held her at the wrist. "I need to use the telephone. I'll let Father Timothy decide what to do with you."

Alta walked, hard and fast, toward St. Michael's, dragging Myrthen behind her. She thought of Gabriel running, wondered why and where he was going, why Danny had left him with Myrthen. Behind her, Myrthen stumbled, mumbling a few plaintive snatches of prayer. Alta increased her pace. When they were within sight of the church, she urged Myrthen to hurry. Then, when they were on the path leading to the closed doors, Myrthen tripped on something and fell, breaking Alta's grip with a yank. Alta turned and found Myrthen in a crumpled pile, her weight on one hip and both forearms in the dirt. Her hair had come undone and hung around her face in black clumps shot through with gray. She sat and sobbed.

When Alta bent down and tried to help her up, Myrthen only dropped her head against her arms and cried harder. "Are you hurt?" Alta asked. Myrthen shook her head against the backs of her hands. "Come on now," Alta said, her voice softening. "Get up." But she made no other move toward Myrthen.

Instead, she cupped her hands to her mouth and directed her voice toward the church.

"Father Timothy!" she called. "Father Timothy!" Then she turned back to Myrthen and said, "Wait here. I'll get help."

Myrthen lifted her head and slowly pushed herself up. Not bothering to move her hair from her face or wipe her nose or brush the tear-streaked dirt from her cheeks, she looked up at Alta and whispered, "Forgive me."

Alta looked at Myrthen, at her filthy, beautiful face, her pleading eyes as the night swirled around them. They had nothing in common but everything: a wedding day, a man, widowhood, emptiness, grief, age. Alta didn't know her at all, didn't know what sins she had committed, what secrets she bore. Likewise, Myrthen, she assumed, didn't know any of hers. But Alta knew this: she'd taken something from Myrthen years before, something Myrthen didn't want but that nonetheless had belonged to her. Alta could just as easily have been the one on the ground, begging forgiveness.

"We're all guilty of something," Alta said. It was as close to a confession as she would come, and as close to absolution as she could offer. Whether it was enough, she didn't know and, quite frankly, didn't care, because at that moment Father Timothy came running toward them, his bathrobe like an unbuttoned cassock flapping at his sides.

June 28, 1969

Father Timothy held Myrthen by the elbow, and she stumbled, glassy-eyed and mute, alongside him to the church. He tried coaxing more information from her to complete Alta's story, but all she would say was, "He ran away, he ran away," in a voice that dwindled to a whisper. Shrinking into herself, she seemed to grow older with every step. They made an odd pair—him with his white hair standing erratically on end; her hunched over her guilt, cradling it like a newborn child.

Father Timothy guided her to the confessional and closed the door after she went in. On his own side, he waited for her to begin the usual way, *Forgive me, Father, for I have sinned*, but she did not. She knelt on the prie-dieu, shivering in spite of the summer heat, then rested her forehead onto her hands, which were knotted together as though in prayer, but no prayers came. Not in her entire life could she recall ever having felt more alone. She had forsaken herself. *I could die here*, she thought. A throaty, gasping sob escaped her, and Father Timothy slid open the window between them.

"Myrthen?"

But she couldn't — or wouldn't — answer. She couldn't beg forgiveness, because she knew that she didn't deserve it. Even if God were merciful, even if He would erase the stain of her sin if she could confess it, she could not bring herself to speak those secrets she had borne and buried. Instead, she sobbed into her fists. When she finished, she looked up through the tiny window at Father Timothy, and by the disappointed expression on his face, she knew that she hadn't buried her secrets deeply enough. He didn't know the details but still, he knew.

Slowly, she stopped crying. She lifted her head and unclasped her hands, pried herself off her knees, and, as she uncurled herself from the confessional, she dropped her tangled rosary beads quietly on the floor. Then she left the church for the final time, without a single word to or from God.

August 13, 1969

Lidia stood with the fingertips of one hand pressed against her mouth, considering the mountain of cardboard boxes in the middle of the living room. They were marked in her neat and sprawling hand: "kitchen," "books," "clothes," "mementos." And "Gabriel." When Danny's acceptance letter from the City University of New York arrived in late July, they had decided — with Alta's encouragement — that he would enroll for the fall semester.

"It'll be hard, I know. But you deserve a new start," she had told them. Alta had come to stay with them after Gabriel's accident, to fend off the intrepid few who were still greedy for whatever Gabriel might have known or seen or remembered. Finding buried treasure or filling in the gaps of history or confirming some treachery or assuaging some guilt. They wanted whatever they could get, even if they couldn't ask him directly. "You stay here and what'll you have? Ghosts. That's what you'll have and that's what you'll become. Just look at me."

"Come with us, then," Lidia said.

Alta wrapped her hands around a cup of coffee and looked out the window. "I had the chance to go to New York City once." She smiled. "A long time ago. My uncle Punk and aunt Maggie lived there. I've told you about them. She was going to take me to the theater." Alta shrugged one shoulder. "But I didn't go and didn't go, and then I was married and had Abel and I couldn't go even if I wanted to. But by then, I didn't want to. Next thing I knew, everyone I ever loved was gone." She shook her head. "I was only thirty-eight when I lost them all. Thirty-eight. That number seems awfully young looking back."

"Why didn't you leave then?"

"Maybe I should have left, I don't know. I wasn't ready. Or brave enough. Maybe that was it." She thought of Maggie and the Silver Palace Theater that she'd never seen and the cigarette she'd tried—and failed—to smoke. And of the life she'd led and the loves she'd buried in Verra, the loneliness of being on her own in the woods, surrounded by asparagus and memories.

"I remember that day," Alta said, turning back to Lidia. "That day two and a half years ago or so when Gabriel got lost in the hollow and found me." She closed her eyes and took a deep breath. "That's how it was. He found me. Not the other way around. I didn't know how lost I was until then. Maybe that's why I stayed. So I could meet you and Gabe." Alta shook her head. "Anyway, it's too late for me now."

The soulful part of Lidia, the maternal, the emotional, couldn't bring herself to get rid of any of Gabriel's things. But the practical side, the one that had governed most of her uncommon life, knew it didn't make sense to take everything with them to a tiny student-housing apartment in New York City. She packed a box of books and stuffed animals, holding each one for a moment before putting them inside. Most of Gabriel's baby clothes—except for a few sentimental outfits and his first pair of shoes, which her mother-in-law had had bronzed—would be donated. There were some things of his that she wanted Alta to have: the firefly jar Danny had retrieved, a crayon drawing he'd done of the cabin, his fishing rod—

"Mama, not that!"

Lidia spun around, gasped. "Gabriel! My goodness, you scared me."

He limped over to her, leaning on his little cane, and pulled the fishing rod out of the box. "I want to keep it."

"But, Gabe, there's not going to be any place to go fishing in the city. I thought we could leave it at Alta's so it'd be here when we come back to visit her. Would that be all right?"

Reluctantly, he put the fishing rod back. "Okay," he said.

She put a few more things inside and sealed it. "It's time. We need to go up and say goodbye. How's your leg? Think you can make it?"

Gabriel nodded. Lidia picked up the box and adjusted its heft. The contents were heavy but the weight was bearable. She stepped out into a draft of warm summer air, waited for Gabriel to pass, then back-kicked the door closed behind her. Slowly, they made their way one last time down through town and across the creek and up the Hollow to Alta's.

The light slanted low already. Katydids and crickets cried out as the pair walked, breaking small, dry branches and scattering the animals that lived low to the ground. How many times had they made this journey, Lidia watching Gabriel scamper ahead, both of them anticipating the warmth of Alta's cabin? The cups of tea and bowls of soup and hours of conversation. Lidia could hardly imagine how much she was going to miss these walks—and Alta.

Here was the knot in the creek where Gabriel liked to drop his line. And here was the old rabbit warren at the base of the red maple he always stopped and peered into, even though they saw a rabbit go into it only once, years before. And here was the stump where they'd carved their initials one summer afternoon, on their way home with a wicker creel full of fish, all of them: L + D + G = LOVE.

A familiar scud of smoke billowed above Alta's cabin, a thread rising from her hearth and into the sky that struck Lidia now as a reliable connection between earth and Heaven.

"You look like you've been working since the crack of dawn. I heard you coming, put the kettle on." Alta stepped aside to let them in, and Lidia took a deep breath of the embedded scent of soup and tea and linseed oil. "Come in, come in."

"I'm afraid if I do I'll never want to leave."

Alta reached out and took Lidia's hand and squeezed it, then pulled her close, and they stood like that for a while next to Gabriel and the sealed-up box, both of them fighting tears and clinging to each other as though to make up for the next loss. Finally, Alta pulled away and held Lidia at arms' length with both hands and looked fiercely at her and said, "I'm so proud of you." She shook her head. "So proud." Then she crouched down and took Gabriel by the hands. "And you. Look at you. So strong! Your granddaddy took good care of you, didn't he? You'll be running all through New York City before you know it." She hugged him until he squirmed away.

"I don't want to say goodbye," he said.

"You'll come visit," she said, then quickly turned. "I'll get our tea." Lidia could hear the muffled sound of her crying in the kitchen.

Alta lay awake in the dark all that night, listening to the sounds that she'd long grown accustomed to: the prattle and rush of the creek, animals on the hunt or on the run crashing through the foliage, insects and owls, the whistle of the train. She looked around at the paintings that had covered the walls for more than twenty years; she hadn't changed a thing. Even the new sheets she'd bought for the bed she'd shared with John were now old and worn. With Lidia and Gabriel, she'd had a reprieve from loneliness for the past couple of years, and now, secluded in the Hollow wood, her substitute family spending their last night in Verra, she felt the stealthy approach of isolation once again.

But the next morning, after making breakfast for one and cleaning up afterward, she stared at the lonesome-looking bowl drying upside down beside the sink, the single coffee cup, and an idea seized her. An unfamiliar sense of adventure overtook her and she laughed out loud. *Why not?* she thought. *Why the hell not?* She found the suitcase that had been John's and threw in a week's worth of clothes, nothing fashionable but she didn't care—she'd buy new ones. Underwear and an extra pair of shoes and her toothbrush. Her paints and a pad of paper. What else? She looked around, wondering if she should take any of the paintings, anything of John's. No, she decided. If she tried to choose from among the relics, where would she stop? Then she realized she didn't need them anymore. She'd been saying goodbye for two decades, hoarding and polishing the treasures inside her sarcophagus. It was time to let them go.

She bathed, put on her nicest dress and shoes, withdrew the cash she kept inside a lockbox in the closet. Then she shut the suitcase and nearly jogged to the door. With her hand on the knob, she took a long look again at the cabin before closing and locking it, leaving the past inside.

Following dappled sunlight all the way to the cemetery, she stopped once to pick a thick bouquet of wild buttercups and daisies. She wanted to say goodbye one last time. But after she entered through the eastern gate, she came upon a familiar shrouded figure kneeling beside a grave under the shade of a sugar maple tree.

Alta was ten feet away; she could tiptoe past Myrthen without being heard, her footsteps masked by the goldfinches singing in their tabernacle above the trees, pay her respects, and go. Yet the sight of Myrthen compelled her to creep forward. Six weeks before, when she'd hauled her from the edge of earth above the mine and taken her to Father Timothy, Myrthen had still been pretty, her dark hair thick beneath her veil. Now she looked shrunken. Her hair had thinned, pronouncing the grays, and she had lost so much weight she seemed ill. Her hands looked gnarled in their prayer knot, the bones of her wrists jutting out. Her back curled as though from a dowager's hump, and she was as still as the headstone beside her. The only thing that indicated life inside of her was a low murmur, a prayer. Alta moved closer until she could hear it: *Talitha koum. Talitha koum. Talitha koum.*

She hesitated just behind her, listening to her mourning. If Myrthen knew she was there, she didn't indicate it. Alta reached out her hand, hovering it above her shoulder to—what? Offer her some comfort? What could she say that she hadn't said already? Though only inches away, Myrthen was unreachable, lost as she was inside private grief or guilt or shame. So Alta withdrew her hand and, instead, placed the flowers she'd picked on top of Ruth Bergmann's grave, rearranging them so that they all faced the same direction. A small thing, but still, it was something.

"Goodbye, Myrthen," she whispered. But Myrthen didn't hear.

Then Alta closed her eyes and sent her love to Abel and Walter and John. She didn't need to touch their graves to do so. Wherever she was—in the cemetery or in the cabin or in New York City—her memories of them rested safe inside her. They would understand that she was ready, finally, to go. They would understand that she didn't want to end up like Myrthen, miserable and shriveling next to their graves.

Alta looked up and saw the kite of steam rising into the sky above the valley, a thread of train-made clouds signaling that the passenger engine was coming. Was it already almost noon?

As she started back down the path toward Verra, a smile spread across her face. Her pace quickened to match the trail of steam puffs coming around the mountain and soon, she laughed out loud and ran hard, her feet flaring unskillfully out to the sides. When she reached the bottom of the trail, she crossed the wooden bridge that arched over New Creek and connected Whisper Hollow to Verra, then made it to the station house with just enough time to climb the few steps to the platform and catch her heaving breath before the train pulled in.

Standing under the noon-struck clock, Alta scanned the crowd. There they were, huddled together at the far end of the platform, Danny clutching their tickets, Lidia holding Gabriel's hand, Gabriel watching the sky.

"Lidia!" she called. "Gabriel! Danny!" All at once, they turned.

Alta, jubilant, lifted her suitcase toward them.

"I'm going with you!"

Acknowledgments

Alta came to me, unbidden, asking me to tell her story, but I could not have done so without the help of a great many people.

I am grateful to my mother-in-law, Geraldine Cander, for sharing her memories of growing up in a coal-mining community populated by first- and second-generation immigrants. Her perspective on the duties and talents of the Polish women in her family was invaluable. Homer Hickham called me "a brave soul to write about a West Virginia coal town without having lived there and then," and patiently answered many questions so that I could try. Thanks go to Bill Richardson for driving me around West Virginia's southern counties for two days and providing essential information on the impact of geology, industry, immigration, and religion on coal-mining communities in the twentieth century. Sonny Schumann led a tour I took of the Beckley, West Virginia, Exhibition Coal Mine, and afterward answered my many questions, drew a hypothetical underground map, and, in a continued exchange via e-mail over the course of several months, helped me plan the catastrophic event that divides the book into its two parts. I was so grateful for his assistance that I named a character after him.

Many thanks to Brother Luke Stone, Third Order Regular of Church of the Assumption in Keyser, West Virginia, for our many conversations that helped me imagine the complex relationships my characters had with God, the Church, and each other. May he rest in peace. I am grateful to Sister Timothy Marie of Carmel for her guidance and wisdom regarding the Carmelite charism and stages of candidacy, as well as the language used during Myrthen's meeting with the Mother Prioress. Thanks to the Reverend Anthony Cekada for his counsel on the intricacies of ecclesiastical authority and the Code of Canon law, as well as his assistance with the fictional letter sent to Myrthen from the Tribunal of the Diocese.

I would also like to thank Dr. Crista Miller, organist at Co-Cathedral of the Sacred Heart, for the demonstration and for answering the kinds of questions only a nonmusical person would ask. Jim Kosnik, music professor at Old Dominion University, graciously explained the tradition of organ music within the Mass context.

I owe a debt of gratitude to my agent, Jane Gelfman, for her faith in me. Her memorable reaction to an early draft was an indispensable gift throughout the book's evolution. I wish to thank Judith Gurewich and everyone at Other Press for believing in this book, and for making important contributions to its final iteration.

I am indebted to my dear friends and early readers for their love, support, and encouragement: Charlie Baxter, Sarah Blutt, Sabrina Brannen, Lucy Chambers, David Eagleman, Stephanie Flagg, Tobey Forney, John Garber, Lee Ann Grimes, Pamela Hicks, Simmi Jaggi, Karen Johnson, Jon Kooker, Andrew Lienhard, Emma Lyders, Marla Majewski, Anissa Paddock, Theresa Paradise, Kerry Shamblin, Katherine Tramonte, and Holly Wimberley.

I am grateful to my sister, Sara Huffman, who always makes time and never lets me give in to despair; and to my parents, Cindy and John Slator, and Larry and Brenda Pullen, for their unconditional love. I thank my sweet babies, Sasha and Joshua, for permitting me the necessary quiet during the writing of the manuscript. My love and gratitude go to my husband, Harris Cander, who abides the countless hours I spend at my desk, sustains me through the ups and downs, and always makes me laugh.

And lastly, I am grateful to the characters themselves. After living — clearly, insistently — for so long in my imagination, they will live ever after in my heart.

CHRIS CANDER is a novelist, children's book author, freelance writer, and teacher for Houston-based Writers in the Schools. Her novel *11 Stories*, published by a small press in Houston, was included in *Kirkus*'s Best Indie General Fiction of 2013. Find more of her work at www.chriscander.com